killing miss love

killing miss love

MARSHALL QUINN BLACKWELL, JR

Snake Ridge Press
Fort Lauderdale

"Forgiveness is the fragrance that the violet sheds on the heel that has crushed it." —Mark Twain

To my senior high school English and History teachers,
Mary Walker and Elizabeth Yielding

PRELUDE

November 2010
Mariah Wolfson Choudrant

CURIOSITY CAN BE A POWERFUL MOTIVE. SO MUCH SO THAT I HAVE TO admit that it was the title of the document, "How to Kill Your Lover," that provoked me to read it and search for any meaning the manuscript might contain. After I took a first glance at the beginning pages, the manuscript appeared at best predictably base, and at worst, obscene. Nevertheless, it caught my attention as the author of the diary of sorts did ask some significant questions. And as I read on, I couldn't help but to rally behind the voice, or better yet in this case, the voices of the author in their attempt to find answers to the questions that were quickly posed. But my early opinions of the manuscript, which in hindsight tend in some degree still correct, were to be revisited as I began to take interest in the story. Even amid the degenerative and horrible subjects of the tale, I began to feel joy. Perhaps what helped me to recognize this sentiment was that at some point during the three months it apparently took the author to transcribe his ordeal, a young man found his voice, if not all the answers to which he searched.

I came across the manuscript quite by accident in November of 2004, after my husband and I decided that our lives in New York would be enhanced by allowing ourselves the pleasures of the tropics on an economical scale. From an estate sale, we had purchased a unit on the 17th floor of a relatively old condominium that we felt was a good deal for the price, considering the unit was walking distance to the beach and directly on the Intracoastal waterway of Fort Lauderdale, Florida. It didn't hurt that the appreciation on these units was stable and predictions from various market analysis showed them to be a plausible investment. With this and our intention to take some time from our careers as editors for two separate publishers in New York, we closed the sale.

But the condo needed some work and my husband and I decided that before we could settle in and relax, we would renovate the unit to our own specifications and taste.

Although we both have had some relative success with our careers, neither Sean nor I were made of money. We had used most of savings for the down payment and closing costs, so there really wasn't enough money left over to hire someone to do the remodeling. Besides, we both enjoy a project and so we took the Thanksgiving to New Year's Holiday season to put our renovation into motion. Sean, whom I'll admit is quite the handyman as he did an excellent job on our warehouse apartment in the city, gave me my first assignment. It was to tear out the breakfast area and counters; the intention was to open up the kitchen to the living room. He had already inspected the area for electrical or plumbing hazards and determined it was safe for me to begin my demolition. He left me to my work and quite enthusiastically set out to do what he had told me on the day of closing, with adamant conviction, his first act of renovation in the condo would be to destroy "Liberace's Tomb," which in short is what he called our master bathroom. I had to agree—it did look like a bad rendition of a Las Vegas casino bathroom. Perhaps the previous owner had gone awry in an attempt to imitate the men's room at Caesar's Palace. It was hideous.

With Sean so indulged, I was left to my own devices, which were a crowbar, hammer, and handsaw. I went to work and halfway through ripping the breakfast bay apart, an envelope simply fell out into the rubble of nails and cheap wood. The large manila envelope, very similar in fact to legal sized envelopes used by the title company at the closing, contained a manuscript. I looked at both sides for a description of its content, but they were blank. Naturally, I took the manuscript from the unsealed envelope. The title, "How to Kill Your Lover" leapt out at me. After the initial shock, I'm sure that a smile came across my face as at the time I was inclined to believe Sean was playing a joke on me. So I thought to myself that I would amuse the child that had come to be my husband and proceeded to read the opening sentences of the document.

The warm breezes coming off the tropical Atlantic and through our windows could not warm the goose bumps that prickled my skin as I read the first paragraph. The journal of sorts continued to keep my attention for the next few days during breaks and before bedtime. This confession or "quest," despite the poor grammar and bad spelling, not to mention the endless red-penned insertions, held an element of honesty tempered by malice that I had not seen before. Nothing genius, simply an honest exploration that I found bizarre, shocking at times, yet humorously alluring. Quite frankly, I never had any intention of publishing the story. Having said this, I'd prefer to let you, the reader, now discover the tale just as I did; to decide for yourself whether the story is base, obscene or whatever adjective comes to your mind.

How to Kill Your Lover

Accounts Written by Mason Harrison Caldwell III

CHAPTER 1

June 1992

Hello

I PICTURE HIS FACE AND I FIND THAT IN MY MIND, IT WOULD LOOK BET-ter were it unrecognizable. I could just push him over the rail. I also know that blood and brains on the cement would draw a sizable crowd and attention, which would inevitably lead to my imprisonment—at the very least. Boy, I can't get caught. After all, this is Florida and the state's biggest rivalry with Texas is not a contest of athletics but capital punishment. Nevertheless, the murder is something that I have planned for quite some time. The son of a bitch deserves death and I feel no pity for him. I can only hope for his agony in his final moments. Yes, I think a fall from his balcony would be too kind. But I have to admit that I do enjoy the idea of the drama that would follow his fatal plunge.

I can imagine the array of tourists that will flock to his body and the immediate commotion from the wail of sirens, and I have to laugh when I think of the irritation that some of these rich pukes in my building will have when they find that both elevators are inaccessible, as the entire building hurries to get to the ground floor to see the carnage.

I know that I am angry. No, that would be putting it mildly. I know that I'm enraged, but for the life of me, I don't think I can pinpoint exactly what I'm so angry about today. Perhaps that is part of the motivation behind this effort. "That" being the urge to specify the core of my rage. I'm not so sure that I didn't come out of the womb pissed off. And I know that, in fact, I am unstable. For the day is near. I have no doubt that I am going to put the motherfucker to death. That I promise.

Would you like to know how it has come to this? I would. (Who are "you" anyway? I ain't no Anne Frank, and "you" ain't no Kitty, her journal. So I talk to myself. I know that's fucked up. So let me see now, I think I will simply call you, "Selectric." My trusty silver steed of typewriter, galloping away on your little electric ball of symbols and letters as you carry me through the canyons of lies and delusions that would thwart my quest for clarity. Anyway that is the primary motivation behind this endeavor. "That" being what? Truth? Yes Truth. I've committed myself to a quest for truth and have been told since I can remember that all a person has to do is seek and he or she will find. So I'm seeking. What do you say, my dated IBM friend? Will I be finding? We'll see. Won't we?)

Selectric, I want to explore the very essence of my obsession with killing my lover, a man that is a huge part of me and a man that loves me. I want to be as honest as I can possibly be. That will be a trial in itself. But I'll do my best.

And the story is mine. Call it a confession, if you will. But one that is true to its core and intent, despite the lack of immediate clarity as I embark on this voyage to murder, shall we call it. Sorry to get so dramatic, Selectric. "Voyage to murder." Shit, murder is murder, and it's nothing new under the sun. I've heard it referred to as the final lust. And anyway, it should not be that difficult as it is not my first murder. But I get ahead of myself, as I often do. Let me back up and begin with my third attempt, as feeble as it was, to kill the prick. I think that is an appropriate place to start since it is recent and coincides with the moment that I decided to keep an account of my quest.

Can you keep it quiet, Selectric? I'm afraid that unlike your predecessor, Kitty who was very quiet, I am concerned not for Nazis but of an unfriendly Indian or two jumping out of these canyons we travel. Shhh.

You're so right, Selectric. You have no predecessor and I am not Anne Frank.

CHAPTER 2

Fort Lauderdale, June 1992

I T WAS OBVIOUS TO ME THAT I WAS IN TROUBLE.

"Andy! Come here would you?" There was a curious tone to that "would you." It had the similarity of someone asking, "I don't know why I'm asking you this question because I already know the answer."

"Sweetheart," he said as I entered the 12-by-12 foot, solid gold marble bathroom. He didn't look shaken or even remotely disturbed, and the only hint he showed of annoyance was a cocked eyebrow as he said, "I really, and I mean really do appreciate you running my bath for me. And the candlelight, Andy? Simply divine," before pausing as he dramatically blew one of those snobby kisses from his own hand as if he were some kind of Italian Heiress.

"Hey! No problemo, Rick," I said. "That's what I'm here for, to make you comfy."

"That's what I'm talking about Andy. But I don't think that a fucking scorpion fish in my bath water is going to feel good pricking my fucking balls," he screamed.

It still amazes me how Rick can go from calm and collected to a red hot hysterical case in zero to ninety—but I have the talent of keeping a pretty good poker face and said calmly, "Scorpion fish, huh? Dude, those things are poisonous, I hear. Like deadly poisonous. Oh, what do you say, Rick?" I pondered aloud as I looked at the dead fish floating in the bubble crusted water. "What the hell is one doing in your bath tub?"

He replied, "For the one hundredth time, you Louisiana Bimbo, it's a spa, not a tub, and you better tell me, you little prick, before you're out working 15th and Sunrise, where I found your pretty little ass."

"Jesus, Rick," I said baffled. "This reminds me of the time a water moccasin came through the plumbing of the tub and bit Aunt Rheda in the twat." I shuddered. "I mean she damn near died on us. She never could hold a coffee cup steady afterward. It taking so long …" He cut me off in mid-sentence. He was scarlet red at this point and screaming.

"Listen, Rose of the Okeefenokee, or whatever swamp they hurled your ass out of, I don't give a fuck about your goddamned Louisiana stories. Just look at this thing. Do you really think it could fit through the plumbing?"

I stood looking at him breathing really heavy and I have to admit that he had a point as we were in a unit on the 17th floor.

"Now get that damned thing out of my house." He said as he threw his towel at me. I damn near couldn't hold back a laugh because as he spun around and turned to walk out of the bathroom, Rick slipped on the wet marble and let loose a healthy fart at the same time. After his tone and the insults the man had just hurled at me, the fucker had the gall to say, "Excuse me," in an embarrassing tone like he was a debutante, belching at a country club dinner.

It really does amaze me that people forget that manners should be used to make others feel better, not to show that they were raised in a certain class and to demean people that don't follow their same etiquette. You might say that Rick's manners, or lack of manners, were warranted due to the fact that there was, in fact, a scorpion fish in his bath water. But let me give you a wink here. I'm not stupid. Although I do come from Louisiana, and I do enjoy taking advantage of people that watch a lot of TV, thus are convinced that anyone from the South is missing a certain x chromosome, or has one added in the wrong place, or whatever it is that causes that horrible Down's Syndrome. And Rick watches a lot of television and definitely thinks that I'm stupid. Or at least he made the mistake of saying so to me.

He's also one of these people that are always exorcising his demons and wants to exorcise mine too. Either he's quitting smoking or not eating meat or drinking only wine spritzers, perhaps even attempting to give up drinking altogether. And for the love of God, "slowing down" on the drugs. Or Jesus, almost nearly as bad to deal with, losing weight. Whatever the case du jour is, he wants me to do the same, and I don't need to lose any fucking weight. Hell! He was pouring us scotch just the other day and he says, "Andy we gotta quit drinking. Seriously."

As he was handing me my glass of scotch, I said, "Fuck That with a capital F and T."

"Come again?" He said in a tone like a first grade teacher responding to a brat that had informed her that he would not be doing any more homework. I took a healthy swig of my drink (and I do love scotch) and told him with a grimace and a wink, "You exorcise your demons, but I'm gonna play with mine."

I thought he really was going to throw me out for a second there. If you haven't gotten this yet, let me make it clear—he's got the dollars; I don't. Okay? Him rich, me poor. And he may be rich, but he's not a bad looking guy for 42. Actually, he's damn good looking.

So why does he keep a 22-year-old hustler in his house? Much less, one that attempts to kill him. (Actually he doesn't know that I'm trying to kill him. I'll explain the scorpion fish thing more in detail later.) So could it be that he has some control issues? Nah, I don't think so. Well, maybe he does, but maybe it's because the man really does love me. In all sincerity, I'm certain that he does—or at least as much as he can fathom the word—and I think that's all anyone can expect from anybody else.

And why do I stay? Why not just pop him with a slug and head out the door? Well, I didn't have a gun on me the first time that I wanted to kill him. But then I ask myself if I stay because the man has cash. Maybe a little. But although the money is nice, I don't think that's what keeps me around either. But would I stay if he were poor? I'd have to say that I'd probably have never fallen for him to begin with, as I would have told him the first time he approached me to "think again numb-nuts," had I even the slightest hint that he didn't have money. In general, I try to avoid anything that makes me crazy. But at the same time, I have to try really hard because, initially, I'm always attracted to what makes me nuts, and nothing makes me more nuts than being stone cold broke. But at the same time, so does the confinement of a home. My apologies if I contradict myself here, but I'm finding that when I'm honest with myself, I tend to do that. But I'm sure of this: money helps to keep me sane, or as sane as any guy that talks to his typewriter might be.

Anyway, fuck the shrinks! And I've been "observed" by a couple, which would tell a guy to take some kind of progress program and to get in touch with himself. I am here to tell you. There just ain't no twelve stepping my ass out of this shit. I know because I've dealt with some of those programs, too. And I tried telling them that nothing makes me more sane than knowing I got a place to sleep and money in the bank, but they just went on about God this and one fucking day at a time that. "Poor fools" I thought to myself as I shook my head in pity for the brainwashed dipshits. "We'll see. Keep coming back. We're glad you're here," they always said. Okay, so we'll see. And I'd rather have my dick pulled off than go to another one of those meetings again.

Sorry, I'm off on a tangent again, but it would take more than money to make me stay with this guy, because this jackass Rick makes me crazy too. So I think an honest answer to the question of why I stay would be to say that, partially, I stay because I know that I love him. Now don't go getting sick on me, Selectric, 'cause I got a little queasy just writing that. And in all fairness to Rick, a good question would be my comprehensions of the word "love" as well. But like I said, I'm attempting to be as honest as I can be, as the truth is what I'm after here.

But then why would I want to kill my lover, AKA Sugar Daddy, Mr. Meal Ticket? I really do love him. I don't think I'll ever love anyone else. (Throwing up your reservoir of black ink yet, Selectric, old boy? I damn near did.) But besides money, there is only one thing in this world that motivates my ass more, and that is revenge.

The first night I meet Rick, what's he do? He fills my head with what I think is coke, but it's not. It's this shit called "K." I have no idea where or who the fuck I am and I wake up with a bleeding bum. I usually get checked every 6 months for the HIV bug, but now that I think I have it, I'm whammed by a fear of needles when I think about getting checked.

Yeah I'm a slut-slash-whore, but usually I just let these guys suck my dick, and once in a while I fuck 'em, and if they really throw out the cash, I let 'em fuck me wearing a rubber. So far, so good. I've been doing it for two and a half years and all's well till I met Rick three months ago. I made an appointment to get tested the other day, and I don't have any symptoms or anything—but I'm scared.

So I asked Rick the next day after our initial meet-and-fuck, while I'm drying off after a shower in that imitation Grecian tomb that he calls a bathroom, "So you did use a rubber?"

The man looks at me while he's taking a piss and laughs out loud, tells me, "Don't tell jokes while I'm pissing." He gives a little humph and continues, "You'll make me miss the pot."

So I'm thinking that this guy is a bigger jerk than me, but what the hell I'll play along with it. So I asked him while he's in mid-stream, "So you agreed to the two hundred?"

"I agreed to nothing, but if you want two hundred, it's yours. What are you doing for lunch?" He asked, shaking his dick.

I answered his question with the question, "You're negative right?"

"Good thing I just finished or you would've made me miss the pot," he said without the slightest hint of emotion.

"Yeah, I'm free for lunch. I could go for Italian." I said with my subconscious obviously guiding my appetite.

"Yeah?" he said. "That's what I had in mind. Maybe we do have something in common."

I had hoped that Italian food was all there was to it. If I'd had a gun, I think I would have shot him on the spot, as I made up my mind right then and there to kill the man. But believe it or not, I knew then that this guy had it bad for me. And, something else: I had it bad for him.

Now I know you are going barfola. But for anybody that has ever felt love at first sight, or almost first sight, you'd understand. I know this. We have no control over whom we fall in love with or when it strikes. I hear some of these dips say it takes at least a year to fall in love, but horse shit, it can take five minutes, or even five seconds. And there ain't jack crap you can do about it. Seriously, not a fucking thing. The only thing that a guy can do is choose how he will react to it, but he can't control what he feels. I know some people would say that I'm full of shit and don't know the difference between love and lust or what have you, but I don't think one can rationalize an emotion, particularly not one that is this strong.

So why stupid things like scorpion fish, murder, et cetera? Because revenge is an emotion that rivals the best of them. The scorpion fish was revenge on the small scale. Nothing compared to what I really have in mind for the guy. But again, I progress too quickly. Let me back up about six months, to get a better handle on what's going on here.

CHAPTER 3

December 1991

I'D NEVER BEEN TO FORT LAUDERDALE BEFORE LAST DECEMBER. LET ME say this: "Connie Francis doesn't live here anymore—if she ever did—but really bad imitations of her do." And these impersonators usually have a dick and balls swinging underneath a lime green dress with size 12 magenta pumps on their feet. I know that ain't a pretty picture. But I guess the reason I think of Fort Lauderdale as a personification of Connie Francis is her frosted hair and dated music. There is something about frosted hair on women that I find incredibly tacky, yet so common on so many wealthy women here. It appears to be a common style with so many of these old gangsters' outdated and hard rode girlfriends. It's like what I heard this lady say, decked out in jewelry, describing the city in her growling nasal accent, imploring her husband to take her back to New York. "It's just so hot, sticky and run down."

I can only guess that that lady was from the Brooklyn. I once read in a magazine that there is no greater form of contraception than a New York accent. If I were straight, I think I'd have to agree. That little crispy punctuation with every other syllable pronounced like an order rather than an accent just gives me the willies.

But despite the abundance of pushy Yankees, I like the city. Actually, I really like New Yorkers who I find are basically a dynamic bunch who don't care what you're story is as long as you produce results. And after living in New Orleans, I find the place pretty fucking clean. People actually get out and exercise here and roller blade everywhere. I'd like to see people skate on the cracked sidewalks of New Orleans. If the tree roots didn't get 'em, the dog shit would. I have a love/hate relationship with New Orleans. Come to think of it, I probably have that kind of relationship with a lot of things and people.

When I left New Orleans in December 1991, I thought I was leaving on a temporary basis. Kind of like a vacation. I had picked up this coke fiend in a French quarter bar and the guy asked me how I'd like to go on vacation with him. I asked him, "Where to?"

He said, "Fort Lauderdale."

I said, "Cool!"

Then I bent him over some Budweiser cases and fucked him in the dry stockroom of my favorite bartender's classy place of employ. Then the dude took me out to the airport and bought us two tickets on Value Jet for the 7:00 P.M. So I get on the plane with this freak, with nothing but my money clip and fake identification, and I mean we were rolling. Not just down the runway, but we were higher than Mt. Everest from this guy's totally pure kick-ass cocaine. I vaguely remember that he put a popper bottle under my nose as we skirted down the runway to take off. The flight was nearly empty and he had put a blanket over us and jacked me off right there on the plane. It was a pretty intense flight with this guy. Notice that I don't call him by his name. That's because I didn't know then, or even now, what the jackass's name was.

So we finally got to Fort Lauderdale after a two-hour layover's worth of cocktails in Atlanta, and the guy didn't even take me to his house or anything, but had the taxi drive us straight to this bar called Jimmy's where these 18- and 19-year-old guys were dick dancing, and to make a long story short, one the these little fucks stole my trick and coke connection. So I was there with nothing but the clothes on my back and my wallet, with all of exactly $32.63. And I have to say that when you let yourself get into a bind like this, you will remember the exact amount of money you had when you realized you were up shit creek, no matter how fucked up you are. And after the last 40 something hours with Co-co man, I wasn't a pretty sight to behold. To tell the truth, I don't think I even knew my own name! Since I go by many names, that can be a trick, no pun intended, but when I'm working, and I'm here to tell you here and now that I was working that night so I'm pretty sure I was calling myself Andy. In all probability, that is what most people I've met these last few years know me as: Andy.

So the bar closed and as I stumbled out alone and dazed, I was blessed with the ability of some cognizance to read a blurred sign posted by the courtesy of the city of Fort Lauderdale that pointed forward with an arrow and announced "Beaches." After about an hour of following the beach route, I hit A1A and saw the ocean for the first time in years. I know many people find it hard to believe that someone from New Orleans doesn't see the ocean often. It is astounding how many tourists make it to New Orleans and are disappointed to find out we don't have a beach on the Gulf. There is no saltwater beach less than ninety minutes from New Orleans.

Anyhow, it was a warm December night with the temperature just right at about 71 degrees so I took off my shoes and started walking down the beach. I came to a part of the beach nearby a parking lot, which was not as well lit as other parts of the beach. I found a lounge chair loosely chained to a life-guard shack and told myself that this was as good a place as any to relax a second. And despite my condition, I remember that I made note of the fact that I was able to see the stars for the first time in ages. The lights from bigger inland cities like New Orleans tend to deny access to stars. So with the gentle surf lapping only 25 yards away and with the possibilities offered by starlight, I was entertaining the possibility that I would hang around Fort Lauderdale for a while, and with that decision made, I dozed off.

I'm not sure what time it was, but it was still dark when a policeman woke me up, and was actually friendly about kicking me off the beach. He offered me the location of a public shelter but politely informed me that if he saw me sleeping on the beach again, he would have to take me in. So I groggily headed down the sidewalk, and by this time, a coke hangover was setting in. I remember praying to myself, please let me find a dark place before the sun comes up. There is something about sunlight that makes me face the reality of my situation, and thinking about this added to the incredible headache that I could feel coming on.

I've heard it said that both God and the Devil look after fools and I've come to believe in this theory. For right there across the street from the beach was a yacht club with reasonably easy access to the boats by pier. But the walkway was blocked by a gate with a guard stand so I walked a little further down the road and said to myself, "What the hell, I've always been a strong swimmer."

So I took my chances and lowered myself into the water and swam toward a boat with the inscription, "Lucky Abe" on its stern. My intuition told me that Abe was not on board and I was right. Lucky Abe even politely extended me the convenience of a rear diving ladder, so I took it. Before I knew it, I had stripped my wet clothes off and slipped under the canvas and into the life dinghy. Pretty soon I was dreaming of having my dick sucked by Tom Cruise.

However, when I awoke, my mouth tasted like Tom Cruise had taken a shit in it. Perhaps this is a bit too vivid, but like I was saying, my mouth tasted like a buzzard had taken a shit in it and my head felt like the depraved bird was pecking at my skull with his sledgehammer of a beak. I could tell it was now daylight because the canvas that covered the dinghy was allowing the light to seep through and begin a smidgeon of what I thought would be the first of my day's torments.

Oh Selectric! But what to me wandering eyes appear when me peeps me disheveled head out of the dinghy? It wasn't eight shiny reindeer, but it was one of the most beautiful sunrises that I had ever seen in my life. The sky was pink and cutting through the silhouette of the palm trees that grow on beaches and of course the ocean was so gentle and green.

I guessed it was around 7:30ish and decided not to test my luck any further with Lucky Abe. So I grabbed my still damp clothes and, grimacing, dressed under cover of the dinghy's canvas. I eased out of the little boat and when I was on deck, looked around and saw that the gate from the pier to the street was now open. So I casually jumped onto the pier and walked on up to the gate and bingo—I was on the street.

I immediately crossed over A1A and headed north and I couldn't ask for any better luck. There were showers right there on the sidewalk for the beach tourists to shower off before going back to their hotels. My problem was that I needed a towel, so I walked across the street and bought a white beach towel, some toothpaste and brush, and some cheap spandex shorts that I kept on when I paid the cashier twelve bucks. I put my damp clothes in the bag he gave me and was in the water of the Atlantic Ocean before I could count ten.

It had been years since I swam in salt water and you couldn't have told me that it, and the relaxing sound of the surf, can cure a hangover better than aspirin, but it does. But the swim was made short because I blew my nose violently and then, like any good redneck that had seen Jaws, I became concerned about sharks when I noticed all the blood from my nose. So I got out and walked up to the shower and rinsed off and brushed my teeth. I decided to catch a few more hours of sleep so I walked back down to the edge of the water and laid out my towel. I blended in with the others that were already starting to dot the beach.

I slept till about noon, when a combination of hunger and the bass of a passing homeboy with his music pounding from A1A woke me up. I gathered up my stuff and walked up to the shower and rinsed and brushed my teeth again, and dried off and put on my shoes. I beheld my first sober look at my new surroundings. There were bars and hotels with restaurants galore across the street from an incredibly wonderful beach, and my intuition told me correctly that I could practice my chosen profession here just as well as I could in New Orleans. Even though I had about twenty dollars left, I knew that I was going to be okay. I rationalized to myself that I was 22, white, hard bodied, well hung, and had a smiling face that can stop traffic. Oh yeah, not to forget piercing green eyes.

So what—I'm conceited.

As I contemplated how I was going to get myself looking good enough to hustle some guy, I laid on the beach, soaked up the sun and took in my new surroundings. I remember very distinctly the moment and how it grabbed me with a stranglehold of reflection. I guess my conceit forced me to place the question before me that if I was such a looker, with so much promise, how in the hell did I get myself into a situation like this? And to put it bluntly, how did I become a whore? I remember that I sat on the sea wall that day and recalled this drug dealer in New Orleans telling me the way they made teenagers into whores down in Brazil. He said that they would simply take them and lock them up in a bedroom and about every hour, a thug would go into the room and rape the poor guy. This would keep on going until eventually, the guy gave no resistance and basically accepted the fact that if he was good, he'd get a drug smack, and if he was non-compliant, or didn't perform well, then not only would he be denied the drug, but perhaps he'd be beaten as well. Basically, the kid would be turned into a dog to do tricks and that even dogs have more self-respect than these poor kids do. At least that's what the dealer said.

"I have self-respect." I told myself as I sat there on the Lauderdale sea wall. I have enough self-respect not to have dirt under my fingernails from digging ditches and besides, I could do anything I wanted, couldn't I? The fact that guys would give me money for sex was just a stroke of luck. Unlike those Brazilian guys, no one had ever stroked me hard, except luck. So as I examined this question of my involvement in prostitution, I thought back further.

Let me back up again to take a look at why I became a hustler—and a good one at that, if I do say so myself.

CHAPTER 4

Louisiana, The 1970s

Let's get to know each other a little more intimately, Selectric. My real name is not Andy. When working the streets, I figured why risk giving out my real name, as there are too many things someone can do with that. I came by Andy when I was homeless and my first trick in Jackson Square in New Orleans asked me what my name was. I wasn't accustomed to the anonymity of a large urban area. So when the john asked me my name, I looked over his shoulder and saw the statue of Andrew Jackson. I thought about saying Jack but before the words came off of lips, I recognized that my trick would think I was being a smart-ass. And Andrew sounded so formal, not to mention it was the name of one of my best friends in the world. So I just blurted out the name "Andy," and it stuck.

My real name is Mason Harrison Caldwell III. Do you think that it sounds like my father wanted me to be a U.S. Senator? Hell, with a name like that, I even think I still have a chance. Well, maybe governor would be more realistic. Do you think the Great State of Louisiana would have a male prostitute as governor? Personally, I don't think it would be anything new under the sun, but we'll get into my pessimistic opinion of politicians later.

Anyway, my father always told me that I was "the butt ugliest" baby he'd ever seen. I kid you not. And he was right. I've seen the Polaroid snaps. My Dad and I were almost like buddies when I was a child and he didn't raise me to be a China Doll. I remember when I was around 12 years old that I was having some friends over for the night and we were all up watching Saturday Night Live. In a fit of laughter, my dad blared out, "God-damn son, those Coneheads look just like you as a baby."

You can imagine how that would stick to someone in the 6th grade, and it did. But he was right. My baby picture looks like Bill Murray with no hair or teeth, playing Mr. Conehead. For those Generation X-er's that are unfamiliar with the Coneheads, I do pity you. (Technically, I make Generation X, but in reality, I view myself more as one of the forgotten ones that came of age at the end of the 70s and early 80s listening to School House Rock.)

And honestly, jibes like the Conehead thing didn't bother me. The truth be known, I knew by age twelve that I was somewhat blessed with an attractive appeal. I made straight As, had three of the prettiest feathered hair girlfriends in the 6th grade, and was a star running back in Gray Y Football of Monroe, Louisiana.

Never heard of Monroe? Monroe's call to fame is that it was, I've been told, for a very long time, the largest deposit of natural gas in the world. And also that Delta Airline began there. Get it—Delta, as in the Louisiana Delta. Essentially, they are crop dusters who have done very well. But a lot of people in that area of the country haven't done well. The two places in the present day U.S. of A that vie for first place in national poverty are Appalachia and the Mississippi/Louisiana Delta. Fortunately for me, I was raised by a lawyer who controlled a 4,200 acre family estate of prime Delta land. Don't get me wrong, we were no Rockefellers, but for North Louisiana, we were some fat cats. But this little fat cat was giving some early signs that he wouldn't be a tomcat that wanted to make babies, but would in fact grow up preferring the company of other Toms. And that shit don't fly in the Delta. Definitely, the gay flags to the future were flapping, to my parents' distress.

I recall my dad coming home for a break from law school in Baton Rouge. Baton Rouge is about 4-5 hours from Monroe and I guess he was going to surprise my mom. Anyway, I was around four years old and I had a red cowboy hat, and since my cowboy boots were black, I used this as an excuse to talk my mom into letting me wear her red high heels. She said, "Well okay, but you can't let your Deddie catch you."

I asked her, "Why not?"

She replied, "Honey, your Deddie just don't understand things like color coordination."

Well, I didn't know what in hell color coordination was, nor did I give a shit. All I cared about was that I had Momma's permission to wear her red high heels. So like I was saying, there I was clonking around in Momma's shoes with my red cowboy hat and my cap-gun and holster when Deddie comes walking in. Well hell, I try and hold him up, and I thought it was all good and fun when I fired my cap-gun at him. By the expression on his face, you'd have thought he'd actually been shot. And a Southern accent is even stronger when you find a rebel in shock. I can still here my dad's voice twanging in its effort to reach my mother in whatever part of the huge house she was in, "Aw Baby, come on now! Look at this! Don't let my boy wear high heels. You're gonna turn him into a queer."

To this day, I think my poor Momma believes I'm gay because she let me wear her high heels whilst playing Cowboys and Indians.

And there was another incident right around that time. My dad would let me watch football games with him and his buddies. If L.S.U. was playing, you could bet your first born child that a passel of rednecks would invade our living room. My mom was always the perfect hostess of these events that my dad would enjoy. There was plenty of beer, smoked sausages off the grill, avocado dips, boiled shrimp, and pizza for all the junior hillbilly's that came over. Ever see kids in November in cut-offs wearing cowboy boots in a yard playing football? Yep, we were rednecks. Luckily by this time I knew that I was not allowed to play football in high heels, though I'm sure I would have tried if they hadn't been put off limits.

And an L.S.U. game is nothing to scoff at. I hear that the screams and jumping in Tiger Stadium in Baton Rouge alarmed some seismologist as the Richter scale registered a small earthquake one Saturday night. Seriously, these Coon-asses lose their minds. L.S.U. is Mecca to many Cajuns. I don't think most realize that the college was founded by William Tecumseh Sherman (SPIT! Toof), the Devil himself. And most of them probably don't know that a Yankee wrote Dixie, but before I go off on a tirade, back to the football game at my wee age of 4or 5.

I believe the game was against Nebraska. The point being, I hated the color yellow as a child, but I loved, and still do the color red. So I'm causing a few agitations in the living room because I'm yelling, "Go Red, go!"

I remember my dad's friend Gary Coats hollering, "Boy, what in the hell you cheering for those God Damned Yankees for?"

"Cause I like red," I shamelessly shot back at the cotton farmer.

L.S.U. was getting the shit kicked out of 'em, and I'm sure some of the Good-Ole-Boys in the house had hefty wages bet on the Tigers, so my dad's protective instincts must've kicked in.

"Come over here and sit with me," my dad said, motioning with his hand on his knee.

But what happened next was really an embarrassing incident for Dad. I'd become a little older and by now my dad had graduated from L.S.U. and had passed the Louisiana State Bar. In the future, I would learn from others that my father would show no emotion in court with electric chair pending or screaming children being torn from a mother judged unfit and what have you. That was not the case in this little incident.

L.S.U. had finally scored, and I was knocked off Daddy's knee as he shot up to run over to his stereo to drop the needle down onto the L.S.U. fight song. Before he was able to get the song going, the television cameras had zoomed in on the L.S.U. quarterback that was running off the field and had removed his helmet at the sideline. So, just as dad is placing the needle in place, I scream out while pointing at the TV, "Oh look Deddie! Ain't he pretty!"

The needle scratched across the record, and the room came to a silence and I can still envision it like a still photo. Rednecks halted their shrimp inches from their open mouth, and I still clearly envision my mom in freeze-frame emptying an ashtray into our fireplace. It was as if someone had a camera and yelled, "Look shocked" and then snapped the flash for posterity.

I think my mom was the first person to talk over the single sound of the T.V.

"Does anybody want a beer?" she meekly inquired.

The only immediate reply was from my dad's buddy, Booger (yes, like something you can pick out of your nose) whose failed attempt to cover up his snicker was followed by Gary Coats clearing the phlegm out of his throat through his nasal passage. The technique in clearing phlegm out of ones throat is a talent many Rednecks work years on perfecting, and Gary Coats was the Beethoven of throat hocking. With his nasal passage clear to give his best vocal effects, he mockingly said, "Mason, I think you need to have a talk with your boy."

Dad did his best to defuse the situation with a laugh, and everybody else hesitantly joined in with my dad walking over to me and saying, "Let's go to the back and have a chat."

"What?" I asked, following at the same time, knowing that walking to the back when company was present usually meant a good talking to at the very least, if not a whipping (only with a belt on the ass—and of those I count the times on one hand. My father never touched me with his hand.)

Back in the bedroom, Deddie sat me down on the bed, then kneeled down to eye level with me and began, "Son, we don't call other boys or other men pretty when we notice that they are handsome, and even then, we don't say it."

"Why?" I innocently inquired.

"Look, Son," he said holding me gently but firmly by the shoulders, and then continuing, "I know you aren't a sissy, and you know you aren't a sissy, but if you say things like that, then other people might think you are."

"So," I said with a shrug.

"So?" my dad repeated stammering for a response then rebounding with, "So they'll make fun of you, and maybe even want to beat you up, and other boys won't want to play with you, and they'll walk around calling you a sissy."

I just replied, "Oh, okay. Then I won't do it again, Deddie. I'm sorry." I said sincerely.

"That's okay, you didn't know, but now you do. Now let's go back and watch the game."

And there were other incidents after that. In the first grade, my teacher sent me home with a note explaining that I was caught kissing another boy in the lunch room. Of course my mom, completely racked with the guilt of her high heels, took the note apologetically to my dad, and I basically got the same talk in the bedroom again, except this time, the subject matter was kissing other boys.

But what really gave my mom a fit was not that I was kissing other boys, but that she rode by the school yard and caught me playing jump rope with some girls. She wasn't worried that I was playing with girls. It was the fact that they were black. Jesus, I still remember their names. Miriam and Jacky. They were my best friends. You have to keep in mind that in 1975, the public schools in North Louisiana had only recently been integrated, and unlike a lot of white parents who had taken their children out of public schools and placed into private "Academies" to escape the "demon of integration," my parents, because my father was running for District Attorney and needed the black vote, opted to keep me in the public schools. But my mother had warned me that while I was supposed to be nice to my black schoolmates, I wasn't to play with them. She assured me that she would find out if I did, and that I would get a whipping when I got home. Well, all had been going well for a while, as I had started by playing with Jackie and Miriam on rainy days during inside recess. Initially, I was really impressed by their coloring techniques and this lead to forming a friendship as the two girls were eager to show me how to, "Color yo pictures right." And before you know it, they had invited me to join them on the playground. Hell, I even remember our jump rope song:

Knock, knock, knock we's calling Jacky,
Calling Jacky to the Do-o-o-e,

We's gonna have us lots of fun,
Cause our girlfriend Jacky's at the Doe.
Shut the Doe.

Then we'd count the times till she would miss, and when she'd miss, we'd get the rope in rhythm again and call out the next jumper substituting her name with the rhyme. I think I was the only boy they'd let jump with them. But that ended. I can remember that morning recess as we swung the rope, and the dread I felt when I looked up to see that the honking coming from the road that ran parallel to the schoolyard was none other than my momma slowing down to a near stop in her white Wagoneer to let me know that I had been busted. And she was true to her word. I got a whipping. After that, I didn't play with Miriam or Jacky again. I didn't even use a black crayon when coloring. I was even hesitant about getting into my dad's car because his LTD was black.

And so there you have it. As a little boy, I liked playing cowboys and Indians in red high heels, calling L.S.U. quarterbacks pretty, kissing other first grade boys in the lunchroom, and singing and playing jump rope with little black girls. And that's just what I can remember. A few weathervanes to the future I'd say.

But by the third grade, my parents had taken me out of the public school system and placed me in a local private academy. The class rooms there held much fewer students. There were only 15-20 kids in each class, with only two teachers to each grade. The kids here were also less aggressive than the children in the public school system. In general, they were raised by professionals, or at least successful business owners. Tuition was not cheap. It cost about $3,000 per semester per child to go to this school. But if any black child's parents could come up with the money, they would also have to buy stock in the academy, and if they could surmount that hurdle, there were entrance exams that could be manipulated to terminate that child's enrollments.

My mom and dad must have thought they had gotten their money's worth because I was playing with other little boys, and was not only a starter in each of the football, baseball, and basketball league teams, but was making all star and winning trophies for tournaments and individual competitions. In addition, my school marks were exceptional, and in the sixth grade, I received detention for playing spin the bottle on the playground and kissing a girl. I thought I heard my mom say "halleluiah" when she got the note. But the reality of puberty would very soon compel me towards my true nature.

I can honestly admit that I enjoyed the locker room much more than watching cheerleaders practice or watching the girl's dance team as they drilled. I never did, nor have I since gotten the tits thing. But did I get the chest muscle, ass, and dick thing! In the seventh grade, it consumed my thought about 90 percent of the time. I loved wrestling in P.E. during the my seventh grade year, due in large part to the fact that there was this guy that was fourteen, in the ninth grade, named Greg that I would team up against on a regular basis. It appeared we had a rivalry thing going on, but in reality, I was getting a real jolt out of this guy and he was getting into it as well.

I remember that when we were in the lunch line after our P.E. class that he was behind me and gave my ass a really good squeeze. Later that day, he asked me to hang around after school behind the football field in the woods. But I had to explain to him that I had to take the bus home, or otherwise my mom would pick me up. He even asked me to spend the night, but my dad said there was too big of an age difference for me to be hanging out with Greg, and that he had heard the rumors of the guy's involvement with pot.

So I played on with my facade that I liked girls, kept a steady, went to school dances, and agreed vehemently with the other guys about certain girl's big tits. I even liked my little girlfriends, but didn't have the foggiest notion about having sex with them. I hadn't even discovered masturbation. But I will never forget my first orgasm. Dude!

It was March of my eighth grade year and I can still recall the dreary overcast day, with a temperature in the upper 60s. It was Saturday and my parents had informed me that the Meeks and their son Scott would be coming over for a barbeque that afternoon, and dinner that night. My dad had asked me to try and get along with Scott this time if I could. I told him that I would, and that I was actually glad to be having some company over other than my usual buddies that lived up and down the bayou for a couple of miles. Scott was fifteen years old, a year older than I was, but had been put back a year in school. I had never really liked him. He was one of those guys who, when we were younger, would come over to the house about every six weeks or so with his parents and we'd usually ended up in a fistfight over something like him wrecking my motorcycle or tearing something up. And come to hear in later years that not many people did like Scott as the poor guy got really screwed up with PCP. But at age 15, he was spending the weekend on leave from Chamberlain Hunt, the military school over in Port Gibson Mississippi. It was the place those "Bad Boys" wound up.

I was back in our game/living room when Scott walked in and the first thing that I noticed was how much he had matured since I had seen him last summer. Apparently, they had put him on a weight lifting program at school, because the guy was built, and his body had matured a lot faster than mine. He looked really good and I was at a stage in my life when I was lanky yet showing some signs of muscle. But again, I had not yet even jacked off to have an orgasm. However, I had been waking up after wet dreams and wondering why in the hell my underwear was sticking to my skin. Of course I had no idea I was having wet dreams and little did I know that today was the day that I would have my first sexual encounter.

It really did start innocently enough. The irony of the whole thing is that Scott's mom, along with the moms of most of my friends, thinks that I'm a pretty good kid and a little gentleman. So I get her blessings when I ask Scott to stay over for the night and camp out and my mom volunteered that she would be happy to run Scott home tomorrow. Most of us Louisiana teens at fifteen had driver's licenses but Scott, poor guy, had already had some brushes with the law and his parents couldn't get him insured. So my mom, being the cool Mom that she was, packed us some sandwiches, chips, and the like. She even gave us a few beers to take with us. And I get out some sleeping bags and a couple of fishing poles and at about 3:30 that afternoon we loaded up the skiff and pushed out to guide ourselves from cypress tree to moss hung cypress tree and through the grove until we finally got out into the channel. Well, we get out there and lo and behold, my little six-horsepower Johnson is out of gas. I explain to Scott that we'll have to call it off or just paddle to the camp sight. He's all for paddling and actually, we got lucky because the current was with us. After all, a bayou is a bayou because of the fact that the current can change flow. This is usually due to the tide. Kind of like some people I know—but anyway, it was working for me that day. Usually, by motor, the trip to my "camp" was about 5-10 minutes, but that day, it was about a 40-minute paddle, and about halfway through the trip, a little spring storm with no lighting or anything came up and drenched us. We were laughing about it and Scott was telling me about some of his outings at Military school. He said he liked the field trips but hated the academy. Ironically, it all sounded pretty good to me from what he said as we paddled along. Finally, we made it to the camp and we were drenched.

And when I say camp, I don't want to give any grandiose impressions here. This camp was made from stolen wood and was basically a glori-fied tree house that my buddies and I along the bayou had built several summers back. It was really cool. What we had done is found one of the few places on the bayou that had a steep bank, and we dug post holes on the edge of the bank and sunk a couple of telephone poles that we had found and sawed in half. We then took a couple of two by eights and ran them from the poles on the bank to two parallel cypress trees so that our camp would hang out over the water. The bank we had chosen was well wooded, and even today when I think of a mental "safe place," this location comes to mind. But the structure was very small, about six feet wide and ten feet stretching over the bayou. We constructed a roof and walls from stolen sheets of plywood and tin from old shacks that dotted the bayou. We even stole some fireplace bricks and made a fire place in the joint. Then in the back, we rigged some chicken wire to a two by four for support and stole some foam rubber and voila, we had a bed!

Looking back, it's funny how we never really thought of this as stealing. We looked at it from the point of view that the builders were moving into "our bayou" and that they owed us something for tearing down our woods, and we justified that whether they liked it or not, they were going to pay homage. In retrospect, we viewed ourselves in similar fashion as a Mafia boss in New Orleans, who would make bar and restaurant owners pay up or fail inspections. We thought this was pretty cool and we were tough guys. Shit, we had even taken a roll of that 1970s shag yellow carpet and decked the inside walls and floor with the stuff, and then wrapped the outside with bisque industrial plastic that contractors use to keep out moisture during various phases of their construction. The place was definitely snug, but the humidity from underneath and an occasional tear in the plastic that surrounded the outside wood and tin, had allowed the place to mold up in the last two years since building the shack. Funny, but I still get horny when I smell molded carpet. Maybe some people would find that sick, but let me tell why I get a boner from this distinct smell.

So we tied the boat to the little pier that ran horizontal to the water and then pulled up under the cabin, to our door. We thought that it was so cool having the door under the camp rather than being placed on the side like a standard door. I thought of this idea that, looking back, was a fire trap. Anyway, one of the rules between the other guys that built the shack and I was that whoever was at the camp last, was to replace the wood supply so that there was already wood handy. And as I mentioned, Scott and I were both drenched and now complaining of a chill as we unloaded the boat, so the first thing I did was make a fire. While I did this, Scott stripped down to his skin and laid the sleeping bags on the foam bed. Keep in mind that the little place is only sixty square feet and as we were both coming of age, and with the exercise from the paddle, I was able to get a good whiff of Scott's musk from his arm-pits and ass. I still wish someone would bottle the smell of mildewed carpet and male musk. They both give me an instant woody even today. But off I go again Selectric, so let me get back to the moment at hand.

I remember Scott asked, "Man, aren't you cold?"

"Yeah," I said keeping my eyes trained on the fire that I had just built then added, "But I don't have a change of clothes."

"Well numb nuts, neither do I, but you don't see me shivering do ya?"

He was right, but at this age I was inhibited by nudity. I wasn't confident with the size of my dick in comparison to some of the magazines I'd seen. I was one of these guys that started puberty early but never really fully developed until around eighteen. And on top of it all, I thought to myself, "Fuck what if I pop a boner and this guy tells everyone I'm a fag?"

But I was fairly quick on my feet even then and the answer came to me with the proverbial killing of two birds with one stone. I offered Scott our safe box which didn't hold any money but something even more valuable to teenaged boys. It contained what I would guess was one of the largest porn collections in the parish. Jeff, one of the guys that was a partner in the camp, had stolen them from his Uncle Woody who lived in a trailer behind his house. So like I said, I'm thinking that if I pop a boner, I can blame it on the porn of women, and at the same time, I had hoped a little more would come of the situation.

So Scott sat back on the bed thumbing through the collection as I undressed and then laid our clothes out in front of the infant fire to help them dry. And the shack was quickly heating up from both the fire and the sexual tension. When I turned around, I noticed that Scott already had an erection and that I would not have to fear any consequences from a show of arousal. And while I was admiring the size of his dick, he was staring in awe at one of the pictures in the book and said, "Come check this out."

So I stepped over and sat back next to him to see what he was looking at. It was typical porn shot of a man with a big dick right before penetration into this woman with her legs sprawled and holding her huge tits. There were several shots of this guy pounding her.

"That mother fucker has a weapon, wouldn't you say?" Scott inquired while pointing with his finger directly on the spot of the page where the model's dick was revealed by a close-up.

I casually agreed, as I had further been coached by my father never to make comments or even look at other guy's dicks. But Scott continued, "Man, I wonder if I will ever get that big?" he said with a hint of doubt, grabbing his cock.

I took the cue and ignored my dad's fatherly advice, saying bluntly, "You're not hurting now."

Nonchalantly, Scott acknowledged my compliment by saying, "Yeah, I'm pretty much tied with a guy in my barracks for first place."

"You have dick size contest at military school?" I asked in amazement.

"Kinda," he said laughing a little. "It's not formal or anything, but we do talk about it. You know, there ain't no private showers or johns like we have at home."

"Oh," I said and I guess the intimidation I felt from the idea came through in my voice.

And, as I was reaching over to grab another magazine from the box, Scott offered, "You're not in bad shape yourself. You'd be in the upper middle part of the pack in my barracks."

I was happy to hear that and I'm sure that the enthusiasm in my voice suggested the relief in my sense of inferiority when I said, "Really?" then quickly rebounded with the average standby, "Cool!"

By now, the afternoon had progressed to early evening. With the verification from Scott that I was of "normal" dick size and the familiarity of the night sound of the bayou starting to break into chorus, I began to feel more comfortable. When Scott questioned me, "You ready to pop one of those beers?" I eagerly replied, "Now you're talking."

Now keep in mind here that, as I said, I had never even jacked off and didn't know what to do with a hard on, but as you can imagine, that was only about to last for a few more minutes. And I remember that it had started to rain again, and we were starting to get a buzz when I noticed that Scott had gotten hold of one of our magazines called The Encyclopedia Sexual. Like the title suggested, it described cunnilingus or fellatio, and would then show very graphic pictures depicting the act. And of course, there was "Homosexuality," or as my partners in the camp in previous previews of this magazine had called, the "H" page. They would quickly flip past this section of the magazine with its black and white photos of men in 69's and one with a guy on all fours taking it up the ass. It would have spelled disaster to even get caught looking at these pages with my other buddies, so when I noticed Scott had stalled at the "H" page, I quickly volunteered, "Pretty sick, huh?"

Scott completely astonished me by saying with a shrug, "They look happy."

Looking back, what I find hysterical is that I was fourteen years old, in a tree house on a foam bed, naked with another guy all horned up, drinking beer, and looking at porn of two guys sucking dick, and I was still worried that this guy Scott would think I was a fag. It is funny to me now at just how naïve I was. But as we were getting down our second beer, Scott asked me if I had ever had sex before and I told him that I had not. I returned the question to him and he said that he had fucked his cousin, who I had previously met on one of his family's visits over. She was a couple of years older than us and not a bad looking girl. I asked Scott, "What was it like?"

Enthusiastically, he said, "Unbelievable Mason, Fucking unbelievable. I mean the feeling." He paused attempting to describe sex and came up with a pretty good description when he continued, "I mean it hurts and feels good at the same time!"

Innocently, I inquired, "How can it hurt and feel good at the same time?"

"Mason, I can't describe it anymore. You'll just have to do it to find out."

I shook my head saying, "Damn, I wish it wasn't raining so we could sneak over to Karen Borden's. I heard she let Gary White finger her."

"Yeah, too bad, but like it shows right here, you don't only need girls to do it Mason."

I don't think I'll ever forget the night sounds of the bayou, the crackling of the fire, and the sound of him gulping down a swig of beer before he sat up to put the empty can of Miller down, then laid down on his side with this mouth only inches away from my dick, and his dick only inches away from my face. Nor will I forget the shudder that enveloped my body as I felt Scott's warm mouth taking my dick. And the light from the fire as I was only inches from his big cock. Really, it was in my mouth before I knew it. Not the least bit of resistance did I offer this guy.

I was simply delirious. But that was broken up in about 30 seconds with Scott exclaiming, "Fuck Mason, your teeth are killing me."

"Oh man," I mumbled with his dick still in my mouth and reluctantly taking it out, I sat up on my elbow and continued. "Fuck dude, I'm sorry."

"Don't worry about it, but here's the deal. I'll suck your dick first and you can see how it's done and then you can suck mine."

Even today, I have to hand it to the guy; there were just no mixing words down on the bayou. It was just that simple even for a couple of young fags.

So I laid back and Scott started back and I can only describe what I felt as complete and pure ecstasy. I remember that I thought to myself that I finally knew what it's about. As I lay back, the subtle yet exquisite pleasure began to increase as it made my breathing become more and more difficult. I could hear the occasional slurp from Scott and his mouth as he gave me this experience. And sure enough, the "pain" came into the picture and I recall my slight concern as my breathing was becoming similar to when I was done running a 440. Honestly, the concern damn near went to panic as it seemed I couldn't catch my breath, and all of the sudden, I actually heard in my ears nothing short of, "Boom!"

The only other time in my life I can recall hearing anything similar to that sound is the time that I was at an air show and a jet fighter flew overhead and broke the sound barrier. As the thunder of the boom subsided, I let out a yell that took me out of my trance and I reached down and put my hands on Scott's head imploring him to stop. My dick was so sensitive that he must have sensed the frantic nature of my tone when he asked, "What's wrong?"

At first I couldn't say anything as I was actually scared that some kind of damage had been done to my dick. And there was no longer any sound whatsoever. The rain had stopped and it was quiet. And the fire wasn't even crackling. It was a quiet that I have never heard again. And things felt different. In fact, they felt amazingly different and I remember thinking to myself, "What is that smell?"

"That smell," for lack of a better description, smelled vaguely sharp and clean yet unique. What does cum smell like? I think the closest that I can identify cum fragrance is the smell of a bathroom after it has been given a good cleaning with Comet Brand cleaner.

By now, I was damn near in a panic. I recall, of all things, thinking about my English teacher, Mrs. Graves and what would she think of me if she knew what I had done. Would she still consider me one of her best students in years? And with that thought in mind, I couldn't hold back a sniffle.

Pretty pathetic I'd say. But I can't think of anything that could make me feel worse than the validation that I was in fact acknowledging that in all reality, I was a cock sucker. Fantasy was past. I had crossed the line. I was completely shocked and ashamed.

But Scott, who had not yet come, just said, "Okay, now my turn."

I'm ashamed to say today that at that time I had no intention of returning the favor and when Scott noticed my hesitation and then caught sound of one of my sniffles, he asked in an irritated voice, "Oh fuck, did you cum Mason?"

"I don't know," I answered, now curling into a fetal position facing away from him, staring into the fire's embers and thinking that for sure, I would know what that felt like before too long.

I have to laugh as I think back to how Scott broke the silence of the moment with the tone of disgust and spitting when he exclaimed, "Hell yeah, you came in my mouth mother fucker!"

He got off the bed and went to the ice chest and since we had drank all the beer and didn't bring anything else, he took out a piece of ice and put it in his mouth and within a few seconds was spitting out the hole in the floor that was our door. Shortly thereafter, he came over to the bed and stuck his dick in my face and after my failure to comply with his gesture he said, "Aw come on Mason, a deal is a deal."

"I can't" is all I replied and Scott's frustration was evident when he said, "Why not?"

"Just leave me alone, I'm serious." I answered in monotone not even recognizing my own voice.

Scott must have recalled me kicking his ass a few years back and heeded my warning for about five minutes. Scott broke the silence with the incorrect insinuation that we had already discussed an alternative to me not reciprocating the blow job.

"Alright then Mason, you can fuck me" he said.

I laugh again now, looking back, but my only response then was to get up, put on my clothes, jerk my sleeping bag out from under him and put them in the boat. He definitely knew that I would leave him and he stuck his head through the hole that was the door saying, "Damn it to hell, Mason, wait. Let me get my clothes on."

He got in the boat and started to say, "Fuck Mason, what in the hell…"

I cut him off lifting my paddle out of the water with the serious gesture that I would knock his lights out and again in a voice that I did not recognize, said, "Just shut the fuck up. Don't say another word. I mean it." He took my warning seriously.

We paddled home that night by moonlight through the bayou and it's groves of cypress trees covered in Spanish moss. It appeared to me as if they were crying as the night birds mocked me with their shrill and eerie cackles. There was also the chorus of the frogs and crickets that chirped and croaked in a new key as if they were telling me that I was no longer part of their symphony. And as we got out of the channel and made our way through the cypress grove, and pulled the boat up on the bank, I turned around to see the silhouette of my house and it looked different as well. I no longer felt welcomed at home. Nothing seemed the same. I didn't think it ever would again.

And to tell the truth, my assumption was correct.

CHAPTER 5

Fort Lauderdale, December 1991

As I sat on the sea wall that December afternoon and compared myself and my predicament to the unfortunates in places like Brazil, I realized that although I had never taken a physical beating to encourage me to cooperate in giving sexual favors to men, I had been repeatedly told that society did not tolerate my desire to engage in these acts. I was told it was unnatural, and I was unnatural, and my ears still pound when I hear the disdain in my peers and family's voice as they pronounce my kind as subhuman by proclaiming, "Those fucking faggots."

I have to admit, I've sung the chorus myself, even believed the damned song. So much so that I eventually decided that if I was on a train ride to hell, I might as well make it a fun roller coaster. And here I was on a fast turn in sunshiny Fort Lauderdale Florida, rather than being in law school and on my way to the governor's Mansion. I was flat broke without a pot to piss in except the public toilets on this magnificent beach.

Luckily for me, the sun on my 22-year-old body had quickly healed any trace of the poison that I had consumed and snorted the night before. After a quick slice of pizza, some push-ups, sit-ups, and three more hours of snoozing, I could feel the night coming the way that I imagine a vampire would recognize the first moonbeams streaming through the dusk. I have always adored the night.

The sky was starting to turn pink through the West as I looked up to hear the cacophony of a flock of wild parrots racing overhead. So I figured that I had best start acting a little social and got on with the night's business. Understand that I was by no means nervous, as I had no doubt that I could score at least one hustle for $100 before ten P.M. I could probably do at least five times that, with any luck. So I walked through the sand to the showers again and washed up, then walked down the beach to the public bathrooms and brushed my teeth, combed my hair, and after taking a good look at myself in the mirror, I figured that I looked like any other kid on vacation ,walking with a beach bundle back to his hotel room. But the difference between the college kid on vacation and me was that I would let another guy suck my dick for $100—or if he was ready to play with my ass and pay double, then I was ready to play double.

And while I was looking at myself in the mirror, I remember grinning when I recalled a buddy in New Orleans chastising me for selling my ass when he asked, "Jesus, Mason, how in the hell can you even look at yourself in the mirror?"

My response to my buddy, a pharmacist, was perhaps a bit harsh, but I think appropriate: "How do you feel when no one will sleep with you, much less pay you for doing it? So go play with your pills, and bang on your typewriter, and be sure you don't forget to clock out. You wouldn't want to cheat the company, would you?"

What can I say? I am just proud of the fact that I have "The Goods" to stay in business. Man, I feel sorry for those guys with little dicks. Men will terrorize the poor mother fucker with a little dick. They'll even laugh at a poor bastard born unfortunate. Hell I'm guilty of it, but I did it only once and I won't do it again. I was never beaten like those guys down in Brazil; but I did take a hell of punch from a john when I let out a smirk at his pencil. Now as I look in the mirror and see the scar on my chin, I feel it's safe to say that I won't go there again. Sometimes it takes a punch to learn a lesson.

But let me get back to whoring. Hell, I kind of equate it with deer hunting, fishing, or what have you. I really was brought up in the woods and I had always enjoyed the hunt. I was the typical little redneck brought up on the simple philosophy instilled by my father that some dogs will hunt, and some won't. And I'm here to tell you, I can smell my prey a mile away. Yep, there are two things I can spot in a heartbeat and they are another fag or a cop. This is an extremely beneficial knack to have in my line of work. I wonder if it is any coincidence that the two things my father has the most disdain for in this world are cops and fags. Oh, and lest I forget, military commanders or preachers, I think the ultimate insult to the old man would be to write him a letter telling him that I am a gay chaplain in the Army MP, and that I might make Colonel this year.

To tell the truth, I don't much care for cops either. I've yet to run into a police officer who doesn't rub my grain the wrong way. Not a one. It is something in their attitude that screams conform that is about the most repulsive thing I can think of. Nevertheless, I guess it is fortunate for me that officers of the law carry this common denominator that I just can't quite tag with a name. Maybe it's assholism? Or something like that—but let me keep thinking. And even when they are undercover, this invariably seeps through their disguise.

For instance, I knew this dumb motherfucker back in New Orleans that pulled up with a crew cut and just opened his passenger door of his Ford F-150 and told me to get in. So I asked him, "Dude, why don't you just protect my head when I get in so I don't come back and charge you with police brutality."

You know most johns are going to be a little nervous but here this guy was with a preconception that gays are fairies and want a butch man that can open car doors for us. And if this officer had a lick of sense, he'd have known that most johns are a little nervous and will at least cruise you a couple of times before they stop and proposition you. And hell, even if I had not been sure that this guy was not a cop, his reaction to my smirk after my comment totally blew his cover. Police hate to be laughed at and this John Law couldn't control his temper for even a split second as he slammed his truck into park and threw my ass against the wall and demanded an I.D. while he slapped my ass around. I guess my point being was that the dumb fuck felt good that he blew his cover and acted like a typical prick of the men in blue. I guess he thought he was in control of the situation. That was alright with me because I went on to score a grand that night.

I have often wondered how I survived the Police of New Orleans. I'm here to tell ya, Selectric, if one of 'em ever asks you to stop typing, you better do what he says. They can be rough. But nowadays, it's some of the younger cops that I have to watch out for. They didn't grow up like their fat-ass, donut-eating, civil-rights-bashing counterparts that held black voters at bay, or attested to "suicides" of depressed Yankees that got speeding tickets in the wrong place at the wrong time. I almost got suckered back in New Orleans by this guy that looked to be a loser, overweight hotel bartender. This guy walked up next to me in black and white bartender garb acting a bit intoxicated and he laid a line on me. He said that today was his birthday and at 38 all he could show for his life was a bartending job. Basically he said that he was lonely. He's was pretty convincing but he talked with his hands, and I looked at them. Most career bartenders I've seen have some beaten up hands due to the lemons, limes, bar soap, and the alcohol itself. I think they called it "Bar Rot," and this dude didn't have it. So before I started talking money to this guy, I looked him square in the eyes and I told him, "Kiss me."

And I puckered up and his response was, "What? Right here on the streets you want me to kiss you? Oh man, kissing just isn't my thing."

I know this for a fact. Cop or no cop, nothing is more repulsive to a straight man than the thought of kissing another guy. They just can't do it. So I just told the cop, "Awe now Teddy, no kissy no sissy. Me no like you?" I told him in my best imitation of a Saigon street walker and I laughed. The same hate flashed from this guy's eyes that I had seen from his older predecessor. As I walked off, I held my nose like something stank to signal my counterparts working the North Rampart that night. I heard the younger, already-chubby undercover cop as he called in on his back up to come pick him up as his cover was shot for the night. As I walked off and laughed at the prick I heard him explain to his Sergeant or what have you, "The little faggot wanted me to kiss him … I'm not sure I wouldn't rather have him suck my dick than kiss me … right, right."

But let me get back to my status in Fort Lauderdale that December sunset. Like I said, it was time to get into action. I had planned to go back to that strip bar and score enough money to get a weekly rental or something, but I knew I couldn't just go in there broke or the bouncers would kick my ass out. I had absolutely no connections in this town. Yep, Selectric, I was alone in new woods without a compass. But if spotting johns or cops was a necessary tactic in my hunt, so was the ability to spot a likely thicket where the johns hung out. I could tell that the ocean front was a bit too tame. It just didn't contain the elements that tingle my instincts into a hustling mode. So I walked up to Sunrise Boulevard. With nothing but a hunch, I took the bus west, which of course was the only direction to take a bus on Sunrise from A1A. And my hunch proved correct. For almost immediately after crossing the Intracoastal, I started to recognize my competition at play. Probably as easily as a deer hunter would recognize another one of his compatriots from his hunter's orange. And a good hustler is about that predatory instinct. The glossy, focused eye is a common look that I have seen in the eyes of every single one of them. There is no mistaking it. It's very similar to the look that a coyote gives a rabbit. It's also common in the eyes of many lawyers, but I'll touch on that later.

I've always felt that working the major boulevards in New Orleans was somewhat stupid, so I decided to use my same philosophies here. They are fairly simple. One, I believe that if anybody is looking for something illegal, he doesn't want to purchase it in the light, like on a major strip. So I like to go off on a side street that has traffic and just a little into the dark. I have heard tales about Sunset Boulevard, but this wasn't LA, and besides, I noticed too much competition on Fort Lauderdale's Sunrise. Maybe they had protection of some sort and again, I knew that I was on my own. So, I opted to walk to the neighborhood just off Sunrise and N.E. 13th Ave.

It was basically a very tacky neighborhood that might have been nice at one time. It was obvious that people in my line of work rented cheap little efficiencies and worked the area fairly hard. So I easily stepped into character. I was just a neighborhood boy out for an evening walk. I couldn't help but notice all of the "For Rent" signs, so I made it a point that I would remember to check some of the places out tomorrow to get a cheap room. I also noticed that some of the cars that drove around were making the block for at least a second time now. These were the same guilty faces in the same cars that could have been cruising the French Quarter, but were now in Fort Lauderdale. I wonder why so many gay men look at other men through darting eyes. Seriously, when a straight man is dazzled by a woman, he has no problem absorbing her for as long as he likes. I've watched men stare in trances for a good thirty to forty-five seconds before the woman giggled interest, walked off, slapped the creep, or maybe all three.

Anyhow, I was definitely in the right spot. Other guys were obviously irate that I was pouncing on their "territory" but the good thing about being a gay hustler is that I don't have to pay a pimp to protect me or my territory. I told the first mother fucker that started to say something to me, "Go take a bath you trashy freak so you and your stink don't have us all out of money tonight."

This was probably not a smart thing to say as I had no idea who this guy was, but what can I say, I can be a real dumb ass at times. Why some of these bottom feeders think they can do this work smelling like the street has always puzzled me. Hell, that's not always the case, but some of these punks smell like a gutter following Fat Tuesday, and they actually think these men want them in their Mercedes so that their lovers, wives, or whatever can ask what they had in the car. Shit, I don't even wear cologne. Some Right Guard, but no perfumes. I don't let myself get to smelling bad. And if a guy took me to his house, I always tried to shower before I left. Now that's class wouldn't you say?

The way I see it, class is having so much of it that you don't worry about showing it off. It just comes through. I know that someone might wonder how a guy like me can think that he's classy, but trust me, there is class in any trade or field. There are classy racehorses and even though the horse may be owned by a thug, the animal can still be a classy race-horse, and perhaps even owned by a classy thug. So I have to ask, is it a contradiction in terms when I question, why not a classy street hustler?

In New Orleans, I always had the choicest cut of pie, so why wouldn't I in Fort Lauderdale. But I had to be careful of cops, and I knew it as I saw a gray Mercedes pass by for the second time, then came to a stop only yards in front of the direction that I was walking. So I approached the car from the driver's side and casually nodded to the man and smiled and continued forward. I only had seconds to size him up before I would start with the bait lines.

He was in his late fifties and was not the fat type, but basically he had all the signs of bad health from smoking and drinking. Frankly, he was smoking a cigarette and I could see the bags under his eyes despite the poor light. But the car was a Mercedes Benz and he was wearing a golf shirt. There are at least ten warning signs that I look for without thinking. But I didn't get any notion that this man was a cop. Nope, this guy had some class. And a New York license tag. So I brought out the exaggerated nasal dumb ass Yuk Yuk that any Yankee would expect from Southern trash and said, "Hey mister do ya think ya could help me with something?"

I tried to place a hint of urgency to my tone. I told myself that most people are good and that they really wanted to do was to help someone out if given an incentive. And frankly, I knew that most johns were just plain lonely. When he slowed his engine and I saw a break light, I gained even more confidence.

"Hey man, excuse me, but are you familiar with the city?"

The man cracked a smile to reveal his yellow stained teeth and replied, "Been here on and off most of my life. I guess you could say that I'm familiar with the place. Why?"

From his response and his demeanor, I was fairly optimistic that this guy was no man in blue. He also slouched in his seat. So I smiled at him with my best "you wouldn't believe it" and said, "Well I just flew in from New Orleans and the airlines lost my bag. So I tell them to send 'em to my friend's house and I haven't ever been here before, but I've been on the phone with my buddy once a week since Labor Day and now I come to find out the sumbitch don't even live here and ..." I threw up my hands in disbelief, still relying on this man's predisposition that anyone from the south had to be a complete idiot.

"How long did you know him before you came here?" the man quizzed me.

"Just since I met him at Southern Decadence festival in New Orleans." I replied then went on with a weak smile, "I can't believe it but he gave me an address that some Mexican woman with little kids was living in, and ..."

Of course the man took a moment to correct me believing me ignorant enough to think that anyone that spoke Spanish was automatically a Mexican stating, "Possibly Puerto Rican or Cuban, Maybe Mexican. Makes no difference, you got scammed. I shrugged to acknowledge his assessment and he went on to say, "I was just driving my pool man home. Seems like you're in a little situation here. Perhaps you would like to make some phone calls at my house?" the man punctually offered with what I assumed was a crisp New York accent.

"Oh man!" I exclaimed with appreciation and continued, "You have no idea how much I would appreciate that!"

The man cracked a smile and said, "Get in"

I did, and even the smell of his cigarettes could not overpower the smell of a Mercedes. It had to be the leather. I mean the damn thing just smelled rich. So the man drove cautiously out of the neighborhood and onto another major Boulevard that took us to what I now know to be the Fiesta Isles area of the city, where I glimpsed the degree of wealth that the neighborhood strutted through, even in the darkness of the night. It seemed like every single house had a yacht behind or next to it. Finally, he opened his garage and we entered the carpeted enclosure.

When we got into the house, I noticed that there were pictures of this Latin stud everywhere. The man motioned me hospitably through the dining area and into a living room where he was obviously set to entertain. And I asked him point blank, "So who's the stud in the picture?"

The man seemed to be a little disturbed that I might be casing his house or something. I mean, he didn't seem insulted or threatened but his disposition definitely changed. He replied to my question, "You know you haven't even asked me my name." His tone was not one of jealousy but of slight regret, and he even smiled slightly as if the act of smiling was a bit difficult for him now. As well, his soft blue eyes, even though blood shot, did not cast menace, but despair. And yet at the same time a plea for comprehension of his torment in an almost telepathic way was extended to me. In an instant, I knew that the man was in incredible pain. The room was too silent.

The old man was staring with reverence at the picture of the young man. I knew that I needed to break some tension here, and fast. As I popped my palm on my forehead, I went ahead with more good ole boy, "Oh man, I'm so sorry. You know I was actually brought up better than to act like this, but with the day's bullshit and all, my manners ..."

The man politely held up his hand motioning for me to stop, then made a fist and covered up his smoker's coughed and continued, "His name is—was—whatever the hell," he said with what I perceived to be a histrionic attempt to place his tense correctly. After gathering himself he continued, "He is Federico Ernesto, and I am Pat Madera." He looked at me. "And I believe you have some phone calls to make."

To tell you the truth, I wasn't really sure who was conning whom. He was playing it pretty hard, or else he really was in love with this guy. Regardless, I could tell by his surroundings that this guy was pure gold. As he handed me the cordless phone, I thanked him and instinctively called the "Time and Temperature" of American Bank in New Orleans and started my spiel.

"Hello Frank?" I asked eagerly as the recording announced to me that the current temperature in the Crescent City was 48 degrees, and then proceeded to encourage me to begin investing in IRA's so I let out a perceptibly frustrated breath of air and continued, "Yeah, it's me Andy … Uh huh … I know … Yep, Yep, Yep, you were right about the dip-shit."

I slapped my hand on my forehead and spun around at the same time to be facing Pat and continued talking to the recording, "Listen, can you just help me get home?" I started to add a hint of desperation to my tone and lowered my voice a bit so as to allow Pat to barely hear me say in the phone, "Come on Frank. Please! Only $125 and I'm on Value Jet back home … Am I good for it?" I spat out incredulously into the phone receiver and continued, "Have I ever not paid you for anything?" I questioned the recording that was now coming to its end.

"So what if it wasn't actual cash, Frank? Hello, hello?" I asked in a quiet panic as the bank recording told me to have a nice day and hung up. So did I and finally looked up at my host who didn't miss a beat asking, "Can I offer you a drink? I'm having Scotch. Johnny Walker Black on the rocks do it?" he further inquired with a one eyebrow raised.

I shrugged and gave a half-ass, "I don't know, Pat."

"Listen!" he quickly injected, and sympathetically continued, "It looks like we could both use a little company tonight. What'll it be?" He asked with a smile and a friendly slap on the shoulder.

Again I just shrugged and looked at him with a "what the hell" smile and said, "I'll have the same."

"Whew!" He exclaimed, then after letting out a whistle said, "Scotch on the rocks at your age? Man!" he exalted enviously. Then he handed me the tumbler and offered me a toast. But I already had the glass to my lips before he could lift his to toast. Even I was embarrassed about my manners and turning red told my host, "Oh Jesus, Pat! I can't believe myself. Please excuse me."

He eagerly held up a hand to motion to me to forget it as nothing, but I continued by telling him while holding the tumbler up to the ceiling lights, "Ya see Pat; I don't just view Johnny Walker Black as Scotch. I mean to say that if we had a Frenchman giving me a confirmative on my attitude to Mr. Black here by calling it the 'Nectar of the Gods,' I'd have to tell him, 'Frenchie, bullshit. I'd have to say sipping Johnny Walker Black is more like giving Zeus a blow job and having the god come in my mouth."

That comment got the first laugh out of Pat that I'd heard all night and I knew then that I had him hooked.

"What do you know about Zeus, Andy?" he asked with the smile still fresh on his face.

I gulped the next bit of scotch down and replied in a matter of fact tone, "history major."

"No kidding!" he gently exclaimed, then with some interest inquired, "When did you graduate?"

"I haven't graduated yet. I'm only a junior," I explained. I didn't feel it necessary to get into the fact that actually I had a G.E.D. as I didn't graduate from Chamberlain Hunt where they put a great deal of emphasis on Greek History.

"At Tulane?" Asked Pat.

"Yeah right. Like I can afford that." I stated somewhat incredulously.

"What Tulane? Why Not?" he asked, then continuing in a fatherly way, "I'm sure that most of the students there are on scholarships, but anyway," he paused by wholeheartedly slapping me on the back, then saying, "Isn't tonight a school night?"

"If it weren't Christmas Break, but I'm not in this semester anyway," I offered perhaps a bit too eagerly and coughing up some of my scotch and continued, "I go to the University of New Orleans here and there you know. Save a dollar here, study some there, and then work, then?" I paused and looked into his eyes and just said, "I don't know. I haven't really made the grades for a scholarship, but right now all I have to worry about is getting home. That flight home won't be cheap."

"Well, when is it?" asked Pat.

"I think around tomorrow morning at 7. Or tonight at 10:30. I hardly remember getting here. But I do remember something of the flight brochure. Don't ask me?" I shrugged.

"How much do you need?" he enquired and looking him straight in the eyes, "One twenty-five."

"That's not a problem" Pat replied.

"I can pay you back when I get home," I explained.

"No, that won't be necessary," he said.

"You know, Pat, you're not a bad guy. I could pay you back now."

The man was lonely, and I didn't have to do anything. He simply walked over and unsnapped my shorts and let them fall to the floor. As he knelt down on his knees, he proceeded to unzip his own pants and masturbate as he gave me a blow job. As a matter of fact, I'd say he gave some of the best head I've had, but wouldn't you know it, I get a talented john but the man turns out to be a quickie-pop. It took him only five minutes and he shot his load in his own hand.

Pat even said thank you as he was washing out his mouth and hands at his living room's bar sink. When he had finished washing and drying his hands, he walked over to where I sitting with a boner still showing through my shorts, and he handed me six twenty dollar bills. I told him that I really appreciated the cash.

"Do you want to stay here tonight and let me drive you to the airport?"

"I think if I hustle, I can still catch that 10:30 out tonight," I replied and quickly added, "I really want to get home."

"I can call you a cab for your trip out to the airport. I would take you but I'm a firm believer that drinking and driving don't mix," he said earnestly.

Within 10 minutes, I shook his hand goodbye and told the taxi driver as we pulled out, "Take me to Jimmy's."

He let out a contemptuous "harrumph," pushed his meter to the on position.

I started to give him directions as I mistook his groan for a 'huh?' and said, "I think it's on West Brevard or ..." But I was rudely interrupted by his gruff Brooklyn voice, "Yeah, yeah, I know where that fag place is."

"Great," I said aloud and then added, "Then you think you could just get us there, Mr. Bunker."

"Yeah sure," he said then lit up a cigarette and turned up his oldies station and I was glad that he had all of the windows down for I figured that the sound of the wind as it came through the piece of shit car would muffle the music so that I could listen to my head.

I'd like to say that tricking doesn't faze me, but that would be a lie. And the truth, as I have stated earlier, is what I'm after here. Rationally, I could always justify my behavior, but honestly, the disgust I felt from the cabby's eyes peering at me through his rear-view mirror only intensified the emotional chords that echoed through me. Which brings me to this question:

Do feelings have anything to do with truth or reality? Did the fact that I could sense that cab driver's disdain for me have anything to do with "The Truth?" If I denied the sentiments I felt that he had towards me, I don't believe that I would be painting an accurate scenario of that night. And exactly what were his true sentiments as they concerned me? I felt sure through initial remarks, gestures, and a mirrored stare that the driver hated me. But I didn't really know. The dialogue that I shared with this complete stranger had been relatively short; I could only feel what I assumed would be this goon's thoughts.

And if I could have by some miraculous gift of telepathy read the true thoughts of my driver, would I have still considered him a goon that hated me? I'm sure that I'll never know what that cab driver honestly thought of me. But I know how I felt. I heard the weak voice of my conscience calling "The Committee" a fantasy that truly exist only inside my mind, validating my feelings. Someone else with an unforgettable Irish accent was shouting and stirring things up over there. So I feel that here is as good a time as any for me to introduce this realm of my existence that, again, without any doubt, allows me to know and remember how I felt.

CHAPTER 6

December 1991

Meet "The Committee"

TELLING YOU NOW LADS AND WHAT FER OF YE WITH CUNTS betweenst yer legs, I want to hear a promising reason for the summons by this turd, Conscience, we just can't seem to shit out our arse. Come now, shall we give the lad a break! Do we want Andy on the beach tonight or worse yet, in jail. At least now we'll not want for proper lodgings."

The ramifications for these maniacal rantings were the evident but weak excuse for a conscience that attempted to bring order to a conglomerate of confused sentiment that had formed in a nerve just off the lower neck. Slowly, the feelings were being sorted by a gathering of emotional and instinctive natures that inhabit my being. These entities fed on the feelings, which in essence were themselves. These were fleeting gatherings, like clouds in the sky, but they always held consequences as a cloud can bring tornados, cause lightning, or provide life giving moisture. Their Essence is validation of any idea or belief presented to the moment. Though unruly and unpredictable, these emotions, instincts and traits were not to be, and would not be taken lightly.

Although he dutifully announced the call with the cold indifference but threatening demeanor of a small claims court bailiff, Mr. Conscience knew he really had no power in these emotional halls themselves. He looked dull as he ceremoniously gestured with an obligatory duty of one that had inherited a paid and cushy position of privilege that had now become work, but compensated well enough not to quit. He held his posture as best he could with the preeminence afforded to a position that at one time might have held some sort of valor and honor but was obviously no longer enjoyed or valued by any of the traits and characters of the emotional realm. For some reason, yet to be satisfactorily explained, the cast of the emotional realm still responded to the decrees of Mr. Conscience with much the same respect the British Parliament would give to an edict from the Queen Mum.

Mr. Conscience had grown accustomed to being customary. A few years back, he had begun to feel like a Catholic Saint's holiday in a Protestant country where annual observations remained printed and highlighted on the Gregorian calendars but, for the most part, ignored by the Lutheran masses. Better yet in the case of Andy's emotional realm, the masses had indeed reconverted to their Pagan past.

Because his voice had become so weak, Mr. Conscience let out a sigh and took his seat at a round table where he was anxiously satisfied by the fluttering arrival of a handful of various characters that were still capable of hearing his pestered cries. That was until the lighting of the room took on a new shade and hue with the arrival of Mr. Slut/Whore.

Mr. Slut/Whore had railed in Celtic fury that would have made the most ornery geezers of Cork blush. And the scarlet and orange radiance emitted by the enraged trait gave the meeting room an air of brilliance that was difficult for Mr. Conscience to bear.

Before Mr. Slut/Whore could sit down, Mr. Conscience, his voice frogged and high, with very little power but still not able to hold back a little of the truth that a glimmer of hope offers, meekly announced, "The reason we're all together again, Mr. Slut/Whore, is because you're here. It would be safe to assume that were it not for you, Mr. Slut/Whore, and the incredible shenanigans that you get Andy into, we'd all be back in New Orleans with Andy pulling himself together and getting back in school. Wouldn't you say?"

Mr. Slut/Whore couldn't hold back a hysterical laugh as he leaned back in his chair then hastily brought it down to look at Miss Addiction. He retained his newly found good disposition as he questioned her, his Irish accent thick as the horrid dark beer of his native land.

"Miss Addiction, is that what yer planning to do with the money Andy and I make after a night on the prowl? Really now I beseech you. A wee wince of honesty Lass. As I know that is difficult for a girl as yourself, but I hope you don't mind my asking you to look Mr. Conscience square in the eye and tell him that our young man Andy was going to advance our night's work to an account fer a future check to the University Of New Orleans."

Since Mr. Slut/Whore's change in mood had dimmed the lighting to a hue that was much more comfortable and familiar to Miss

Addiction, She had relaxed to a momentarily tolerable degree and was now free to remove her hand that she had used to protect her sensitive eyes from his previous rage. Miss Addiction extended her dark, blood-red polished nails to grab her cigarette pack, casually withdrew an unfiltered stogie and after packing it delicately on the table, finally lit the stick. She took a huge drag and exhaled an atomic cloud of smoke.

She addressed Mr. Slut/Whore in a tone that did away with whatever doubts any entity at the table could have held about the familiarities between the two as she abandoned his formal saluta-tion and calmly expressed in the low country gentility that a mistress on a delta plantation might use to tell her 22-year-old 'boy' to rub her back, "Don't patronize me Slut/Whore. It really isn't necessary." She flicked her cigarette ashes onto the floor and took her eyes off Mr. Slut/Whore so that she could address the expressed disapproval of Mr. Conscience towards her filthy habit. With her own face that was now as bland and casual as that of a billionaire spending a hun-dred dollars, Miss Addiction didn't have to utter a syllable to Mr. Con-science. Communication between many emotions and characters of mind didn't require the use of words, as words are simply trivial instruments used to send messages to the mind of the host.

Expressions of various means such as light, color, facial contor-tions (or lack of such) were more than adequate to communicate thought between Miss Addiction and Mr. Conscience. As they sat around the table of the committee now in session, her menacing and stellar Conveyances towards Mr. Conscience expressed her complete disregard for his disapproval of her disposal of ashes and her con-tempt for his not having an ashtray on the table. Miss Addiction was certain that Mr. Conscience knew full well that she smoked and as she blew a cloud of smoke directly in his face, she made him fully aware that he should have accommodated her habit before he even considered calling the group together. Mr. Conscience too sheepishly lowered his gaze back to the table. Miss Addiction took another drag of her cigarette and blew another cloud upwards into the air as she returned her attention to Mr. Slut/Whore and stated calmly, "You know I've pretty much kept Andy off the hard stuff. There has been no heroin and very little crystal. I'd say that's a favor I extend to you Slut/Whore for we all know that Andy's dick gets the size of a newborn's when he's on crank and let's face it, that's not good for business."

She took another puff and continued talking while exhaling directly at the lame duck chairman and, simultaneously running her eyes up and down him, stated flatly, "and a little dick is not even good for you, Mr. Conscience." Miss Addiction flicked her cigarette ash on the floor again and coldly stated with a slow and luscious emphasis on the last three emboldened words.

"A little coke and some booze won't kill the boy so all of you can just pucker up pretty as you like and politely kiss my ass."

Mr. Conscience took his hand off of his face revealing the bags under his eyes while he casually pointed out to the group, in a voice that moment by moment had begun to resemble the resolute whimper of Hanna Barbara's cartoon character Droopy.

"Excuse me Miss Addiction, but I believe the reason that you heard my voice calling you to today's round table is precisely because you and Mr. Slut/Whore do indeed seem to put Andy in dire circumstances."

"Well Slut-Whore is a bit of a looker wouldn't you say, Sugar? You wouldn't hold it against a lady for wanting to spend a little leisure time with him would you?" She questioned Mr. Conscience who blushed at the insinuation made by the smoky cunt.

Miss Addiction gave a subtle wink to the Mr. Slut-whore and after she casually acknowledged his airborne kiss, Miss Addiction returned her attention to Mr. Conscience who had glowed a pale red from the embarrassing truth brought to light that he did in fact find Mr. Slut/Whore attractive.

"Why really, Chairman Conscience, will you never recover your wits and accept the fact that you find men attractive. It is becoming quite boring and frankly, I'm growing tired of the little damper you put on our parties. So please, kindly make your point obvious and say what you must and let us alone with our nature."

"Well," Mr. Conscience began, then paused and drew in a breath so that he could trudge on, "you all may remember that young man that Andy was in fact getting friendly with. I think Andy was even making some plans with the law student. What was his name?" Mr. Conscience silently pondered the young man's name with such focus and determination that his face had contorted to resemble a heroin addict letting go of a dump after a six day constipation.

Suddenly he exclaimed the lone name. "Michael!" in a voice that actually held some vitality but quickly faded as he plodded on.

"And anyway, Miss Addiction, intentionally or not, introduced first Andy and then Michael to the pleasures of meth and Michael mistakenly snorted a gram of crystal that he thought was cocaine, in one sniff. Remember how this popped the bright kid of 26 with a heart-attack that put him in a coma?" He gingerly asked, but upon receiving no response from any of those sitting at the table continued.

"The poor guy came out of it but now only eats puddings and apple sauce. You would think he was born with MS. Although I can't explain why his memory came to me, I think we're all here today because I remembered Michael and I don't think any of us wants to land in a state institution of some type eating mush."

"Talk to Slut/Whore about eating pudding." Miss Addiction cackled as she dangled a fresh new Pall Mall from her lips and used both of her hands to cuff the lighter and light another cigarette. She left it dangling from her mouth as she crossed her arms and took stock of Mr. Slut/Whore's feigned attempt at shock.

"Miss Addiction! How dare you!" exclaimed Mr. Slut/Whore. But he was unable to hide a smile and a guilty glint in his eye as giddily tried to defend himself.

"I had no idea the man was about to shoot his load. As we all know that rarely do I take us to the act of eating cum, but again, I have to place some of the blame for my lack of control in that particular exception on a little white pill that Miss Addiction did ingest. And it removed any inhibitions that might usually annoy me. Ah me Las, if memory holds true, I think the pill was called ecstasy." He ended the sentence extending a debonair smile and wave of hand to the round table.

"Shut the fuck up both of you!" bellowed an older feminine voice from the haggard yet vibrantly bitter face of an old woman that along with some of the other entities called to the round table had heretofore kept silent. Miss Love stood up now and the woman pointed first at Miss Addiction and then at Mr. Slut/Whore and intermittently looked at each one of them while scolding them, "You've taken an All American boy with some sexual confusion and turned him into a whore."

Mr. Slut/Whore brazenly stood up and bowed to Miss Love and greeted her with an almost sincere, "A fine top of the morning to you as well Miss Love but would you mind me quickly asking you, what's Un-American about being a whore?" Mr. Slut/Whore's face was shining innocently. He still gave it his best to speak as if he were familiar with the Emerald Isle, although Andy had never been to Ireland or any other nation in Europe for that matter.

But Mr. Slut/Whore stood up with the temper and righteous conviction of the Celtic patriot and poised, "Honestly here is a nation that sold her secret of nuclear science to Communist governments whose very constitutions stated their mission as the destruction of free enterprise while another American freely sold dangerous biological information to Islamic militants. Here is a country that has repeatedly said that if it feels good, do it. Rock on gang! Here is a country that has worshiped a 'Material Girl' but at the same time has sent troops to protect women circumcising, homosexual killing Dictators as long as, 'His Hines or El Duce or whoever the fuck sends the oil. Here is a country that literally makes heroes out of whores. Don't fuck with me fellas for if Andy is blessed with the goods, and that's what keeps the food coming and the show running, don't expect me to lend you a serious ear today."

He looked around the table and realized his Irish passion had begun to absurdly light the place up again. He only wished that he had a brass band playing, "America, the Beautiful" as he closed his soliloquy with a contemptuous and arrogant, "And quite frankly, PISS OFF!"

"Thank you Mr. Slut/Whore. Your Patriotism is duly noted," Mr. Conscience meekly consoled, then added, as he saw that his soothing words were having some effect on the Mr. Slut-Whore's aura, "It's just with all of his intelligence..."

Mr. Conscience was interrupted by Mr. Slut/Whore's rude exclamation, "And speaking of Intelligence, where is that old mother fucker today? You called the meeting and I had to show up. Are you possibly implying that he is excused from these little soirees you call? Dare I say that there is, in fact, an implication that his time is more valuable than mine?"

Through pursed lips, Miss Love came to take Mr. Conscience's slack saying, "He said that he's going to have to just watch the table from that video camera as he can't see the reality of his being able to properly communicate in the same room dominated by Mr. Slut/Whore and Miss Addiction." She was still sitting as she pointed up to a small camera anchored in the vice of ugly metal. As she lowered her hand back to the table, she stopped talking and returned her face to its perpetual pout only to be addressed by Miss Addiction as she walked over to her and kindly placed a hand on her shoulder.

Miss Love sat frozen and looked out into space while she did her best to ignore Miss Addiction whom now inquired, "Well, well, well, Miss Love; did those pictures of the boyfriend all over the John's house tonight inspire to you to the summons of our little meeting this evening? Bless your heart," continued Miss Addiction as she looked over at Mr. Slut/Whore with a glum face to extend him an invitation to join the mimicking pity-party she had begun for the benefit of Miss Love. The old woman suddenly rose to shake off the hand that Miss Addiction had placed on her shoulder and spun around to spout to the belligerent characters, "One of these days, Intelligence is going to come in here and kick both of your asses with the truth."

"Really Miss Love?" Mr. Slut/Whore calmly asked then further inquired, "He and who else?"

"Me!" shot back Miss Love.

"Love's not truth honey," Miss Addiction sympathetically extended to Miss Love.

"The fuck it's not!" stated Miss Love with the conviction of Churchill. She stood up and pushed Miss Addiction aside to walk out of the meeting.

In a grated and off-key voice that had been pickled from Vodka, Miss Addiction began to sing a song in her best imitation of a torch diva, "Hey lady, please lady, don't just walk away, 'cause I have this need to tell you, why I'm all alone today"

Mixed with the wild cackles of Mr. Slut/Whore's laugh and the clicking footsteps of Miss Love's geriatric shoes as she departed the room, Mr. Conscience's pleas for the old woman to stay at the table were interrupted by my memories of reality's taxi driver as he crudely, but truly, got back to the business at hand—money

"That'll be twelve-seventy."

I reached in my back pocket and produced the wad of twenties Pat had given me for letting him suck my cock.

CHAPTER 7

Fort Lauderdale, December 1991

I MUST HAVE CAUGHT THE DRIVER'S ATTENTION WHEN I EXPOSED THE wad of bills. Perhaps he had picked up hustlers from Pat's house before. I really don't know if it was that he felt he could trust me, or if it was his general lack of fear of getting busted that allowed him to simply proposition me. I just remember that my entire attitude changed towards the guy despite his gruff Brooklyn voice asking, "Hey kid! You want some nose candy?"

"Fuck yeah!" I replied before he even finished pronouncing the word candy.

"Sixty bucks," he said with a look that, despite what accent or language the man communicated to another person with, any fool would know to be read as "take it or leave it." But he asked for it as easy as a teller in the hundred dollar minimum window at a horse track would request a well-dressed gambler, "Two thousand please sir. Can I ask you to hurry so that Miss Costanza behind you can beat the bell?"

"You got it," I said to the taxi driver and quickly handed him three more twenty dollar bills. And about just as quick, the taxi driver slapped a white baggy in my hand. I quickly put the baggy in my front pocket of my shorts and shut the door, said thanks to the driver. He nodded and drove off.

I looked around and took stock of the building that I was about to enter for a second time in my short but eventful trip so far to fabulous Fort Lauderdale. Only this time, I swear it looked different. I was hoping that I didn't cause any kind of a scene the last time I was here as I took stock of all of the expensive foreign luxury cars in the lot. I took that as a good sign for my present situation. I remember that I thought to myself that I was reasonably sure that I didn't cause any problems here last night, and with that thought in mind opened the door and walked into the joint. And although there was no one asking me to pay a cover charge, I was greeted with a look of contempt by the door man. His emaciated face brought back to my memory this total bitchy fourth grade teacher. And although I was not in any of her classes, she still figured me for rotten and glared at me with eyes that silently said, "I've got my eye on you."

I gave him the same "what the fuck" that I have always felt for jackasses and walked with no trouble up to the bar. I wanted a drink really bad. But my thirst wasn't from anxiety, because despite the initial greeting from the door man, I felt really comfortable. I think I probably relate to gay bars in much that same way that a gay catholic would relate to a cathedral. No matter how bad I'm treated, I feel at home in them. Bars that is. And this bar was full.

While I looked for a break in the crowd to get to the bar, I had already casually started to canvass the place for the most strategic place to score a quick hit. The boys had all the old men hot and ready tonight. It felt like people were having a good time. So while I made a lap around the bar to find an opportune free space, I couldn't help but notice that all eyes were on this guy on the bar top that looked like he was no older than sixteen, but was showing major tube through his g/string. He looked like he could have come off an Iowa farm. He had short dark brown hair with the wildest green eyes that equated with a famous National Geographic cover that featured an afghan girl with the same outrageous emerald gleam. And as luck would have it, the stars over South Florida were going to be kind to me again tonight. The dancer glanced over and smiled at me. I smiled back and he danced over to my side of the bar and crouched down while dick teasing this old geezer standing a little to my left. When the old man had to reach over to put a five in dancer's pouch, he gave me the break that I needed to step up to the jammed bar. I gave the dancer a nod of appreciation and held out my next to last twenty across the bar to catch the bartender's eye, and when he looked over I loudly asked him for a Johnny Walker Black on the rocks. The bartender looked to be a fellow of about my age or maybe a little older, and he wasn't hard on the eyes either, but still couldn't hold up to the kid on the bar.

As I reached over to pay the bartender, I couldn't help but catch a whiff of the dancers crotch musk, and I was immediately aroused. And I don't care if you're cool as motherfucking James Dean, a turn on is hard for any guy to hide. The young stud dancing just kept a shit eating smile on his face and modestly looked at me with the assurance that he was accustomed to turning people on. And better yet, there was no doubt that he enjoyed his work. He was a party boy, through and through. And I liked him at first glance. I knew he was what we termed on the bayous as "good people."

I reached back and changed my drink to my left hand and with the right elbow holding my place at the bar, I extended my hand and tried to keep rhythm with the song "Knock on Wood," but being blessed with about as much rhythm as a hunk of granite, I was unsuccessful. Lucky for me the song ended within 20 seconds of my failed hand dance. My embarrassing predicament was broken by an unenthused voice questioning the men in the bar through the house P.A. system, "Okay, what about Mark?"

And when the patrons of the club responded much more enthusiastically than the M.C. had asked them for, Mark looked up at the DJ booth with the best "Eat Shit" gaze I've yet to see matched. The fact that he held one hand on his crotch to keep the bills, that were sure to fall out if he didn't spare the necessary attention only made the effect better as he leaped off the bar with the agility of a cheetah. He was definitely feline but with the masculinity of a big cat. Although his balance was that of a cheetah, his spirit held the aura of a cougar. I could tell he was one tough motherfucker but he wasn't the type to fuck over people. You just knew it.

And to further serve the MC more insult, the crowd gave a cohesive groan to express their disapproval for some shitty Rick Ashley MTV song and this skinny, rail of a kid that he had introduced as Raymond, who sluggishly attempted to dance. The old-man that had been crowding me earlier pronounced loudly as he walked off while contemptuously ignoring the new dancer's motion for him to, "come on." "I got to take a piss" the old man said to the unpopular dick dancer.

I appreciated the room the geezer's absence now gave me, but my free space and relief was soon interrupted by Raymond and his skinny legs. When he leaned down to crotch dance for me I rudely told him to piss off. It wasn't necessary but I was sure I didn't want to have anything to do with the guy. Sorry, but the guy made me grimace and since I'm being honest, I know that it wasn't right bitching the guy out. But it's what we do. Anyway my attentions were soon diverted by the unmistakable sound of a man with confidence asking for what he wants.

"Horace, would you give me a brandy and seven," I heard someone request from my immediate left and when I turned to face him, I remember thinking to myself, "I bet he doesn't get told no very often."

Mark caught me again gawking at him. Horace the bartender brought Mark his drink and motioned to Mark to look at the well-dressed business man that had purchased it. As Mark acknowledged his appreciation by holding up the glass to the man that had bought his drink, I noticed that he looked older and even hotter in his change of clothes. He was wearing khaki cargo shorts with construction worker's boots with thick socks to pronounce his great calves. He wore a peach colored tank top that accentuated his tan and muscular shoulders. And I'll have to go against my dad's earlier counsel and just say fuck it because this guy was absolutely beautiful. He was still damp from his dance and again, his natural scent was intoxicating. The guy was turning me on. And I'll never forget the first words he ever said to me.

"Hello, Lucky."

"Hell, I guess so," I tried as casually as I could to say.

"Where are you from?" he half laughed out.

"Louisiana. You gotta problem with that?" and I couldn't help but to like that he appreciated my sense of humor. He grinned and held out his hand to introduce himself.

"Mark, and I don't have too many problems with much of anything."

"I reckon," I replied in an exaggerated southern accent. He took my extended hand and shook it vigorously.

"You know I've heard rumors from some guys that were on the set of The Beverley Hillbillies that Max Bayer had a big dick. So how about it Jethro, do you have a big dick?"

"Well I'm sorry to report that I guess we'll never know about Max because if memory recalls, he's passed on." I replied and as he continued to firmly grasp my hand, He stated with humored arrogance, "I didn't ask you about Max Bayer's dick, did I?"

"No, you didn't," I answered, and then further granted to the cocky dick dancer, "You asked if Jethro had a big dick. My name is Andy."

"Well I haven't heard any rumors from the cast of Mayberry but what about you Andy? Do you have a big dick?"

"You wanna see it?" I volunteered.

"Follow me," he said with a big grin and calmly laid a twenty dollar bill on the bar telling Horace, "Thanks for keeping the bar dry for us to dance, buddy. We'll be back in a second."

While I followed Mark to wherever he was taking me, I noticed that Horace had marked that our spaces were not available to others by placing a napkin over our drinks, and he turned down rocks glasses to assure any seat vultures that we would be back for our places. The fact that Mark had the good grace to generously tip a bartender in a bar he worked in only further reinforced my opinion that this was a smart party boy.

He took me into the bathroom of the change room and I silently thought to myself, "Alright." And I pulled my shorts down and let my dick fall out.

"Good man," Mark said.

"Thanks. Uh, do you want a bump?" I clumsily offered.

"Cool, dude," he acknowledged.

I reached down and took out the white baggy the driver had given me and, not even bothering to explain to Mark that I hoped it was good, I reached for my usual keys that I would have—but were not with me. And Mark caught my predicament and I'm sure its implication, but was cool and quickly offered a straw from the side of his cargo pants. I took the straw from him and with a hint of concern in my voice, I told him, "It might be a good idea if you let me try this first."

"No problem Andy," he simply replied.

I took a smaller than usual snort in the straw and after about a second or two from the blow hitting home, I just let out, "Oh yeah!" and then packed the straw for the stud. He filled his nose, then I gave mine the necessary attention. Luckily, it was actually really good blow. I got a boner that would knock a horse over and Mark just held it about as firm as he had grasped my hand in our previous introduction and said, "How would you like to come to a party that a very good friend of mine is having on his very nice yacht. The kind of party with lots of blow and dough for a guy that has some talent—and something tells me you know how to perform at a party like this."

"Just that quick, you're going to let me in on your action?" I asked with sincerity.

"I know you don't have any rhythm," he replied with a laugh, "You can't be in here to dance. And I'd say by the common fact that it takes one to know one, you, my friend, are a whore."

I didn't say a word. There was a good ten seconds of silence while Mark just looked at me and continued to hold my dick. Finally, he said, "And you could probably use a place to stay tonight."

"Thanks," is all I said.

"The pleasure will be mine," he said.

"Hey! What gives?" a whiney voice questioned from the other side of the bathroom door.

"Oh fuck off, Raymond. I'll be right out, okay?" Mark said unable to hide the aggravation in his voice.

I had pulled my shorts up and Mark said, "Just walk past the little fuck and let's go finish our drinks. Mike will pick us up before too long."

"Cool," I said and we walked past the little shit without giving him the time of day and took our saved spots. Horace walked over and said, "Hey Mark, Mike just called and said he'd pick you up outside in 20."

"Cool. Thanks dude," Mark replied.

We finished our drinks in about 10 minutes and though I was short of cash, I thanked Horace with a five note.

"Thank you," he said sincerely.

"My pleasure," I replied and walked out to wait in the parking lot with Mark.

"So who is Mike?"

"Probably one of the best guys I've ever known."

"Cool," I said, then offered Mark another bump.

"Let's wait for Mike. His windows are tinted. Fort Lauderdale PD central is just around the corner, dude."

"Thanks for the tip."

"Like I said, Hello Lucky," he offered with a reassuring smile then raised his arm casually to catch the attention of a black Lincoln Town Car saying, "There's Mike."

I threw my cigarette onto the gravel parking lot and as I exhaled, I thought to myself, "What the fuck? Sounds like a good deal. If nothing else, I've met this cat."

CHAPTER 8

Fort Lauderdale, December 1991

My New Friends

I FIND IT INCREDIBLY AMUSING TO LOOK BACK AND ACKNOWLEDGE HOW I have met complete strangers and within minutes of meeting them, they completely alter my life. I guess it's one of the perks of being a vagabond hustler. And Mark, whose last name I later found out to be Kosko, a man I'd meet later named Martin VanDerman, and of course Mike Talbot would definitely play a large part in showing me a different world.

As Mike's car pulled to a stop, He rolled down the driver's side window and I couldn't help but think he was a cop because he looked way too much like this actor that played the ass kicking, club swinging sheriff in the movie "Walking Tall." But just as obvious was the man's keen intelligence. Not that there aren't any intelligent cops. I wouldn't want to deny the boys in blue that. But to tell you the truth, there are very few that are keen. They may be "driven" or "unblemished" and perhaps altogether "incorruptible" but on first thought of it, I can't think of a single one of the fuckers that I've ever met that I'd define as keen. I think that to be keen is the ability to rationalize and think for oneself despite the disadvantage or optimism that a situation may present. Most of the cops that I have met usually subscribe to some type of "—ism." And when a guy prescribes to any "—ism," he abdicates his ability to be keen. To be keen, a guy has to be razor sharp and any form of idealism prescribed and ingested by a guy and nourished by him as absolute truth would only serve to dull the edges of a keen individual. And there wasn't a fucking thing dull about Mike Talbot.

To begin with, he had a smile that cut through the night and that just gleamed money. His teeth appeared natural and although they were straight, his smile contained the confidence that would assure an individual that making a buck was far too easy for him to bother with bleaching his teeth. And I knew right away that if he knew I were judging him on his smile or anything else, he'd probably just keep on smiling while he told me to go fuck myself.

When Mark opened the door to get into the car, the vehicles inside lights came on and I couldn't help but notice that Mike's eyes were a deep blue that drew me into his psyche the way that deep water can lure a sailor from a hot and sundrenched deck for a soothing break and relief offered by the harbor's depth. And his gaze held a twinkle that confirmed the possibility of much more optimism.

I instantly recognized that Mike was healthy, but he wasn't a gymgod either. He had a big muscular neck and big forearms and he was not reluctant to exude the energy to extend an open hand towards the passenger's back seat that I was now settling into. I happily shook the man's hand and returned his smile and I'm sure that it by no means whatsoever held the same confidence that his held. And he was still able to convey to me in one quick glance that I had nothing to fear from him. Before I released his hand, I knew that I liked him. Mark's voice broke the telepathy with the simple introduction, "Mike, this is Andy. Andy, Mike."

"Pleasure," is all I could manage to say. I don't think that the man intimidated me in a fearsome way, but at the same time, I was not able to find words as easily as I am usually accustomed while I'm engaged in ordinary conversation. I think I had a huge crush on him and it made me nervous. I'm sure that he tapped into my uneasiness, but he had the good manners to put me at ease by all but mimicking me and returning my greeting with the same, "Pleasure."

And the fact that there wasn't even a hint of condescension in his voice only made me like him more. I was all about Mike from moment one. I wasn't in love, but I believed in the man. I hardly knew him, but I knew the man was good for his word. And that is a one hell of a trait for anybody to have.

Looking back, I have asked myself, "Did my initial trust of Mike Talbot in fact dull my ability to be keen, or perhaps even force me to any pretense that I have to the claim of being keen. I don't think so because Mike never did try and think for me. He would present a situation or question, but from day one, I always felt that he left the answer to me. That's also the quality of a good sales person.

And I was about to learn firsthand what the guy was selling. Actually, I already knew that he was planning on selling my ass, but I was still a bit vague as to how he would do it.

As we drove off, Mark broke the exquisite silence of the Town Car by abruptly asking Mike, "So are you taking the Dick out tonight? I've already told Andy how nice and big it is and he agreed to get on it."

"Dude! BE COOL," I growled at Mark. I was a bit unnerved as I don't like people putting words in my mouth. I had already acquired a good amount of respect for Mike and was taken aback a little by Mark. But my obvious discomfort was making both of them chuckle.

Mike managed to stop laughing first and said, "Andy, 'The Dick' is the name of my boat."

Then he reached over into his glove compartment and took out his car phone and in a second was speaking, "Martin, How are we in terms of stock on Scotch? Yep. Okay. Go ahead and blow the hull out. I'll start up when we get there." And he hung up and put the phone back in the glove compartment asking, "Martin says we need Scotch and Rum. Is anybody particular about any certain kind?"

"Johnny Walker Black," I quickly volunteered.

"Black it shall be, Mr. Andy."

I was embarrassed at my quick response to Mike's generosity and also the polite servitude he was extending. So I said, "Jesus, I'm sorry! Where are my manners?"

"No need to apologize for good taste my boy. I'm happy I asked you. I need a change from Dewar's."

"Dewar's is fine." I volunteered

"Don't make me change my mind about you. Johnny Walker Black is on his way."

Mark added, "And don't forget the Captain."

"Ask and thou shalt receive. Captain Morgan this way cometh as well."

Mike pulled into the parking lot of a liquor store. As he got out of the car, he asked, "Smokes?"

"No thanks." We both said in unison.

As Mike shut the door and walked in, I asked Mark, "So who is Martin?"

"Martin is Mike's Afrikaner boat boy that lives on The Dick."

"Whoa, dude, I don't think I've ever done a black guy. Not that I'm a racist but I was brought up a redneck." I shakily volunteered.

"Whatever dude, but you and Martin will probably have that in common. He is Dutch. Afrikaner is what the Dutch South Africans call themselves." Mark further explained then continued to describe Martin further.

"He's got sandy blond hair, Greenish eyes that can be grey, the personality of a turnip, a little dick but one of the prettiest asses I've ever seen."

"Nice guy?" I asked.

"Probably not a nice guy but if he is your friend, he's a good friend. I think you guys will get along."

"Sounds like it." I said

"Would it sound like it if he were black?" Mark asked in a slow, quiet yet crisp pronunciation that broke the mood of the evening. I didn't answer.

"Dude, you need to get over that. That shit don't fly in Fort Lauderdale."

"I hear ya, Mark. And you're right."

No sooner than the words came out of my mouth than Mike was opening the door. He handed the bag to Mark and when sitting down and buckling up asked, "Alright, I think we are ready for a party. How about you guys? You men ready for a good time?"

Mark quickly restored the previous joviality with a simple, "Fuck yeah!" then he smiled at me.

"But of course" I said matter of factly.

While he brought the town car out onto Broward Blvd, Mike asked back in the same matter of fact tone, "Well, let me ask you. To what angle of destiny do I owe the pleasure of extending the hospitality of my boat and crew to you this fine evening?"

I didn't even hesitate. I shot totally straight with the man. I told him everything that had happened to me the last two days. By the time I was finished we were pulling up into the same marina that I had trespassed on the night before.

"Well, I'd say your luck has changed, Andy. Give Mark a hand with some of the bags in the trunk. Welcome aboard," said Mike as he flashed that lottery winning ticket smile of his and made me feel like he had known me all of my life. I had known pimps in New Orleans and most of them were bad motherfuckers. I had never been under their thumb. But I was allowing myself to be taken in by Mike Talbot on just a simple hunch. I thought to myself, "Even a blind pig finds an apple core once in a while."

As Mike had mentioned luck, I carried two stuffed bags down the pier and passed right by Lucky Abe. Except tonight, the fine vessel was not vacant. She was having a party of her own. As I walked a little further, I could see the dinghy that I had spent the previous night in and right next to it was the barbeque pit smoking away with some fat ass shirtless old man with an extraordinary hairy back grilling something. The sound of our footsteps on the wooden pier of the boat were interrupted by a wild scream of delight and when I glanced in the direction of the merriment, I saw through a rather large crack in the curtains of Lucky Abe's forward bow the silhouette of two naked women dancing together. Instantly, my mind presumed that the boat was owned by some rich and retired furniture tycoon from New York that was now having the time of his life in his golden years. I thought that he was probably married to some snip-snap bitch that tried to keep him on a diet back in New York and wouldn't let him have steaks or butter, but that she probably was clueless that Abe even owned a boat in Fort Lauderdale.

"Good for him," I caught myself saying aloud.

"Amen," Mike agreed.

Silently, I thanked him for the refuge he and his boat had given me the night before. I took note of the stroke of luck that he was not having his party the night before. Man, I'd rather be lucky than smart any day. As well, I pondered the idea that he was in fact a lucky man to have the money and health to live this way at his age.

"How old was Abe," I wondered silently to myself.

With that thought in mind, I made a mental note to myself that that was exactly the reason that I had to make some real cash before I got up there in age myself.

To myself again I was silently saying, "Nothing more pathetic than an old fag with a skinny wallet, fat gut and a saggy, old man's ass."

And with that thought in mind, Selectric, I can tell you The Committee that inhabits my mind once again called a meeting to order.

CHAPTER 9

Committee Meeting Number Two

NOT A SOUL HAD ANY IDEA WHERE HE OR SHE WAS. EMOTIONS among instincts sat helplessly staring at one another in the void that they recognized instantly as their parlor, but once again were completely faint in there cognizance of place or time. It was the same every time. And then as always, a voice would emerge and shortly would follow the materialization of a board room or at least an interpretation of something similar to a boardroom.

"Alright, alright! Get with it, will ya. Which one of you afterbirth of a Her Majesty's Navy Bastard put the notion of a future into our man Andy's head?" An Irish voice proclaimed.

Although the idea of an oval office began emerging, there was still only silence from the parties sequestered. But quickly to follow was once again the original voice and no doubt the empowering bell that tolled for the reality of the emotional parliament. Mr. Slut/Whore resumed in a bellow, "Who did it? Come, come nothing to fear."

Still there was nothing but silence. Then Mr. Slut/Whore stated his vigilance in a bit more soothing tone.

"Kindly speak up, will ya? Surely I'm not the only one present. We all know what the happenings at hand are, but I want to know who perceived that there was anything wrong!"

He ended in a thundering boom to which, again, there was no response. And although time was nothing in this sphere, it was at the same time (for loss of a better word) everything. Mr. Slut/Whore again presumed his authority and again demanded a response to his personal enquiry by declaring.

"So help me, as you all know me, I will keep each and every one of us here with a six month erection for 50-year-old blonds on horseback if someone does not stand up and take responsibility. Now GOD DAMN IT! WHO CALLED THIS MOTHERFUCKING MEETING?"

A smirk emerged from the silence and as the light evolved, the figure of a hand placed dramatically across a mouth appeared along with the entire silhouette of Miss Addiction and the implications of her guilt spawned into full view. As the emotional realm slowly materialized, the grin on the guilty perpetrator's face casually evolved and stood out to volunteer for the blame associated with this evening's get-together.

"Miss Addiction, really!" Mr. Slut/Whore exalted then continued unabashed, "When one is so much to blame for any feelings of remorse or guilt and with all parties involved usually yielding to Andy's mercy for your effects, I hardly see reason for any of us being removed from our personal agendas for your sake."

He took a breath and with a stronger Irish accent demanded, "Well woman, what say you?"

Still, Miss Addiction said nothing, but the shade of the room was definitely becoming more realistic and so was the silhouette of Miss Love. Consequently, Mr. Slut/Whore began hovering ferociously over the antiquated and weak, yet cotton candy blue emergence of Miss Love and subsequently began demanding in a verbal barrage, "You again! Will you never rest?" Slut/Whore demanded of the old girl as the perpetual pout that formed the outlines of her face slowly emerged.

"I have nothing to do with the cocktail quaffing, pill slugging, powder snorting, ass-injecting plots of that rouge' unto whom you have placed the deserving title of Miss Addiction."

However, there was no denying that the shades that made up the aura of the two were emerging into one color. In fact, a color that promised power. In response, Mr. Slut Whore feigned aghast for he recognized the illegitimate nature of this phenomenon but continued his inauthentic gesture and stated, "Well, well, well! What have we here? Perhaps a little coup de d'état arising from an alliance of the most bizarre of bedfellows? If nothing else, what a strange alliance."

"Whatever Slut/Whore!" Miss addiction proclaimed then continued, "I know that you know better than to take in the mix that quickly." The colors finally began to separate but as they did, the feint but unnerving shade of Mr. Conscience began to pervade the room. But only for an instant. His weak purple aura was quickly diminished as his silhouette stood no chance to evolve as he did not decree any invitations to this soirée due to Miss Addiction's dominance which had become pervasive earlier in the evening. When Miss Addiction completely had his lavender shade out of her hair, she began to dust her clothing in disgust as she swiped, akin to a dandy subjected to spider webs, at the remnants of Miss Love still intertwined in her.

"Miss Love! Could you control yourself? Kindly call in the remainder of this baby blue doo doo that you insist in draping your essence, for as you can see, Scarlet/Orange and that baby's puke breath just don't work precious."

"I'm blue you cracked out freak," shot back Miss Love.

"It is not blue, Miss Love." Miss Addiction gently stated, then continued with a tone of utter contempt. "As a matter of fact, I'd say you're some form of chalky pastel, but that would be pushing the envelope as far as I can see. Like Mr. Conscience, perhaps you see yourself alone again, despite the obvious misinterpretation by Andy between the competitions of our auras for the same space."

Miss Addiction took a deep sigh then continued, "And alone you should stay as Mr. Conscience is now powerless to call any future meetings. Things are going far too well Miss Love. Can you even remember your old ally?"

Miss Love was having difficulty even contemplating Mr. Conscience. Weak as he had become, he could always be counted on to at least provide her a podium or venue of sorts but his essence was not even present at the moments meeting. She was puzzled but she was still around. That she knew.

"Then why am I here?" Miss love proclaimed, "And why are you and I the culprits fingerprinted by the combination of our aura's glow implicated as a union that called this meeting?"

"Exactly!" proclaimed Miss Addiction, "Mr. Conscience is only concerned with the past. And you have the nerve to intertwine your interpretation of Andy's future with me. I ought to beat the shit out of you now." Having said that, Miss Addiction lunged at Miss Love and began pulling the frail emotion's short cropped Buster Brown Hair from her pastel light blue bass.

"Sit down this instant! Both of you" Raged Mr. Slut/Whore as he brandished a foot long black dildo from inside the podium that he now stood behind. Both Miss Love and Miss Addiction sat down immediately remembering the past time that Mr. Slut/Whore had beaten the shit out of both of them with the bacterially infected instrument that had left them both in an emotional infirmary for five days.

As they took in the effect of Mr. Slut/Whore's threat, Miss Love crossed her legs while she gathered her composure and Miss

Addiction grabbed for her purse to get some tissue and placed them in her nostrils to sponge blood caused by her neurotic nose bleeds that always erupted when she was distraught. Her present condition caused by actually being associated as the originator of the evenings meeting with a clear implication of her aura blending with that of Miss Love's.

"Now that I have your attention, it is I that is obviously placed on the stand and being called on to defend myself this evening. The question is, why am I defending myself against interpretations sent by both of you to our lad Andy?" He put the dildo down and gestured to hold his chin as if in deep thought and then out of the blue, a very deep dark voice whispered one word.

"Future."

"Who said that?" Mr. Slut/Whore nervously asked as he looked at the array of emotions and instincts that lightly dotted the forum headed by Miss Love and Miss Addiction. Both of them only shrugged their shoulders in a sincere gesture of ignorance.

"Oh I see. Well, who said 'future' is beside the point. I think I know now why we are here." He blew the bangs of his hair out of face and while tapping his fingers on the top of the podium, Mr. Slut/Whore asked Miss Addiction, "Pray tell Miss Addiction, for you of all, why do you see a future for our man Andy?"

"I was only looking out for both of our interests Slut/Whore." She extended as honestly as she could. "I mean, after all, we're having so much fun and all that I just don't see any reason that we have to take unnecessary chances."

"Unnecessary chances?" He quizzed her aloud.

"Yeah you know. We need to be careful and all and try to store up a little money sugar." Miss Addiction cooed in a voice that would have made Vivian Leigh sick. She further explained, "You know the boys won't come running for you in ten or fifteen years if we don't have money. I mean really, look at these boats. Do you really think we could have gotten on here tonight if we'd left things up to Miss Love?"

Miss Addiction and Mr. Slut/Whore both laughed as Miss Love Sulked and kept silent.

In a moment they both ceased and Mr. Slut Whore began to speak then stopped himself and continued after he had chosen his words a bit more carefully.

"So you both want to stay around a while and both of you have entertained the notion that I am the reason Andy's Longevity may be a problem?" He paused again and Miss Addiction quickly injected.

"I don't mean to judge you or anything, but just remind you about rubbers."

"You just keep us off the needles and I'll keep a rubber on anything going up our ass Miss Alabama." said Mr. Slut/Whore.

"Well I'll try." Miss Addiction whined in pestered conviction.

"Do." He succinctly snapped at her then quickly added, "But you Miss Love, why should I explain my action to you. To be truthful, I don't really see you around too much in our future so why in the world do you even show up at these little get-togethers much less call them?"

Miss addiction snorted and as she did, the blood soaked tissue came out of her nose.

"Fuck you all!" is all Miss Love could say. She felt tired and wasn't even sure that she had an answer for the man.

"That's what we're getting on this boat to do Miss Love. TO FUCK. MY SPECIALTY!" He thundered then continued, "and before we do get on, I want to make sure that we're all in the same mind and that is to have a good time and not think too much of the future." He paused to take a breath for a moment and then looked directly at Miss Addiction and gazed into her as if he were Harry Houdini and asked her, "Between the two of us, how long do think we have. It's no lie that you have been increasing our dosages a great deal lately. Come clean now. Well honest as you can. What say you? Ten or perhaps fifteen years?"

There was silence but it was only momentary as he mocked her in her own accent.

"Come now, Swamp Pussy, tell me. Do you really see us all here in ten years?"

Miss Addiction tried in vain to look serious for a second but then it was useless. As she contemplated her plans for the next five years, she was certain that all present would be lucky to see that much time. With that thought conveyed she shyly raised her hand to hide the smile from her mouth as the only sound that came from her was the single word sentence, "No."

She was utterly shameless and the next sound all could here was that of Miss Love's chair falling backwards and hitting the floor as the decrepit emotion clogged from the room. Mr. Slut/Whore jumped down from the podium and grabbed Miss Addiction's hand and they proceeded to dance circles around the pathetic hag. Somehow the music of the Virginia reel was pounding as they sashayed and swirled around Miss Love. Miss Addiction posed, "Does she really look like she's getting older or just plain grey? Come dance with us if you can darling?"

"Miss Love, really do stay for the party. But I'd have to ask you to change out of that sweater that you insist on wearing. Dear woman, we are in the tropics so if you're going to stay, I'm afraid the sweater will have to go." And having said that, he ripped the grey and wool treasure from her frail body and her tattered bra did its best to hide her saggy tits as Mr. Slut/Whore twirled her moth balled garment around like a banner.

"Slut/Whore!" Miss Addiction mocked, "Now that is a bit cruel don't you think."

A tear came down Miss Love's cheek which only served as rocket fuel to the vibrancy of the compatriots that were dancing around her.

"Grab your partner and dozy-doe" hollered Mr. Slut whore, still unable to hide his Irish accent despite his best efforts. Nevertheless, The Virginia Reel blared on as reality set in.

CHAPTER 10

Fort Lauderdale, December 1991

H EY ANDY, NOT HAVING SECOND THOUGHTS ARE YOU?" MARK ASKED, as he momentarily grabbed my arm.

"Huh?" is all I could reply

"Earth to Andy, don't freak on me dude," he said with a hint of concern.

"Oh no man, really, everything is fine. It's just been so long since I've been on the ocean. I got really sea sick the last time." I replied.

"Not to worry, dude" Mark said as he pulled a bag of cocaine that would hold a tuna sandwich, from his front pocket. "The Dr. is in," he jeered.

I heard a "hell yeah" from somewhere in my mind that I couldn't suppress, and am sure that I said it aloud.

"Beautiful isn't she?" said Mark.

"I'll say." As I said, not taking my eyes off the bag.

"I mean the boat," Mark corrected me.

I took my eyes off the bag and looked up to see the boat that would be taking us on our cruise. Even though I could barely make out the boat due to the darkness, I could see that it was a modern craft, and I wholeheartedly agreed.

"Looks really nice."

"Wait till you see the inside, totally first class," Mark added.

The inside of The Dick was extraordinary. And the same could be said about the physical appearance of the craft's cabin boy, whom I saw immediately when I walked through the bow's front door. He obviously took good care of the spotless white carpet that ran the length of the boat; the brass that decorated the boat and the polished wood was just as unblemished. As I took in the impressive charcoal nudes that covered the walls, the cabin boy casually walked over and shook my hand with very little or any stated emotion.

"Hello, my name is Martin. Can I get you something to drink?"

His accent reminded me of the American actors of the 1950s portraying WWII Germans. And, he had a very curious body smell—not a bad one, but just very much male. As I still held his hand shake, I said, "Andy. Yes, thanks. A scotch on the rocks."

He released my hand and walked off to get my drink. As he did, Mark stated, "You're up dude".

He was still sniffing hard to clear out his nostrils. I walked over and saw the huge lines of coke that he already had laid out on the coffee table of sorts. I patted him on the ass and said, "God Bless ya."

His only response was a smile as he smacked the shit out of my ass loud enough to make a crack. I turned around quickly and as I did, I saw that Martin too was smiling. Feint as it was, it was the first show of emotion that I had seen him express. Somehow, I remember thinking that it was probably difficult for him to smile.

"It looks like the party is starting without me," Mike said as he stepped into the front cabin from doing whatever it was that he had been doing. Martin walked over and handed me my Scotch, for which I thanked him. He gave me no response but walked over to Mike and gave him one of the most sterile kisses I'd ever seen given and told him, "not for long."

Martin was simply a man of few words.

"What's the forecast for tonight?" Mike asked Martin.

"Good," Martin replied.

In my mind I had to agree. The world was certainly a very beautiful place to be this evening.

"You blew her out already?" Mike asked Martin.

"Yes." Martin replied.

I choked a little while in mid sip of my scotch at this question to which Mark patted me on the back a bit histrionically stating, "Martin always blows the hull by opening several hatches and as well, turning on blow pumps prior to starting the boat. That way, we don't go boom-boom from electric currents mixing with gas fumes."

"Oh," Is all I could manage to say.

And with that, the engines of the fine vessel cranked with a muffled purr. It was as if the sound was an invisible cue, and Mark went outside and started making himself busy releasing ties from the pier. Soon he and Martin were pushing us off. I felt somewhat ill at ease as I was doing nothing, so I went up to Mike to ask if I could help with anything, but he was definitely pre-occupied and hollering at Martin.

"Push the back out a little farther. I need a little more room to turn and miss our neighbor."

Mike turned the boat's wheel sharply and I looked up to see Mark make an incredible jump from the pier back to the boat just in the nick of time. Before I knew it, we were on our own, slowly cruising through the docks of half million dollar yachts, at the low end, and multimillion at the high end. As I looked at them, I was again amazed that only the night before, I had been a stowaway on board one of these. I remember thinking to myself, "Just goes to show what good looks and some nerve can do for a guy in this great land of ours. That, and other people's generosity."

These guys were generous. No sooner were we on the Intracoastal when Mark walked up to Mike and said, "Time for your vitamin E Captain."

Mike opened up his mouth and Mark placed the capsule in Mike's mouth and handed Mike his own drink to wash it down. When he took a swig, he squinted and pointed at my glass with a grimace. I rushed to his rescue and after a brief moment to recover, he said, with a sense of humor, to Mark, "Don't do that to me again" he said referring to Mark's Captain and Coke.

We all laughed.

"And how about our new friend? Le gusto, amigo?" Mark asked.

"Would I look a gift horse in the mouth?" I said opening my mouth.

"I hope not." Mike countered while Mark fed me the pill and I took a healthy swig of the fine Scotch that Mike had bought for us. Mike continued, "I hope that you don't have any plans for tomorrow."

"Nothing pressing," I said with a smile, as I had already told him of my dilemma.

"Well. Make yourself at home."

I took his comment, like him, at face value and I immediately felt even more comfortable. Hell, I felt like I was in heaven. Being on a yacht with three hot guys on tropical waters with X, coke, and good scotch was about as close to heaven as I had ever believed that I could come, I remember thinking to myself.

"So what if they turn out to be murdering pirates. At least I'll die a happy man," I thought, and then I decided to do what I usually do. I sat back and enjoyed the moment.

CHAPTER 11

Fort Lauderdale/Miami Coast, December 1991

M ARK SAT DOWN NEXT TO ME ON THE LUSH BLACK LEATHER SOFA, which looked great next to all of the stained wood throughout the cabin. And, I'm here to tell ya, so did the cabin boy, Martin. Seldom have I seen such a good looking male specimen. He had dark green eyes and a flat top crew cut of sandy blond hair that highlighted the perfect complexion of his face, which sat on a square jaw. His lips were thin and pursed and his nose thin and straight. As I admired his flawless ass and shirtless torso that comprised his Adonis six foot build, I couldn't help to think that had he lived in an occupied country of Europe during WWII. He would certainly have qualified for the "Lebensraum Project" that Hitler had set up for "Aryan-like" children to be adopted by Nazis.

"Martin?" Mike called as he held his glass up to show that he needed a refill and Martin was there in a split second to dutifully grab it and fetch another drink.

"How long have you and Martin been together?" I inquired.

"We're not. He just lives here. He's my friend." Mike replied keeping his eyes ahead as he steered the vessel. I could tell that he was concentrating and the focus of this concentration was revealed by the lights now apparent on the upcoming bridge. He was navigating his approach to a draw bridge. Martin returned shortly with another tumbler of scotch for Mike, who simply said thanks and turned the glass straight up and downed it before Martin had a chance to reply, "You're welcome."

"Can you get her through the bridge?" he asked Martin.

"Yah," Martin grunted. And just that quickly, Mike handed the wheel of the boat over to Martin. He then walked over to the couch where Mark and I were sitting, pulled out his dick, and slapped me on the face with it.

Now, that kind of shocked me. Whore or no whore, the dick slap made an impact on me. I recall how it conjured up visions of this woman in Arkansas that had pressed charges against the state's governor. He was now running for president. I remember her crying and her allegations that she could prove that he did it because she could tell exactly where Governor Clinton had a wart on his dick.

So what's the big fucking deal? I would vote for the man. All these women were getting up and crying about how horrible he was. Please! I'm sure it's not like the wart had a hair in it that told the poor gal that she was never going to win the Miss America title.

But I go off again. So sorry. But I can assure you that Mike's dick had no warts on it. And since neither was I in the habit of looking a gift dick in the mouth, I was all too happy to put his beautiful dick in my mouth. Great drugs, yachts, big dicks, scotch—this was better than heaven and I hear ya, Selectric, 'Waive a dollar through a trailer park…' Well fuck off, I am a whore!"

So with Martin at the wheel and with Mark now sucking on Mike's huge balls and myself indulging on Mike's nine inch cock, The Dick took us into open waters. And The Dick was big enough to handle open waters without making me seasick. The seas were as easy as I was that night and, Mike, who was also concerned about making me sick, was gentleman enough not to come in my mouth. I can say this now about Mike— anybody that he ever caught having unsafe sex was immediately asked to leave the boat. After he came on my neck, he playfully slapped me in the face with his hand and walked up to relieve Martin from the wheel.

With me still just sitting on the black leather couch and the X kicking in, the next thing I know is that Mark's dick replaced Mike's in my mouth. I felt Martin pulling off my pants and over the sound of my own slurps I heard Martin's monotone Germanic accent say again only one word, "Nice."

I was rock hard and in an instant I recognized the distinct feeling of a rubber being placed on my dick quickly followed by the sensation of Martin balancing himself to sink his beautiful ass down on my cock. Mark took his dick out of my mouth to walk around and straddle Martin's face to give him my previous job. Martin responded with gusto. That allowed me to give my full attention to that firm South African Adonis's ass. I was now plowing it as he sat on my lap, sucking Marks big eight inch perfection. I was able to look up at Mike, who with us being in open water did not now have to be as diligent as he had been before, as there were far fewer maritime obstacles. I could see that he was smiling and enjoying our pleasure as he slowly sipped his scotch. I guess the show went on for about another ten minutes or so before I picked Martin's ass off my dick and Mark pulled his dick out of Martin's mouth. He threw Martin down on his back on the plush white carpet. I ripped the rubber off and after a few strokes started to spew a gusher of cum onto Martin's solid, smooth, and hairless pecs. About the same time I heard Mark wail out as he added his load to the manmade lake that had been made on the sternum of Martin's chest. Martin continued to lie on his back and slightly arched it so that he could stroke his dick and finger his own hairless hole that I had been fucking only seconds earlier. Then, Martin's six inch cock contributed to the genetic pool that was being made on sternum of his concaved chest.

Mark and I lay back on the couch exhausted while Martin was the first to get up and shower. We both sat breathing heavily, taking in the slight hum of the boat's engine. In a minute or two Martin had returned.

"Next," said Mike from the control panel and wheel as he lifted his glass to Martin and Martin took the glass to get him another drink. Mark grabbed my hand and said, "Come on. I'll help you rinse."

I gave no argument.

CHAPTER 12

December 1991

Life as a whore on "The Dick"

I THINK THAT IT IS SAFE TO SAY THAT BY THAT TIME IN MY LIFE I WAS A big enough boy to know that there is nothing, but nothing, for free. But then again, without beating the gift horse expression to death, I don't like to pass up a good time. Here I was on this boat, a 21-year-old run-away (22 with my fake ID), a fag, a college drop-out, a whore—being shown the time of his life. I could only guess that with all of that coke and ecstasy on the boat that there was probably some type of dealing and involvement in the drug trade. That didn't bother me at all, as I reasoned that the closer one was to the connection, the better off one was. And since I had been selling my ass for the last two years, I didn't have any problem with the engagements that would be required of me to stay in this arrangement with Mike for next month or so.

To be honest, I thought it was a lot of fun. Basically we just continued for a few weeks to do what I laid out earlier. Sometimes we were a show; sometimes, a guest would join in. Actually, there were a lot of times that the guest that Mike would return to the boat with, by way of The Dick's runabout, would join in. The parties would usually go on as long as the "friends" kept shelling out the cash for drugs.

It could get pretty dark at times. Needles, and even an occasional overdose, but thank God, I never saw anybody actually die from an over-dose. I know I saw Mike dash back to Miami in The Dick's runabout with this one guy who had shot up something. Mike said that he called a cab at the dock and left the guy. He said he found out later that the guy was alright. I saw no reason to question Mike. As far as I knew, neither he nor the guys ever lied to me.

I got to know the crew and Mike pretty well relatively fast. Mike owned a couple of car lots in Pompano Beach, and Mark had graduated from the University of Colorado with his undergraduate in Geology. He even had his own condo in Fort Lauderdale, although I never saw it. He was on board for all of the "party days" and would skip off for the 4-5 "chill days." Martin was here because Mike said he could be. Just like me. And Mike would throw each of us anywhere from four hundred to six hundred dollars a week. Martin and I kept our cash in the boat's safe and Mike would pay for the all the food, drugs, drink, what have you. But only he knew the safe's combination. Once, I asked him to get out a thousand for me and he did and gave it to me, with no question, on one of our chill days. I left the boat that afternoon with my money without Mike even raising an eyebrow. I drove up a little later with a motor cycle and asked Mike to come take a look at it. He told me, "Looks good."

When I explained to him that I had not bought it yet, he said that he could probably find me one for less than what the owner of this bike was asking. So I took the bike back to the owner and told the guy that I would have to pass on it. I went back to The Dick and gave my money to Mike to put into the safe of the boat. I knew I was free to go anytime with my money.

But why the fuck would I want to? On Christmas day, we sailed to the Bahamas and fished. Martin actually landed a decent sized Dorado and Mike brought it back on ice and gave it to a taxidermist to be mounted. To be honest, it was the first Christmas in a couple of years that I had not spent alone. We cooked steaks and had some nice wine and just the four of us passed the day together. On other chill days, Martin and I would go down A1A to the gym, and once in while we would see Mark there. Then Martin and I would come back and maintain the boat. I didn't mind at all. And then we'd party for a few days. Mark, I knew, still danced at Jimmy's, but I really just threw off the bars and stayed on the boat, or sometimes would catch a cab to a movie. Martin and I ate on the boat all the time with a primary diet of grilled meats and fresh veggies. Martin was a genius on the grill. We'd smoke a little pot and have some wine and a lot of the time, Mark and Mike would not even be around. That was our basic routine.

CHAPTER 13

Fort Lauderdale, Florida, January 1992

To be totally honest, I still am not sure what happened on New Year's Eve, 1991, which was the night of the incident—and calling it an incident is a major understatement. Because an explosion that sank The Dick left my memory a little shaky, this is what I only hazily recall.

I know that we had been partying for a couple of days and had rung in the New Year's with a major party on The Dick. Sometime around 2 A.M. of the New Year, we docked in Miami and dropped off our johns. We were all flying and there was no sign of any of us coming down soon. So Mike put it out there to go to an after hours club off Collins on South Beach. We all got dressed, grabbed our wallets and caught a cab from the dock to the Club. After an hour or so, we picked up a couple of guys Mike thought were hot and headed back to Fort Lauderdale. I don't remember the two guys' names just that they were both in their mid twenties. They were good looking guys wearing tank tops who seemed like any other club fags I'd seen. To be honest, I don't know if they even had anything to do with the boat going up with a bang. All I remember is this: Mike stopped the boat and turned off the engine. We were just off the beach over a coral reef that was just twenty feet or so down. We then turned on the underwater cameras with lights so that the images of the reef and fish would come up on the screen in the cabin. A little good music and the party started up again. It was the usual: poppers, coke, ecstasy, no clothes—and sex.

Call it dumb luck or what have you, but I didn't join in right away. Still dressed in the same clothes that I was wearing at the nightclub, I needed some air and was really feeling the snort of coke that I had just inhaled with gusto. I stepped out on the front deck to enjoy the brisk moonless night and the stars, and my enhanced speculation of their possibilities due to the drugs flowing in my inner space. But that delusion of serenity was changed in an instant.

Without any warning, the darkness was lit up and the silence of the night was broken by a blow horn, then the announcement, "This is the U.S. Coast Guard. We are declaring our intention to board your vessel. Stay anchored and do not start your engine."

I couldn't see a thing as my eyes just didn't adjust to the beams and I still remember the voice on the blowhorn like some dream. In fact, my memory of New Year's Eve 1991 is just like a dream. Then there were voices, something like, "Fuck—Mark, flush the stuff. Hurry! Mike, get the stuff out of the safe." Then I remember someone frantically said, "Let's get going," and someone else screamed, "Oh Jesus Fucking Christ, hurry."

Next thing I vaguely recall is the sound of the main engine as it briefly attempted to turn over. Then everything else was just a blur, blended with the sound of a bass note, "WaWaWawawawaawaaWaWaWawawawa."

It could have been a second, or it could've been twenty years. Time stopped, or caught up with a light bursting brilliance that hurled me through the air over the Atlantic coastal waters off Fort Lauderdale. The experience seemed like a lifetime independent of my own. There was an explosion, then I knew I was in the water. Or, saying that I knew anything at that moment would not be an accurate description of the situation. I recall that I gasped for air and my face stung like someone had slapped the shit out of me, and when I tried to scream it was like being in a dream where the person dreaming tries to scream but can't. There was only a sense of silent awareness.

With unconscious vigor, I started swimming and I couldn't tell you today how I knew which direction was shore and which was open ocean, so I just swam away from the light of the burning particles of boat scattered here and there, with the conviction that I didn't want to drown. Simple sheer dumb luck and the surreal environment can be the only answer I can apply here that allowed me to avoid the Coast Guard in my initial minutes in the water.

And in no time it was so dark. I still couldn't hear anything, not even the sound of my own strokes. As I write this, I can taste salt water, and I shudder with a tenth of the fear I felt upon realizing that something alive had bumped against me in the water. But for whatever reason, whatever it was didn't do any damage to me. It only increased the adrenaline that was fueling my strokes. Swimming and swimming, at last I felt the sensation of sand in my hands and the relief of just lying there when I reached the beach. And for a little bit, I think I did just that. I just lay on the beach and hugged it and dug my hands in it like it was some kind of lover. In every sense of the term, I guess you could say that I just washed up.

I stood up and walked in the moonless night toward a light. Today, I know that it was the light of a restroom and changing room at John U. Lloyd Beach; at the time, I didn't know what it was. I was deaf and apparently in shock as I walked through the sea grass on a little path through the Florida pines, oblivious to cones that must have caused the cuts on my feet before I finally reached the public facility off of the beach. I apparently just walked in, still in my clothes, and turned on the shower, got under it and started drinking the water. Then I must've simply passed out away from shower's edge.

"Hey Boy, you still with us?" A gruff southern accent, coinciding with a sting in my face, was my wake up to reality. It was an elderly white Park Security Officer and he stopped slapping me only long enough to turn off the shower. Then with what I remember as considerably more force, the officer resumed his slapping. When I started crying and crawled to the corner of the shower in a fetal position he finally stopped slapping me.

"What's your name, Boy, and what the hell are you up to."

I didn't do anything but continue to sob and cry hysterically. So he came over and picked me up by my underarms. Then, with one hand, he pulled out my wallet and threw it on the ground and continued to check out my pockets with his other free hand with which he found my bullet full of coke. He then gently set me down and walked out of the shower into the change room with my wallet which had my fake I.D. that I had used in the club, and my bullet full of Coke that had apparently made it intact with me through the swim. He opened my wallet in a tone of authority questioned, "Darren, Darren White, That you boy?"

At first I didn't answer as I had to think for a second. Then it hit me that I had the fake ID that I had used since high school to buy booze with. And although the picture was me, I certainly wasn't Darren White. Darren White had been a classmate, two years older than me, who had died of spinal meningitis while working on Governor Edwards's election drive and voter registration for my dad. I was able to easily assume my dead buddy's identification. Believe me when I say the dead do vote in Louisiana.

"Yes sir," I sobbed pathetically.

Holding up the bullet of coke, He continued his questioning and asked, "What is this and where did you get this junk?"

"This man," Is all that I said and resumed my sobbing.

"Oh for Jesus' sake" said the security guard as he walked out of the little building through the doorway that revealed the light of coming day. I heard him on his radio, "Hey Cheryl, Max here. Yeah looks like I got a junkie out here, or somebody in a mess." The female voice on the other end replied, "Another homeless one, huh?"

"Naw, this one is in decent clothes and looks like he's well fed. Might be a sweet boy. Looks like he's been date raped or what have you. Just get the sheriff out here will ya?"

"10-4," came the feminine voice from the other end.

Next thing I know was I'm in a Broward Sheriff's Office squad car being given a chauffeured tour of dazzling and star studded Dania Beach Florida. I've seen worse.

CHAPTER 14

Fort Lauderdale, January 1992

M Y RIDE TO JAIL IN THE BROWARD COUNTY SHERIFF'S CAR AND THE sunlight took me little by little out of the haze that had been my mindset for the past few days. As the haze lifted, it was replaced by a total sense of emptiness. Although I soon found myself in an eight by ten holding tank with six other guys, the feeling of being alone in a total abyss only grew stronger. Luckily for me, these people seemed to be nine to five working people that had been stopped for DWI. There was only one dude that looked like he might be bad news, but he stayed pretty quiet.

As the plight of my present circumstances sank in, the previous night's events began to come into a coherent perspective, although I could barely remember them booking me with trespassing, possession of an illegal substance, and drunk and disorderly conduct. I hear that people have nervous breakdowns, and I don't know if I had one, but I think that this had been the closest I'd ever come. I was tied to reality by the last thread of ripped cheap cotton fabric that comprised what was left of my mind. It was like being in a hollow, infinite shell. But even here, as ridiculous as this may sound, various aspects of the physical world such as my clothes that by now had dried, but were incredibly wrinkled, kept me from completely falling into the abyss. And although I needed to shave, the feel of my beard against my hand as I rubbed it maniacally kept me together I realized that I didn't have a soul in the world to call accept my mother back in Louisiana, and that was out of the question.

It must have been six hours before a guard came by and told me to follow him. I compliantly went along as he took me to a shower area where we were alone. He handed me a bundle which consisted of an orange uniform, socks, and on top a small packet with a miniature toothbrush, toothpaste, comb, and small pack of antibacterial soap.

"You've got three minutes to shower and get dressed." He informed me with no hint of emotion whatsoever, then asked in the same manner, "What size shoe do you wear?"

"Eleven and a half."

He left the small locker area and I quickly undressed and got into the shower.

I had been arrested at least five times in New Orleans, but was always out on bail within two hours, and had never been convicted of prostitution. I was even caught with a joint once but my lawyer and two thousand dollars got me out of that. So I had an inkling of what was going on, but I had never been put into state clothes before. I felt like a highway sign as I pulled on the bright orange jump suit. When the guard returned with standard issue converse low tops, I attempted to joke with him.

"Hey man, you know where I can get some of these to send to my hunting buddies for Christmas?" I asked, with a slight grin, in my best redneck straight bass.

He replied, "My name is Officer Cohen, and if you ever address me as 'man' again, I'll be taking you to dental emergency and you should see what lousy work they do."

I quickly wiped the smile off of my face and said, "Got it."

"Got it, what?" he barked back

"Got it, Sir."

Then he cracked a smile. But you know what? Maybe blessings can come in a jailhouse stay. At least I was getting my wits back.

When Officer Cohen then took me to the mess hall, it became apparent that it was dinner time and the day was coming to an end. Officer Cohen told me to get in line and left. That's when it really sunk in that I was maybe the fourth or fifth Anglo Saxon in the room. Everyone else was either Hispanic or black. Really, nothing was different than I had been used to in New Orleans, but I had only ever spent short amounts of time in a holding cell. I had never eaten jail food before.

I got to the back of the line and no one else lined up behind me and I guessed that perhaps Officer Cohen had done me a favor; there were some incidents that went on further up the line as other prisoners were being pushed around by other guys. When I got through the food line of canned vegetable medley and canned chicken over rice, I grabbed two of the rolls that were offered at the end of the line and joined the few other white guys, sat down, and didn't say a word. Luckily, nothing happened and I finished the food without incident. Officer Cohen came up and grabbed me and told me that I was to go with the Blue group when the cafeteria was being cleared.

You know, Selectric, for some reason, the guy was looking out for me. Like so many people that I have run across, it does boggle my mind to look back and see that they were kind to me for really no other reason than just to be so. And me being a hustler and all, I tend to take it from them. Don't get me wrong, I can be nice and usually am, but generally, I want something for it. I simply don't trust people enough to believe that anyone is truly good to someone for nothing. Time and time again, I have run into so many people that just want to help others, and I can't explain their motivation being anything other than honest compassion. I'm beginning to wonder. Perhaps, Selectric, Anne Frank was correct after all about people being basically good at heart.

And here I was in a lockup without a dime, or even shoes for Chrissake. I was in a relatively alien city and no one from New Orleans was going to fly here to help me on a drunk and disorderly charge with drug possession. As I walked down the florescent corridor to my cell, I was relieved to know that I would share accommodations with a whacked out skinny white guy who was too emaciated to harm anyone. But my state of relief was quickly fleeting as a panic sat in when I asked myself, "What in the hell are you going to do now?" I was terrified, alone, and I felt subhuman as the lights dimmed and I climbed into my bed.

I don't intend to try to make more of jail than it was, but honestly, it totally sucked. I think I learned this while I was there. I remember someone quoting, "I'm not afraid of death. I just don't want to be there when it happens." I'm sure that I agree with these sentiments. But jail, on the other hand, from any angle, completely terrifies me. I'm afraid of jail, the thought of it, and the reality of it. I swear I'll never go into one again.

And this stay would have been longer but for, again, nothing but sheer dumb luck. To begin with, nobody even tied in the fact that I came off the exploding boat and so I wasn't ever questioned about it. And to add silver to gold, the cocaine that the BSO found in my pocket had become lost. When the public defender contacted who she thought was my mother from my fake ID, the poor lady on the other end of the line truthfully replied that her son was dead and my attorney hung up the phone and looked at me with the most sympathetic look I had gotten in years.

"I told you, since they found out I was gay they don't even acknowledge me." I explained.

The next day, when I went before the judge and the DA, was the first day they were back from the Christmas and New Year's holidays, and their dockets were full. I suspect that my Public Defender told them about her phone call to my "mother" and when she pled guilty to my charges of public drunkenness and trespassing, he sentenced me to a $1000 dollar fine or 40 days and 30 hours of drug and alcohol treatment/education. So naturally, I took the 40 days and so began my short stay in the tidy accommodations of the Broward County Sheriff's Hotel.

About two days into my incarceration, the guard came by my cell in the morning and explained that I should start working off my substance education and that today I would be in luck, as a program volunteer was coming into the jail to chair a meeting at two P.M. I told the guard thanks and that to make sure I was on the list after lunch so that I had hall clearance from the common yard. I pretended to be eager and I'm sure I didn't fool the guy. To tell you the truth, I had heard about drinking rehabilitation groups but I had never been directly involved with them. One of my buddies, a literal street whore, in New Orleans got in with them. I saw him two years or so later while I was walking in the Fauborg Marigny as he pulled up a for sale sign out of the front yard of a duplex with a big red "SOLD" sticker on it and placed the sign in the back of his new Toyota Camry. When I approached him, saying, "Damn Johnny, you look like a million dollars. What gives?"

"Just living life on life's terms," he said matter of factly and never strayed from his work, regarding me as incidental.

"What's that supposed to mean?" I asked skeptically.

"I just gave up the drinking and the drugs Andy."

"Shit Johnny! Sounds to me like you found Jesus or something."

As he shut the trunk of his hood and got into his car, he handed me a business card and said, "Andy, when you get ready to give up the high price of cheap living, give me a call."

And then he just drove off. As I stood there alone on the broken sidewalk holding his card, I distinctly remember gawking aloud, "Motherfuck." Because for real, this guy was one of the worse cases I had ever seen at our age. I had heard that he had gotten busted with possession but had gotten out early, and word on the street was he'd gone straight, but this was utterly amazing. I was shocked that someone so absolutely certifiable would be able to be the man that I had assumed, more or less, just told me to go fuck myself.

So that afternoon as I walked to the jail library and thought about my old chum Johnny, I wondered what kind of meeting this was going to be. Was I in for thirty hours of fucking Sunday School? Or would I have to learn paragraphs verbatim from the Bible? I really didn't know. I only knew that the judge was serious about me doing what he said for me to do and I didn't want to go in front of the man in black again and tell him I had not done the ADE—Alcohol and Drug Education.

And all was gradually revealed. When I entered the library meeting room, I noticed offhand that there were about ten other inmates who were already sitting down, and that the guy that was obviously from the outside and overseeing the meeting was in front of the room. He had set up a coffee station and stated in a no nonsense tone, "If you would like, please help yourself to a cup of coffee, then find a seat. We're going to get started here in a moment."

"Thanks," is all I said and took a cup then headed for a chair in the back of the group. I didn't want to appear too eager.

The chairperson began the meeting and announced that his name was John and that he was an alcoholic.

"Motherfuck!" I thought to myself as I reflected on the matter of fact and nonchalant manner that he revealed this to ten or so other people. Then I continued to think to myself. "I hope he doesn't expect me to say things about myself like, hi I'm Andy a gay whore that actually enjoys getting a big dick pumped up my ass. Anybody gotta problem with that?"

Really, I was stunned by John's frank attitude. But as I know, there is something to be said for shock value so I listened to the words that he was reading aloud with interest. What I remember most is that the word God kept popping up here and there and I was immediately suspicious of the entire motivation of the chairperson. Anyhow, John asked if there were any people new to the meeting and that he didn't want to embarrass anybody but just to get to know them. So I raised my hand and said, "Yeah, I'm Darren. First night in my ADE." (I almost fucked up and said my street name, Andy.)

And I was really taken aback when everyone in the room replied in unison, "Hi Darren."

"Yeah, uh hi," I said back. I remember that I thought that this guy at the front must really be like Jim Jones, from Guyana, and that they were going to pass out the Kool Aid any second. I almost got up and walked out, but I reminded myself about the judge and kept my ass down. Fortunately, I kept my mouth shut and listened to the guys in the meeting open up and be honest; it really got kind of interesting. I mean I thought I was a fucked up drinking and drugging son of a bitch, but I'm Junior League compared to what I heard. And heartache abounded. Man I'm here to tell you, there was some serious shit that was said in that room by some of these guys and I vaguely got a glimpse of what was going on in these meetings. Finally, the chairperson, John, told his story, stating what he had been like and what his life was like now, and he was serious. He had the same attitude and look in his eyes that my buddy Johnny back in the Big Easy had that day I saw him in the Marigny. He announced that he had some literature that was free for the taking and that after the meeting, anybody that would like a book should please help himself. Before closing the session or meeting, or whatever, with a prayer, he informed the group that he would be back Saturday night at 6 P.M. and to please bring a buddy or come alone. I knew, from his story, that this guy Johnny was no dummy and I also knew that he would be useful in getting by the judge, so without saying a word, I walked up and grabbed the book and walked off with it.

I spent the next few days going through it. The book described the principles that these guys lived by and how they claimed to have been delivered from the virtual nightmares that had been their lives. Some of the stories that I read made me take a good look at myself and I thought, "I don't consider my life to be a nightmare. Not before now. As a matter of fact, it was a dream, until the boat blew up."

I recall that while I lay in bed that night reflecting on my deceased friends and the fun and parties, I got really depressed and bitter that all of them and the good times were gone. I really couldn't blame the loss on alcohol or drugs. The real blame lay with the fucking police. I got more angry and depressed, so much so, I that I stifled my crying so that no one would hear.

CHAPTER 15

Broward County, March 1992

DESPITE THE SELF-PITY AND ANGER, I DID MAKE IT TO THAT MEETING Saturday and within a week, I was opening up and putting on quite a show. To be honest, I'm not sure if I knew myself if it was a show. I think that during this time I first learned about self-discovery and the profound awareness that can come from an individual being honest with himself. Perhaps it is from this small fraction of time in my life that I got the motivation to pursue writing. Either way, I didn't miss a meeting for the remainder of my time in jail. It was during this time that I became very close with John, the chairperson of the meetings that was coming in twice a week.

I can only describe John as the type of truly good and compassionate man whose motivations were truly based on helping other individuals. He was a heterosexual married man in his early forties with two little girls, ages five and eight. He made his living as an AC repair man and liked to bass fish and play softball for his company team. Of course, he gave of his own time, bringing two meetings a week to the Broward Jail and it was, as I said, during these times that I got to know him.

Although I went to Drug and Alcohol Education class every day in jail, it was during the ones sponsored by John that I was able to talk to him on a personal basis afterwards. He agreed to show me the ropes of staying sober. After a month of these talks, he told me that if I was serious about staying off the junk and the streets, that he had discussed with his wife the possibility of my staying with them in their home for a while when I got out of the pen. The only conditions would be that I could not drink or drug, and that I had to be gainfully employed. Abiding by that, John said that I could come and go as I liked and would be welcome until I got on my feet.

Eventually, the day came around that I was released. After the meeting and well wishes from the other prisoners in the program, I walked out of the place, with John at my side, a free man.

It was an absolutely beautiful day. The temperature was around 77 with a mild breeze and probably the bluest clear sky I had ever witnessed. We got in John's truck, rolled down the windows, and headed to a K-Mart store where John bought me some essentials like underwear, socks, and jump-suits for work—I was going to be a cleanup and errand boy in their AC shop—and razors, toiletries and such. Then we headed to his house in the little town of Dania.

We pulled up directly on his lawn, as his garage had been converted into the room that I was going to be staying in and the rest of his driveway was taken up by his fishing boat and his wife's small Honda Civic. When he shut off the engine and got out, I took a brief account of my surroundings. I knew that we were only two or three blocks west of Federal Highway and that his house was no different than others in neighborhood with sparse lawns, Florida Oak and Australian Black Olive trees. It seemed that everybody, like John, parked in their front yards. Most of the home's garages either had boats in them or had been converted. The driveways housed canvas covered boats and trailers.

My observation was quickly interrupted by the sound of his screen door that creaked open immediately followed by squeals of joy and excitement as two little girls came rushing at him, hollering, "Daddy, Daddy, Daddy!"

He caught each of them with one arm and he pulled them up from the ground as they leapt at him. They gave him hugely exaggerated smacks of kisses on each of his cheek as though the girls were in competition with each other over which one could give John the best kiss.

"How are my two best girls today? Huh." Then he looked at me and said, "What do you think Darren? Do I have two of the prettiest girl-friends you ever saw?"

Before I could answer, the older of the two said, "Oh Daddy, Momma's your girlfriend, but I love you most."

"Nah ah!" quickly countered the younger continuing, "I wuvs you the best."

With that he gave each of them a big kiss on their cheeks and let them back down to the ground, stating, "Lord you girls get bigger every day. It's all that good cooking your momma is giving us. Speaking of which, what is that I smell coming from the kitchen?"

Both girls shook their heads and raised their shoulders, declaring their ignorance of their mother's menu for the evening.

"Who's that?" the youngest girl asked, pointing at me.

"That's Darren, whom I was telling y'all about. Can you say hi?"

She walked over behind her father, putting her thumb in her mouth and shaking her head "no" while hiding behind John's leg. Then the oldest spoke up bravely, "Hey Darren, I'm Connie and I'm in the Third Grade."

"Wow!" I said and then continued, "I bet that you started learning multiplication tables already."

"Uh huh," she said then started going down the line of multiples of three to digit ten.

"Dang Connie, That's good. I don't think I remember what three times nine makes. I bet you make A's and B's."

"Straight A's," she quickly corrected.

"I make stwaight A's too," the youngest one meekly offered from behind her father's leg.

"Nah ah, you don't get A's in Kindergarten," Connie the elder of the two objected.

"She sure does." John said rushing to the younger's defense adding, "Abby's the best finger painter in Florida. They even hung one of her pictures up in the Broward County Library for Art Festival last year."

Abby stuck her tongue out at her sister and before Connie could counter, John stepped in and said with quiet but authoritative enthusiasm, "Hey, why don't you two run inside and see if you can help your mother with anything while I show Darren his room and get him settled in before dinner."

"Okay Daddy," they both said in unison and scampered off back into the house.

Laughing a little, John said, "Grab your stuff and follow me to your room and we'll get you set up here before dinner."

"Sounds like a plan. Man, you don't know how much I appreciate this, John."

"Yeah, I do Darren. I've been in the same spot, more or less."

"Well you seem like you've got it going on now what, with all of this and those two and I haven't even met your wife yet," I said while waiving a hand at his truck and boat and general direction of the house and air.

"Darren, all of this, as you put it, is nothing but a miracle and a gift that I know I couldn't keep if I didn't try and give it back to you and others like us. I only hope that that you get to do the same."

Then we were interrupted by Connie coming into the garage.

"Connie, now you are going to have to start knocking on the door before you come in to visit Darren from now on."

"Okay, sorry, I forgot, but Momma says for y'all to wash up and come eat."

"Thanks sugar. Tell her we'll be right there." And Connie ran out of my room with a sense of satisfaction that her mission had been accomplished.

"Man, John, you don't know how much I'm looking forward to this meal. I've eaten nothing but jail food for some time now. I get a whiff here and there of whatever she is making and I really salivate."

Laughing a little and shaking his head, John corrected me again, "Boy I hate to tell you twice, but I know what you mean again. As you know, I was in the Salvation Army for a couple of years and although I was lucky to get the meals that I got there, they can't hold a candle to what Karen whips up. Get washed up and come on in through the front door and we'll be in the kitchen. You're in for a treat, Lucky."

He laughed a little more, then headed out and left me to my devices—emptying a bar of soap from one of the bags on my bed and then fumbling for the light in my small bathroom that I was using for the first time. I washed up and did what I was asked.

When I walked through the door and the spring on the screen door slammed behind me, I was hit by the smell of home cooking that I had not enjoyed since I was a boy of 18. It was homemade southern style cooking. There was simply no mistaking it. I don't know if it was the love expressed by the little girls earlier, or the initial delight from inhaling the aroma, or if it was the distinctly Southern accent in the woman's voice calling from the end of tiny foyer and from the arch that separated the dining room from the TV room.

"Darren, come on back and take a seat at the table. I'll be with ya in a minute. I got my hands full at the moment."

I couldn't see Karen as the kitchen was off in a nook from the dining area, but my mind instantly reeled. I find that smells or scents can send me into a flashback far more effectively than any usage of L.S.D. ever has. It was as though I was back home before dinner and I couldn't control the memories that hit me. Whether memories flew at me or flew me to the year of 1982 doesn't matter. But I might have as well been back in my boyhood home, and so I was in an instant. Selectric, let me describe the flashback I had in Karen's kitchen that brought me my last meal with my momma and daddy.

CHAPTER 16

Ouachita Parish, Louisiana, January 1987

IT WAS THE FIRST SATURDAY OF MY JUNIOR YEAR IN HIGH SCHOOL, AFTER classes had resumed from mid-semester and holiday breaks at the local private school I attended. Momma had made a huge meal of smothered steak, okra and butter-beans, rice and gravy, and a yellow squash casserole. As well, there was a fresh baked skillet of cornbread and a full pitcher of iced tea. It was absolutely one of my favorite meals and the aroma filled the house with an underlayer of bacon, meat, and onions mixed with the natural aroma of the vegetables they accompanied. Most people would consider it comfort food, but even this meal could not subdue the anxiety I felt when Momma shouted through the house that afternoon to come and eat.

I was the first to the table and as I sat down, Momma came in and I could see that she had been crying. She tried to hide it, or better yet, tried to pretend she was trying to hide it as she produced a weak smile that I recognized as the "Shot Smile." When I was a little boy, it was the smile she always gave me when we got out of the car at the doctor's office and I had made her promise me that I wouldn't get a shot. And even though I got a shot every time I walked through the doors of my pediatrician's clinic, I would somehow try and fool myself that I would not get a shot because, "Momma promised." But Momma had promised nothing before this meal, and I knew my father was pissed. And, pissed was an understatement. Actually, it was one of the few times in my life that I saw him out of control with his emotions.

I had fucked up quite a bit since the summer of my freshmen year in high school, and most of the time it had to do with pot and alcohol. Let me give you a brief account. I got my driver's license on my fifteenth birthday two years earlier, and with it in my wallet only two weeks I had bottomed out Dad's Grand Wagoneer in Hog's Bayou. Being a total dumb fuck, I'd put the vehicle in low four wheel drive. I kept pumping the engine and needless to say, I threw out the rods and burned the engine up. I had a buddy with a Ford Bronco tow me and my dad's mud covered, top of the line S.U.V that now had no engine, into the front yard of our house. I was falling down drunk when I got out of the vehicle to help my buddies undo the chain riggings when Dad walked out of the house for an explanation. I was too drunk to explain what happened so one of my friends gave a brief account and then my dad laid down on his back and went under the Wagoneer, to see for himself the extent of the damage. After seeing the busted oil pan, which confirmed that the engine was indeed blown, he got up and looked at me and said simply, "Start making plans to get a job. You're going to pay for my new engine."

"No big deal, Dad." I hiccupped.

So I got a job, or better yet, he got me a job that spring working on weekends for an oil and gas case cementer, and it continued through the summer. I was a yard hand and washed the filthy concrete and pump trucks when they came in from a job and then reloaded them by forklift on pallets holding the various chemicals needed with the order for their next job. By the end of the summer I had the money in my dad's sock drawer to pay for the fiasco. When I presented it to him, he said, "Well, now you know how costly these things are. Keep the money, Son. You might want to put it up for college."

I didn't put it up for college. I spent it on Mary Jane, alcohol, water skis, gas, and horse racing. Needless to say, Baptist fathers of fifteen year old boys and girls were not thrilled when one of my little girlfriends confessed to her parents that I'd supplied fake I.D.'s to her and the couple we'd doubled. A she blabbed that our out date had not been to a chaperoned Saturday school trip to the Vicksburg Civil War Battlefield, but to Louisiana Downs which was about a hundred miles in the opposite direction, both geographically and metaphorically speaking.

Actually, Dad played this incident down with a bit of a sense of humor, even though it did put him in a sticky situation with some of the lawyers at the courthouse. I actually overheard him telling my mother, "Horse racing and pussy, or being chaperoned around a monument to fools of the past. I don't think that was a hard choice for the boy."

"Oh, good God" she exclaimed, then continued in exasperation, "he failed algebra last year and now he's failing biology and I really think this has all got to do with his drinking. He always made A's and B's before he started drinking. You've got to put your foot down."

"The bars and beer brewers aren't going to close because your baby is growing up. He's going to have to learn for himself how to live here with them. He'll sink or swim, baby."

And I was sinking fast. I was on my way to making All State Defensive End in my sophomore year—but this almost never came to be, The principle of the school did not share my father's attitude towards drinking at that year's Football Homecoming Dance. While I was inside dancing, or attempting to dance, he opened the door to my momma's Lincoln town car and found my fifth of Crown Royal. Thank God he didn't really know the anatomy of the car and the "secret compartment" in the door, or else he would have also come across some Jamaican Gold that would have made a Thai Stick shudder. But the Crown was enough to make for the evening's drama as he turned up the lights in the gym and then interrupted the band, marching on the stage with the purple velvet bagged bottle of whisky and asked for me by name. I walked up to the stage and after a short soliloquy on how alcohol would not be tolerated at school functions, and that this was found in my car, he asked me to leave and noted that measures would soon be in place to assure my expulsion. As he walked off the stage motioning for me to come along, I took the microphone and slurred, "Great game guys. Sorry about the break in the music here but it looks like my momma left her bourbon in the car again."

Principal Stelder was furious.

Thank God Daddy hated the man. He was an Uptown New Orleans dandy who had been recruited by some of the country club parents to bring more prestige to our little private academy. But the "Headmaster," as he preferred to be called, was good for his word and on Monday morning, when I showed up for school, I was handed my suspension with an invitation to the board of directors meeting to be held the following week. If I cared to, I would be free to say anything on my behalf before I was expelled and my parent's portion of stock in the Academy purchased back by the board. Daddy's answer was swift and decisive.

He bought stock in a private school in an adjacent Parish, and let the owner of the Logging and Perforating Company (whom he used in his contracting of natural gas) that I would be attending that new school— with my current football playbook in hand, and that the coach of my new school had already assigned me a locker and jersey for their team so that I could suit up when the two schools played in a couple weeks. It was no coincidence that Mr. Claxton, the owner of the Logging and Perforating Co. had a boy a year my junior who played football with our team. Mr. Claxton was also Vice President of the Board of Directors for the Academy. That evening after dinner, Mr. Claxton came by to ask Dad to be mature about this thing as, after all, I had broken school rules and had been implicated in several other situations.

"Claxton, like my boy said, that was his Momma's Crown Royal and I don't care for that two bit piss ant calling my office up and leaving a message with my secretary about the vouchers of my stock to be present at "his" board of directors meeting next Thursday. So Claxton, as you know, I've bought ample stock to enroll Mason in River Crest Ridge. So here's my stock for you to return to Principal Stelder," Daddy said as he handed him a legal envelope. Then, handing Mr. Claxton another envelope, he continued, "I'd also like for you to explain the contents of this envelope to Principal Stelder. In this one are my offices legal right's to the mineral deposits that lay beneath 'his' school. The best access to those rights, to which I'm lawfully entitled, happen to be smack on the center of the fifty-yard line of 'his' football field. If Mr. Stelder has any problem understanding the documents therein, just ask him to call 'my' office. Oh, and if I don't have the time, my secretary will explain to him that there will be a Christmas Tree drilling rig placed there Thursday night and within a few weeks, a permanent measuring grid so that the revenues accrued from this venture might pay for my son's new stock and tuition and inconvenient drive to River Crest Ridge, whom Mason will play football for. And I have to say Claxton, I'm going to enjoy Headmaster Stelder and 'his' school. Because, his school won't be having any home games for a while. I'll see all y'all at River Crest."

I've not witnessed too many educated men look as dumbfounded, silent, and shocked as Mr. Claxton's was that Monday night.

"Mason you can't be serious," Mr. Claxton finally said.

"Never more in my life, Claxton."

The board of directors never met that next Thursday, and expulsion proceedings were never taken towards me. I was back in class by Friday noon and with my suspension resolved, was allowed to play football Friday night. Then I went out drinking at the bonfire on the levee to celebrate our slaughter over our rival. We ended up beating River Crest Ridge the next week by twelve points, thus winning our district title. I passed biology and even my second shot at algebra and got a job as a lifeguard that summer at the Bayou DeSieard Country Club. The only real trouble I got in that summer was for my little baseball booking I did at the club among the teenagers; when I got caught—or better yet "implicated" for that—I wasn't even fired. Perhaps the Club, of which my family were not members, nor did my dad have any wish to be part of, was afraid of a drilling rig on their golf course. And even that fall went well during my junior year without much of an incident other, than me still drinking heavily on weekends and not doing well in geometry. I even made All State.

But then I really blew it at the winter dance.

Four days after Christmas, the Country Club had its Winter Formal, to which one of the school's young ladies invited me. It was on an absolutely freezing, nineteen-degree late December night. I was doubling with another couple, and after the dance my buddy and I decided to use my dad's houseboat to see if we could score with our dates. I was up for it even though I was more interested in the bar on the boat than getting into my date's panties. When, after several drinks, my buddy and football teammate took his girl back to one of the boats cabins and left me and my date in the front to drink alone together. It took about twenty-five minutes before his date, a girl from the local Catholic school, returned to the front of the now darkened boat to demand that we take her home "immediately." We got into a big hurry as the Catholic girl went into hysterics and hustled off the sixty foot, two-story house boat in a hurry. And I forgot to turn off the water pumps that I had turned on so that our dates could use the restrooms, which of course used river water. As I said earlier, it was a freezing cold night and it was even colder on the river. I was about to learn the extremes and consequences that arise from the dreadful mistake of not properly shutting down the boat the next morning at home.

"Wake up Mason." My father's voice cracked through the eight A.M. air like it was the voice of God Almighty himself. At first I thought I was dreaming until I realized that the covers had been ripped off of me and the lights turned on by my father. His glaring silhouette hovered only inches above me, all too clear in the electric light. I remember distinctly the smell of his morning smoker's breath.

"Were you on my houseboat last night, Boy?"

"Uh, yeah dad," I groggily confirmed, then continued as I knew something heavy was up here. "But we didn't leave the dock or take it out or anything like that."

"Get dressed you little bastard—and I'd wear some old clothes if I were you. You're going back down to the dock to see if you can help save my boat, which is now listing and about to pull the dock and five other small houseboats with it."

"What?" I enquired as I sat up and rubbed my eyes. My father slapped my hands from my face so that I could see how angry he was.

"Someone, and I'm assuming that is you, forgot to turn off the water pumps. The water froze and busted a pipe. Then it thawed and pumped the fucking Ouachita River into the hull of my boat. You little son of a bitch—get dressed and be down on the dock in twenty minutes or I'll throw you in the water myself."

"Jesus Deddie, I'm coming, but when did you find this out."

"Edgar and Winston were going over the Ouachita River Bridge just fifteen minutes ago to go rabbit hunting and looked over and saw the boat leaning heavy. They just called me."

Edgar and Winston were two Cajun brothers that ran a local women's clothing store with a third brother of theirs. They were hunting buddies of ours, and also close neighbors on the bayou. Then dad called the dock keeper, Mr. Grayson. Thank God the old man was there. He rushed down and boarded the sinking vessel and was able to turn off the pumps so at least the water quit flooding in. Mr. Grayson asked my dad if he wanted him to cut the Cypress Lady free so that she wouldn't bring five other boats down with her as she pulled the dock over. I later found out that Mr. Grayson was able to hook up some bilge pumps on the pier to get enough water out so that complete disaster was avoided.

I truly believe I owe my life to that man.

Nevertheless, I spent New Year's Eve manning the pumps as they purged the rest of the water from the various flooded compartments of the boat. The worst fact was that the engine room was flooded and had spread oil everywhere, not to mention that the motor and generators were ruined. I spent New Year's Day with a sponge and bucket down in the hull doing the best I could to wipe up any extra water that was there. Hell, I guess I know now that I ought to stay off boats around New Year's. However, the boat was saved and no other boats were damaged, and nobody got physically injured.

But as I mentioned earlier, I had never seen my father as completely out of control of his emotions as he was that morning. He stayed angry throughout the week. Anger was something that he pretty much stayed off of. And at breakfast the following Saturday morning, I was to learn just how pissed he was, and to what level of exasperation I had brought him. Finally he came to the table and after my mother sat down, he said, "Honey, this looks wonderful." And she started to tear up immediately as he continued.

"Son, your mother and I have been talking about your grades and the trouble that you have continuously managed to stay in, and to a large degree keep us in." He took a deep breath, then looked me square in the eyes and continued. "I try not to make any major decisions when I'm in a state of anger, and it is only now that feel myself somewhat in control of my emotions. I've decided that we're all going to take a ride over to Port Gibson this afternoon and have a look at Chamberlain Hunt."

My mother now added loud sobs to her visual tears, and for a second, I thought I saw my dad's eyes start to glisten. With the exception of her sobs, the table was quiet. I didn't dare say a word. Really, what could I say? I just ate without saying a word and so did Momma and Daddy.

Two hours later, we were driving through the Academy grounds. I kept quiet. My mother did too. After getting out and walking over the grounds with Colonel Westin, my father sent my mother back to the Wagoneer. He asked Colonel Westin for a private moment with me and we walked together on the parade ground. It would be the last time that I talked to my father.

"Son, I'm at a complete loss here. You seem hell bent on destroying yourself. I don't know what else to do." Again I didn't say a word. I somehow knew that to plead with him would only make matters worse. And he continued.

"I'm gonna leave you here, Son. They'll issue you quarters and clothing. The last thing I ever wanted for you was to have someone thinking for you, but I honestly don't know what else to do. I love you, Son."

I was stunned. As we walked back over to Colonel Westin my mother came running out of the Jeep screaming "No, no, no," in hysterics, my father ordered her back to the vehicle before she could get to me and she obeyed. They drove off.

Two months later, I got high and drunk with a couple of my classmates and was caught red-handed, naked with both of them in "the act that dare not speak its name," as Colonel Westin described over the phone lines to my father. I sat with the Colonel and my two comrades in the Commandant's office as Colonel Westin called each of our fathers and gave the identical speech. I was informed that I would not be expelled but that I would have all privileges revoked, including summer leave

When I called my mother to beg her to help me her only answer was, "If I had known you were going to be like this, Mason, I would have never had you."

Then she hung up. Two days later given first chance, I was off of the Academy grounds with a thumb out, heading for New Orleans.

CHAPTER 17

Fort Lauderdale FL, March 1992

A ND IN AN INSTANT MY MIND RETURNED TO THE KITCHEN IT HAD never physically left. The same present composed of the smells and verbal accents created by Karen's dinner, which had just moments before thrown me back to my mother's and my last exchange of words. They were only words from the past. Nothing more than a memory. But, I had the reality of a home-cooked meal again, I took my seat with John, Karen, and their two little girls. John's description didn't come close to describing just how good the meal Karen served actually was. Nor could I tell you in words how good it tasted, but only that my body and mind absorbed every bite as though the baked and stewed pork chops were the first that I had ever eaten. Or that the rice and gravy might have validated every reason I had for living. And I must mention the homemade corn-bread and a squash casserole with a side of pole beans; Karen couldn't have done any better.

And I asked Karen and John, "Do y'all eat like this every night?"

"Am I lucky or what?" he said with a bite of something still left in his mouth.

"Incredibly," I answered. Then I continued, "Karen that was absolutely the best meal I've had since I can remember. If I had a thousand dollars, I would pay that amount for the exact same meal again, but I don't. Is there anything I can do to repay you?"

She smiled humbly and then said in her strong Georgia accent, "Aw you're too sweet. I'd imagine anything would taste good, though, after what you've been through."

"Please don't even attempt to sell yourself short Karen."

"Well, you are welcome," she said and then continued with a slight giggle, "and since you don't have a thousand dollars this time, you could help me wash dishes."

"My pleasure," I said with sincere enthusiasm.

So I picked up my plate and Karen's and brought them into the kitchen where I found the garbage can under the sink. She followed me in with the girl's half eaten plates and when she saw me scraping the plates she giggled asking, "Do you think you might have a thousand next week?"

"If I don't, I'll have it next month. Thanks again, Karen."

"Well if you just keep your nose clean, that would be worth more than a thousand dollars to me. You hear?"

"I do."

"Then good." She said with smart satisfaction. Then she hollered at John, "Honey can you start the baths for the girls while I put the left-over's up."

"Sure thing, baby," he answered, then asked, "is my softball uniform in the dryer? I got a game at eight over at Mill's Pond."

"Oh, that's right." Then under her breath said, "Damn I forgot to change my wash over." She continued shouting through the house, "Oh honey, walk out to the utility closet and put 'em in the drier. It won't take but a minute. You've got plenty of time."

"No sweat baby, thank you."

"You're welcome," she hollered back to him, then smiled saying, "never a dull moment around here. You going to the game with him Sugar?"

"No, He was talking about dropping me off at a drug meeting over by the tracks somewhere, then picking me up on his way home. How about you, you going to his softball game?"

"No, not tonight. I'm gonna be doing service for the Ladies Institution's Service, and help chair a meeting for the Broward Counties Ladies Ward."

"Christ, you too," I said in disbelief as I loaded the dishwasher.

"Freely taken, freely given," she automatically responded, then added, "you'll see some day. I can tell you're a good soul down deep."

I didn't say anything to respond to her comment. I just let it sink in, and then I pondered to myself whether what she said was true or not. While I was silently asking myself this, I came up with another question. Do I even have a soul? Does anyone? No answers came.

I guess I wasn't watching what I was doing, because about this time, Karen handed me a wet plate and I dropped it on the linoleum floor and it cracked and shattered into a at least ten pieces.

"Oh shit," I said aloud without thinking and then thought about talking like that in front of Karen, much less her girls. Then I panicked with the thought of one of them running through the kitchen with bare feet and hollered aloud, "John, I broke a dish and there's shards all over the floor. Keep the girls outta here." There was a brief hesitation in response then, a holler from the back of the house, "Don't worry, they're safe and sound with Mr. Bubble."

"Really, Darren," Karen said coming over with a broom and a dust pan and sweeping everything up in two seconds.

"Relax a little, but I appreciate you thinking about my babies."

"Sorry if I got a little excited," I apologized.

"Just a broken plate," she said, then adding as she put the shards in the trash can, "it all works out if we let it. I got the rest of this. Feel free to just watch TV or whatever. We'll be heading out just as soon as Tara gets here to watch the kids."

"Thanks again, Karen."

"Now you are welcome again." And with that she turned on the dishwasher. I went back to my room and just laid on the bed and took two or three deep breaths.

I contemplated whether or not I was in reality, telling myself that this was all fine and dandy for John, but that I would never have a wife and kids.

"For crying out loud," I silently exclaimed, "who the hell am I kidding? I'm a gay hustler who will never live a Father Knows Best sweet TV lie."

A tinge of guilt shot through me, but in an instant I knew I wouldn't be staying here with John and his family. Best to get my happy ass back to New Orleans, the sooner the better. I wasn't sure just how, but then, in an odd twist of logic, I remembered Karen saying that things would work out if you let them. And then I heard the doorbell ring and the girls giggling over Karen as she explained to the baby sitter that they had already bathed and were ready for bed. She told her to feel free to use the phone, TV, or eat anything in the kitchen that she would like.

"Just put 'em to bed whenever you get tired of 'em but no later than nine, please"

There was a knock on my door and I said, "Yeah, come on in."

John entered in his baseball digs, saying, "You finding everything you need?"

"Just fine John. You've got a great place here."

He smiled and said that we had better head off, as he needed to drop me and Karen at county. We went out the front door of my room and Karen was already in John's truck and we took off. Within a few minutes, we were pulled into a really bumpy gravel road by a train track. John stopped the truck and said, "Alright here you are, we'll pick you up about 9:30. If you don't want to hit a second meeting, just hang out and shoot some pool or sit around and drink coffee." Then he winked at me. While getting out of the truck I told them sincerely how much I appreciated them. I almost started crying because I knew that this would be the last time that I ever set eyes on them again. I closed the door to the truck and Karen scooted over and they took off. I walked up to the building through the small crowd that was hanging out in front of the shoddy facility and decided to walk in just to put Karen and John's mind to rest for the night. But I knew I wouldn't be there to meet them at 9:30.

No sooner had I walked in when I heard Karen's voice, "Darren, hey Darren," and she was breathing hard like she had been running, then continued, "John didn't know if you had money for the basket, or would want a Coke." And with that she handed me some money and dashed out before I could even count the bills she had handed me.

"See ya in a couple" she said.

It was three dollars.

"Thanks," I hollered back but she was already gone.

That was the last time I ever saw John and Karen. Who knows how this story would end or whether it would have been written had I stayed with them. But I gave it another five minutes just standing in the foyer of the meeting hall, then walked out and over to Federal Highway and caught the first bus north to Sunrise Boulevard. I was going to turn a quick trick and get back to Louisiana. I got off the bus and I felt lucky.

I was Andy again.

CHAPTER 18

The Committee

When I got on the bus as Andy, I could tell The Committee had been at work and was concluding a new musical composition. Mr. Slut/Whore was banging on a baby grand piano that sits in the back of Andy's mind; on the piano sat Miss Addiction in a stunning and strapless black dress, with her legs crossed and her shoulders swaying in tempo to Mr. Slut / Whore's rendition of, "If You Knew Suzy." He wailed with his exaggerated Irish accent, "Oh if you knew Andy, like I know Andy, oh, oh, oh."

As he brought the song to an end, Miss Addiction gently put down the Champagne flute and clapped a polite applause and dramatically exclaimed, "Bravo Slut/Whore, Bravo!"

Mr. Slut/Whore sat up quickly, knocked over the piano bench like he was Jerry Lee Lewis, and bowed as he held both fist clenched to his chest and let out a smug, "Thank You."

As he walked away from the piano, he let his hand trail down the keys to produce a trill as it progressed from the high keys to the low keys. Miss Addiction promptly offered him a flute of Champagne but Mr. Slut/Whore replied in mock earnest, "Oh no, I never touch the stuff."

Miss Addiction, taken off guard, could not disguise her mixed expression of shock and insult. But within seconds, Mr. Slut/Whore could no longer maintain a straight face. A small crack in his demeanor created a smile, at which Miss Addiction burst out laughing. Then she handed the Champagne flute to Mr. Slut/Whore's waiting hand. At the conclusion of her healthy laughter, Miss Addiction took a heavy sigh and said, "Oh Slut/Whore, I gotta admit, you almost fooled me there for a second. I thought you might have let some of that Drug and Drunk School get to you."

"Sunshine, you should have seen the look on your face. Priceless Cheri, simply priceless. He kissed her hand with French design then continued, "Speaking of fooled, where is our incorrigible old lady, Miss Love?"

"I haven't seen the dear since our little memory ride into the nostalgia down Mommy Lane."

Mr. Slut/Whore dashed over to the piano, carefully put down the champagne, and announced, "I guess the trip down Mommy Lane helped to rekindle some memories of ..." he broke into verse with piano backing him up "The Way We Were."

He kept the musical intro to the verse of the song going on the piano and they both laughed aloud at Mr. Slut/Whore's wit. Miss Addiction took a quick sip of her Champagne and complimented him, "That was brilliant, Slut/Whore, how you just simply let Andy keep reminding himself about the fact the he was nothing but a whore and he'll never know love."

"Thanks Doll, but you needn't underestimate your contribution to the victory. Twenty to one says Andy is on the streets tonight looking for a trick to finance a high, as well as a ticket back home."

"Oh Slut Whore," she said, waving a hand at him with simple southern belle modesty, "those would be entirely conservative odds. You can give me a hundred to one and you would still just be stealing my money you little rascal, scalawag you."

"Come on Sugar. For Daddy now," He said in his best southern accent, which wasn't very good. "Just one dollar."

"Well then, alright, for the sport of it," she replied.

They lifted their glasses and sealed their wager with a toast, which created a clang in the recesses of my mind that Miss Love couldn't help but overhear.

But she was not crying. The southern accent of Miss Addiction combined with the Irish tune that came along with every word out of Mr. Slut/Whore's mouth reminded Miss Love of dialogue from Gone with the Wind, between Gerald O'Hara and "Katie" Scarlet. Miss Love knew that if any trait or emotion in the mind of Mason Harrison Caldwell had half the strength and resolution of Scarlet O'Hara, it was her. Miss Love recalled an episode in the movie when Scarlet announced, while she counted money and denied credit to her old friends in her husband's hardware store, "I'm going to beat these Yankees, and I'm going to beat them at their own game."

Miss Love hadn't thrown in the towel yet. She'd let them carry on. And they did just that. Mr. Slut Whore tore into the Piano and for the benefit of Miss Love, mocked another Barbara Streisand song, "Songbird."

"Who sings for songbird?" He theatrically wailed.

Miss Addiction tried to join in but found it completely out of her key. She couldn't sing for shit anyway.

CHAPTER 19

Fort Lauderdale, March 1992

WHEN I GOT OFF THE BUS ON SUNRISE BOULEVARD AND N.E. 15TH Avenue, I realized that I was on the hunt again, and it didn't take long for my natural disposition to whore (or unnatural, depending on your point of view) to surge. Actually, I felt little if any remorse. I had gone through shock, met some people that wanted to change my world-view, and now had returned to my natural habitat. I felt vibrant and sure of myself with respect to the fact that I could score. I would have enough money to get out of here and get on the bus home with a buzz. I wanted a bump. And to get a bump, I needed to score a chump. I walked north down 15th, then just east, and found myself in a neighborhood which offered me no competition to speak of on the streets.

The sun had gone down and the streetlights were on so I took off my shirt to let my strong and toned body speak for itself. And I started walking. It wasn't five minutes until a local police car cruised by me and I waived at them and they waived back. I guess the recent life of clean living worked, as they must have thought that I was just a local guy on an evening walk. Whatever the case, they didn't give me any shit. All signs were pointing to a score.

Another five minutes of walking and I took a right and headed back to Sunrise Blvd. And little did I know at the time that Lady Fortuna was about to lay a pretty little trick on me.

He was driving a 1991, brand-spanking-new, midnight blue Mark VII with tinted windows. When I saw his break lights hit, I thought to myself, "Alright, here we go. Play the dumb 'visiting Uncle Tony walking to the video store routine.'"

He had pulled over about 20 yards in front of me and I walked by and gave an intentional nervous look at the window of the car. The tinting allowed me to see nothing inside, and I walked on by. Within five steps, I heard the electric window rolling down, and a voice that didn't sound too old at all ask in monotone, "Do you think you could tell me how to get to Ruby's Guest House?"

I came to a stop and turned to look at him, putting on my best good ole boy yuck yuck face and replied in an exaggerated Southern accent, "Who me?"

He pulled the car up to dispose of the space between us and turned on his map light; I turned to look at a man that had the most subtle good looks I had ever seen. He was nothing but radiant. He'd probably never been, nor would he ever be, a model. He had light brown hair that was receding and vaguely parted to the right. His eyes were blue with a grey hint, and a natural squint. They had a cunning look to them and I guessed that he might be a lawyer. I would later learn that he had a law degree but did not, in fact, practice law. His smile was predatory, which made me initially want to give up the dumb ass routine, but with a quick hunch, I decided to stay on it. I quickly ran my eyes over the rest of his character and took note that he wore a white polo shirt and that he had no jewelry around his neck. I could smell the cologne, "Quorum." He smiled with a perfect set of teeth when he said, "I haven't noticed anybody but you. Do you know where it is?"

I kicked the gravel on the road and said, "I'm not from around here. I live in Louisiana. Just visiting my Uncle Tony. He and his buddies went out for the night so I thought I'd walk up to the video store."

"Yeah, what kind of movies do you like?" he asked.

"Action," I replied a little too quickly.

"Get in. I think I have some videos at my condo that you would like." He quickly stated and flashed that great smile.

"I live right up Sunrise, off the Intracoastal. I can drive you back or you could walk back after the movie. You got nothing to lose and a lot to gain."

He gave me a wink.

"Alright." I replied and I heard him unlock the passenger side with the auto lock. So I walked around the car and got in.

When I opened the door, the overhead light came on and as I was getting in, the smell of his cologne overwhelmed me. As I settled into the deep blue leather seat, I was able to see the man's navy blue worsted wool pants and a ring on his right hand, which was perched on the wheel. I guessed it to be onyx or opal. I had no idea really, but the guy literally reeked of class. In a nutshell, he reminded me of a toned down Ed Harris.

He put the car in drive and asked me, "What is your name?"

And as soon as he asked me, I wanted to suck his dick. I wanted to play with his ass, fuck him, and for him to fuck me. I wanted him to sit on my face and play with my ass and then fuck each other some more and when I'd had enough, I wanted to fall asleep with my head in his crotch. The guy was sex in a bottle.

In my state of lust, I thought for a second about giving the guy my real name but quickly came to my senses when he asked again, in a really bad imitation of a southern accent, "It's not Bubba, is it?"

"Yeah, it's Bubba. How'd you guess?" I replied, then quickly gathered my wits and returned to a yuck yuck by saying, "No man, it's not Bubba. Andy." And I held out my hand to shake his. He was being a true smart ass and took his hand off the wheel and with his knee steered the car, feigning out of control into the next lane, and shook my hand. I have to admit that he scared the shit out of me and I really let it out, "Man, look the fuck out." My accent was no sham here.

He laughed and said, "Guy, if that's not a Louisiana boy in panic, I don't know what is. What part?"

"Northeastern part of the state. Ouachita Parish, right off Bayou DeSieard."

"Whoa shit! Right out of the swamp. What brings you here?" he inquired with a slight laugh.

"Just heard it was a fun place to be, so I called my uncle and he sent me a ticket from New Orleans to stay a couple of days."

He laughed a little more and looked in his rear view mirror, like he might be covering ass for what he was about ask, "Uncle Tony won't mind if you stay with me tonight, will he?"

"I don't know. I might have to call and tell him where I'm staying, and with whom. And by the way, who might that be?"

"Rick. Rick Gurnee," And he held out his hand again to shake.

"Nice to meet you again, Rick, but I'd rather not see you drive with your knees anymore."

He cracked a slanted smile and then I asked, "What movie did ya have in mind Rick? I really love movies like Indiana Jones or Double O Seven, things like that."

"Got em all." He replied as we were about to cross over the Intracoastal, but the red light indicating that the draw bridge was about to come up lit bright.

"Goddammit!" He grunted and stopped the Lincoln. As I gave a sigh, he shot a look at my crotch as he must have noticed the bulge that was already making an outline through my pants. He reached over and grabbed my dick through my pants and I sat motionless; he looked me square in the eyes and with no hesitation whatsoever bent over and kissed me. I guess he kissed me the whole time the bridge was up, because the next thing I knew, the people behind us were honking their horns. When we looked up, the bridge was back down.

"Fuck 'em," He said with a laugh of contempt. He took out a vial with a white substance from the console under his arm rest and put a big scoop of powder under my nose. I didn't hesitate and sucked it up like a Hoover. He then treated his own nose.

"I never knew draw bridges could be so much fun."

"They can be," he said while the car behind us was still blowing on its horn. He punched in a cassette and Flock of Seagulls came to life. "Wishing" ran through the premium sound system of the car. I felt like we flew to his condo. Then we took the elevator.

And so the night began in a rage of pure carnal attraction. Rick shifted his eyes from mine and then up and down my body all the way up in the elevator. When the doors finally opened, we walked quickly to the end of the hall without saying a word. He unlocked his door and I stepped from harsh lighting and the industrial carpet of the hallway onto white marble that soon met hardwood oak that separated the living area from the foyer. All of which was accented by carefully placed, dim track lights. Only a few steps into the living area, the fully windowed western wall of the living room allowed me to see the spectacle of moonlight and electric light dancing off the water of the Intracoastal; it allowed for the shady silhouettes of yachts and sailing vessels to emerge.

"Nice view, don't you think?" Rick asked.

"Very," I replied in a matter of fact tone.

"I really enjoy it here." He stated, then motioned by waiving his hand over his huge L-shaped black leather sofa, saying, "Please make yourself comfortable. Would you care for anything to drink?"

"Sure, scotch please," I replied, probably a little too quickly.

He had a small grin when he said, "I've got Chivas or Dewar's."

"Oh, Dewar's sounds great thank you." Then I added, "On the rocks please."

I saw his smile increase as he walked away and as I listened to him put the ice in the glass, I settled into the sofa and absorbed the smell of the natural leather mixed with the cologne Rick was wearing. The design and décor exhibited from his smoked glass and black granite entertainment center were impeccable. It was interlaced with scattered original paintings, sculptures, and various glass pieces. In a moment, the sound of cracking ice was replaced by the seductive and sexual surround sound music that came forth from a track by the group Enigma.

I could hear his footsteps on the hardwood and he presented my scotch from behind and walked around the sofa and carefully sat very close to me. He gave himself enough distance just to look me up and down. As I took a sip of the scotch, I heard him earnestly proclaim, "I'd have to say you are probably the most handsome man I've come across in years."

And by the way he said it, I felt that he believed his statement. He made me feel like a million bucks and he looked like the million figure incarnate. He bent over and kissed me again and I instantly liked the smell of his breath and texture of his skin and lips. Everything about him was distinctly masculine yet refined and smooth. He took the scotch out of my hands and placed it on the glass table and unbuttoned my jeans and I thrust my hips up to allow him to take them and my underwear off in one easy swoop. The feel of the leather against my bare ass and his hands between my legs and my balls as he clasped my butt gave me an instant erection that was more intense than any I had felt since I could remember.

That was the beginning of a night that was full of every form of complete and total ecstasy that I had ever known before or after. Emotions stirred that I'd never felt or recognized. He was like a magnet that took my very soul into his interior being and allowed me to touch all the atoms necessary to create a current that revolved around and began a new creation that was us. And all I could speak was his name. There were no questions with these feelings and my mind did not allow for any elaborations of options or possibilities. What happened simply happened, and the feelings were absolute emotional truths.

Yet I didn't know the man. I'd only set eyes on him an hour earlier. But again, I was certain. Somehow, I was ecstatic, yet melancholy. I knew in an instant that I was leaving the old world behind. I understood that nothing would ever be the same. I had touched on something few people really ever know. It's like the color blue. Do we all see it in the same shade or form? My guess is no. Does it strike the same emotional cords in each individual? I don't think so.

And likewise, I don't think "love" deciphers itself through any prism from which we all see or feel the same shades or hues. I can assume that there are different classifications such as puppy love, lust, romance, desire—just as there are such differences in turquoise, navy, or indigo blue. But just the same, are all blue. So which one is "true blue" and what is "true love?" We only see through our own eyes. We only feel through our own hearts. Timing is everything.

And as the night progressed, so did the sense of time. It was obscured by the effects of the white powder from an ornate crystal container that Rick later spooned out for us. It heightened the degree of pleasure that was already beyond description by twenty times. I can't think of any medium or language that can accurately describe the rapture and bliss that ensued with the complete and total wild abandon that we embraced.

I can remember but very little. Vaguely and through time, the memories come back to me in a hazy dream. I suppose it ranged from jungle gym sex where he picked me upside down by my ankles and sucked my dick. Then he would lower me a little and penetrated my ass with his tongue. The man had the physique and strength of a middleweight boxer. He would prop my ass on a pillow on the edge of the bed and bang his nine inch, uncut dick in and out of my hole for 45 minutes. He would share a hit of poppers or snort of the powder then he would lay down on his stomach and have me fuck his hot and hairy hole as I lay on top of him with my arms clasping his chest and pinching his tits. I imagine that we carried on all night in every imaginable position and tasted each other as we came in each other's mouth. We were carnal pigs.

So when I awoke the next morning and said to Rick, "Whoa, I feel like a Mack Truck has been driven in an out of my ass, but I don't have a headache or stopped up nose. I don't remember much either. What was in that coke?"

He replied saying, "It wasn't coke ,butt boy. It's special K." He smiled and kissed me and teased, "Want some more?"

"Better hold off," I replied.

"Have it your way." He replied and added, "Like I said, make yourself at home."

"I would, if you could point me to the direction of the john," I said.

As I got out of bed, he pointed me in the direction of the john and he laughed lightly at me as I walked and absent mindedly massaged my ass. When I turned around to flip him the bone, I remember thinking to myself that the man still looked incredible. And while I was pissing, he came into the bathroom butt naked and looked even better running water over his face in front of the huge mirrors that reflected his naked and enticing body from several angles. He had just walked in when I had finished taking a piss and had applied some toilet paper to my ass, noticing the blood.

***

It was during this time that we had our exchange of dialogue I explained earlier in this endeavor, regarding the cash. We switched spots at the commode. And like I said earlier at the start of the story, while he was pissing, he told me he was HIV positive, and that, knowing this, he had fucked me without a rubber anyway. Not worried about it in the least was he. I never will forget what he said when I inquired if his HIV status was negative.

"Good thing I've finished pissing or you would have made me miss the pot."

I got in the shower and wondered how in the hell I could even think that I was in love with this guy—but I was. There was absolutely no denying it. And yet I literally wanted to kill him.

As I turned on the water and sank into the meditation that comes from a fantastic shower, The Committee that inhabits my mind was squaring off like two Civil War armies, each secure in their own beliefs and in their ultimate victory.

CHAPTER 20

Good Bye Mr. Slut/Whore, Hello Mr. Revenge.

I COULD FEEL THE TENSION THAT WAS BUILDING WHERE MY SPINAL cord meets my neck and it was there that Miss Love, as if she were Khrushchev at a U.N. Council, was unceremoniously banging one of her geriatric abominations (only one from an eastern bloc country or Irish nuns in nineteen fifty-six could describe as a shoe) on the podium. Wherein the last meeting found Mr. Slut/Whore presiding, Miss Love called the gathering to order. It was obvious that she was outnumbered since Mr. Conscience had not been able to assimilate for some time now, and for all practical purposes was eliminated. But Miss Love was one tenacious bitch and while simultaneously banging her shoe, she shouted to the rest of the emotions and instincts primarily associated with Mr. Slut/Whore and Miss Addiction that were now assembling in the nerve, "Sit the fuck down and listen up you bunch of Maggot Pukes!"

Mr. Slut/Whore reeled and faced the old biddy of an emotion with a cocked eyebrow. While not by any means frightened by Miss Love's histrionics, he was nevertheless curious and wondering what could possibly be the source of the old woman's self-confidence and look of accomplishment, which surrounded her in a radiant shade of deep purple. At exactly this time Miss Addiction, in a glowing hue of magenta, was making her grand entrance and walking heel to toe towards Mr. Slut/Whore in a stunning strapless red dress and a red feathered hat that made her look like a Las Vegas show girl.

"You look like a whore," Miss Love snapped at Miss Addiction as she daintily took her seat next to where Mr. Slut/Whore was still standing.

As Miss Addiction looked up and gazed a smile at Mr. Slut/Whore, she absently acknowledged Miss Love by replying, "Dress for success is my motto honey."

"Yes, speaking of whoring and success," Mr. Slut/Whore now interrupted. He stood and cleared his throat then continued, "I have to wonder what has gotten into your mind that you, of all emotions, Miss Love, have the gall to bring us into this nerve so close to Andy's brain and to call a meeting. I should think that you would be hiding for your life in Andy's lower intestine, not up here, where Miss Addiction or I could easily rub you out once and for all like we did to Mr. Conscience."

Miss Love let a sadistic smile come across her face as she mocked Mr. Slut/Whore by doing a very good imitation of Mr. Conscience's droopy voice.

"Oh Dear."

Mr. Slut/Whore, a bit stumped, replied, "Very good, Miss Love. I am delighted that you have found some talent—but back to the matter at hand. You do recall last night's little scenario, don't you, Darling? Come lass, remember drugs, prostitution, unprotected sex, hmmm?"

"Go ahead and try rubbing me out Slut/Whore. You don't have the power. Only Andy has that power, and let me show you what he has decided to share with me." Miss Love replied.

With only one shoe on and the other still on the podium, where only days before Slut/Whore had brandished a Dildo at the group, Miss Love hobbled in her ratty panty hose over to where Mr. Slut/Whore was standing and poked him in the chest and growled, "You're on borrowed time, Slut/Whore. Care to arm wrestle?" And when she reached out, effortlessly squeezing his unsuspecting right hand, all in the room—including Miss Love—were a bit stunned by the grimace of pain that was featured on Mr. Slut/Whore's face, and the although foreign but unmistakable sound of fear in his voice as he grunted, "Damn it to hell, yer cunt."

Miss Love just smiled and looked over at Miss Addiction, who had hesitantly risen out of her seat, as if she might come to his aid, and give a half ass show of support to Mr. Slut/Whore. But she thought better of it when she became aware of the sincerity of Mr. Slut/Whore's agonizing condition, and she sat back down.

"You made a good choice sister," spat Miss Love while shoving Mr. Slut/Whore over to the chair next to Miss Addiction. Mr. Slut/Whore took his seat and applied pressure to his now throbbing hand by sticking it between the makeshift pressure vice given by both of his knees.

Miss Love continued, "Like I said Kiddies, only Andy has the power to rub any of us out and, although I might not have the power to kill you, I might—as you contributed to the decision made by Andy to do away with Mr. Conscience—have some say in your eventual demise. But as you can see, I could cause you extreme discomfort for some time."

A sadistic smile now enveloped Miss Love's face as she pulled a Barbie Doll from the podium where Mr. Slut/Whore had, on many occasions, pulled so many of the props that he had used to antagonize Miss Love. As she held the toy up to her breast she looked directly at Miss Addiction and stated in low seething passion, so that all gathered in the meeting could hear, "Oh Miss Addiction, how I would love to pull every strand of blond hair out of your head which holds that chemical infested brain of yours together."

Miss Love looked nothing short of a raving lunatic enacting a voodoo spell as she clenched her teeth and held up the doll and began pulling strands of hair from the plastic icon's head. Miss Addiction, who had a very short memory indeed, and had already forgotten the grimacing figure presented by Mr. Slut/Whore only moments before, was not impressed by Miss Love's histrionics and muttered in disdain, "Oh, please."

Miss Love gave a quick response. With a simple flick of her wrist, she sent the mutilated doll hurling at gunshot speed. Her aim was right on target, so that the head of the Barbie popped the center little gap in Miss Addiction's upper front teeth, knocking them out, while at the same time sending the lady in red and her chair onto their backs. Mr. Slut/Whore could only look at the soles of Miss Addiction's new shoes as he heard her subconsciously muttering from the floor, "Motherfuck."

Stunned, but her anger quickly rising and bringing her to her senses, Miss Addiction pulled her legs over her head, rolled slightly backwards and then sprang up to her feet. Due to her teeth being knocked out and the excess of blood which now occupied her mouth, she half lisped and half slurred, "Now wait just a God damned minute!"

Miss Addiction looked at Mr. Slut/Whore for support, but rather than making a fool of himself, or incurring Miss Love's wrath again, he could only allow himself to meekly offer the lady in red some words of wisdom.

"I'd just sit back down if I were you, Darling," he said.

"But Slut/Whore," Miss Addiction declared as she wiped the blood from her mouth with one hand and pointed at Miss Love with the other, "let's just see what the old girl has to say."

Mr. Slut/Whore replied and then began further explaining in a voice that postured something more than a man who might be just a little tired, "I'm sorry but I'm feeling considerably week today. Perhaps it's just a bug of some sort. Whatever the case, I don't feel myself."

"You don't think she's going to kill us, do you?" Miss Addiction inquired with a hint of panic.

"Now calm down, Lass. Like the invigorated maniac already stated, only Andy can do that. She would have already, if she could."

He offered her a handkerchief so that Miss Addiction could wipe the blood and when she took it from him, he gallantly bent over and pick up her overturned chair. Very slowly and still recovering from the initial shock of the Barbie bullet that had knocked her over and her teeth out, Miss Addiction sat down with one hand still holding the handkerchief against the vacant bleeding spaces of her gums.

Miss Love, who had not laughed in ages, could not hold back at the sight of this and blessed her two villainous counterparts and all subsidiary traits and emotions with their first earful of Miss Love's high pitched whinny that was not that dissimilar to the nay of a Shetland Pony mare signaling the same breed's little stud to please come and massage her twat with his fifth leg.

Mr. Slut/Whore knew that now was the time to act, if he were indeed going to have any hope of putting Miss Love back in her place. He needed to rally and quickly was on his feet and, with caution and manners he brought up the simple facts. "Andy was picked up last night by a John with cocaine and ..." He was at a loss for words, as he wasn't sure of the new drug.

Miss Addiction nonchalantly said the single letter, "K."

"Thank you, Miss Addiction," and he went on. "By a cocaine and K snorting forty-two year old, co-dependent, homosexual. Miss Love, you are forgetting the man is HIV positive and completely unconcerned about Andy's welfare."

Miss Love quickly countered, "I'm not so sure he's not concerned about Andy's welfare Mr. Slut/Whore. As you know, many people think that a young man in Andy's line of work will automatically have HIV. But I will grant you Rick could've at least told him."

"Miss Love," Miss Addiction, with a tone of total contempt, felt the rally and quickly chimed in, "I doubt Andy would've cared last night too much about anything Rick told him with my little kitty K purring in the boy's ears. And even without K, I don't recall Andy ever asking any of his tricks their HIV status. Blame it this time on drugs or the moon; I don't care. The simple fact is that he threw caution to wind and if not now, it would have been sooner or later. The damage is done, Miss Love. All you have to do is to travel down to our little Andy's asshole to validate what good time 'LOVERBOY' had with Andy's ass."

Miss Addiction thought she could feel her teeth growing back in, and reached into her purse to take out her cosmetic mirror. Her teeth were growing back, but when she saw herself and the actual mess due to the Barbie bullet incident, her tone became even more visceral as she stated coldly, while wiping the blood from her face, "We probably have AIDS. Deal with it, bitch."

Miss Love was actually speechless at this, and although she was still quite virulent, she did feel some of her strength deteriorating. Mr. Slut/Whore, although not feeling so well himself, picked on Miss Love's dilemma and announced.

"We will deal with it. Oh yes, we have no alternative. We must go forth—but how will we do that? Will we let the nice gentleman show off his cash and order hundred dollar bottles of Bordeaux at fancy Italian bistros? Of course we will. As we're toasting we'll think of the revenge that we will take on him if he is idiot enough to take us into his house to enjoy his comfort, protection, and due justice, which is of course ..."

Mr. Slut/Whore let two to three seconds pass for effect and looked around the room feigning a need for secrecy then whispered one word, "... murder."

Miss Addiction let out a loud gasp, then quickly chimed in, "Oh please. Not before we are on the man's insurance policy. And I can't stand the thought of going to jail. But we will need money, and why let Rick, bless his heart, go to the grave with the it? Hell, let's make sure we're in the will. We probably have at least a couple of years to party before we get Kaposi Sarcoma, or pneumonia kicks in. With the money, at least we can still have some kicks."

"No one is dead yet," Miss Love intervened, then added, "although no one knows what dead men do, we do know that dying men do love."

Mr. Slut/Whore cursed under his breath and gave it one last shot, "Haven't you been listening to the news? There is nothing but this AZT crap, which is in and of itself nothing but chemotherapy in a pill. It may be lethal itself, and AZT may or may not only buy a short amount of time in which to live a pathetic existence. And the specialists tell us that it will be at least ten years before any decent forms of treatment can even be hoped for. The bad boys are dropping like flies, Miss love. Face it, you old cunt, we're dead. It's just a matter of time."

Miss Love, with the semblance of a stiff British upper lip, let Mr. Slut/Whore's insults and fatalism in one ear and out the other. With each word he had spoken, his entire essence waned and she brought this to his attention with her response.

"Yes Mr. Slut/Whore. As with all things it is simply a matter of time. And you need to seriously deal with the fact that as of today, Andy is not going to be whoring or behaving like a slut. Just look at the resilience in his eyes, bouncing back from the mirrors. You have to see the blatant truth that he perceives that he is really in love, and along with this is the obvious revelation that this man Rick has it bad for him, too. Look in the mirror, Mr. Slut/Whore."

Mr. Slut/Whore was left with no choice but to view his own reflection as the entire meeting room was transformed into a house of mirrors. There was absolutely no denying the truth of Miss Love's words.

"Good bye Mr. Slut/Whore," said Miss Love.

"Perhaps," said Mr. Slut/Whore.

"Slut/Whore!" Miss Addiction screamed in sincere concern as she witnessed his essence decline, and she sensed his acceptance of his own demise. She knew nothing else to do other than reach in her purse for her bumper and took two huge snorts of the drug left from the previous night's party. It was the only thing that she could think to do in such a crisis. That, and create her own selfish drama. She wondered without the help of her old ally and partner in crime, how Andy would be able to support her expensive habits.

"I don't think I'll be able to make it without you, baby" She whispered to the now utterly hazy outline of Mr. Slut/Whore. She then raised her voice at her own realization. "How else will Andy make any money unless we are being nice to the gentlemen."

"You needn't worry, my precious vixen. Miss Love, willingly or not, and Andy have ensured that you will be well taken care of."

"Still sweetness, you can't leave me alone with her. I'll go out of my own mind. I can't even stomach the thought of it now." And she wasn't lying. In fact, she barfed violently all over the floor directly in front of her. Then, after taking out the handkerchief that she had been using to wipe the blood from her face, she wiped her mouth and was truly a pathetic figure when she all but screamed, "Slut/Whore you've got to stand up and fight!"

"Now, now, my lass" came the soothing words from the vague black aura of Mr. Slut/Whore. His face was no longer visible, yet he was still barely audible with his Irish cantor and accent, and he continued to assure Miss Addiction with these comforting words.

"Don't you worry, you'll not be alone. You know you and I are made of the same stuff. You, myself—all the fun emotions stem from one pool, Darling. I'll just be changing me name. You'll see me again soon enough. You'll be fine."

"But you won't be you! I want you," exclaimed Miss Addiction in a tone and ferocity paramount to that of a five-year-old girl demanding her favorite dolly.

"But I love him!" bellowed throughout the emotional domain in the same omnipotent voice that had in an earlier meeting declared, but the single word, "future."

None of the emotions present, not even Miss Love, could claim ownership of the proclamation. And it was clear to all that Mr. Slut/Whore was no longer around. The only part of him that remained was his left shoe. Perhaps it served as a token reminder to Miss Love that he had been there and might return given the correct conditions. Whatever its significance, it was all that remained of Miss Addiction's once gallant partner.

Miss Love almost felt sorry for Miss Addiction who was now reduced to a crying mess that sobbed violently. She was bent over on the floor of the room, tearing out her own hair as if she were the widowed love of a Native American warrior.

As if things could not get more out of hand, all in the meeting were nearly scared completely shitless by the sudden ignition of a small fire over the direct spot where Miss Addiction had hurled only minutes before. And from the fire boomed like thunder the audible translation to all, "And we're gonna get even, I promise!"

"Slut/Whore is that you?" queried Miss Addiction, still bent on her knees and looking into the fire with the same reverence and awe that had to have been expressed by Moses when he gazed upon the burning bush. But from the fire came no audible response. In fact, something much more astounding than a voice emerged from the flames, to completely shock the wits out of all present in the current emotional meeting hall.

And no, it wasn't a phoenix of any type. It was in fact a little man, only an eighth the size of all the other committee members, who simply jumped out of the fire. He was wearing a blue and magenta sequined jump suit and sported dark red knee boots. With his thin red eye and face mask, he looked like a miniature version of a Marvel comics superhero.

"Oh my God!" mumbled Miss Love in a bizarre state of shock.

"Slut/Whore is that you?" questioned Miss Addiction once again. This time she got a reply.

"Tis not," said the little man in a confident tone, and in the accent of an elder British statesman. Then he let out a shout with reverb and clarity that would have made Dudley Do Right or any comic hero envious.

"I am MR. REVENGE."

The sound echoed through the chamber like thunder, and with such intensity that were all present ears not hurting, they would have had difficulty believing that such racket could come from such a little man. When the reverberations subsided, Miss Love, still at the podium, looked down on the little man and said with some degree of authority, "I'm sorry Mr. Revenge, but you won't be any more victorious than Mr. Slut/Whore. You must understand that Mason, or Andy as you may, is now in love."

"Tis my absolute favorite stage upon which to play," Mr. Revenge replied with his guttural sincerity highlighted by his hand over his heart. He then made a sweeping bow as if to imply that he was at her service.

"He won't murder," Miss Love said, convinced in her own words, although she did have to stop and ask herself if the little man was actually growing in stature. She wasn't sure but her train of thought was interrupted by the man.

"Oh really? And why not? Think very hard Miss Love." He had rolled his R's in "really" and "very" as he addressed her. Then he continued, "Before Andy started drinking, or going deeper into denial about Miss Addiction or Mr. Slut/Whore or even his inclination to members of his own sex, what was our young man's most dreadful secret? Is it coming back to you? Remembering are we? Correct!" he exclaimed, then said as if he were an attorney resting his case, "This isn't Andy's, or Mason's as you may prefer, first murder."

"Sweet Jesus, not that again," said Miss Love shaking her head in disbelief.

She was sure that Mason had long ago absolved the guilt he had held for his Grandmother's death, but Mr. Revenge certainly was right on mark.

"Oh yes, Miss Love. Since you know how honest love is, please get honest." He said lunging at her with an accusatory finger.

"Oh my God" is all Miss Love could say again.

Miss Addiction was speechless but getting happier by the minute and clapping her hands together in joyous glee. She knew full well that guilt of this magnitude would definitely be instrumental in the facilitation of a medicated frame of mind that could bring on a month's long binge. She ran over and kissed the little man, for she had concluded that Mr. Revenge had indeed grown in stature right in front of her eyes. He was at least half of her height now.

"Oh my God" is still all Miss Love could say.

"As I said earlier, Miss Love, my name is Mr. Revenge. Please don't worship me."

"Sweet Jesus," said Miss Love again.

"No. Mr. Revenge," Mr. Revenge again corrected her.

"Sweet Jesus!" I agonized aloud from the confines of Rick's modern shower.

Rick hollered from outside of the shower, "You saying something?"

I turned the water off and thought fast on my feet, "Ah yeah, ah, do you have a towel?

Rick opened the shower door and threw in a towel. As I dried off, I couldn't help but revert to the insinuation of Mr. Revenge about my first murder. Or was it homicide. Whatever the case, I caused the death of my Great Grandmother. Before I was dry, I'd relived the entire episode of my boyhood days in my Great Grandmother's home and care.

CHAPTER 21

Ouachita Parish, Louisiana, 1975

THE HOUSE IN WHICH I KILLED MY GREAT GRANDMOTHER CALDWELL had beautiful columns with cast ironed bars in front of each window and doorway that announced the paranoia and mistrust held by generations of my family. Still, the place was absolutely beautiful. Although it is certainly not antebellum, as it was built in 1908, the home does carry the grace and ghosts of days gone by that some would classify as post reconstruction, Louisiana Bourbon. That reflects the point in the State's history after reconstruction when there appears to have been an effort to recapture the agonizing splendor of antebellum years, and to some extent, there was a degree of success. Of course, that would depend on your definition of success.

Let me back up and describe my home as I remember it, Selectric, so that you and I and can get a better picture of the events that occurred there. I feel I can trust you and I believe that the nature of this sordid episode plays an important part in who I am today.

The house sits on a ridge on the banks of Bayou DeSieard, which is nothing more than an ancient riverbed, now filled in with Cypress trees covered in hanging Spanish moss. The bayou itself now runs into the Ouachita River; before the levee systems were put into place it flooded annually and deposited layer upon layer of sediment, year after year. As one approaches the house, he sees on his right that the fields running off the ridge are planted with either soy beans or cotton annually. Before fully grown they show the barren dark brown earth that almost looks black when the plows roll through it. On the left side of the drive, huge live oaks cradled with gargantuan Azalea bushes sprawl majestically and randomly on the lawn, which creates the bank sloping gently down to the bayou, clogged at certain times of the year with endless water lilies in and out of bloom. The driveway is tightly lined on both sides by 80-year-old crepe myrtles sprinkling their fire-red petals on the gravel that leads straight up to the stairs of the front porch of the house, which itself sits about eight feet off the ground. The house is a single story but because of flood possibilities sits on at least fifteen red brick pilings. On the front and back of the house these pilings continue to extend upwards about another twenty feet to create columns that support the front and back porches respectively. The four bay windows on the front porch are covered with wrought iron and tend to give the house eyes of a suspicious nature. The eyebrows of huge wooden storm shudders can be closed anytime if anything or anybody didn't look acceptable as he approached the huge white wooden house. With the exception of the lofty camellia trees that surround the bottom of the house to act as windbreakers (they are very successful), the only other adornment on the side of the house are the dark green storm shutters that can be slapped against the wrought iron covered windows at a moment's notice.

From the back porch the staircase leads down to a small backyard that hosts three small tenement shacks that are now used as sheds but used to house maids, grounds keepers, drivers, or hired help and their families. They are actually part of the fence line that leads into a twenty acre pecan orchard and pasture that is cradled by the winding bayou and fenced on the edge of the cotton field with barbed wire. There is also an old chicken coop in the backyard that led into the pasture. Through out this part of the yard are pear and fig trees and next to each shack's outhouse are planted wild plumb trees.

Although nobody lives in the shacks anymore, during my early boyhood years Ella still lived in the last remaining inhabitable structure and I loved spending time with the old back house keeper I still consider my mother of sorts. Ella was nothing short of a saint.

I used to get in trouble when Mammaw Caldwell would catch me using Ella's outhouse. I thought it was great that the old wooden structure was still in use, although poor Ella still didn't have modern plumbing in her house and used a manual pump for the sink in the little kitchen that comprised the second room in her two room house. But the outhouse that sat on a fence line under old wild plumb trees about fifteen yards from Ella's back door was vaguely in sight from the back porch of the main house and I had been caught exploring the structure several times by Mammaw Caldwell, who was convinced as many white Southerner of her generation black folk carried diseases that were different white people and that I might catch something. My mother even spanked me the second time that Mammaw informed her that I had been in Ella's outhouse again..

Nevertheless, I found the adventure worth the risk as Momma didn't spank that hard anyway for inside the little wooden shelter, Ella had stapled the walls with all the wilted and worn out old cardboard church fans with their exotic pictures of bible stories and scenes from the Middle East and Mediterranean. Their were Psalms and scripture within the illustrations which as a young beginning reader I could try and decipher as I did my business. Really, the light would seep in from the gap provided by the slant and angle of the top tin roof and at times, it was nothing short of a religious experience in the little space. With cows just outside and with fragrance of plumb trees in bloom, I can only guess that I came up with my first impression of serenity and heaven would be like. Yes Selectric, it is somewhat twisted but maybe that's why I find these modern marble and bright designer restrooms such an abomination.

Anyhow, Mammaw didn't like the idea of me spending too much time at Ella's but of course, Ella would spend a lot of time with us in the main house. Even in her "private hours," as they were referred by my mother when she would implore me to leave Ella alone, Ella would be knocking at late hours of the night on Mammaw's bedroom door that ran into the back porch. With all the windows up to allow the cool Autumn breeze to rejuvenate the house and all of the souls at rest, I could hear the familiar routine dialogue that played between Mammaw and Ella about every four or five weeks. With Ella being as quiet as she could be but as urgent at the same time with her quick little taps upon the wooden door, I could sometimes hear the sniffles of the frightened woman before she would "Thank Gawd" when Mammaw would finally open the door.

"Hell's fires Ella, you gone wake everybody in the house."

"I'm sorry Miss Caldwell, but I know for sure Ole Scratch, he back in the attick out there."

"Come on. Just be quiet now," Mammaw would try and whisper but the 90-something-year-old dear didn't know how.

"Yes mam. Thank ya Miss Caldwell," would more or less be the standard reply depending on the amount of sniffles Ella tried to hide in her relief from her terror.

I didn't understand how a person who, during the waking hours, always had a chuckle if not an out and out, heartfelt fit of laughter could convert to the frightened and sobbing wreck that I felt so sorry for on nights like these. I asked her once what "Ole Scratch" was and she quickly hushed me and in one of her few stern moments with me, told me that I was never to say that name again. Perhaps this was my first concept of hearing a loving individual in a state of fear.

Luckily it was at about this time that my dad returned home full time from graduating law school in Baton Rouge. Mammaw's mind was beginning to slip and instead of being afraid of the Devil, (My Mammaw chewed "Day's Work" tobacco and if she ever met him, she would've spit in his face) she would keep us all up late at night as she walked hardwood floors with her cane from door to door shaking them and rattling her old timey keys that looked like a jailer's key ring as she relocked the doors of the old home over and over. She'd told me of a couple of attempts made during the depression to break into the house so I guess the trauma of those events was giving us a glimpse of pro-longed effects. I still remember my father's voice as he explained to her in early morning hours that she had already locked up and to go back to please get her needed rest. Sometimes she'd go back to bed then at other times, she was up and about with her cane announcing her vigilance.

I had been given my own bedroom that had been an adjacent room to Mammaw's. At one time, it had been occupied by my deceased grandmother's (my dad's mother) crippled sister. There was a door that connected directly to Mammaw's room so that in years gone by, she and her husband, Dr. Caldwell, had easy access to assist her cerebral palsy-afflicted daughter. But the door today was never used and remained locked. Mammaw had a huge desk from which she managed her 4000 acre estate and she also slept with two pistols, .38s to be exact, under her pillow in case anybody tried to steal the silver/gold she horded as a result of her complete distrust of the Federal Government. And she told me stories of a ghost and a wolf that lived in her room and that it was only safe to go in there when she was with me. She didn't want me in her desk or anywhere near those pistols.

Looking back I can't believe Mom and Dad would have left me with her but I guess they felt I was safe enough with Ella there. It was Halloween weekend, 1974, and L.S.U. had a night home game. Mom and Dad were to stay with a couple they had met during law school in Baton Rouge for College sport extravaganza. Come to think of it, there was nothing unusual for Ella to just stay in the house and look after me when at times in the past, Momma would go down and visit Dad while he was still in school. And I was perfectly comfortable being there without Mom or Dad, and to tell you the truth, I was certain that nothing would happen to me with my Mammaw around, and I could be sure of good company with Ella.

I was in the first grade that year when our teacher, Miss Bowden, was explaining the significance of Halloween and that it was all for fun as there were really no such things as ghost and such. I raised my hand and proceeded to correct her.

"Miss Bowden, Ella say's there's Ole Scratch. I think he's the worst one but after my Mammaw saw me in her room picking up her pillow and just looking at her guns, why she assured me she got to me just in time before that ole ghost would've got me."

Miss Bowden had noticed that I had really grabbed the other children's attention with my outburst and so for the sake of her recovering their trust in her previous explanation of Halloween, perhaps she felt it her duty to argue the case and set me right. In her high pitched nasal voice and a smile on her face with a tone of amusement Miss Bowden asked, "Mason, now, your Mammaw? She is a Christian isn't she."

"Yes Mam. Really Christian!" I expounded.

"And Ella? She is too?" Miss Bowden, with a quizzical look, further enquired.

"She sure is. She wouldn't miss church for the world and takes me when Momma and Dad are out of town," I replied.

"Well then honey, they believe in their salvation by Jesus Christ. Mason, they're not worried about any old ghost or demons. They're just joshing you," she stated with a chuckle in her voice then started laughing. And all the other kids started laughing with her and the next thing I know are pointing at me and hollering names like "Scaredy-cat" and "Baby-baby." Then the teacher took out a bag of wicked looking pumpkin masks and passed them out with candy and made a 'WHOooo' sound at me and all the other kids joined in more. I was pissed.

To make matters worse, I took the bus home that day, which was unusual because Momma usually would pick me up. Adding salt to the wound, the kids on the bus teased me even more and by the time I got home I was nearly in tears. Nevertheless, Mrs. McDonald who was a close friend of Momma's, came by and picked me up that night and I went to her house for a little party and trick or treating in their neighborhood with her little girl. After she checked my candy and drove me home, I was in a little better spirits from all the games and joining in the fun instead of being made fun of. I was still in my little cheap black drug store skeletons outfit when I got home and Ella was quick in getting me out of it and into a running bath.

After I got out of the tub, Ella put me to bed in my room with prayers and she left my door cracked as she always did as it was my request. I heard her turn herself into the cot kept for her in the center hall that ran the length of the house and into which each adjoining room had an open transom at the top the door to allow for circulation of air prior to the days of A.C. I also heard Mammaw and her cane come into the hall and ask Ella, "Ella? You alright before I start locking up and turn out the lights?"

"I'm scared Miss Caldwell," I heard Ella attempt to whisper then explain a little louder, "And it be All Saints. They's bound to be haints 'bout this evening."

"Ella! There's no such thing," I distinctly heard Mammaw all but growl then with resolve she continued, "I keep trying to tell you this. Now hold on and I'll get you something so you'll sleep."

I listened to Mammaw's footsteps as she went to the bathroom and then return to Ella's cot.

"Here Ella," she said, "two spoonfuls of the some of this tonic and we'll all get some sleep."

While this scenario was playing out, I couldn't help but think about my teacher telling me that Mammaw was just joshing me and after the teasing I had endured, I was sure that it was only fair of me to play a little trick on Mammaw and my idea of a reprisal quickly came into mind. I knew that she would be walking the floors late into the night as she checked and rechecked the locks on the doors and the open window's iron bars. I caught myself giggling out loud and quickly muffled my laughter just in time as Mammaw opened the door to my room and said, "Sleep tight now. You're not too cold with the window open?"

"No mam. Night Mammaw," I replied.

"Night now honey. Sweet dreams."

Next thing I heard was the door leading from her bedroom to the front porch being shook then locked, and her routine had begun. Within five minutes, I could already hear Ella snoring from the hall. The timing was perfect. Mammaw had already made her way to the breakfast area of the back porch and was checking that door. I knew from past experience that she would next go into Momma and Dad's room and check their window and the door that led from their room to the back porch.

Barefooted and in my underwear and night shirt, I slipped out of bed and quietly walked on the huge Persian rug that covered the hardwood floor in my room over to the chair where I'd laid my school things. Carefully, I took out the mask that Miss Bowden had given myself and all the other children at the end of the school day. I slowly put it on and proceeded to the hall and tiptoed right past the snoring heap of covers that was Ella, to the door that led to the main sitting room in the very front of house. With the skill of a cat burglar, I navigated my way around the antique furniture and Steinway and Son's grand piano to hide behind one of the huge beige portieres that draped from the ceiling to floor of one of the large bay window closest to the double front doors to the front porch. It took a few minutes but what seemed hours when I finally heard Mammaw and her cane come from hard wood floors of the kitchen to pass on the huge rug of the main dining room and then to back to the hardwood floors of the sitting room where I then laid in wait.

I remember that I was worrying she might hear my breathing through the slit in the little covering over my nose and about that time I heard the door shake and could feel the iron bars of the window rattle a bit as Mammaw checked to be sure that the front door was securely locked. It was at this time that I threw back the huge portiere and jumped directly out growling and roaring as loud as I could.

"RRrrrrr, Roarrrrrr, Rrrrr!"

I instantly saw her drop her cane and it went rattling to the floor as she reached up and clasped her chest. She didn't have a look of shock. I don't really know how to accurately describe it. It was as though she were gazing far off, as if I wasn't there and it was not me that was scaring her but something else. She fell back onto the piano bench and with one of her arms, she hit the piano keys with a loud bang when she landed in a heap on the floor.

I knew that something was terribly wrong and I went over to her and started tugging on her nightgown saying, "Come on Mammaw, come on now. You know there are really no such thing as ghost or goblins. Please Mammaw! Talk to me."

But she didn't. She just breathed a few more breaths and then a couple of what I could only describe as wheezes, then lay there through the moonlight with her eyes wide open and still staring far away. This absolutely terrified me.

I ran in to wake up Ella and as I started pushing on the clump that was underneath the pillows and covers, Ella just grumbled. She was out cold. It was at this time that I remember that I still had my little mask on and I thought to take it off and throw it in my room that I wouldn't scare Ella too. I wonder, was I covering up my guilt as well. Either way, I came back out to the hall and started pushing and screaming and finally Ella woke up in a very groggy state and said,

"What's wrong Mason? Settle down chile"

"Ella hurry please! Get up please" I begged.

"Law's sake, what is baby?" she further enquired as she slowly sat up.

I was tugging on her now and nearly pulling her out of her bed. Somehow between her own wooziness and the hysterical pitch of my random screams, Ella was able to understand my plea,

"Come see quick! Please Ella. Come see Mammaw. She fell. Oh please hurry!"

Now sensing the urgency, Ella got out of the bed and turned on the hall light and I pulled her to the front sitting room where she finally saw Mammaw motionless on the floor.

"Miss Caldwell! Miss Caldwell! she hollered out loud and then went and bent over the still body and picked up her hand and started slapping it as she further exclaimed," Oh Law, Miss Caldwell, Oh my Lawd"

But then Ella quickly gathered her composure and was on the phone begging for an ambulance. It got here with the Sherriff and I vaguely recall telling him that I heard her up like always and then I heard the piano bang which was different than all the other times, and that I went in to check and that that was where I found her in a heap on the floor. I told the same story to my mom and dad when they got back and I understood from talking to Dad that the County Coroner wrote the cause of death as a heart attack. I have never admitted the truth to anyone until right now. Maybe not murder, but at least unintentional homicide. But either way, I did kill my grandmother. I guess I got even with her. Way more than even.

My mother and father had long talks with me about how old Mammaw was and that death is what happens when people get that old. I told them that it scared me but that I was alright now. Ella wouldn't come back in the house for weeks. Eventually she died herself of a heart attack out in her shack. But I had nothing to do with that one.

CHAPTER 22

Fort Lauderdale, March 1992

WHEN I GOT OUT OF THE SHOWER, RICK GAVE ME A QUICK KISS AND said that he had laid some clothes out for me on his bed that I was free to wear if I liked, and added with final insistence, "Be sure you put on the Speedo if nothing else."

I dried off and, sure enough, the clothes fit. He had also topped the pile of elegant summer wear with a pair of adjustable sandals that looked as good as they fit. I took a step out of the bedroom directly onto the balcony that runs the length of the condo, from the living room to his bedroom door. As I breathed in the warm air, I let my senses enjoy the breeze, the bright blue sky and view of opulence that surrounded me from this vantage point. There were million dollar yachts and private luxury sailing vessels along with fast cigar boats docked up and down the Intracoastal, alongside well-manicured back yards that led to mini mansions—or real ones. In other spots sat classical beach houses next to high rise condominiums and, for as far as the eye could see, there was an eclectic oceanside view of luxury, wealth, and recreation.

Within a few minutes Rick had showered and was standing next to me on the balcony in clothes that were only different from what I was wearing by color.

"You look great!" I told him.

His only response was a raised eyebrow and a smile. Then he said, "Let's go. I'm starved."

We took the elevator down to the lobby and, rather than taking off for the parking garage, Rick gently pushed me in the direction of the building's pool and patio area, then led me to the staircase that ran down to wooden docks. There, he pulled back the canvas on a smart boat and motioned for me to get in. I was only briefly hesitant, remembering the last time I was on a boat, but to be totally honest, I didn't have any apprehension whatsoever after about ten seconds. Something in my head told me that if the last time didn't kill me, nothing would. After a few clicks and make readies, he undid the boat and jumped back in and we were out.

The motor drowned out any need for conversation, so I just took in the sights and in no time he had us tied up to a really nice restaurant just off the Intracoastal that had some of the best Italian food I'd ever eaten. We laughed a lot and just talked movies, books, football, and genuinely had an easy time communicating and getting along.

After lunch we got back in the boat and headed down to Miami and a nude beach. Part of the way down, Rick took it really slow as we got baked with a fat joint that he had stored in a console of the boat. We listened to Flock of Seagulls again. At the beach we really didn't say a lot. We just relaxed. He looked great there in the buff and he thought it was funny that I wouldn't take off my Speedo. He laughed saying, "What's this? A modest call boy?"

"I just like my tan line, and so do most of my customers." I mumbled without opening my eyes or turning my head to look at him. But I immediately noticed that he quit laughing when I referred to my customers. He quickly asked, "Are you booked for tonight?"

"That depends on you," I said while still lying on the towel in the sand with my face away from him. I let myself smile as I felt two of his fingers on the corner of my face and he didn't say anything. And again just this touch of his sent me reeling head first through the new cosmos I felt I had entered.

We spent a good two hours on the beach rubbing each other down with tanning lotion and sun block. When we couldn't stand the tension any longer, we got back into his boat and went out a couple of hundred yards and dropped the diving buoy. We got lost devouring each other like it was our last moments on earth. We came on each other after shooting ropes. As the afternoon began turning to evening shade we dipped into the clear green water and rinsed ourselves off, then smoked another joint and headed back to Fort Lauderdale. We stopped on the way at a restaurant and had some shrimp and a great bottle of chardonnay and were back at Rick's dock by just past nine. After showering off together, we settled in on his bed with his television on. I have no idea what we were watching as I fell asleep with my head in his crotch.

It just pretty much went on like that for about another three days. We hung out, did drugs, had sex, went out to eat, went on boat rides and took walks. At times, there would be hours of incredible silence with sunrises or sunsets or simply a good movie. At other times we would talk non-stop. And a lot of the times, I would do most of the talking. I really hadn't shared too much personal history about myself, other than I grew up in Louisiana on a bayou. The way I had described it, Rick was probably under the impression that I was raised in a swamp shack. Usually I would ramble on about history and what comprised my worldview. Rick was a good listener and seemed genuinely interested and at times fascinated by my sense of history.

On about our third morning together he confessed, "I'm basically pretty ignorant about all that stuff, Andy. I find it incredible just how much of a handle you have on history, particularly American History. Really I'm more of a man of the moment. And I have really enjoyed the recent moments with you."

"Me too, Rick. I hope I haven't talked your ears off," I replied, not really quite sure how to take his compliment.

"Not at all." He said, then continued, "and I hope you are enjoying yourself as well. But you haven't even asked me how I'm paying for this. Aren't you curious?"

"Well I'll let you in on a little secret. I'm not charging you," I teased.

Rick shot me a haha, good one smart-ass grin then patronized me further, "I mean this, Andy." He said raising his voice while turning in a circle with his arms extended, pointing to all the luxuries of his condo's main living area. "The boat, the car, the dinners, the drugs, and the booze—how do you think I pay for all of it?"

"You said you were a business man. I took you for your word. Really I didn't think it was my place to pry. And to boot, I wasn't and am not about to look a gift horse in the mouth. What are you getting at anyway?" I now asked with some suspicion and then continued with a playful laugh, "You want me to wash your car, wax your boat, and mop your floors? Maybe I should do a little laundry and some dusting?"

Rick laughed out loud and walked over to the balcony and was quiet for a second, then turned around and said, "You're a bright guy Andy, and I'm only saying that I'd like to help you out. You've obviously had some schooling, and it's also obvious that you're at least on some kind of break—for lack of a better way of putting it. You ever think about going back to school?"

"Maybe. I mean sometimes," I stammered, as I was a bit taken back by the sudden implications that I sensed he was making.

"What would you like to study if you went back?"

"English" I replied without hesitation. "I'd switch my major to English, concentrating on writing a novel."

"Did you ever have any ideas about going to law school?"

I laughed aloud as I shook my head.

"I meant no offense," he quickly offered.

"None taken. It just seems like everybody that I've ever talked to thinks writing is such a pipe dream. It's like people are always spouting the great American dream. 'You can be anything you want to be, a doctor or a lawyer.'"

Rick smiled and said, "I know what you mean."

"Really, Rick, why in the hell would I want to be a lawyer? Lawyers work too damn hard. And frankly, I think I'd be bored spending all my time reading statutes and cases."

He turned around and said, "My, but we are honest at times. I'm sure my profession would bore the shit out of you, and since you haven't asked me what it is I do, then I'm just going to have to tell you. I'm a real estate genius. What you see here is the results of my investment and marketing abilities—but don't be mistaken, I've worked my ass off."

"Me too," I spouted.

He smiled a somewhat disheartened smile and after briefly hesitating to catch his thoughts he said, "Despite both of our lifestyles, Andy, there is the possibility that we may be around a while."

He was quiet again. It was the only other reference he had made of his HIV status, and obviously was very uncomfortable talking about it and didn't say anything else other than, "Anyway, as I was saying, I would like to help you out. It's a bit late to get you in for the spring semester, but I'm sure we could get you in Broward Community or Nova for the first or second summer semester, depending on how fast you could get transcripts switched. I take it you could get transcripts here."

It was a full-fledged proposal, and just that quick. I thought for a moment that after easily passing my G.E.D. I had only taken a couple of part time, six-hour semesters at University of New Orleans as a major of history. I had barely kept my average to a C as I only went to class when I wanted. But other than my failure in math, I had okay grades.

"No difficulty whatsoever." I said, and walked over to him and undressed him. He sat down on his sofa and I took off my pants and we lit a joint. Next thing I knew I was in his lap, riding his nine inch dick for at least a half-hour. Things were going good. Real good.

CHAPTER 23

Fort Lauderdale, March 1992

WITH IT DECIDED THAT I WOULD MOVE IN WITH RICK AND ATTEND Broward College, I found myself with free time on my hands, as it was now March and the summer semester would not begin until June fourteenth. I wrote letters to U.N.O. and got the forms for transfer credit, while at the same time looked at the requirements of study at Broward College for a major in English, and I was delighted that I would no longer be forced to take mathematics and that emphasis would be replaced with a foreign language. I was grateful that I had taken two years of Spanish in high school as it would come in very handy for the minimum eight hours that I would need in Spanish to finish my degree.

At the same time, I had rationalized and told myself that going back to school was just a sham. I was going to die of AIDS, so really, why bother? I reiterated to myself that the sham of school was necessary in order to stay in close proximity to Rick so that I was able to ensure that he doesn't live longer than me. It would allow the time needed for me to carry out the revenge that I had in mind for the man. That is to say, a murder in which I would not be sent to jail for committing.

And yet here I am on, nearly a daily basis, continuing to have unsafe sex with the man I have condemned to die. I think I looked at it in much the same way that a lung cancer patient smoking cigarettes in ICU would. The damage is done. He feels he might as well go out with a bang. It isn't that the cancer patient would intentionally ignite his oxygen panels. He or she might, but it is unlikely. And at this point in his or her plight, it is also unlikely that the patient is going to get out of the hospital and grab a thirty-eight and sneak up on a big tobacco executive and blow out his brains. But that doesn't stop the cancer infected addict from indulging in the love of his life. Oh no, smoke away boys and girls. And that's what I decided that I was going to do. Unlike the cancer patient, I still had the ability to sneak up on my nemesis with a .38 and blow his brains out. Although I don't know when I'll start showing signs of this dreaded disease, there is a good chance that I might find myself in prison hospitals verses public charitable institutions. Although I doubt there is too much difference, once I'm in a bed. It's the difference in the atmosphere of the public doctor's waiting room verses that of the prison doctor's. The time prior to getting sick time is what concerns me.

And besides, I thought that I might be able to do the murder trick in the three months before school starts and not waste my time or Broward College's. But in the meantime, I knew that I would have to make a show of it. And as people know, life and school cost money. Rick was going to help but he made it clear—when he returned home from work about three days after making his proposal, and found me with my feet up, lying on his couch watching television—that I was going to offer some financial assistance as well. When he walked through the door and I looked up from the television with my pot glazed eyes and flashed him a smile, I could tell the by the look of exasperation on his face, his disheveled hair, his tie already undone, and the very fact that he didn't return the smile, that Rick had seen a very difficult day at work. So as he walked to the bedroom, without acknowledging me whatsoever, I decided to be a little ray of sunshine and roll him a joint from his wee stash that I had been helping myself to all day long. I quickly completed the task and met him in the bedroom just in time to see him flinging his shirt off and throwing it half-hazardously toward the hamper in his closet, then sit down on the bed so that he could take off his shoes. I jumped on the bed, which I had made, and was about the only useful thing I had done all day, and laid back and lit the join. After exhaling a huge puff of smoke, I extended the joint to Rick. He reached up and without looking at me aggressively grabbed the joint from my hand and put it out on the marble top of the nightstand that was next to his bed.

"So did you find a job today?" Rick asked.

"Only figuring out your cable," I replied in a goofy laugh at my own joke. When he turned and looked at me, I could tell that he was in no mood for my shit.

"Thanks for your honesty, at least. I wish I had been dealing with people as fucking honest as you all day. Do you know that I nearly lost eighty thousand dollars today in a lawsuit by the attorneys representing tenants of mine and their little girl who claimed she had split her head open on my apartment building storm shutters while playing in the back gardens? In fact she had been running around the grounds, unsupervised, in the dark, at nine P.M." He took in a huge breath then exhaled.

"That's it. Good air in. Now bad air out. And repeat," I half-seriously consoled.

Amazingly enough, he followed my instructions about three times and actually regained some of his composure. He managed to get one shoe off before he looked up at me and stoically returned to the subject at hand as he enunciated the numerical value when he said, "Andy, did you hear what I just said? Eighty thousand dollars? That's not chump change!"

"Well, it ain't a million dollars either. Let me suck your dick"

Man, he blew up and shot off the bed with one blue Neiman Marcus sock still on his foot and walked over to the balcony door of his bedroom and screamed, "God damn it to hell! You are too smart to be an imbecile, you little fuck. What would you do if I did lose eighty thousand dollars? I have to start driving you around in a used Honda?"

Although Rick keeps some powerful weed in his house, somehow the words that he screamed at me got me mad enough to balance out the euphoria of the pot and to create not an angry of expression, but a blank poker face .When I glimpsed in the dresser mirror, it was the same expression that Rick was looking at when he gazed upon my actual face for several seconds of silence.

Finally, I felt that I was able find a civil and calm tone, but I was very serious when I said, "Rick, as far as what your drive me around in, at this point I really couldn't give a frog's fat ass. Just don't let your ass get too fat. And Rick," I said pausing for a second, "are you still with me here?"

"Yes, I'm here," he said, matching my even tone.

"Listen to me now and listen good," I commanded, and noticed him cock an eyebrow. When I saw him with his one blue sock still on his hairy ankle, I may have let a slight smile creep on my face, but I am sure the he understood how serious I was when I continued, "Don't ever assume that I am anything like an imbecile. Rick, do you understand me?"

He didn't give me any response whatsoever. So I added, "I'm only going to give you this warning once. Please don't ever refer to me as stupid or imbecilic again. Otherwise, I'm not sure that I can be held responsible for the actions that would follow such a dressing down from you. Do you understand?"

He just sat there looking at me for a couple of seconds, then asked in the same even tone that he had been using earlier, "Let me fuck you."

And I did. Without a moment's hesitation, I pulled off my shorts and before I knew it, he had my ass propped up on pillows on the edge of his bed and he was spitting on my hole. Then he fucked me silly. Yes essentially, hysterically silly. I kid you not when I say it was a "take me to another universe out of my mind fuck." That man is all that and then some.

Finally, after what could have been a hundred years or only two seconds, as I really don't think either one of us was capable of fathoming time at the moment, we shot simultaneously. After lying on each other and coming to our senses for a little while, Rick asked, "You hungry?"

"Yeah, I'm starved. Take me to Houston's for a steak. Do you mind?" I queried

"Sounds good to me, since. by the way, my lawyer did settle and I'm not going to lose eighty grand. Not even close," he said with a wink.

"Then why the fuck!" I let out in exasperation.

"Because I could, Andy," he answered. And after pausing briefly he asked me, "And then what would you have done?"

"The exact same thing we just did," I replied.

I guess he liked the answer because he gave me a big kiss and with a smile said, "Let's go. And try to find a job tomorrow, will you?"

And we went out to Houston's Steak House where he casually outlined, in various parts of our conversation, what type of job he would prefer me to find for employment. Of course, he didn't want me working for an escort service, nor did he want me in the service industry as a bartender or waiter, as he wanted me to feel comfortable with his friends and to "get away from that environment."

"Really Andy, I should think that you would be very good in the capacity of some sort of a sales position. You really do have a way of endearing yourself to people quickly, and you are a really good listener." Then he said with a laugh, "you talk too much sometimes, but after losing a couple of sales, you would learn to keep your mouth shut."

"Just for that, may we have a ninety dollar bottle of Cabernet?"

"Of course. Maybe I'll learn to keep my mouth a little more restrained as well," he graciously conceded, then hollered, "Waiter!"

He ordered the wine and great steaks. Although I did want to kill him, he had my heart on a string. It was a great dinner.

CHAPTER 24

Fort Lauderdale, March 1992

S o I GOT UP THE NEXT MORNING AND, AFTER KISSING RICK GOODBYE AS
he went off to another day of real estate negotiations, decided that it
was getting boring just sitting around the house. Rick had given me a key
and introduced me to the doorman, Ivan, so it was official that I could
come and go as I liked. I put on some off-the-beach wear that Rick had
bought for me and slipped into a pair of his flip flops, then set the alarm.
There was even an open elevator waiting for me as the apartment door
closed behind me. It was as if all omens were pointing towards a wonderful day. And they were.

The second I stepped outside and felt the breeze coming from the
ocean, my nostrils caught some of the salt and flora scents simultaneously
riding the breeze of delights. I felt my nerves stating, "Oh hell yeah!"

It was as if someone had given me a valium, but I was actually drug
free this morning and was still feeling refreshed from the sexual release
Rick had brought me to the night before. Overall, it was one of those
sunny late winter mornings that can only exist in South Florida. The
kind of day a freezing millionaire in Chicago will pay serious cash to get
his cabin-fevered ass absorbed into. As weather goes, I don't think that
the day could have been better.

I wasn't even making a conscious decision as once again I was instinctively pulled toward the ocean and I found myself walking towards the
beach. Within five or ten minutes I was on A1A with the waves of the
Atlantic providing a gentle bass to the perfect weather. I stayed on the
west-side of the road to avoid all of the tourist and spring breakers that
were crowding the beach-side sidewalk, which is very narrow at this part
of the beach. I really had no agenda of any kind and I suspect that I was
right where I was supposed to be. For as I was walking, I couldn't help but
notice the colorful scarlet and outrageous dress of a skinny black woman
who was manning a kiosk about thirty yards ahead of me.

Even from a distance, I could feel her sense of self-dignity. She held
her chin just a notch higher than most people, yet her posture seemed

perfectly natural. As I got closer, I noticed that her head, which appeared like it might be two sizes too big for her skinny vein-protruding neck, was over shadowed by a large and floppy straw hat with a vibrant red sash about two feet long that flowed wildly in the sea-breeze. The hat completely shaded her tiny five foot tall frame from the rays of the sun. The dress she wore was more like a Greek or Roman toga and, to add to this classical appeal, the woman wore red sandals that were very dainty and feminine and laced over her ankles.

And I'm here to tell you, Selectric. This woman was black! Charcoal colored jet black! Her skin simply accented the rich and scarlet linen dress that shimmered in the sea breeze and I instantly found her vibrant and alluring.

She had stationed her kiosk close to the wall that lined the sidewalk and prevented the public from encroaching on the grounds of an old and huge private estate known as the Bonner House. The iron bars that filled the gaps between large and square ten foot high, stucco columns and also topped the three foot stucco walls that ran between each column were ideal for the woman to hang her paintings. So, upon reaching the Kiosk, I automatically stopped to examine the woman's public exhibit. All the paintings were what I would later learn to be called "Caribbean Art" and each was an original. I was taken by their vivid color and obscure symmetry.

Shortly into my viewing, the old woman caught my attention out of the side of my eye and while looking at me while arranging some pieces on her kiosk, she acknowledged me with a polite and formal, "Monsieur."

I returned the greeting with a simple smile and slight nod of my head and she returned the smile and went back to work. We connected instantly but before I could pursue her attention any further, the voice of a squat and fat middle aged man with heavy white sun block on his nose, wearing Bermuda shorts with black socks and walking shoes honked out a demanding question in a New England accent, "What do you want for this one?"

He was pointing to the painting that I had also been admiring. It was truly fascinating. I'll try to describe it fairly in words. It resembled a cotton field at the base of a volcano, but it wasn't a cotton field. Instead of people, it was populated by obscure creatures who more closely resembled mice, yet they held definite human characteristics. And instead of cotton bolls on each plant were what appeared to be vague varieties of cheese that the mice-people were harvesting and placing in bizarre baskets upon their backs. And, there was a cloud in the sky that resembled the shape of a cat with a malicious smile on his face with a paw about to grab one of the mice that was upon the volcano's top. This mouse-man, unlike the others in the field, had whiskers and really carried little if any expression on his face. It was obvious that the other mice much closer to the base of the volcano, and out of reach of the cloud cat, were enjoying their day and their whiskers had been replaced with expressions that had been painted in such a meticulous way as to give each mouse-person his or her own personality. They seemed happy and content in some form or another. I would guess the scene to be taking place somewhere in Central America, as there were definitely Latin influences and suggestions in various aspects of the painting, which left no doubt that the area was tropical.

So the black lady managing the exhibit turned to face the man who had more demanded than asked the price and, looking him squarely in the eye, replied without a trace of emotion in her obvious French accent, "3000 American dollars, Monsieur."

"What?" he exclaimed in astonishment.

She did not give him a reply or acknowledgement. She walked over to her kiosk and began busying herself arranging some little wooden carvings. The man followed over and, attempting to regain some composure, asked this time in a more level tone, "No really, all kidding aside, how much will you take for it?"

"The price is not negotiable Monsieur; three thousand American currency is the purchase price," the lady replied, and as she did so, she enunciated the "s" sound in "price" to where she almost sounded as if she were a snake hissing at the end of her sentence.

The man laughed and shook his head, took out his wallet and withdrew two one hundred dollar bills, then put his wallet back in his back pocket and stated matter of fact, "I'll give you two hundred."

"You will not, monsieur," She replied matter of factly. Her tone matched the short and fat little New England man's pushy tone.

Once again, the man took his wallet out and this time he produced three hundred dollars and without saying anything, fanned the bills at her as if he were exposing a hand of playing cards. The black lady, without saying a word, took a small, little paintbrush and little jar from her drawer in the kiosk and walked over to the painting. What happened next literally astonished me. The woman proceeded to paint whiskers on a mouse that was highest up in the main crew of mouse-men at the base of the volcano. The scary thing was this—the mouse-man's caricature was so close to that of the stubby obnoxious tourist that it made my eyes do a double take back and forth from the painting to the pushy tourist so that my mouth must have just opened in astonishment. When the lady had finished her addition to the painting, she turned with a look of satisfaction on her face and looked at the man and stated, "It is a work in progress, no?"

The little man's white complexion was now turning red with rage, and the hate in his eyes was apparent. But he remained speechless for the moment as the black lady admonished him, "You do not deserve my exquisite painting, monsieur. Oh no, you do not," and she reiterated her vigor by waiving the little paint brush in the air and pointing the brush at the man with each waive stating, as if he were a child, "No, no, no."

Clenching his teeth hard and holding his breath, the man gave me the impression of someone very close to having a heart attack. Finally, he released his teeth and let out his breath stating simultaneously only one word with visceral passion, "Bitch!"

That was all he could say, and as soon as he had said it, the lady let out a loud laugh and bent over as if she might lose control of her faculties. Then, gradually, she came to gain some control of herself, but when she looked over at the man again, she burst out again into hysterical laughing and turned around waiving her hand at him in a gesture that implied that she was pleading for him to please go away as she couldn't take much more of it.

The man stomped off and he must have walked a good twenty yards before the lady, still chuckling to herself, regained her composure and took a piece of Kleenex from a little drawer in the kiosk and wiped the tears of laughter from her eyes. I found myself engrossed in the spectacle that had so entertained me. I knew I could learn something from this lady. I only wished that I had three thousand dollars to give her for the painting, so while she was still wiping her eyes, I walked over and told her so. She took one last sigh from her laughing, looked up at me and nonchalantly she told me, "Take it. It's yours, Monsieur."

"What?" I asked incredulously and continued expressing to her in amazement, "You are going to give me a three thousand dollar painting?"

From the gut, she released a sigh that produced an "uh huh," mixed with a little chuckle and a slight smile that expressed her amusement at my reaction to her generosity. And she walked over to the wall and took the painting down from its place and brought it over to me and pointed to the little mouse at the top of the volcano with whiskers that was in reach of the cloud cat and said, "This painting has been waiting for you."

And then she extended the unframed painting to me and I took it.

"Jesus, thank you, Miss ..." I said dumfounded, as I didn't even know her name.

"Madame Dieux Dieux," she said formally.

She then extended her hand and while I was placing the painting with care under my left shoulder and cradling it against my side with my left hand so that I could return her handshake. All the while, I was asking myself if I had heard the woman correctly because she had pronounced her name like "doo doo," which is a child's term for "shit." As I reached out and shook her hand, I remember that I was thinking to myself, "Did she say doo doo like poop?" and simultaneously I announced my name aloud, "Andy."

"No," she said and smiled to reveal her alabaster perfect teeth and asked with her heavy accent, "what really is your name?"

"I should be asking that question. Really? Doo Doo?" I meekly stated.

"It means God God in French, and basically my nickname dat dey give me back hom get lost in translation from Creole to French den to you. But you are no Andy."

I was floored once again by the little woman but without a second thought, I told her my name and she repeated it aloud in her thick French Creole accent. When she pronounced it, it almost sounded like "Mai-son" or "My-son" and after she had repeated it once more, she smiled tenderly and said, "I like that. How did you come of this name Mason?"

I told her that it was a hand me down and she pulled a couple of Dr. Pepper Bottles out of a cooler that she kept in her kiosk and popped them both and gave me one.

"Thank you," I said.

"Tell me about yourself, Mason, and what has brought you here to me?"

And with that we stood in the shade of the umbrella over her kiosk and I began telling her, a total stranger who felt like a long-lost friend, about my trip from New Orleans up till that moment, without skipping a bit except for my intentions of murdering Rick. She listened without interrupting except to excuse herself a couple of time politely asking me to "hold dat thought" when she needed to assist a possible buyer, then coming back asking me to continue. By the time I had told her about the past few months and the spin cycle Fortune had set for me, it was nearly one in the afternoon.

I felt like I had just taken off a two hundred-pound sack of rocks off of my back. Astounding to me that it was just that simple. By talking to a lady that I hardly knew but had immediately considered a friend, I had relieved my mind of stress and found myself once again in a strange new state of peace and clarity. And to make matters even better, Madame Dieux Dieux put the proverbial cherry on the ice cream by patting me on my arm as she stated simply, "So you have experience in sales and need work. Well, I need a salesman."

"You do?" I asked. "Why?" I further inquired as I had seen just how effective she actually was with other customers—other than the jackass she had run circles around—and I couldn't imagine her needing more than one person to operate the kiosk. She explained in her Creole English, "My business is growing. My nephew works my cart for me on South Beach. I got to shut this thing down every time I go to the Islands or Guatemala to buy or to drive down to the beach to check on or restock him. I'll give you twenty-five percent of everything you sell here."

She held out her hand to seal the contract and without hesitation, I took it. She then instantly took me over to the product and explained to me the backgrounds of each painting, its artist, his or her background, such as the country and city or village of origin the artist was from. And while she was training me, a small crowd gathered and she sold three paintings. While she was taking care of the third sale, she saw a lady looking at some work hanging from the fence, and silently, Madame Dieux Dieux motioned for me to go and help the customer. I walked over and asked the lady if she had any questions and she asked me could I tell her where the piece was from.

"That piece is from a village in the Dominican Republic, painted by a 14-year-old girl who is already defining new theories in the usage of shadow. The artist has received acclaim from two shows in two galleries in New York. We were fortunate to get these before those shows."

"Oh yeah?" the lady asked with a hint of doubt, but quickly added, "Well I like it either way."

"That's what counts," I replied.

"It says you want a hundred and twenty five. I only have a hundred cash on me. Can you cut me a break?"

I asked her to please excuse me for a moment and I walked over to Madame Dieux Dieux, who had been listening anyway and she said mildly that she would make an exception for this lady. I walked back over and apparently the customer had heard Madame Dieux Dieux and with a smile handed me the bill and said, "Thank you."

"Yes Ma'am, and have a nice day," I replied.

The lady started to walk off but Madame Dieux Dieux stopped her and placed the painting in a plastic bag. The woman thanked her again and went on her way. Madame Dieux Dieux then walked over to me and took the bill from my hand and said, "I'll bring you a notice of independent contract employment tomorrow. You have to keep up with your own taxes." When I cocked an eyebrow to hint that she might be crazy, she let out a giggle and I couldn't help join in. It was an honest laugh over the dishonesty of cheating the American Government of some money. It felt good. Shortly thereafter, Madame Dieux Dieux handed me $25 from her cash drawer and asked me to be back tomorrow at ten A.M.

"Ten A.M. it will be. Thank you and I'll see you tomorrow," I said.

"Good-bye," she said and she turned and started back to work.

It was the first honest buck I had made in some time, and that night when Rick got home and I told him that I had a job as an art dealer. When I showed him the painting that Madame Dieux Dieux had given me, he was somewhat reserved in his enthusiasm.

"I hope you won't allow this to replace your plans for going to school," he commented.

"No, but it will keep me out of trouble and into a little money until school starts," I replied.

But Madame Dieux Dieux had already begun a modest education of sorts. I was pleased. Things were falling into place.

CHAPTER 25

Fort Lauderdale, April 1992

T HROUGHOUT THE LAST DAYS OF MARCH AND APRIL, I ENJOYED MY evenings with Rick. These nights usually contained a little party atmosphere consisting of one if not all of a little coke, Special-K, pot, wine and/or scotch, and awesome sex. By day, I hung out down by the beach working with Madame Dieux Dieux, who generously instilled in me the techniques of selling art. She told me that I was a natural.

"You are da first American boy I've met dat knows to keep his mouth shut and listen," she emphasized.

I told her that I credited my father for this trait, since he had told me that it's amazing the information people give you if you keep your mouth shut. He always said, "If you do this, you can ask questions that you are already confident in assuming their answer."

"Exactly," Madame Dieux Dieux had said with authority and almost quoted my father verbatim while she allowed, in her excitement, her Creole influence to run wild, "If you say it, den it eeze a lie, but if dey say it, den it eeze da truf. And dey put out da money on dey own truf, no?"

"Jesus, did you ever think of going to law school?" I asked her, remembering again how assertive my father had been in his belief that a good attorney never confronts a witness with a question in which the attorney doesn't already know the answer that will come out of the mouth of the person on the stand.

"I am a salesman and curator of art, along wid some oder tings, but da law—" she turned and looked at the ocean, then continued regaining the posture of her speech, "I make my own laws. I live here and got to get along and all, but I believe in what I want. Even in Haiti, I did this. I'm not sure I can be a big enough whore to be a lawyer."

After saying this, she immediately caught herself and was apologetic but smiled at me and continued, "Not that there is anything wrong with being a whore. It is what it is. I just am not. Who gone to pay for dis?" she said laughing and gesturing to herself. She quickly added, "Anyway, what is best, and that is not my thing. My thing is my thing," she concluded.

Then she moseyed over to a tourist who was admiring some of the art hanging from the fence.

I had made only six sales by the end of the first week but, in general, had worked just four or five hours per shift for Madame Dieux Dieux's kiosk. So I had made a little over Two Hundred Dollars in cash by Friday, and when I returned home around six that evening, the first thing that I had noticed when I walked through the door was that Rick had taken down the painting that Madame Dieux Dieux had given me. Granted, I had not asked him if I could hang the painting in the foyer, but I reasoned that he wouldn't mind as, being in sales himself, he would surely recognize the motivational implications that the painting hanging in this location would have for me as I left for work each day. Not only that, I considered it to be a very good painting. I reasoned that it might be good advertising, as the painting in this location was certain to catch the attention of any guest the we would have over.

I was in a little bit of a huff when I entered Rick's bedroom and the second thing that I notice was the shower running in his bathroom. (Seriously, I have always found people's bedroom bathrooms to be a place of inner sanctuary and perhaps even a glimpse into their souls. Do they have good reading materials? Are the colors relaxing?) So when I walked into his solid gold abortion and I heard Rick humming an off-key version of "Those Were The Days My Friends," I found my opinion of his sense of taste further waning, to the point of disgust. I couldn't help but grow angrier as I thought to myself that he really had some nerve. With the shower running and steam covering the glass so that he could neither hear nor see anything, I caught myself interrupting his verse with perhaps too much edge to my own voice, "Rick, how—" but I was cut off two words in my sentence by one of the nelliest, high pitched screams that I can remember coming from a butch man. It sent shivers down my spine and was so intense it made me scream. Then Rick hollered aloud, "Aghh!"

After the brief exchange of screams in the golden tomb, I said, "Jesus Rick! It's me, Andy. Remember, you share your lovely home with me?"

"Fuck's sake, dude! Do you think you could knock before coming in here and scaring the piss out of me?" he yelled from the steam.

"Sorry guy, but the door was open. I'll try—" I replied loudly but he cut me off.

"Let me turn the water off so I can hear you without us screaming at each other." He yelled back as he turned the shower off, then added, "Can you throw me a towel over the door?"

I went to the hamper and grabbed one of the huge golden towels and handed it to him over the door and his arm reached up through the steam and took it from me.

"Thanks," he said then quickly added, I'll be right out."

I went to the bedroom and waited for him and shortly he was mostly done drying but came into the bedroom naked still drying off and apologized to me, "Sorry for the commotion in there, but I'm just not used to people walking in on me in what I consider to be a very private and personal room."

I bit my tongue again and thought to myself what a gauche and hideous display of wealth and bad taste he displayed by defiling such a sanctuary with such a constipating golden gleam. But I did manage to keep an even tone when I replied, "Once again, Hon, my apologies. I'll try and remember to have a little more respect for your privacy. As well, I guess I should ask you before I hang anything from your walls."

He didn't say anything, but walked over to his dresser and took out some underwear and put them on and took an appraised stock of himself in his mirror. So I broke the silence.

"Rick, you with me?"

"Yes, of course Hon," he said putting a strange accent and sarcastic emphasis on "Hon" then he turned around from his dresser's mirror and gave me a quick kiss on the lips and said, "I just didn't think that the painting went with the scheme of things in my foyer, Andy. Did it occur to you that you might want to check with me to find an appropriate place for your little orgy of colors in my house before just hanging it in my foyer? Okay?"

There was no mistaking his condescending tone for anything other than what it was, as he proclaimed mastery of his house.

"Okay, I take it you don't like the painting that Madame Dieux Dieux gave me?"

"No, Andy, I don't particularly care for the painting. And I'm not sure I want it to be the first thing people see when they come into my house."

"Rick," I went on, "I am very well aware of the fact that it is your name on the titled deed of this condominium. But in case you haven't noticed, I live here now as well. Let me ask you, since we don't have a contract or lease per se, am I entitled to kitchen and living room privileges after I'm through sucking your cock? Perhaps I should ask you before I heat up a pop-tart in your toaster?"

"Don't you think you're overacting a bit, and being perhaps a little unreasonable?" he asked evenly.

"No Rick, I don't. Not one bit. In fact, I think you were rude."

"Whoa, wait just a Goddamned minute" He bellowed as loudly as any redneck I've ever heard bark the command. I could tell he was really angry as he continued, "You haven't been here even three weeks, and without even asking my opinion, you find a hammer and a nail, and put up and unframed picture in a room that has nothing in common with the picture, and then have the nerve to barge in on me in a tirade like a brat that was just told he couldn't have a pony."

"That's crazy Rick. It wasn't in a tirade. I just asked you a question then you got so shitty," I countered.

"Yeah, but no 'how was your day' or sneaking into the shower to shower with me. Oh no. Right to the point for you: 'where's my painting,'" he said, making a bad imitation of my southern accent. But he did have a very good point. So I asked simply, "Well Rick, where might hang my little orgy of colors?"

He cracked a smile and said, "Now that's more like it," then gave me a kiss and continued, "Wherever you like, as soon as it gets back from the framers."

Jesus I felt like a compete jackass when he said this, and I'm sure he knew I did because he pulled me down on the bed and tore off my pants and playfully spanked me.

Next thing I knew, we were having sex.

After showering up, Rick got some steaks out of the refrigerator and I sautéed some mushrooms and put some potatoes in the oven. Rick got out a good bottle of wine and we had a terrific dinner. It was one of those totally satisfying evenings where we left the dishes on the table and got on the couch and I laid down with my head on his crotch. Rick turned on the TV and within thirty minutes, I was out like a light. It was just blissful. I don't even remember him waking me up from the couch and putting me to bed.

The next morning when he was already up and putting on his tie, I woke up groggily and he came over to kiss me but I turned my head in fear of my bad breath. But he forced my face back towards him and grabbing my face, he landed a big kiss right on my mouth and then playfully said, "Don't turn your head from me when I'm kissing you."

"Must not be too bad," I said holding my hand to my mouth.

"Never," he said with a big smile.

"Yeah, right," I yawned, then added, "just wait till I use a little too much garlic."

His response was disgusting. "Don't you worry, baby cakes. I'd still kiss you and eat your ass the morning after all you can eat taco night."

"Christ! That is true love," I let out in disgust.

"And don't you forget it." He said, finishing his tie and spraying some cologne for his finishing touches, then added, "Speaking of forgetting, I almost forgot to tell you. Some buddies of mine reminded me of a lobster dive that we had planned some time back. I told them about you. They're looking forward to meeting you."

"Dive?" I questioned, then asked, "Like a scuba dive?"

"Yeah, you know, like looking at all the pretty coral and fish, except we're going to try a get a few lobsters as well. Do you dive?" he asked.

"Never been. Sorry dude, but I'm clueless about the sport."

"Not a problem. I know that you can drive my boat, so you won't be useless. Anyway, it'll be a blast and you'll have an opportunity to meet some of my friends," he assured.

"Well, when do you have this planned? Madame Dieux Dieux wants me helping out most afternoons," I asked.

"Andy, Sundays are Us Days, okay? And I want you with me on this dive."

"Okay," I yawned aloud, not sure if I would have a problem with Madame Dieux Dieux or not, but I was sure I would with Rick if I didn't go along with this.

He gave me another quick kiss then said, "I gotta run. See you tonight—and remember to set aside Sunday."

"Okay," I replied again.

But before he could even exit the room, The Committee that inhabits the emotional realm of my mind were at play and despite the happiness that was weaving its way into the fabric of my life, I couldn't hold them back. I barely heard the front door close when I could hear Mr. Revenge with a full chorus singing, "She'll be Coming Round the Mountain." And the Chorus and Mr. Revenge were loud and clear in their intentions.

CHAPTER 26

The Committee, April 1992

AS IF THE SONG "COMING ROUND THE MOUNTAIN" IS NOT HORRIBLE enough, the neurotic overtones of Mr. Revenge's guttural overcompensation and slight English accent, replacing the western twang, made the tune that was now stuck in my mind unbearable for everyone there. Even Miss Addiction was rousted from her satisfaction with the present situation of her new life. She was completely irritated for having her caffeine/marijuana craving interrupted by the enthusiasm and obtrusive operatic singing that was blaring through the central nervous system. No long able to tolerate the intrusion to her routine, Miss Addiction threw down her rendition of "High Times." And with no regard for the fact that she was still in her house robe and curlers, she stepped out of her nerve and into the direct blood flow until she found the cell of Mr. Revenge. After she made a decent enough connection with the peptides of Mr. Revenge's hot cell, she began angrily knocking on his door. And to assist in overcoming the all-pervasive jingle of Mr. Revenge's voice, she hollered as she pounded, "Revenge, goddam it to hell, open this door. I know you're in there."

After several rounds, she took a moment to catch her breath and while looking down at the welcome mat on which she was standing, she noticed that her slippers were tapping impatiently on a design of roses that were shaped in the fashion of thirteen knots culminating in a hang-man's noose. She rolled her eyes at the obnoxious décor and with renewed vigor, once again began banging with clenched fist non-stop on the cell door. When the music finally ceased, she stopped knocking, expecting there to be a response to the door but after another minute there was still no answer.

The consternation on her face must have been obvious to Mr. Revenge as he suddenly and unexpectedly opened the door at the exact moment that Miss Addiction had raised her fist to resume her hail. Dodging her fist from what might have been a nasty punch to the top of his head, Mr. Revenge, still wearing his blue sequined super-hero mask, was otherwise naked and dripping except for the towel that he had hastily wrapped and was scantily covering his middle area.

"Miss Addiction," he said formally but with a hint of surprise. As he appraised the condition of the lady, dressed only in her house robe now on his public doorstep, he further apologized, "I was just getting out of the shower. I do hope you haven't been at my door for too long."

He paused momentarily to allow Miss Addiction to respond but she was still breathing heavily from her frantic knocking and was unable to make an explanation in time before Mr. Revenge, as if perceiving a divine revelation stated, "Oh I see. You must be having problems with your plumbing and wish to use my necessary rooms. I was just getting out, as you may have perceived, but by all means."

Not wishing to argue with him and realizing now how ridiculous the public display that she and Mr. Revenge might be making, she clutched at her house robe to cover a breast that was exposed due to her ranting and banging and asked in simple exasperation, "May I come in?

With much enthusiasm and cordiality, Mr. Revenge threw the door wide-open and said, "Of course, of course! Please come in make yourself at home." And he added with a slight Chuckle, "Mi casa es su casa" and then quickly explained further, "I've been taking a little Spanish. You know, now living in South Florida, I find that it helps."

"Perhaps ,Mr. Revenge," Miss Addiction let out in exasperation, then after catching her breath continued, "but I must admit that I didn't come here just to chat in either Spanish or English."

"Oh, of course not. Please make yourself at home. The shower and the necessary rooms are right down the hall and then to your direct left," he offered extending his hand to give her the right of way.

"Honey," she said as she held he hand up as if she were a school crossing guard. And speaking quickly before he could get in another word, she implored him, "Relax Dear. Just please for one second, relax."

"Relax?" Mr. Revenge repeated in a quizzical tone while slightly tilting his masked head as if he were not sure what the word meant.

"Yes, dear. Breathe in deeply. Let me show you, like this," she said, then took in a deep breath and slowly exhaled the air while motioning for Mr. Revenge to do the same. He attempted to emulate the bathrobed vixen but as he did so, he began coughing outrageously.

"Are you okay?" Miss Addiction asked with a trace of sincerity in her voice.

"I, I don't know if I've ever held that much air in me at once. I rather accustomed to short and quick huffs," he replied. After a quick inventory of himself he added, "But now that you ask, I might have to try that again. I must admit that I do feel invigorated."

He took another huge gulp of air then slowly let it out. He coughed ever so slightly this time as if he were smoking pot for the first time and not quite accustomed to the ritual. Miss Addiction was totally thrown off guard by his reaction to this simple exercise, as he acknowledged in a state of quaint revelation, "Yes. Quite nice really. Now let me see." He took another huge gulp then began his vocal scales, "mi, mi mi, MI, MI MI, MIliii."

He was about to begin with "La, LA" chops when Miss Addiction, pulling out a couple of her curlers screamed, "Whoa! Whoa God-damn it!" then changing her strategy to implore him, she screamed, "Please! Just one second."

"What?" Mr. Revenge asked her innocently enough.

"Please" she sighed regaining some composer and, as if talking to a child, she asked him, "Just look at me for one second. Don't say anything or do anything. Just look at me. Okay?"

"Okay, Love." He answered good naturedly, but unable to disguise his concern for her hysterics.

"Okay. To begin with, can we start by removing that mask of yours? There's no need for us to hide anything from each other." As she stated this, she extended her hand to his face to remove his mask, but quickly withdrew her jungle red fingernails just in time to avoid the snarling snap Mr. Revenge made at them with his mouth.

"Motherfuck, take it easy Fido!" she shrieked.

"So sorry my dear, but the mask stays on. I've been told one too many times that I'm not that pretty to look at."

Miss Addiction's only response was to roll her eyes.

"I'm sorry you feel that way Miss Addiction but really, it's just not good for a man such as myself to allow anyone to perceive me as I really am. Not good at all for business, if you can imagine?"

"Then perhaps I can get you a valium" Miss Addiction responded with new hope. Then she pointed out, "That and a good massage with a little time in a sauna should do wonders for ..."

"I don't do drugs Miss Addiction," he said stopping her before she could go any further.

"Excuse me?" she asked now thoroughly confused. And when all he did to respond was shrug his shoulders, she continued her inquisition in shock, "What do you mean that you don't do drugs? You live in this body and mind, don't you? I know I do. Therefore honey, you do drugs. I assure you."

"Nope," he answered in his best American accent, then in natural British tones he continued, "Seriously, they have no effect on me. Once I'm here, no drug can calm me. Nothing, and I mean nothing but the act can calm me darling."

"The act?" Miss Addiction queried.

"YESSSssss," he sang out with operatic vigor.

She held her hands up to cover her ears and screamed, "Stop it, just stop it".

"My apologies. Really but those breathing exercises of yours are simply wonderful. They just make me want to sing. But I'll try and restrain myself. Okay? But just picture it."

"Picture what?" she asked again.

"My enemy, the subject of my wrath, submerged in ocean water and unwary of my motives and designs whilst I, above in a boat, innocently on the lookout, doing nothing really, but throwing rotting melt in the water."

"Melt?" she further asked.

"Yes, darling. The same thing those Cajun relatives of Andy's use as bait for catching crawfish and catfish back in the swamps of Louisiana."

"You think this 'melt' might attract lobsters on Sunday's dive?" Miss Addiction asked with sincere confusion.

"Oh Miss Addiction in that fog of yours, I guess you really can be innocent, even if that is a contradiction in terms to say of you. But really Love, think about it. The lining of a cow's intestine left to sit out in the hot Florida sun then, still bloody and stinking, thrown near the dive sight. It might attract a lobster or two. And it might attract something else. Come now dear and put that little anesthetized brain of yours to use for one second."

"Oh God! You're not serious are you? Sharks!"

"We gotta winner ladies and gentlemen. What'll it be for the little trollop in curlers? The Raggedy Ann or the squeaky duck?" he patronized.

Miss Addiction didn't say a word but only looked at the masked brat with an open mouth.

"Yes darling, sharks" he repeated and mocked her further, "Perhaps one or two with mouths that can open even larger than yours is now. Man killers. Big Boys, and Mr. Jaws ..."

As he was smiling and stating this, Miss Addiction was giving him only half of her attention, as she began analyzing just how comfortable her life had become since Andy and Rick had begun their thing. She saw no reason not to leave things as they were, and although she reasoned that death was imminent, she could see no reason as to why it couldn't be in the comfortable abyss of an overdose lying snug and comfortable in a penthouse bed. This Mr. Revenge was insane; she realized there would be no reasoning with him. Nor would she ever enjoy the snug relations that she had enjoyed with Mr. Slut/Whore. Not only that, she knew that she held no power over Mr. Revenge. Perhaps it was time for a new alliance. Miss Addiction, referring to Miss Love, silently thought to herself, "How much would it hurt just to talk to the bitch?"

"Now what was it dear?" Mr. Revenge asked aloud to Miss Addiction then again answered his own question, "Oh yes! You wanted to use my necessary facilities."

"Oh no!" Miss Addiction quickly corrected, then thinking on her feet said, "You've misunderstood. The reason I came to see you was for my coffee."

"Excuse me?" Asked Mr. Revenge?

"Sugar!" explained Miss Addiction, I'm out of sugar. I thought you might be able to help me out."

"Well of course dear!" bellowed Mr. Revenge then began chuckling, "Nothing is sweeter than revenge. Let me look in my kitchen cupboard, I'm sure I can help you."

And he walked out of the foyer through a door that led to his kitchen, humming the tune of "She'll be Coming Round the Mountain." But little did he know that Miss Addiction had already casually walked out of the front door and into the blood stream. He was dumbfounded when he walked into the foyer of his home to find her gone, his front door wide open.

"Curious sort of bitch," he thought to himself, then said, "Oh well."

And without giving it a second thought, he took the cup and raised it about three inches from his mouth, then poured its entire contents down his throat as he thought to himself, "Fuck me without rubbers, knowing full well that you have AIDS, will you?"

After savoring the sweetness, he resumed the breathing exercises that Miss Addiction had just taught him. It never occurred to him that at that very moment, she was getting dressed up to the nines to pay a visit to Miss Love. He only wanted to sing. And with his newfound vitality from the breathing exercises and the sweet taste of sugar, he found passion for his song let it rip, "She'll Be Coming Round the Mountain When She Comes ..."

CHAPTER 27

Easter Sunday 1992

Iawoke on Sunday morning cuddled nest to Rick—spooning, if you will. We had slept without the air on as the temperature that April evening was an incredibly perfect 68 degrees, and the day's high was expected to be around 84. The rain had fallen pretty hard the day before and for that reason, Madame Dieux Dieux had not opened the kiosk and I hadn't had to work. Rick and I enjoyed the Saturday afternoon lazing around naked, doing K, drinking, with intermittent sex and a porn movie or two. We had ordered Chinese but neither of us really ate and we had called it a night by midnight.

Upon awakening Easter Sunday, I looked over at the clock. It was nine A.M. so I gently untangled myself from Rick and got out of bed and went to the kitchen and put on some coffee. While it was brewing, I found our pot bat still loaded and stepped out on to the balcony and lit up. I took a huge hit and enjoyed the beautiful calm of the day after the storm. Actually, it had stopped raining hard around four P.M. the day before. But the silence of peace was short lived. The phone rang.

Before I could get back inside to answer it, Rick grabbed the call from his bedside phone and I couldn't help but overhear him talking.

"Hey Jay. Yep. A-ha. I'm still up for it."

I had walked into the bedroom with the bat still in my hand, and while he had the phone to his ear, he motioned for me to bring it to him. I went back to the living room and filled it for him, and when I returned, he had propped himself up on the pillows and he silently lipped out a "thank you" as he took the bat from me and lit it while listening to Jay on the other end of the line. I heard the muffled sounds of a voice on the other end and saw Rick hold off a laugh while smiling big through a billow of exhaled smoke. Then he addressed the caller, "Sounds like you guys had a good time."

Then he got out bed and, in his customary histrionics, tied on his bath robe and walked with the cordless phone onto the balcony, leaning all his weight against the rail while stretching grandly with all but the one arm that he used to hold the phone to his ear. As he leaned his back to the rail, he took another huge toke from the bat and addressed the caller, "Well, it looks like visibility will be down some but we still ought to have at least 15 to 20 feet to see. It really didn't get that windy yesterday and it quit by four or so. I'm hungry for some lobster. See you guys over here around noon. Yeah. Cool. No, we have everything. Just bring your tanks and gear. Bye."

So it was settled. I walked to the kitchen and poured our coffee, mine black and his with cream and sugar; it was just the way he likes it, with the cream pre-heated. I brought it to him out on balcony and he was sincerely thankful and reached over to grab my face and put a big, wet kiss on me—morning breath and all.

"I love you" he stated out of the blue. And, he was sincere. I was still butt naked and after the statement, I thought my guilt at my contrivances would flop out of my mind in a caption over my head, but the voice in those crevices whispered to me that conscience or guilt were no longer an issue.

"I love you too, Rick," I said. He just looked me in the eyes and was silent for about three seconds, then put the coffee to his lips and took a healthy swallow.

"It's gonna be a great day. I know you are going to like Jay and Steve, but I just wish you were PADI certified and could dive. But we'll work on that."

"And maybe we won't," I said then started sing aloud the music from Jaws.

"Would you knock it off? I hardly ever see a shark around here and when I do, it's only nurse sharks. But anyway, I really do appreciate your coming along. I'm eager for you to meet some of my friends."

"Are they both diving?" I inquired knowing full well that he had already mentioned that this would be the case.

"Oh yeah, absolutely! So roll some big ones. You'll be by yourself for about an hour or more, so you'll have to entertain yourself. But, I really do appreciate your making the time and coming along. You'll get to know them on the ride out to the reef."

It had occurred to me that other people other than Rick would be in the water, and I might be instigating a multiple murder, attack, or whatever. But somehow, I seemed to know that only Rick would be hit, if I had any success at all. I was starting to believe some of Rick's bravado about there being no need for fear of sharks. But my curiosity about possible side tragedies was raised, so I innocently asked Rick what Jay and Steve were like.

"Let's see," Rick said as he walked back from the edge of the balcony and sat down on a patio chair and lit the bat again and filled his lungs with smoke. As he exhaled a huge cloud, he gave a small cough and said, "Jay is probably one of the best looking guys in South Florida. He's a model, 27 years old, body like a god with somewhat exotic looks. He has blue eyes, black hair and Asian features. He's a Buddhist, totally good-hearted guy that grew up in the Keys. Sometimes, he bartends a little when he's not on the set or in New York. Steve is a Realtor from Tennessee."

"Christ," I thought to myself, "I'm going to be baiting a Buddhist and a fellow rebel."

But a little voice in my head whispered, "Not anything to worry about. You already killed your grandmother and who are these guys compared to her? Shouldn't bother you should it?" I heard myself answering the voice, "Not really."

My thought were quickly interrupted by Rick, "Go ahead and shower would ya? I'll start packing the ice chest and getting the gear ready, then you can bring it down to the boat while I shower. They should be here within an hour or so."

"Sounds good," I answered.

Actually, it was perfect. It would give me time to double inspect the situation and my first priority would be to insure that my weapon of choice had not given itself away. And I could pack the boat. Things were going well and when I got out of the shower, quickly brushed my teeth, and was out, Rick brushed past me in a hurry to the john and locked the door. He spoke from behind the door as I heard the seat to the toilet plop down.

"Go ahead and put that stuff in the boat, okay?

"Yeah sure," I replied through the bathroom door.

"Thanks," I heard him say with a sigh. His coffee must have kicked in.

So I grabbed the ice chest first, as it was the bulkiest and most difficult and I thought I would get that out of the way. There was even an elevator car waiting with the door open when I walked out into the hallway. I started whistling after I put the ice chest down and punched "Ground Floor."

When I got down to the boat and put the ice chest into its designated area and strapped down it down like Rick had done in our last outing, I lifted up the seat where I had stored the melt. There was only the slightest odor of rotting meat over the smell of mold, common in any water vessel. When I closed the seat and vigorously sniffed the air, I smelled nothing.

"Here we go," I said softly to myself and walked up to the condo. I think I was smiling as I thought about how cool Madame Dieux Dieux had been about giving me Easter off and was even sweet enough to take me out to a meat store in her car to buy the melt. They just don't sell that stuff anywhere but I promised her I would bring her back some crabs, which is what I lied and told her the nasty meat was for.

When I got off the elevator, Jay and Steve were at the apartment front door. Just as a hand knocked on the door, I said, "What up, guys? You must be Jay and Steve." I held out my hand to offer a hand shake and said, "Andy."

When Jay turned around, I must admit that I was taken off guard. He was nothing short of stunning. I shook Steve's hand as I was till gawking at Jay, and although Steve was no slouch in the looks department, Jay was Michelangelo's conception of David in the flesh. Steve must have broken my gawk with his southern accent saying, "Sorry we're early, but Jay didn't want to dive sober. He said Rick mentioned something about having some kick ass weed."

"Ah yeah, sure he does," I replied, coming to my senses. "We do, come on in. I'm sure Rick is still in the shower."

"What I figured," said Steve while looking at Jay who had walked straight into the unit as if he might as well live there and at the same time saying back to Steve, "Would you let it rest?"

Steve just took in a heavy sigh and I motioned for him to go on in before me. I walked in and Jay had already taken a seat on the couch. I told Steve to make himself comfortable and he went and sat next to Jay. I told them that I'd be right back and when I walked back to the bedroom to get the bat, I heard what I thought to be a whispering quarrel and upon returning to the living room I distinctly heard Jay saying, "Rick is my best friend. He acts the same at my house."

When I laid the bat on the coffee table, I asked, "Want a beer?"

"Some of that Chalk Hill Chardonnay would be great," Jay said.

I replied, "Sure," but when I went to the fridge, the bottle that I was sure had been chilling for two days was gone, so when I returned to the living room, I told Jay, who was loading the bat and motioning for Steve to hand him the remote to the stereo, "Sorry guy, but I thought we had some. Come to think of it, I bet Rick packed it in the cooler. I just put it in the boat before you guys got here."

"Beer is fine," Steve said with a hint of agitation towards Jay.

So I popped three Molson's and sat down with the guys to make light conversation. Really, it was that civil. Even though I knew I was about to bait the water for sharks and these relatively total strangers would be in the water, I was going to be a perfect host. And it was actually a very comfortable first introduction for Jay and me, if not for Steve. Jay was perfectly at home and he began discussing how long he had known Rick. He explained that it was two years ago that he and Rick had had met while Jay was bartending at a Las Olas club. Steve had only come into Jay's life three months earlier and Steve really didn't contribute too much to the conversation. I got the feeling that he was somewhat suspicious of Rick and Jay's relationship, but I found humor in Steve's discomfort. I could see anyone being initially attracted to Jay, but he was also to me a "for real" type guy. I was in no way jealous or suspicious of Jay. Actually, I liked him right off the bat and hoped that the shark would let him slide. I couldn't really make up my mind about Steve though. Don't get me wrong, I wasn't cheering for a Great White to come and chop off his dick or anything, but he said very little and was somewhat reluctant to smoking the peace pipe, so I was wary of him. For some reason, I could see him as a closet case Kappa Sigma at some prep college. Although we were both Southerners, I surmised that he wouldn't want me in his fraternity. Later, on the ride out to the dive site, I would just chalk him up as a moral simpleton. (On the ride out, a careless boater shot over our bow and when I flew the bird at the guy and had hollered aloud, "Take some boating lessons mother-fuckers and then go eat some shit for lunch," Steve looked at me somewhat aghast and said, "Potty mouth.")

So finally Rick got out of the shower and sauntered into the living room looking at the gear still not in the boat and walked over to Jay while giving him a big hug and said, "Happy Easter guys. Good to see you. Hope you won't mind the boat not being loaded. Would you be offended if I asked you to help me carry some of this down?"

Rick had said "down" with a hint of a growl in his voice, and I decided not to even attempt to explain. The sharks would be enough. So I smiled at him apologetically and said for the first time that morning, "Yes, Happy Easter Darling."

"Oh, no problem, happy to do it!" Jay exclaimed. The guy was right out of an Up with People cast. Everything was happy, happy for this cat and I wondered what in the hell he and Steve had in common, but figured it was none of my business.

Within ten minutes, we had all of the gear in the boat and Jay and I pushed us out and jumped in. We were on our way to the dive site and my being called a "potty mouth."

The Intracoastal was very crowded that day as tourist season was at its peak, it being Easter Sunday, but we all chatted and had a fairly pleasant conversation and a really nice buzz going by the time we got out into open ocean.

"I hear the Jacks are still surrendering a few lobster to us land dwellers," Rick shouted over the roar of his engine, now at full throttle.

Jay replied compliantly, "Sounds good to me. I'm a little familiar with some of the crevices there too. Who knows, we might get lucky."

I was at a total loss to what "the Jacks" were, so I asked. Jay shouted over the engine, explaining that the Jacks were actually huge anchors left in the water from World War II that had been used to tie down American submarines while they were being restocked before going out on patrol in the Atlantic, Gulf, and Caribbean. They were left down there and had turned out to be the building blocks for a new reef.

There were about three boats in the area when Rick brought our boat to a slow speed. He kept the boat at a very low idle and I saw dive buoys that were close, or around thirty to one hundred yards from the boats. Jay commented, "Doesn't look like we're going to be having as much company as I thought."

Rick replied, "I bet yesterday's storm persuaded a lot of people that the visibility would be low."

"Looks like it'll be okay though," Steve chimed in at about the time Rick brought the boat to a stop. No sooner had he stopped, Steve grabbed a mask from a bucket of water that all the guys had sunk their mask into and he jumped in the ocean.

He went under for about ten seconds, then came up and said, "No way it's thirty feet visibility, I'd say closer to twenty or a little less."

"That's good enough," Jay said with enthusiasm, then added, "Hope you didn't already pee, it would have helped warm up your wet suit while decompressing."

"Jay, that's gross" said Steve.

"Just a fact of life, going down, that the pressure fucks with your bladder. Anybody says they don't pee on themselves when diving is a liar."

"Sounds fun," I said and Steve gave me a grimaced look as he was climbing back into the boat.

As they were suiting up, Rick addressed me. "Really Andy, just relax and listen to some music. Don't stay right over us, but stay around thirty to fifty yards away. If it looks like an idiot is going to drive over our dive buoy, just bring the boat a little closer and point towards us. Either way, we should be down for no more than an hour. It's shallow enough we won't have to worry about nitrogen problems."

"You got it. Y'all bring me back something good to eat," I said with enthusiasm, rubbing my stomach.

"Love you," Rick said, then gave me a quick peck and jumped into the water. The other guys who were now about ready followed soon and plopped in. While they were making last minute adjustments, Rick said, "See ya on the bottom" and he disappeared.

Steve finished helping Jay with what I thought I heard was a belt problem, and then they started descending together.

I lit a joint and thought I would let the dive buoy get about 25 yards away, and then I'd create the Ya-Ya seafood gumbo that any type of marine carnivore would come for. At least that's what I thought.

It took the guys about ten minutes to get to what I judged would be a safe distance from me so that I would not be detected baiting the water. I took the melt out from under the seat and a little voice in my head said, "You better be sure they can't see you throwing the bloody stink in the water."

So reluctantly, as I'd become terrified of deep salt water, I got a mask that was also stored under the seat and said a quick prayer and jumped in. I could not help but take in a deep breath and have flashbacks of my earlier experience of my night swim in horror from the explosion aboard The Dick. But I put the mask on and dove down about six feet or so and was immediately enthralled by what I was seeing. The reef was only twenty feet below me and I could see the beauty of it from there as I looked around in all directions, trying to see if I could spot Rick and the guys. But Steve had been correct when he said that visibility was about twenty feet or less, and they were not even a haze in my view. I surfaced, crawled into the boat from the rear as I had seen Steve do earlier, and went immediately to work.

It didn't take twenty seconds after I threw the first handful of meat in the water for the commotion to begin. I was holding my breath as I threw the raunchy concoction, but eventually I had to breathe. I hurled and threw my head over the side of the boat to add my own puke to the mess around the boat. But the action in the water was picking up. After another two minutes, I saw what I had been hoping for: a fin. And it was a rather good sized fin at that. I still had about half of the melt in the bag left and as I dispensed the remainder, I puked again as the stench was terrific. This caused more commotion right by the boat but the big fin stayed about twelve yards away. With the last of the melt in the water, I spotted some other large objects swimming closer in the area of where I had seen the large fin and I smiled, knowing that I was attracting what I was looking for. I was in awe at all of the swirls in the water and by now counted three large fins yards from the boat. I looked over to the buoy which marked where the guys were and I'd say they were about thirty yards from me. Still, I saw no other signs of blood in the water other than what I had thrown in. Carefully, I leaned over the edge and filled the bag that had contained the melt with water and let it sink.

Then I heard it, a scream so chilling and high that it had to come from a woman. It reminded me of the scream that my mother had made the night my great grandmother shot the intruder in our house. But it wasn't coming from the direction of the dive marker Rick and the guys were floating under. Instead, it was from a marker about a hundred yards away.

A woman had surfaced and was waiving frantically to her dive boat, screaming, "Get me out, oh God, come get me! Sharks, sharks," she yelled. Soon another figure emerged beside her. He seemed much calmer and their dive boat raced over. The driver of the boat yanked the lady out of the water and I watched in horror as I imagined that I would see her coming out shooting blood from broken arteries, but she was up and walking. And the man that had surfaced with her was casually getting himself out of the water and I could see that he was now next to her and coddling her while putting a towel around her. I looked around still waiting to see a blood pool near Rick's dive marker but nothing still.

The water around the boat had grown calm and I could not see either of the big fins around any longer, and I wondered if Rick had been hit. I thought to myself that surely one of the guys would surface and scream for me to come get them if that were the case. But such was not the case. In fact, about forty minutes after I had thrown the melt, I noticed that their buoy was now getting closer, perhaps only twenty yards from the boat. Then I saw bubbles and soon after, one of them appeared on top of the water and exclaimed.

"Woo hoo!"

It was Steve. About fifteen seconds later, Rick emerged and tearing off his mask said in an excited tone, "Man what a lucky day. I've never seen the lobster so active. Dude, I mean they were on the move."

"I got two!" Steve said with excitement and about that time Jay surfaced.

"I got three," Rick exclaimed holding up the nylon bag displaying his catch.

"Did you guys see that bull shark whiz by us?" Jay let out.

"Oh man, was he beautiful or what?" Rick said with awe.

"I thought I saw something," Steve said in agreement, then added, "it's been a long time since I've seen the reef so active. The storm must've stirred things up or something. How many did you bag, Jay?"

"Two," Jay proudly replied holding up the bag.

"Hey Andy, Bring the boat over and help us out," Rick ordered.

I did, and when everyone was in they started getting out of their wet suits and their excitement was evident in their conversation concerning the activity in the water. Jay swore that the bull shark must have been an eight footer.

"No way," said Rick, "You know the mask makes anything look bigger than it really is."

"I'm taking that into effect dude. Remember, I grew up in the Keys."

"I wish I had seen it," Steve admitted with an air of disappointment.

"So how you doing?" Rick asked me.

I explained that I was worried sick about them as I told them about the lady from the adjacent diving boat come out of the water screaming.

"Stupid bitch," said Jay then he added, "she's clueless that people pay big money to see sharks on a dive."

"Come on guys, pipe it down will ya," Rick implored then said, "I'll never get Andy in the water now."

Jay teased me when he started to sing the "danh dah, danh dah" from Jaws and pinched me on the ass while Rick bent down in the ice chest and brought out the wine. Steve kept on about what a blessed day for lobster diving they had been given. Rick gave us each a glass of wine and said, "A salute to a grand day of lobster and a beautiful Easter with good friends." He flashed me his adoring smile and we toasted each other's glass.

Jay said, "Hear, hear" and I meekly followed by saying the same.

As we headed back, Jay went on and on about the beauty of the shark, and as I sat and listened, Jay insisted that I take a scuba class. We got home and unpacked the boat and steamed up the day's catch and had a party.

Yep, we had a party.

CHAPTER 28

Fort Lauderdale, April 1992

Iawoke to a Monday morning, alone in bed. Rick had already slipped out. I was not feeling enthusiastic about meeting the day as I had a hangover from the previous day's Easter celebrations. I turned over to look at the clock to see that it was already ten A.M. and in disgust, but with no energy to panic, I forced myself out of the bed and into the kitchen to make a pot of coffee. Rick had left everything set up so all I to do was turn the coffee maker on.

"He is good to me," I thought to myself. But nevertheless, that thought did not diminish my mission of murder and revenge. As far as I was concerned, the course was set.

I cheated on the coffee maker. It had barely made a cup when I pulled the pot out from the under the drip and quickly poured the strong liquid into my favorite cobalt blue coffee mug. I put the pot back on the burner to the sound of hissing steam and quickly wiped up the slight mess that had been made. This act was small torture to Rick when he witnessed it and he had bitched at me on past mornings for my impatience. Of course, I would cheat the coffee maker on purpose and when he bitched, my reply to him would always be the same, "Why don't you buy a model with the auto drip cut off when the pot is removed?"

"I need to buy a new boyfriend," he'd say.

I would reply, "You're not through paying for this one yet."

He thought that was romantic and was off the mark on the intent of the statement. When he would kiss me after this ritual, I would almost feel sorry for him.

Anyway, the coffee kicked in and I went to the john. I hate to keep beating a dead horse, but the bathroom immediately killed the effect of the coffee. I became constipated when I walked into the room. The gold was bright and reflective and in effect, nearly blinding as if the sun were blaring in through a portal.

Seriously, I think of a bathroom as a place of meditation and peace. This bathroom is the antithesis of serenity and destroys any connection to the soul. I had gotten into the habit of closing my eyes and thinking hard about the outhouse behind my great grandmother's housekeeper Ella's shack, that sat on the edge of the pasture. As a little boy, I had risked many a spanking as it was simply unthinkable for a little white boy to "go" where black women went. Remember, Selectric, this was the early seventies. North Louisiana was a little behind Mississippi, but we were being forced to catch up.

And so, Selectric, you must understand that the visits to Ella's outhouse were worth the risk of the strap. I don't think I have yet to find a place of more comfort and calm or more close to God than this little structure. Don't get me wrong, I'm not a scat queen and I detest shit, but this place was actually one of the sweetest smelling places I ever remember. It was made of cedar and sat under wild plumb trees that were as old as my family's title to the property. When the trees were in bloom, it was incredible. And in spring, white bells and yellow daffodils that gave off an incredible aroma would blossom all around the structure, which was actually part of the fence line of an adjacent pasture. There was also a huge Camellia bush just off the edge of Ella's little shack that couldn't have been more than ten yards away. Inside the little structure, Ella had tacked, for insulation purposes I presume, all the worn out hand fans from the hundreds of Sunday church services that she had attended. And these had colorful pictures from various Bible stories and Psalms on them that were lit up from faint sunrays that filtered through the slant of the tin roof. The walls were literally covered in scripture and art. All I had to do was choose the smaller hole on the wooden bench inside the little structure. I probably regress and repeat myself, Selectric, but I can't emphasize enough how freaking unholy Rick's golden abortion was to my senses.

But back to reality, and after finishing my business, I jumped under the brass elephant's nostril that supplied the water for my shower. Did I really love a man that could commit such an affront to good taste? I'd have to say yes but while I was showering, I reminded myself of the slow bullet he'd shot me with and was thinking that although the shark gimmick didn't work, I'd figure out something that would. So I dried off and puffed on a roach left over from the previous night's festivities, got dressed, got out of the condo and met another beautiful day in paradise.

When I got to the corner of Sunrise and A1A, I could see Madame Dieux Dieux pushing the kiosk. I was glad that I wasn't the only person running late, so I jogged up the block to meet her and said, "Good morning, Sleepyhead. What gives?"

"Don't ask, I don't feel so well. I don't see you bring me any crabs boy!"

She caught me totally off guard, as I thought we were going through simple civilities such as when a neighbor sees another washing a car and he says "wash mine when you're through."

"What?" I asked to buy time and nudged her out of the way so that I could push the kiosk, to which she gave me no quarrel as I could tell by the look on her face that she was in pain.

"What you say! I pull my damn back helping my granddaughter to find a yellow or blue or whatever colored egg. What a waste of food in this country."

She threw her hands in the air then continued, "So I make those kids eat some of them eggs but they don't want it. No!" she said raising her voice. "They want to eat the chocolate rabbit that lay colored eggs."

I shrugged my shoulders, to which she replied in gesture by rubbing her lower back. Then she smiled and said, "Oh but we had a good time, and I make a heap of egg salad and I think to myself, 'I be eating egg salad for a month but at least tomorrow, I have it with some crab.' So where my crab, boy?"

"Well, well. Well ..." I stuttered and she stopped walking and crossed her arms and raised an eyebrow that would have made Gloria Swanson envious.

"We went lobstering," I said.

"That even better! Now I'm gonna have lobster," she exalted and feigned happiness to which I looked at her apologetically and said, "Sorry, we ate them all."

"What! You not think of Madame Dieux Dieux and her lust for crab! Den not one lobster! Oh poor Madame Dieux Dieux," She dramatically exclaimed in exaggerated Creole while wiping away make-believe tears from her eyes. Then she looked at me suspiciously and said, "You didn't bring me a sandwich made that stinky meat I took you to buy?"

Apparently my expression to this jab aroused some suspicion from Madame Dieux Dieux and she further feigned, "Oh Mason! That all you think of poor Madame Dieux Dieux."

She was clutching her lower back as if in further pain. She looked over at me to see if her display of self-pity was having any effect, and I think my own guilt was boiling to a breaking point. Then she held out her hand and said, "Fine! Den hand me the stinky meat sandwich and I'll eat the damned thing."

As she said this, I felt as if my guilt with what I'd done with the melt was causing twenty pounds a second to be hung on my shoulders.

I remember just letting go of the handles to the kiosk and slowly sinking down on the sidewalk and starting to bawl. Selectric, I cried! Cried like my mother was in a casket in front of me, and being void of any hope and filled with despair that could be seen for eternity. I put my head in the cup of my hands and just cried.

Madame Dieux Dieux did not say a word. She obviously knew that something very serious was wrong here, and she simply put her hand on the top of my head and gently massaged my scalp. After a few seconds of this, I looked up at her, but she was not looking at me. She appeared to be lost in a trance looking out over A1A past the beach and into the soul of the ocean itself. Her actions had a very soothing effect on me, although the despair I felt was still infinite.

I just started confessing, "I tried to kill him, and nearly killed other people yesterday. I love him, Madame Dieux Dieux. I'm going to die. Soon! I know it and …" I told her everything. How I took the meat and attempted to entice a shark attack and my intentions of killing him, if I could do it without getting caught—or even better, mangling him so that he would suffer in his final days without a leg, foot, hand, or disfigured in any other way. I explained to her that he knew he was sick and without any regard or semblance of concern, had infected me. Yet we fell in love. And here I was.

Her silence as she listened was even more soothing than her hands had been while she softly massaged my scalp. Once again, Madame Dieux Dieux's ability to listen and seemingly become absorbed in my crisis had the effect, from a rational vantage point, of anesthetizing the pain and bringing it to a manageable level. As my sobs became sniffles, she came out of her trance and walked over to a little drawer in the kiosk and took out some paper towels that she usually kept for her lunch.

"Well, since you didn't bring me no crab, I won't need these today for my lunch," she said.

We both had a light laugh and she continued, softly and with an air of understanding in her voice while handing me a paper towel, "Wipe you eyes Mason. Madame Dieux Dieux gonna help you."

I was completely perplexed, because I had expected her to admonish me, if not for the actual attempted murder of Rick, at least for putting other people's lives in danger. Or at the very least, I expected her to tell me that I should seek psychiatric attention. So cautiously, when taking the paper towel from her hand, I asked her, "Really! How Madame Dieux Dieux? Your listening, I appreciate. That's been more than enough. What do you mean you are going to help me?"

"Child!" she exclaimed, then continued, "What, my little Sally Field here think she the only one in the world with a knack for revenge?" She looked at me hard and started shaking her head then shouted, "Whoa! And a mean streak too. OooWee! Sharks! Tell me Sally, you think a little black Haitian woman not be knowing anything about revenge and murder?"

I was perplexed from several angles as it is my nature to ask the least important questions first, then build up to the more important points (dyslexic question disorder, but it's what I do). And she had said murder so loudly and with such ferocity that I looked around and found myself relieved that there was no one around. With a hint of irritation that I'm sure I couldn't disguise in my voice, I quietly asked her, "Why are you calling me Sally?" and I motioned with my hands for her to keep it down.

"Oh sorry," she whispered, then continued in her natural volume, "I watched HBO at my daughter's yesterday. You know that movie Steel Magnolias. You know, most of the time, I find tears are cheap. But you and that Sally Field, chile, you two make believe. You ever tink of going into the movies?"

"No."

"Well, good, 'cause your tears are real and that Sally Field, I believe hers too. Even though I know they are fake, they come from somewhere. They were true and so are yours. I wish I could help that woman in that movie yesterday. I know how she feel. But dat just a movie. But I can help you. Yes?"

"How?" I simply asked.

"I'm going to help you kill this Rick!" she whispered in my ear.

I couldn't think of anything to say. With the warmth of her breath still present on my ear, she backed up away from me and asked, "You hear me talk of my daughters and grand babies, but you don't hear me talk of any Mr. Dieux Dieux?" She stopped talking and turned around abruptly and looked me hard in the eyes. Her gaze was telepathic and there was no mistake in what her eyes were saying to me. She had killed her husband.

She grinned when she caught my own eyes returning their astonished gawking of disbelief. But her response to my initial disbelief, from what I had assumed to be a harmless woman, was a lone right eyebrow that raised itself so high and the malevolent expression that she exposed showed me another side of Madame Dieux Dieux. And in an instant her face had quickly told me that I had acquired a serious ally in my quest to kill Rick. Just loud enough that my voice rose over the sound of the surf and the cars passing on A1A, I asked her aloud, "Why, Madame Dieux Dieux? Why?"

"The exact same reason you have, Mason," she soberly and quickly replied.

"AIDS?" I whispered.

She nodded her head in affirmation and added quietly but with conviction, "That cheating, beating, no God in himself man back in my country rotting in a grave next to my baby princess."

Now it was my turn to listen and as I listened I saw a glimpse, and only a glimpse, of the pain this woman knew. As she solemnly spoke, she looked out again into the blue and green of the ocean, as if only something so visibly large could give her the strength to tell of her agony aloud.

"For eighteen months, I hold my little angel, so skinny and sick, and my little princess, she have the heart of a tiger. She have more courage, this little girl, than any man I ever know! And she try in vain to hold on to her precious life. I tried to help her, him staying out drunk the whole time, but she finally died. My soul never felt such pain. I have a soul like a rubber balloon that somebody put an acorn in and then blow up the balloon; that little nut sharp point just keep on pricking and I can't get out. But the balloon rubber won't break and set me free. The pain still there, but after killing that man, the prick from the acorn, it not so bad. I think my balloon is crimson. I want to fight. I think the love of my two daughters here with me and my grand-babies keep me alive, red and fighting! And I feel that prickle in my soul every second, but him dead and rotting take away some of the hurt."

I remember her turning from the ocean and looking at me, then saying, "But you want to kill your love. That's strange, but I'll help you still. Maybe you find another love, keep you alive too. Maybe not, but either way, Madame Dieux Dieux will help you. I'll get you this weapon before too long."

"Weapon?" I whispered.

"Yes, chile," she exclaimed, then continued, "you don't see me behind any bars. I'm free and rich and in the good land of America. God help me!"

She sighed and was silent for a moment then asked, "Tell me Mason, this Rick, he wear any jewelry? Bracelets, necklace, or even better, earrings?"

"Yes, he has a diamond earring," I admitted.

"What I'll give you is a very fine crystal powder, made secret in my country. It come from sea fish poison, and chicken blood, and a few other things I don't know and don't need to know. But what you do—" she stopped and looked around to make sure we were still out of earshot of anybody, then continued, "you going to have to be very careful. Buy a face mask like a painter or surgeon mask, and wear rubber gloves. You sniff this stuff or get it on you and you be the one rotting. But this stuff have tiny, teeniest crystals you barely able to see. You dip the needle of his earring in the powder and Rick gonna slowly come down with a killer flu. The doctors, they gonna throw up their hands in disbelief, but he have AIDS anyway so there nothing no one can do, and he gone."

She snapped the fingers of both hands to bring home her point then continued, "It gonna take a month or so, but my Mason not gonna get caught. He gonna be here free with Madame Dieux Dieux. Yes, yes!" she exclaimed with confidence and conviction.

And as I heard her say the final yes with such resonance, the committee was coming to order.

CHAPTER 29

The Committee, April 1992

MR. REVENGE WAS TRIMMING SOME SPECIES OF RARE FLOWER YET to be genotyped, that grows only in my lower intestines, when Miss Love seemingly appeared out of nowhere and tapped Mr. Revenge on his left shoulder. With a startled gasp, he turned around but she wasn't there. Miss Love let out a little snicker and when Mr. Revenge turned to his right he was greeted by a sneering woman in a man's button-down white shirt, wearing overalls nearly two sizes too big for her. Covering her feet and most of her mid-legs were rubber boots to protect her feet from the shit that inevitably composes the paths of this part of the body.

"Sucker" she jeered to the masked man now facing her. Mr. Revenge was still in his sequined super hero uniform but Miss Love noticed something decidedly different about the Captain Marvel dwarf, who had so recently entered into Andy's spirit and emotional realm. So she asked him directly, "Are you getting taller?"

Mr. Revenge, while reaching over the hedge that he had been trimming, clipped from the bush a royal purple flower that resembled a hydrangea flower with a color scheme similar to human hazel structured eyes which, instead of gold, was streaked with quaint pink and violet highlights.

He took in a luxurious whiff and while slowly exhaling, he simultaneously answered Miss Love's question, "Um huh." After contemplating what a delightful fragrance the flower had delivered to his senses, he looked up at Miss Love and asked, "What do you think I ought to name a flower that is as truly divine as this? I should think this a simple task for you. After all, I surmise that this is the sort of thing that you would do best. Naming flowers, holding hands, writing ballads are all part of your historic repertoire."

He held out his free hand for Miss Love so that they might stroll through his garden together. Instead, Mr. Revenge was surprised to feel a sharp sting across his face from one of the rubber dish gloves that Miss Love nonchalantly had removed while he had been exulting over the prize flower that his garden yielded. A welt instantly appeared just under the mask of his right eye. Even Miss Love was a bit astonished, as she was still unaccustomed to her new strength that had grown with Andy and Rick's relationship growing stronger and stronger. Mr. Revenge noticed her expression and casually released the flower he had been revering, allowing it to flutter down to the shit that composed the garden path that he and Miss Love were standing together on. Then wiping his eye, he turned to Miss Love and casually stated to her, "Shoemaker, know thy lass."

"What?" Miss Love shouted.

Mr. Revenge took in a deep breath, and using the breathing exercises he had whole-heartedly been applying from his earlier session with Miss Addiction, he exhaled with refined patience that barely disguised his inner exasperation with Miss Love, and explained, "It's a quote from somewhere darling basically stating that one should stick to the things that one knows best."

"It's funny," Miss Love said forcing a sharp smile. Then she continued, "while I stand here next to you, ankle deep in shit, listening to you and your assumptions of what you THINK I am, that nevertheless, I can't help but to want to humor you. So if you think that holding hands and naming flowers, or sending them, or whatever the fuck it is that you think I'm all about, so be it."

With that, she took the rubber glove and backhanded Mr. Revenge across the opposite cheek than she had previously popped, and stated abruptly, "Morning dumps, I think that is the perfect name for these little beauties that grow from the hedge you are grooming. And although I certainly can't deny the intensity of color and richness of hue, neither can I fail to see that these flowers are the product of a hedge grown in shit tended by a little fiend who wallows in the same."

Mr. Revenge, who had endured the slap and verbiage in a cavalier manner now allowed his tone to reveal that he was losing patience. He looked her square in the eyes with a warning stare and spouted, "Lest we forget, you little trollop, most thing do grow best in shit."

Miss Love, feigning boredom, let out a huge belch, then covering her mouth with hands timidly said, "Excuse me," then the giggling continued with a brief and insincere explanation, "wrong orifice for this occasion."

"Oh please!" replied Mr. Revenge, rolling his eyes through his mask and exalting in a tone that was as butch as is possible for anyone inclined to speak with an English accent.

The sight and sound of his reaction only increased Miss Love's confidence and she pointed a finger at Mr. Revenge. And while wagging it told him with staunch conviction, "You forget, as you are prone to forget the truth, Mr. Revenge, things grow best in shit and sunshine. Honey, at the risk of proving myself a simpleton, we are in a place where they say in slang, 'the sun don't shine.' These divine beauties, as you so eloquently put it, grow in darkness and a literal crock of shit. They won't bloom in any environment other than an intestinal tract."

Mr. Revenge, who had stood completely motionless and silent while providing Miss Love the courtesy of speaking without interruption, now with little effort and no warning held up his hedge clippers and with one swift motion snipped Miss Love's wagging index finger off. Completely caught off guard and in a state of shock, Miss Love expelled an agonizing scream that could be heard throughout the deepest corners of Andy's emotional realm. As a result of the sudden wound, the blood spurted onto the revenge bush causing the Morning Dumps to miraculously thrive on the combination of shit, Mr. Revenge's care, and Miss Love's blood.

Mr. Revenge was now in a state of awe and ecstasy and gleefully exulted, to the wounded emotional hag who was still screaming in tenors unbeknownst to the human ear, "Oh yes, Miss Love, they hold up in the light of reality. Why else would you be making your little voyage on this fine day, except for the fact that your attention has grasped the intentions displayed in the conversation between our boy Andy and Madame Dieux Dieux. Brilliant woman, is she not? There is probably no coincidence in her name and the realm where our 'Morning Dumps' grow. You in your brilliance, Miss Love, allowed this woman into Andy's life and now she will supply the ground for my garden to evolve into an exquisite reality."

Miss Love, now able to control her hysterics and pain after the initial shock caused by Mr. Revenge's attack, had taken off her shirt under her coveralls and was using one of the sleeves as a tourniquet around her wrist to stop the flow of blood to her hand. She just listened to Mr. Revenge and his rationale, as she dared not betray Miss Addiction's self-centered treachery to the little monster by the cracked out vixen's warning to Miss Love of Mr. Revenge's plans. Miss Love knew she had no true ally in the form of Miss Addiction, any more than Churchill had held regards for Stalin as a chum. And yet, she wasn't sure that she could write off Andy's new acquaintance, Madame Dieux Dieux, for an acknowledgement of friend against her metaphorical Axis foe.

And she knew, deep in her heart, that she had not made a mistake in placing Madame Dieux Dieux into Andy's life. Despite the woman's name, Miss Love knew that the little Haitian lady was a creature of love, hope, and art. That somehow her designs would help Andy for the better. But at the moment, wearing only overalls that exposed her sagging tits, Miss Love could only focus her attention to the matter at hand, or better said, the hand missing a finger.

Apparently, her screams had awoken a number of emotions from their slumber. One of the first of the inquiring minds of the emotional realm to arrive in the intestinal garden, to investigate the awful screams, was Miss Addiction. She was wearing only a skimpy magenta two piece bathing suit and was daintily prancing barefoot down the path with no regard for the shit squishing between her toes. As she approached the hedge of Mr. Revenge's garden, she clasped her hands together over her mouth like a gleeful child as she examined the "Morning Dumps," then picked one and brought it to her nose. Momentarily ignoring Miss Love and her state of agony, Miss Addiction squealed with delight to Mr. Revenge, "Oh Revenge, they are beautiful. No, they're gorgeous."

"Are they not, Miss Addiction?" Mr. Revenge conceded. He then took the clippers with which he had only recently assaulted Miss Love, and quickly cut a half dozen of the Morning Dumps from the hedge. Then he reached down on the ground and picked up the remains of the blood soaked shirt that Miss Love had ripped up and he tied the flowers into a bouquet. He handed the arrangement to Miss Addiction and stated chivalrously, "I hope that you will enjoy these at your little party that you undoubtedly will hold this evening. They produce an effect that would make the poppies of Afghanistan envious. We must celebrate a day such as this. As you can see, the end is coming and I expect nothing less from you than to, as they say, 'party till you drop.'"

"Oh they smell so good," Miss Addiction said, while smiling at Miss Love.

Then doing the best she could to be sincere (as much as that was possible for her), Miss Addiction looked at Miss Love and knelt down, still clutching the flowers whose fragrance had her in a heroin on steroids high. She then gently caressed the wounded and half naked wreck's hair, and said, "Bless your heart."

Miss Love gasped for air and heaved in convulsions, which were caused by the combination of excruciating pain in her hand and the opaque concerns of Miss Addiction. She then released a spray of vomit that would have impressed and possibly shamed the producers of The Exorcist. But Miss Addiction had seen it coming in time and was able to step out of the way.

"Oh my!" exclaimed Miss Addiction.

With a sense of regret for the condition of Miss Love that was quickly nullified by the sensations supplied by the bouquet of the Morning Dumps, Miss Addiction decided to live in the moment. Any sense of allegiance she had previously displayed to Miss Love by telling her of Mr. Revenge's intentions would have to wait. Highs this good only came along every so often. And Mr. Revenge, with a sense of satisfaction and no hint of regret whatsoever, held out an arm to escort to Miss Addiction as an invitation for her to stroll through his garden with him. Completely flattered, Miss Addiction took his arm with her free hand saying, "Why thank you sir. Always such a gentleman."

And as they sauntered down the path, they paid no heed to the wounded, disgusted, and wretched Miss Love still kneeling in pain and incapable of doing anything but watching their reunion and leaving. She was, she thought, alone but still resonant in her will to get through her trials. In a truly sick anomaly to the closing scene of part one in Gone with the Wind, she pictured herself in her mind as Scarlet O'Hara on the verge of losing Tara to the carpetbaggers. Slowly she arose in theatrical pose, from the shit of the masked fiend's garden path. With the symphony in full rapture, she lifted her bloody hand and gestured but did not speak the famous pre-intermission lines of the movie classic, "As God as my witness." After all, Miss Love wasn't all that convinced with the fact she was not God. Why should she talk to or witness to herself? Gestures, in her case, were more than adequate. She hoped.

CHAPTER 30

Fort Lauderdale, April 1992

I WENT HOME THAT AFTERNOON WITH ONE HUNDRED AND FIFTY DOL-lars. I had had a successful day with my art sales, after the cleansing of soul I had experienced with Madame Dieux Dieux. It seemed I had a solution to my quest that had ended the not knowing "how" exactly I would pull off the execution of my lover. And Madame Dieux Dieux's answer to my quest was plausible and solid. In a way, knowing this was more calming than a good pop of Ritalin, in its manner to relax me. To be honest, my mind functions much more smoothly. And as I've said before, that can be a scary thing, depending on my motives. But as I also said, my motives of the day had also been moving art and it felt good when I got home to show Rick the cash that I'd earned.

And surprise of surprises, when I walked in the apartment, I found Rick blowing a doobie. He graciously got off the couch and walked over to me with the joint and gave me a sincere kiss while massaging my ass with his free hand. After releasing his love lock on my mouth, he quickly replaced his lips with the joint and while I was inhaling the pot, my mind also inhaled his words.

"You know I love you?" he stated in a tone of affirmation and questioning whether I actually knew this.

I exhaled the smoke and looking him in the eyes said, "Yes."

And I started kissing him again. After we released each other, he asked me, "So did you have a good day?"

I didn't say anything but I pulled the cash from my back pocket and counted it out for him.

"Wow! Not bad for a college boy," he said.

"And where might my man of eternity like his boy to treat him to dinner tonight?"

Rick suppressed a smile, but it was too late as he tried to act arrogant and overconfident by teasing, "Daddy of the universe is quite taken off guard by his boy's invitation and generosity—but with all heartfelt gra-ciousness extended in his invitation, this 'man of eternity' will, and can only accept the invitation, if his boy will put the money away for school and allow me to incur the expense."

"Agreed," I selfishly answered without hesitation, but quickly added, "But since you are paying for the date, Daddy must choose the place. Any ideas?"

"I do. Ever had Zuppa? Maybe a little wine?"

"I've never heard of Zuppa, much less eaten it. What is it?"

"Basically a seafood stew. I think my bayou boy would enjoy it very much," he said as he gave me the joint and slipped his hands down the back of my shorts and started playing with my asshole.

"Sounds great," I said exhaling the smoke from the joint.

"Well, while you're displaying such good manners," Rick said as he pulled down my shorts and finding that I had worn no underwear, he shook his finger that he had just rubbed in my hole at me as if I were a naughty boy and continued, "would you be so good as to bend over the back side of the couch?"

"This couch?" I asked as I pointed to the black sofa and stumbled slightly stepping out of my shorts, which had confined my ankles.

"That would be the one," he said taking the joint from me and taking a quick puff off the dying roach.

And so I leaned over the backside of the sofa, fully exposing my ass in the air as my face sank into the soft aroma of the leather.

"Like this?" I muffled through the cushion.

"That would be the way," he said and nearly simultaneously, I quickly felt the five o'clock shadow parting my ass cheeks, immediately followed by his tongue shoving spit up my hole. Rick had left the blinds up so I was free to look at the breathtaking sunset in the west as he was eating my ass. It was bliss. The pot was really kicking in and I felt him stop eating my butt. I lay motionless as I heard his throat pull up a luger from his throat to lube up his dick with, and bam, I was seeing stars before the sunset. No doubt about it, the man could put me into orbit. Apparently, I did some good for him too as I've yet to meet a guy that can fake an orgasm. It wasn't long before I could feel him coming up my ass, and he convulsed and grunted in a manner only he could do. I can remember thinking, "I'll never forget the way this guy cums, never!"

Slowly he let his hard-on retreat from my hole, and as he took it out, I squeezed my sphincter, to which he playfully slapped my ass and said, "Give it back now."

I released the grip and he sighed as he pulled out and then went to the kitchen to grab a wet rag to clean off with. I was still bending over the couch and enjoying the last of the sunset and the feel of him still in me when he walked over to the couch to hand me the wet rag, Rick again slapped my ass and asked me, "You ready to eat?"

"Uh huh" is all I could muster as I arose from my previous position.

"Come on let's shower off and get dressed," he said.

We showered together, lathering each other's ass and balls and massaging each other's shoulders and back. When we got out of the shower, toweling in the steam, I was in a complete state of relaxation—which was brief, as the phone rang. I told Rick that I would get it, which he quickly said that he appreciated, and that if it were a client, tell them that he had gone out to dinner with a potential listing and that he would return the call tomorrow. However, I picked up the phone to recognize Jay's voice and I couldn't help but grin as he went straight into to telling me what a great time he and Steve had had and how much they really enjoyed meeting me. His voice was sincere and I couldn't help but feeling a tinge of guilt when I replied, "Yeah, me too. Maybe I'll have to get PADI certified so that I can go down with you guy's next time out."

"Dude, you gotta do it!" Jay enthusiastically agreed.

"Well, we're about to go out for something call Zuppa. You and Steve wanna join us?" I asked feeling confident that that would be agreeable to Rick.

Jay explained that Steve was out of town and that he would like to but that he had just given most of his money to an attorney who was attempting to get him off his second DUI, and that had taken most of his cash. Like I said, I genuinely liked the guy so without hesitation, although Rick had already said he would pick up the tab, I told Jay, "Don't worry about the cash. It'll be my treat. I had a good day."

"You sure?" he politely asked.

"Yep. No problem whatsoever."

"Well, I would say that I would like to meet you, but then again, I'm not supposed to be driving with everything going on with this damned DUI."

"Rick knows where you live?" I asked.

He casually replied, "Of course, but are you sure that it wouldn't be too much out of the way?"

To reassure Jay that the he was more that welcome, and the fact that I had no idea about what restaurant we were going to, I took the phone from my face a little and hollered to Rick who was still in the bathroom, "Rick, you mind picking up Jay to join us? Steve is out of town and Jay's temporarily stranded."

Rick sounded excited as he hollered back to me, "Not at all. Sounds like an excellent idea."

I was sure that Jay could hear Rick's reply but I went ahead and told him, having no clue as to where exactly Jay lived, "We'll pick you up in about a half hour or forty-five minutes."

"Sweet!" Jay exclaimed and then quickly added, "You guys wouldn't have a spare roach laying around would you?"

I smiled as I thought to myself; "I knew I liked this guy," then verbally stated over the phone, "For a handsome guy like you, who I'm sure never gets told no, and I don't want to be the first—of course."

As if he had read my mind, he replied, "I knew I liked you from first glance." He giggled a little then added before hanging up, "See ya soon."

"Hope you didn't mind," I said to Rick after I had hung up the phone as he entered the bedroom still butt naked. He walked over to me and gave me a kiss while slapping my bare ass again said, "Uhm, uhm, uhm."

The guy made me feel that he was smitten with me and grinned as he said, "Not at all."

I didn't mention to him that Jay was short on cash. We got dressed and I picked up the roach that Rick and I had left from our previous exaltations from the ashtray and put it in my shirt pocket. As it turned out, Jay didn't live that far from Rick at all and Jay lit the doobie on the way to the restaurant, where we had a really terrific dinner. The lobster, fish, and scallops that made up the French specialty were so fresh and prepared to such a perfection that it would have made many of the chefs of my native New Orleans jealous. As well, Jay was shameless volunteering his knowledge of wine, and he did pick out a perfect bottle to accent the meal.

When we had finished our last bite, the waiter asked if we would like coffee, to which I declined, still enjoying the wine. Rick said that he would take some and Jay ask the waiter for decaffeinated and quickly added, "That was simply a perfect meal. Really, thank you both so much."

"My pleasure Jay, and we're both glad that you could make it with us. We'll have to make sure Steve joins us next time," I said.

"Absolutely. He thinks the world about both of you and before he left, he told me that we need to make at least one Sunday a month with you guys our 'family day,'" said Jay, making quotation marks in the air with his fingers as he said "family day."

Rick added quickly, "If not more than one Sunday would be fine with us, right Andy?"

"Hear, hear!" toasted Jay, holding up the small portion of wine still in his glass that the waiter had not yet removed, then said, "That's what it's all about, being around people that matter to you."

"Where'd Steve go?" I asked Jay.

"Oh he works for Big Blue Real Estate corporate and had to be over to Sarasota for the monthly state business meeting or something like that. Anyway, he's always on the road for them. Makes me nervous. I mean can you imagine? A pretty boy like him breaking down at night on Alligator Alley."

"Not a good thought," replied Rick.

"Why?" I asked innocently enough, not really familiar with their notions.

Jay humorously volunteered, "Well despite the fact that I seriously doubt Steve cold fix a flat tire, much less the lack of State Troopers out in that desolate place, this is still Florida and gangsters and rednecks are still plentiful. And Steve, although Southern, could never fool anyone into believing that he is a "good ole boy." I just worry about him in general. He can be naïve and despite some pretty hardcore rednecks that live in some of the areas that he travels, he refuses to keep a gun in his car. Says he doesn't want to be like his cousins. Anyway, I just wish he didn't have to travel so much."

"I bet it's not any fun for him either," Rick chimed in, then added, "I'll have to leave Andy for a couple of days this week. There's a gas station just north of Naples that I'm giving it hell to get the listing on. Gonna have to be there first thing Thursday morning, so I will have to go over on Wednesday night."

Before he could get the consonant sound of 'T' from the word 'night' off his tongue, my mind was reeling with visions of this place called "Alligator Ally." A place in and of itself that I was completely unfamiliar with, but with descriptors such as desolate, alligators, rednecks, lack of State Troopers, I had to admit that it caught my attention. My mind began to drift from the conversation of the table in the comfortable French bistro, as my imagination brought me to a place I had never physically seen but could only vaguely picture through my familiarity of tourist post card stands. As I was thoroughly familiar with the desolate bridge spans that cover the bayous and swamps leading to New Orleans, I could only guess from the post cards that I had seen of the stretch of I-75 that runs through the Everglades known as Alligator Alley, that it was swampy. But the major difference between these two roads was that I-75 was not a bridge but paved road on flat earth, separated from the swamp only by

a cyclone fence. And as Jay had pointed out, both places were geographically desolate and certainly not the type of place a person, much less a fag,
would want to have a flat tire.

It's not like we're afraid of getting raped—"don't act like you like it
or they'll stop." Just kidding, Selectric, but back to the point at hand as
I was not thinking of a flat, but of the possibilities of a serious blowout
of the front passenger wheel. I knew that Rick drove the Lincoln like a
bat out hell in town and I had seen his radar detector, so I could only
guess, since I had never ridden with him on a freeway, that he would hit
at least ninety miles an hour on an open stretch of flat interstate. Cyclone
fencing probably wouldn't hold back a car hurling into the swamp at that
speed. And if the windows were up, perhaps the electrical circuits would
die and with the pressure of the water, there would be no way to open the
doors and get out of the car. I shivered at the thought, but I was brought
back to the present dinner table conversation as the waiter asked if he
could bring us anything else.

"Anything else guys?" Rick volunteered.

"I'm good," answered Jay and I motioned that I was finished as well.

"Just the check then, when you get a free second," Rick said to the
waiter who nodded and promptly placed the tab encased in a booklet to
the right of Rick.

"Let me at least get the tip, Rick" I said.

"Not tonight, Cupcake," he playfully said as he winked at me and
continued saying, "The pleasure has been all mine tonight."

"Thanks guys, I really do appreciate the night out," Jay chimed in.

We left the restaurant and when we got into Rick's Mark VII, I voluntarily got into the back and left Rick and Jay in the front talking about
some friend they knew, which allowed me to further indulge my fantasy
of Rick having a blowout in Alligator Alley. I was thinking to myself,
"What if he is blowing a joint and has the window partially rolled down
when the tire explodes?"

My mind pictured the Mark VII going through the cyclone fencing
and all the mud splattering as the car eventually hydroplaned deep into
the shallows, then eventually coming to a stop. The lights of the car not
yet going out as the electrical facets of the car are still in working order,
although the engine, being water logged, has died. And the sound system
actually still works, probably playing some new age music similar to the
chanting of monks that I know Rick enjoys. The dark water stirred up
with the muddy sediments from the impact of the car has now finished its
cycle of gushing in through the cracked window and is settled. Rick who

of course has his seat belt on, comes to and is surrounded by the murky water, eerily illuminated by the dashboard lights and chanting music. And after the initial shock and disorientation clear, he begins to regain his senses and slowly realizes the predicament that he is in; what really grabs his full attention, stronger than any medic opening an ammonia tablet under his nose, is a very peculiar and disgusting smell coming just from outside his half cracked window at his own eye level.

"What is this?" he thinks to himself as he sniffs still dumbfounded and not exactly sure where he is or what has happened. Then all of the sudden, sheer terror strikes as he realizes that right outside his rolled down window, only a couple of feet from his face, the cause of the stench reeling in his nostrils, is nothing less than fucking alligator breath.

I started giggling aloud in the back seat of the Lincoln as my imagination and fantasy had gotten away from me and my mind gave its best imitation of Porky Pig: "That's that's all folks."

"Care to share with us?" Jay asked.

"Ah, what?" I asked, caught off guard.

"What has gotten into you?" Jay further inquired, with a hint of amusement.

"Oh fuck," I expelled then took a quick breath and said, "Just the pot and wine. I was thinking about something Madame Dieux Dieux said today."

"Who? What?" Jay laughed aloud.

"My boss. She's a real card. She was talking about Easter today and how we manage to put a man on a cross and equate that with chocolate rabbits that lay colored eggs."

"Twisted" Jay said as he exhaled the last of smoke that anyone could drain from the roach he had lit and finished.

"Well, you asked him," Rick added then continued saying, "never a dull moment with this one around."

I kept silent and enjoyed the music as we took Jay home and then we got home and went to bed.

I had another idea.

CHAPTER 31

Fort Lauderdale, April 1992

I WAS AWAKENED EARLIER THAN USUAL THE NEXT MORNING BY RICK'S ritualistic, and quite dramatic, morning greeting of the sunrise. However, this morning, he was exceptionally loud. I quietly got out of bed so that I could observe him unnoticed. Once again, he was leaning on the northern rail of our balcony in his bathrobe doing push-ups and stretching with exasperating and loud yawns and groans. I watched his gusto as he took in the day and I saw a smile come over his face. He looked beautiful. He looked satisfied and happy and I startled him when I asked, just a step or two behind him, "You looking forward to the day?"

After a little jump, he walked over to me and said, "Yes. As a matter of fact I am. You?"

"Could be interesting. Another absolutely beautiful morning," I replied.

And it was. The temperature was around sixty-nine degrees, light humidity, and breezy. I was looking at him with the northeastern morning light and the panoramic view of the Atlantic Ocean behind him. The breeze from the same direction faintly carried his scent to me. When he smiled at me, it appeared to be the smile to beat all smiles that I'd ever seen. He must have noticed me admiring him and he walked over to me and asked, "So you wanna be my boyfriend again today?"

The way he asked me was almost as if he and I were in the third grade and he was asking me to "go with him."

So I answered him as innocently as I could, "Yeah. You wanna fuck me?"

"Uh huh," he said and kissed me. He was giving me a hard-on, but about that time the alarm went off in the bedroom. His eyebrows furrowed and he seemed genuinely peeved when he said, "But gotta get going. We've got a serious phone conference scheduled for that Fort Myers deal; we should be closing on Thursday. Can you keep that offer up for me till tonight?"

"Looks like I'll have to hang around here another day then," I answered.

"Good, you better," he said.

I don't know what came over me but I felt so enamored by this guy, I involuntarily blurted out, "I love you."

"I know you do." He said looking at me with an expression that I can only describe as truth. He just took another step closer to me and added, "I hope you never doubt that I love you, Andy. I didn't think it would ever happen, but it did. The day I set eyes on you. I don't know what happened, but it happened."

"It happened," I said, with my eyes getting watery. And he smiled again, his facial muscles relaxed and eyes open with serenity and truth.

"I'll get some coffee made. You better get in the shower," I said.

"Bring it to me will ya?"

"Sure, Rick" and as he was walking off, I don't know what came over me but I blurted it out. Not in anger, not in spite, just even toned, "Rick, Why'd ya fuck me and cum up my ass, knowing full well you were HIV positive, if you fell in love with me at first sight?"

I was looking west when I asked him and though I could not see him, I heard him stop dead in his tracks. It was as though nothing in the world could be heard now but the wind. It was like being in a time warp in still frame. Only the wind kept us in the present reality.

"Andy?" he asked and I heard him take a deep breath, as if he was about to say something but he stopped.

"Yes?" I answered not turning around to look at him.

There were a couple of seconds of more silence before he continued in a slow stutter, "I'm sorry Andy. I just assumed tha, tha, tha that," he said in a vain attempt to find words.

It was the first time I had ever heard him stutter. He turned me around and when he did, it was the first and only time I had ever seen him with tears in his eyes.

"We gotta talk Andy," he rebounded. "Seriously, but I need more time and I have to be at the office. A lot is riding on this conference. And …" He paused again and took a deep breath. "I wanna think before I say another word Andy."

I nodded my head to say okay and looked at the floor. Gently, he raised my chin and looked at me, "Okay" I said, "We'll talk tonight. You better go get showered."

Rick left the house quietly without saying anything else. I was sitting on the sofa watching the news report when he left and as the door was shutting, it was just one of those little coincidences when the newscaster urgently announced that the rate of mortality due to AIDS was dramatically on the increase. He further expounded on "The Quilt" that was being planned in D.C. and how the major obstacle was that the memorial was getting too big and that in fact this may be the last year for the event. As well, he announced that there was no cure in sight, although the announcer said that researchers were giving reports a vaccine might be possible in a few years.

I was thinking to myself that I could be on that quilt next year, contributing to its getting so large. God knows how much of Rick's cum I had up my ass. God knows, I let him put it up there. I asked myself why I finally gave into this. And my mind, totally in conscious mode, told me that it was inevitable and that eventually there would be a break in a rubber, or a sore in my mouth, or infected cum in my eye. All in all, I believed that somehow, the bug was going to get me—or did I simply have a death wish?

"Old age is not an option for you," a voice in my head stated in a resounding tone. And in the same instant, something told me that I already had the bug before Rick ever started pounding my ass. But at the same time, I knew that I had tested negative at least nine months prior to our initial K-Hole butt play.

But I thought, "It was inevitable. What with the drugs, sex, and prostitution, what in the hell did I expect? Of course Rick happened to be in the right place and in the same frame of mind to assume that a male street hustler would be HIV positive."

But we never even discussed it. I now know that he simply assumed that to be the case. But it was his arrogance that day that drove me to seek revenge; perhaps it was his arrogance that was part of the reason that I fell so hard for him. But it would not elude my logic and sense of justice that rang out for me to kill him.

"Make him suffer."

I couldn't escape this voice. Tragic yes, but it had to be, and every time I heard a small voice calling for restraint, my mind would revert to a raging "how dare he?"

"Unfair," I uttered aloud. And with that word on my lips, I rolled a joint.

After a few tokes, I decided that I would just get high. I would not go to see Madame Dieux Dieux today. I would, and only could, stay home and get high.

"Yes, unfair," I thought again as I took another toke. I continued my reasoning, "And I will yield my own justice."

I knew what it was. I knew that I would be in control. I smiled, knowing that I would be in control. It would be interesting to hear what Rick would have to say.

"Unfair," my mind uttered again.

And out of the blue, or haze is a better description, I recalled what my Old Man used to say to me whenever I whined the word—"Yeah unfair. That's just the way things are. Elvis got his ass and I got mine. If anything in the world is unfair, nothing beats that. But that's just the way it is."

I laughed out loud when I thought of my Old Man's fat ass and then thought to myself, "I gotta a prettier ass than Elvis ever had. And when he was young, that was a pretty ass. I probably got sick using mine."

I was passed out on the couch when Rick got home that night. I had been smoking pot on and off all day, so when the door's closing woke me up, I was groggy when Rick eased down and sat beside me. I was actually very relaxed and casual as I was rubbing my eyes and asked Rick, "So you had a good day?"

"No. I didn't. I mean things went well with the phone conference and all that, but I have to be very frank with you right now."

I reached over to the ashtray to grab a roach but Rick took my hand and literally took it away from me. He said, "Andy, why didn't you tell me? Why have you been letting me fuck you all this time without a rubber when you know I'm positive?"

"Well, I kinda figured there's no use slamming the gate after the horses are already out of the corral."

My tone had an edge to it both from the fact that he had taken the joint from me, and from the way he just sang right into the main chorus without any kind of bridge. I reached for the joint again and this time he didn't stop me. After I lit it and exhaled a plume of smoke into the previously clear air of the living room, Rick still remained quiet. And I spoke up and asked him, "Who let the horses out Rick? You or me?"

He still didn't answer, so I commented further, "Last time I heard, it takes at least two to fuck, and I didn't exactly ask you to stop. I'm not sure I could have or would have, but you didn't give me an initial choice to make a decision either."

"You had a choice, Andy," Rick said quietly.

"So did you," I answered back.

"Andy, I'm sorry, but I just thought ..." he hesitated then continued, "Well no need in mixing words, but one of the reasons that I was going to the street at that time was because I just assumed that I wouldn't be spreading this shit to anyone that didn't already belong to the club."

"I remember you didn't mix words the next day either."

He was quiet again for a moment and was about to say something but didn't. Then he took a deep breath and announced, "Look! I want you to go get checked. We'll wait about six weeks to be sure but in the meantime, I want to start using rubbers. Let me make you an appointment with my doctor."

"Suit yourself," I replied.

"Andy, you may still be alright. This shit is funny. Some people get it, some people don't, and some people get it and don't get sick at all. I've had the bug since eighty-six and there is not one sign of anything out of order, other than an antibody in my test. But to be honest, chances are, you—with the way we've been going at it—will have a positive diagnosis. But then again, maybe not. Either way, I'll pay for the checkup."

"How generous," I retorted.

"Yes, it is generous, Andy, and I don't know where you think this attitude is going to get us, but I'm not putting up with it."

He was serious and he got up and went back to the bedroom. I heard him messing around in his closet; in a few minutes, he was back in the living room and sat down on the sofa part that was perpendicular from where I was lounging and said, "I'm going out Andy. I don't care for shit right now, but I want you to know I'll do whatever I can to help you, but I need you to warm up. I don't know what to say. You know how I feel about you."

"I know, Rick. You're right, but I can't help how I feel. I don't know how to say or describe it, but I know I love you. I'm going to get in bed and turn on the tube. Have fun," I said with a bit too much sarcasm.

"Andy, stop it!" he demanded in a raised voice.

I didn't even look at him as I walked to the bedroom—his bedroom—and shut the door. I heard the front door close. He was gone. I went to sleep.

CHAPTER 32

Fort Lauderdale, April 1992

I AWOKE ALONE THE NEXT MORNING AND IT WAS CLEAR THAT FROM THE undisturbed side of his bed that he had not slept here. I got up and pulled the curtains aside from the terrace door and he was not on the balcony either. The unit felt empty; I didn't even bother to check the rest of the house, as I knew Rick would never sleep anywhere here but in his own bed. I pulled the drapes closed and plopped back into bed.

I wanted to go back to sleep but couldn't, as my mind took over and began with all of the projections of where Rick could be. I can't say that I'd blame him if he had gone out and tricked, but I didn't think he had then, nor do I believe so today. My guess was that he had gone over to Steve and Jay's place, or maybe just gotten a room at some hotel as many of them would be empty and inexpensive as Easter had passed, marking the end of the tourist season. I wondered if he were eating breakfast with Jay and what they were having. My imagination told me that Jay was up and about in his kitchen with a huge copper skillet making an omelet with every exotic cheese known to man and serving it with French toast made from sour dough bread with homemade strawberry preserves. A breakfast menu that I, of course, would never serve to Rick. I guess this scenario sparked my contemplation of the prior evening's fantasy in which I had served Rick as the main course to an alligator. Where was my infatuation of feeding him to something coming from?

"Yeah!" I thought with excited optimism.

I would put Rick into a guilt trip and suggest that I should not be alone and take the ride with him over to Naples. I could wrap a couple of joints and within the hour, we'd be baked. I would put on a good tape, and when the water looked prime for reptilian homesteading, I'd just grab the wheel and into the murky water we'd plow.

But instantly my optimism waned as I was able to deduce several reasons why this particular strategy was not the best way to proceed. To begin with, I would be in the flooded car with him and I can't help but think that, should I get out of the Lincoln, perhaps an alligator might prefer me above Rick. I can't think of a worse way to go than to be grabbed kicking and screaming into the slimy depths by a scaled monster with a serious case of halitosis. (Perhaps this is the reason for my infatuation of feeding Rick to something?) And second, if for some reason we didn't end up in a deadly situation and simply had a bad wreck, I could wind up with a broken spine, paralyzed, or a smashed face from hitting or going through a windshield. And to boot, Rick could simply over power me and stop the accident from occurring altogether, and that would in all likelihood spell the end of any hope for my justice.

"Nope, that's not the way to get Rick into the swamp. You'd end up in jail or hurt yourself," I silently said to myself.

"Fuck, this blows!" continued the exasperated dialogue in my head.

And then it hit me, as if Jimmy Durante had connected a right hook to the jaw as he laughed aloud and watched me sink to the mat as he grunted, "A blowout! Dat's the ticket."

The scheme flowed within my mind like milk and honey through the fabled Promised Land. I'd just get my little ass out of bed and walk down to the True Value and buy some industrial razors and some sandpaper, then hide them in the garage. When Rick got home, I'd come up with a dramatic excuse to leave on an errand so that I didn't have to be around him or something of the like, then take the elevator down to the garage and do my thing. My guess was that after some high speeds around 80 miles an hour for about twenty to thirty minutes, the sliced side of the front passenger tire would give out to the intensity of the heat caused by the road friction. Now being neither a physicist nor a tire expert, I was feeling pretty optimistic as I walked into the living room and lit a roach; that only increased my good spirits as the stale earthy fragrance came through my nostrils and further ignited my imagination. I remember taking a huge drag and thinking, "It might just work. Even if he doesn't meet Poppa or Momma Gator, or if the crash of the car into the water thwarts their curious aggression, then at least we still have a car accident from high speeds with at least the possibility of serious injury. And besides, what's more accidental than a blowout?"

I didn't bother with a shower, but I quickly brushed my teeth, threw on some shorts and a shirt, then slipped into my flip-flops. After grabbing some loose cash from Rick's dresser, I walked down to the trusty True Value just west of the draw-bridge. I thought twice about the sandpaper and decided not to bother with that. Just the large razor and plastic stick for the razor would do. As I walked home, I thought to myself that Rick would at least have to come home sometime today or tonight to get his business clothes for tomorrow's sales pitch in Naples. So I had better not go to the kiosk today; I was sure that Madame Dieux Dieux would be just fine without me. I'm sure I was smiling as I got home and went into the garage and saw that Rick's parking space was still empty. The meter box room just about 20 yards from his space was unlocked as usual, so I put the bag in the dark corner of the dusty closet and closed the door and caught the elevator up to the suite.

"Perfect" I thought to myself as I entered the still-empty apartment, "I'll just sit here and do what I do best till Rick gets home." And with that I lit another roach and turned on the T.V.

The Price is Right lit up in Technicolor glory as I plopped on the couch and inhaled away any anxiety I had left. The smoke seemed to have a voice all its own as it said, "What the fuck were you worried about?"

"Beats me," I heard myself silently answer the voice over Bob Barker exalting through Rick's surround sound, "Mildred, here is your showcase, as you are today's top contestant on The Price is Right.

As the curtains opened and revealed Barker's Beauties displaying some bourgeois dining room, I thought to myself, "Fuck, Janice sure is getting old. Or is that Janice? And Bob doesn't look so great himself."

I took another drag as the scene on the T.V. announced to the delight of the now squealing contestant Mildred that she would be serving dishes that she would learn to prepare from her fabulous trip to PARIS! As Johnny Olson explained through surround sound that the Price Is Right would fly two, round trip with accommodations, to the City of Light, I caught another glimpse of Janice and remembered as a little boy how beautiful I thought she was.

"Nope, I don't think I wanna get old. Not that I'd mind going to Paris."

I decided that I would bid on that showcase and I took several more heavy tokes as I waded through the commercials of Lemon Pledge and Blue Duck toilet cleaners to see if I'd be hypothetically going to Paris. As Mr. Barker returned and quickly read aloud the price of the showcase that Mildred had passed over, he disclosed to me that I had over bid my showcase but Mildred had come within one hundred dollars, and would not only be going to Paris but also win the Cadillac from her opponent's showcase as well.

"What the fuck? Mildred you ain't gonna have no fun in Paris and you sure as hell ain't gonna ever cook anything more complex than cheesy tater-tot casserole," I thought as I drifted off for my mid-morning nap.

I slept hard until around three P.M. when I was awoken by the sound of the door locks being turned. As I sat up Rick walked through the door and said, "I see you you've been getting your rest. That's good."

Barely acknowledging him or his words, I said, "I'm hungry, I'm gonna run down and get a sandwich."

As I slipped into my flip-flops, Rick glared at the roach and walked passed me to his bedroom. I lit the remainder of the stub and burnt my lips and finger but managed a nice wake me up and went down the elevator.

Within three minutes, I was under Rick's car. Nobody had driven in or was going to their car as I exited the utility room, so as I was working with the blade on the edge of the tire, I was generally relaxed as the blade made easy work for me as I shaved a large spot on the inside of the front passenger tire down to the metal. Less than what I guessed was another three minutes or so, I got out from under the car undetected and replaced the blade in the bag and walked over to the garbage chute closet and threw the bag in.

I'm basically positive that no one saw me walk out of the garage and onto the sidewalk. Within two blocks of the bridge, I walked into the Subway sandwich shop and used their bathroom to wash the tar and dirt off of my hands and face. I then ordered a foot long "Sicilian" to go, and headed back to the condo. When I got in the lobby, the clock over the elevator noted that it was now 3:24, and as the elevator door opened at our floor, Rick was waiting in the hall with his suit and shirt for the next day over his back and his small overnight bag hanging from his shoulder. As I walked silently walked passed him only to make eye contact, Rick informed me, "I'll be back tomorrow evening around six. Your appointment with Dr. Ball is Friday morning. I'll take you around eight."

"Okay," I said without turning around.

As I walked to the unit door, I heard him say, "You're welcome."

I stopped, as my blood pressure soared and my rage gripped my very essence. As I turned to throw the Goddamned sandwich at him, the doors to the elevators had closed and I swear I could almost hear them laugh as I aborted the throw.

I caught hold of myself and probably even grinned as I was unlocking the door and was sure that there was a good chance I would have the last laugh today. I got into the unit with the sub intact and grabbed a Coke from the fridge, then settled down on the couch. (Jesus I love that couch.) And I was loving the sub and a particularly funny episode of Bewitched, where Samantha was giving Darren's mother, Mrs. Stevens, an extra dose of aspirin due to Mrs. Steven's inability to cope with consequences of Aunt Clara's witchery. Aunt Clara's was unable to remember the antidote to the spell when my amusement was interrupted by the phone ringing.

"Hello," I answered.

"Andy!" I heard Rick attempting to bring his voice over the noise of traffic.

"Yeah, what's up?" I asked as casually as I could with a knot forming in my stomach.

"Damn it Andy, can you hear me?" Rick barked over the traffic.

"What? What do you want?" I asked pretending to be annoyed at his tone.

"Sorry. I'm not yelling at you Andy. Just, it's a rotten stroke of luck," Rick yelled then continued, "I was driving over the railroad track just up at Sunrise and it looks like a loose spike in the rail grabbed my tire, and to make a long story short, I've got a flat tire and I don't have anything but that little temp tire and sorry to bother but could you get me Jay's phone number off our phone pad? I don't have it in my Day-Timer."

"Sure, why?" I answered as I felt the air come rushing out of my stomach when I realized he was as of yet clueless that I had sliced his tire.

"I'm going to see if he'll let me take his car over to Naples since he's not driving anyway."

"You need me to come down and look after the car? Change the flat?" I volunteered.

"I was going to just have it towed, but you could be a huge help. Do you mind?"

"No, I think you're only about a quarter of a mile or so up Sunrise, right?"

"Exactly, the tracks by Sears," Rick confirmed.

"Cool. Here's Jay's number," I said and read off the phone number and told him that I was on the way and hung up.

Within ten minutes, I had walked down Sunrise and was talking to Rick in the parking lot of the fast food burger joint that he had managed to pull the car into. He hadn't even attempted to change the tire, so I guess he hadn't taken a close look at the tire whatsoever.

"I'm going to go ahead and call a taxi to get to Jay's," he said as he got back into his car and used his car-phone.

"Cool, I got it from here," I said as I pushed the trunk release button from inside the Lincoln and took my time getting the jack and spare out of the trunk. Before I could get everything assembled to jack the car, the cab was there and Rick managed to take a second to give me a quick kiss and I gave him back a reluctant smile.

"You have a driver's license?" he asked.

"A couple," I replied.

He just shook his head and got his clothes and bag from the back seat of the Lincoln and got in the cab. I put on the spare and drove the car to the Firestone on Andrews Avenue and paid for the new tire. No one new anything for the better. What the fuck? I guess I over bid my showcase again.

CHAPTER 33

Fort Lauderdale, April 1992

WHAT IS IT ABOUT A DOCTOR'S OFFICE THAT CAN PUT THE FEAR OF God into a man ten times quicker than a Baptist Preacher on his best hell-bound sermon? I think the answer is simple—the truth. I for one, know that I will believe a doctor before a hell-bound preacher. Or maybe I will believe them both. Perhaps on my death bed, I might try and believe a heaven-bound preacher, but I know I'll believe a doctor telling me that there is a really good chance that I'll be dead before the year is up. No doubt about it, a doctor is going to force me to look at the truth and get entirely ready to deal with situation. Or, I might even try to a believe a preacher telling me if I trust in the Lord, as Lazarus trusted and was cured, that I won't die before the year is up.

I can picture the scenario in my head as the black polyester suit of Reverend Dickhead extends a hand aglow with radiance and domination as I squint from a hospice or hospital bed to make out the face of the voice that is commanding, "Now in the name of Jesus Christ, get up and walk."

I say to the man, "Hold on Preacher, a little patience while I pull this I.V. out or whatever the fuck it is that is flushing whatever the fuck. There got it. Messy, huh?"

I still can't make out Reverend Dickhead's face to see his expression as the body fluids from the open wound extend to the sheets; but I obey his firm command as he tells me, "That's it. Yes, get up Son. Come with me right now. We'll leave here together."

As I arise, I'm shocked that I am actually up, and I can't quite make out the sound of some type of alarm or trumpets of glory as I begin walking towards the hand and voice that are beckoning me. I also feel the sensation against my butt cheeks as the hospital gown allows the breeze to reach my air-deprived backside that has been stuck against the mattress for God only knows how long. I'm exalting in my new found experience but shame quickly sneaks in as I look down at the sticks that were once my legs and I proclaim to the Reverend, "But Reverend Dickhead,

I'm not wearing any underwear. Don't get me wrong, I'm not shy about showing my ass, but take a look at some of this shit growing on my skin."

I turn around so that the commanding blur in black can see my slit and I hear nothing but silence. So I turn around and, finally, I can see Reverend Dickhead's face. He is in shock and the once vibrant optimism has escaped his voice as he is saying, "Yes, Son, I see what you mean. K.S.? Kaposi's sarcoma is cruel and I wasn't figuring on you being this far along. You may want to reconsider and get back in the bed. On top of it all, I'm not sure I want you sitting on my bucket seats with that shit."

I'm crushed at this and as I scream at him, "But I'm fucking walking. If I can walk on these concentration camp survivor sticks, surely the K.S. can be dealt with, you fucking dick."

Another much more clear and commanding voice brought me back to the reality of the moment and within an instant, I was brought out of the daydream and back to the doctor's office by someone speaking my fake I.D. name.

"Mr. White? Darren White?"

It took me a second to recognize that I was Darren but in an instant, my senses were flushed with sterile smells, bright white paint, and eclectic furniture of the medical waiting room.

"Mr. White," the young lady again stated aloud, but much more calmly as she had seen my unconscious reaction to hearing my name. She slid the smoky glass window that doesn't allow anyone to see through a bit wider so that the note that warned that we were to ring the bell once, became hidden by the adjacent grey glass. The much wider space now revealed the face that I knew she had called my name and her expression might as well cast comic book captions that read, "I don't want to be at work today."

She indifferently held out a clipboard with a pen chained to it in my direction and before I was at the counter she ordered, "Fill this out for me. Set it right here when you're done."

She patted the ledge of the counter to strongly indicate the correct place to return the finished questionnaires, then sternly raised one eyebrow and curtly stated, "And no need to ring the bell."

I returned her a weak understanding smile which might have attempted to extend an understanding of how much anxiety that bell must cause her.

"Thanks," she all but whispered with little if any change of facial expression and she shut the sliding dimpled smoked glass window with what I comprehended as a little more force than necessary. But who am I to say this?

As I walked back to my chair to complete my new assignment, I couldn't help but think that if perhaps she would leave the window open, then people wouldn't have to ring the bell. She could put her name, "Miss Bitch," in print on a name block right there on the counter for all the world to see. And then I or any other patient could just stick our heads lightly through the window and quietly say, "Oh yoo hoo, Miss Bitch, I've finished the assignment you've given me. Now I have a few questions I'd like to ask."

But that would completely defeat the purpose of the smoked and dimpled sliding glass window, wouldn't it? Maybe not? Instead of the bell and glass system, Miss Bitch could hand out a second clip-board with a piece of paper that could read, "Please note that we will be with you at OUR convenience. We've got one of the few medical degrees and licenses needed to run this racquet, and you are one of the many that NEEDS the FEW and you better have medical insurance, or a shit-load of cash, or get the fuck out. If you qualify as one of the two above, we'll be with you when we get to you, so read a Goddamned Bible that is next to last year's medical magazines to your kid and if you don't have kids, kindly sit the fuck down. And NO, we don't have a bell."

After I sat down, I marked the box that explained I would be paying cash. I also marked no on all the other fifty-two questions and found that I had told at least three lies. I didn't see any reason to admit that I used illegal narcotics, engaged in unprotected sex, and imbibed more than two glasses of red wine per day. On the line that asked for the reason for my visit today, I wrote, "dire concern." I couldn't even bring myself to write it down, yet I knew that Rick must have already discussed the situation with the office. Nevertheless, I knew I would have to simply say it when they got me back there and I found that it would now be easier to write down the reason for my visit rather than say it. In true dramatic form, my hand shook as I scratched out "dire concern" and wrote above the black mark, "HIV test."

I thought about it as a "test" and asked myself, like every other time I had taken a test, if I was ready for it. I knew the answer to the questions that were going to be asked on this test as well as any good lawyer knows the answer to his question before the person on the stand responds. And I knew that in about twelve to sixteen days, Dr. Ball would give me the damned thing back, graded like some first grade test where you only get a check or a minus. And I knew there was going to be nothing negative about this paperwork. I tried to think about what Dr. Ball was going to look like. At least on the ride over, Rick had said that he was a good doctor.

"He's really up on this thing, Andy. But even better, you might not have anything to be worried about, okay?"

I replied to his optimism with the major word for the day: "Okay."

I had not heard Rick when he got into bed the night, before and I didn't bother to ask him about it when he woke me up. He had showered as usual before me, and I had stayed in bed while he was in the tomb. I didn't bother to make coffee for him. When he pulled back the blinds and walked out onto the balcony for his morning meeting of the day, I grabbed his pillow and pulled it over my head. When he had finished blessing the morning with his usual routine, he had walked back into the bedroom, sat down next to me on the bed, and took the pillow off my head.

"Andy, I know this is a hard day for you, but it's better to know," he had said and waited for a response, but I didn't give him one.

"No matter what, I'll be here to do what I can for you. You know that? Right?" he further inquired.

"Okay. Thanks," I said with a small degree of sincerity, but yawning.

"Andy, I didn't invent HIV. And I didn't know, Andy?"

I sat up and patted Rick on his knee and said, "It's okay, really."

"Okay," he said and took a big breath and raised his hands up then clasped them back on his knees. He had gotten up off the bed to disappear into his walk-in closet to get dressed for the day. I got in the shower and was dressed and ready within ten minutes and we got on the elevator. I remembered those sounds so clearly. There was nothing but the hum of the winch that let us down nice and easy. And then there had been the echo of our feet through the exaggerated acoustics of the garage. Finally there was the assault of his cologne as we got into the Mark VII. Thank God for the radio as we went towards Federal Highway, north towards pompano towards the medical complex which even looked like courthouse. Inside, I knew that my judge, trial and jury awaited.

"I'll be back in an hour. He's on the second floor," Rick said.

When I opened the door to the building, the cool air, laced with the smell of disinfectants, rubbing alcohol, and floor polish assaulted me like a verdict of guilty being read from a courtroom head juryman. And my unconscious response to the memory of this verdict brought me out of my daydream's and conjectures back to Dr. Ball's office as my own voice verbally said aloud in its best imitation of a Hell's Kitchen street punk, "Yeah, yeah, yeah."

A wealthy looking middle-aged man who was also waiting in the tiny reception area gave me the worried look given by those that see and hear another person talking to himself. I got up and as I brought the clipboard back to the spot where Miss Bitch had shown me to place it, I treated the man to an encore of, "Yeah, yeah, yeah".

The man just shook his head and went back to his dated Men's Health magazine. I don't think he saw me shrug at him. I was doing my best to be a punk and guess I didn't have to try real hard. And the man was not to be blessed with another performance of my neurosis, for I had sat down only a minute or less after returning the chart when the milky white glass flew back and a different lady peered through and picked up the chart and sweetly asked me to come on back.

"How are you today, Mr. Caldwell?" she asked.

"Okay," I replied as the word of the day ding, ding, dinged again. The nurse or what have you took me through the routine of weight, temperature, and blood pressure. The needle to draw the blood didn't even sting and the sweet lady explained in her southern accent that she had been a "vampire" for years. I tried to manage a laugh but could not engage the lame joke.

"You just come over here and sit and Dr. Ball will be in to see ya in just a sec."

And she wasn't kidding, for as she was walking out of the room, a young man, probably in his late thirties with the facial features that easily allowed me to assume what he would look like as an old man, walked into the room and picked up the charts. He didn't even look at me as he asked, "So you've been having unprotected sex with Richard Gurnee?"

"Yes sir," I said as my imagination still obsessed at the prediction of what time would do to this man's features.

"Okay then," (ding, ding, ding) he said as he walked over and put his bare hands around my neck to check for lymph node enlargements and then further inquired, as the smell of coffee poured from his breath, "are you in any pain or discomfort at this time?"

"No sir," I answered sincerely.

"Okay then," he said as he proceeded to wash his hands in the sink, then turned around with the expression of what I assumed was an amateur poker player holding a full house and having a hard time hiding his elation, "I'll see you in two weeks. Make the appointment with Dee Dee before you walk out."

"And?" I asked him.

The doctor hesitated a moment and then tightened his lips and shrugged and said only, "Okay then."

"Okay," I said and he walked out.

I got off the table and walked alone, and apparently Dee Dee was Miss Bitch.

"Okay we'll see you May 12th," she said with what I thought was coincidently too close of an imitation of the good doctor's pursed lips and shrug.

"Okay," I replied.

As I got off the elevator and went through the doors outside, Rick gave a quick jab to his horn to let me see where he was parked. When I opened the door and was getting in the Lincoln, Rick asked, "What'd he say?"

"Okay then, see you in two weeks," I answered in an attempt to imitate the emotionless pentameter of Dr. Ball.

Rick dropped his head a little and as he placed the car in drive said with a heavy breath, "Okay then."

"Do you think you could drop me off at the beach?" I asked.

"Okay, no problem."

"Okay then. Appreciate it, Rick"

Rick turned on to A1A from Sunrise Boulevard and as soon as he did I could see Madame Dieux Dieux standing on the sidewalk behind the kiosk with most of the day's exhibits already hanging from the Bonner House wall. Rick had never seen the kiosk, but being a commercial Realtor and familiar with the strict street vending laws of Broward County asked aloud, "You know, I never asked you about this Dieux Dieux woman ..."

"Madame," I interjected.

"Madame Dieux Dieux is able to skirt the local ordinances and peddle this shit on the sidewalk and make the Bonner House historical site her gallery."

"Well 'this shit,'" I enunciated, then continued, "was highly prized by old man Bonner and before he passed he left huge amounts to promote Caribbean art." I explained as Rick was now fast approaching the kiosk.

"Here is good," I told Rick, and as he was stopping I went on to further explain, "Anyhow, the old man met her 'peddling her shit,'" I further emphasized again to his utter disregard, "down in Miami at her street kiosk and basically wrote her in when the Bonner Foundation was established."

"Jesus, you weren't kidding! That woman is jet black!" Rick said as we pulled up. Madame Dieux Dieux returned my wave, when I called her name.

Before I got out of the car I scooted over and kissed Rick on the cheek. I think he actually flushed a little as Madame Dieux Dieux had walked over and was peering through my open window. She arched one eyebrow magnificently high and brought a hand rolled cigarette that looked like a joint to her lips. She was wearing a bellowing and flowing red dress, accessorized by her bright yellow beads on her wrist, and this all was accented by her black skin. Again it made me think of a coral snake saluting its prey, as she silently acknowledged Rick by bringing her cigarette free hand to act as a visor against the sun so that she could accurately inspect Rick. When she exhaled the smoke, the gleaming white of her teeth, unfazed by her tobacco habit, barely appeared like hidden fangs. Apparently we were creating a traffic problem and a car behind us angrily honked, but the rude intrusion over the sound of the nearby surf did not distract Madame Dieux Dieux's gaze on Rick. When I attempted to open the passenger door of the Mark VII, the door swung out and the grinding sound of the chrome glancing upon the curb brought a grimace to Rick's already perturbed face, as he was glancing in the rearview mirror at the honking jackass.

"Shut the door, Andy" he commanded somewhat angrily then further explained, "I'll take you up to Del Mar and let you out."

I did as I was told and we drove down a hundred yards or so and I could see Madame Dieux Dieux in the side mirror watching Rick whisk me away, and I couldn't help but think silently to myself again of the old saying distinguishing a Coral snake from a King snake: "Red on black is one happy jack. Red on yellow, will kill a fellow," or something to that effect.

"Okay then," I said as I got of the car.

"See you tonight," Rick said just as the low beefy growl of the Mark VII's oversized Ford V-8 took him away.

And the sound of the surf and wind through the palms mixed with easy going engines of less powerful cars on A1A helped me to exhale a rather held breath. As I walked to the Kiosk and display, I was momentarily in a relaxed state, glad to be free of Rick and the earlier morning events. But no sooner than reaching ten yards from her, Madame Dieux Dieux brought my thoughts squarely back to Rick as she asked with a loud approval, "Dat is your Rick? Como se va!"

I don't think Madame Dieux Dieux was aware that I understood the exclamatory Cajun expression (similar to the American slang, "What's up") when I replied, "Well what'd ya expect? Chopped liver?"

"He cute," she said as she burrowed her forehead and shifted all her weight to one leg as she quickly went on, "Hell Andy! He a MAN! And good looking to boot. Mmm Mmm!"

But her enthusiasm quickly waned as she flicked her cigarette to the ground and said in even recollection, "But den so was dat son of a bitch who called himself my husband."

She didn't have to look down as her Roman-style sandals found their mark and showed no regret, as if guided by the cracked yellow toenails that resembled her jaundiced eyes to insure that foot easily snuffed the remaining life out of her discarded cigarette. The wind seemed to pick up and the sound of her sandals meeting the sandy sidewalk were amplified as she walked to the kiosk to diddle with this or that on the crowded shelf. I found the sudden lack of dialogue and the quick change in her demeanor uncomfortable. I walked over to her and when she briefly glanced up at me, and I noticed again, and with more concern, that the color of her eyes were not that far from the shade of her golden stained toenails.

"So how are you today?" I asked with honest pessimism.

"Okay, I guess. And you?" she attempted as our eyes met.

"Okay," I lied.

"Oh Donkey shit Mason, I not doing well either. Why we lie? Huh? You look into my eyes! Shit boy, I feel like my stomach gonna explode today!" she exclaimed then bent over and rubbed her belly with one hand and weakly confessed, "I feel bad today."

"Did you see a doctor?" I asked with sincere concern.

"No, but you did. What da man say Mason?" she snapped back.

"He said 'Okay then,'" I replied, doing my best mimic of Dr. Ball.

"I don't need no doctor to tell me I drank too much beer last night and give an olt woman with AIDS some liver problem," she said as she was grimacing and rubbing her abdomen at the same time. Then she quickly added, "I wonder what he tell me if I walk in dat office with yellow eyes?"

"He'd ask you if you had insurance," I answered in the true tone of a smart ass.

We both started laughing, but Madame Dieux Dieux bent over with pain as she continued to laugh. This cut my sense of humor short and I walked over to her and put my hand on her shoulder. She was still laughing though, but when she straightened up, she couldn't have been more serious than Moses demanding Pharaoh to let his people go. Her yellow eyes now seemed to glow, like a demon's eyes holding the yellow fires of hell.

I stepped back from her as she said, "You going to be 'okay,'" as she did her best to sound like an American using the overused word. Then she quickly enunciated each coming word by pounding her right fist into the palm of her left hand, "Yes, Yes, Yes! My Mason will be okay. He will have justice."

She reached up and grabbled both of my shoulders as she hissed the words, "Justice! Yes Yes! Justice in his own hands"

She could have been communicating with snakes. When she released her grip on my shoulders, I'm sure I stepped back a little. This brought her some amusement as she tilted her head ever so slightly from side to side and let her gaze on me weaken. I felt like a sleepwalker who had been woken up only a few inches before taking the final step off the edge of a cliff when Madame Dieux Dieux said in a much more recognizable personality, "Justice in his own hands, yes. Given to him on the most appropriate day."

"You mean the powder will be here soon?" I all but whispered.

She answered me matter of fact now, as if it were no big thing, "It here. I get it for you at church this Sunday. I say a prayer for you too."

"You might say one for Rick," I breathed out in monotone, while I silently celebrated the news that Madame Dieux Dieux had just delivered to me.

I knew that I was going to do it. The day was turning around quite nicely. In an instant, I was jubilant and I could feel the emotions stir. The committee had been called to order. And as I looked down at my own feet, as if to assure myself where I was, I swear, coming from what I guessed was a nerve on the end of my right toe, I thought I could hear someone smugly say "okay then."

CHAPTER 34

Fort Lauderdale, April 1992

The Committee

MR. REVENGE, HIS BODY AND MIND NOW IN SUPERB CONDITION, was nearly bursting the seams of his sequined red, white, and blue comic book hero's ensemble.

"Okay then," he remarked in confidence to himself.

His face, despite the mask that covered one third of his features, flashed a cocksure expression towards the jury-pit, already inhabited by the nine jurors that had graciously volunteered their precious time. Even with the fact that this was the Emotional Circuit Court of the Right Big Toe, the physical foot was, after all, placed firmly on Fort Lauderdale, Florida soil. So in this hearing, the traditional twelve were replaced by the legal custom of only nine representatives prevalent in Broward County juries.

This custom had come about, in part, due to the lack of civic duty possessed by the fun loving and wealthy alcoholics, drug addicts, bartenders, Realtors, mob bosses, smugglers, prostitutes, ad infinitum that comprise such a large part of the populace of the south Florida county. It had become nearly impossible for the Broward County legal system, weighted down with the area's rampant crime, to conduct its affairs with the twelve-member jury system, and to alleviate some of the jury selection problem, the county had dropped the number of required jurors necessary to nine. Hopefully then an unbiased verdict could be found and, much less, there could just be a trial. And in this similar scenario, the apathy that pervaded the pool of possible emotional participants that made up the psychotic realm of Mason Harrison Caldwell III, aka Andy, was on equal par with the good citizens of Broward County.

And in fact, there had not been any type of a selection process necessary, as there was no pool to select from. The court had lucked out as exactly nine emotions responded to the sequester who were remotely interested in sitting through the shams that had historically become most emotional courtrooms. The constitution and law of

Mason's psychotic realm, to say the least, were already absurd and weak. In the past, things at these "legal" gatherings had really gotten out of hand. But the emotional courts were necessary.

As he made himself busy straightening his files and paperwork in an important fashion, Mr. Revenge looked up in disbelief while Miss Love politely but noisily pulled back a chair for her unlikely ally, Miss Addiction, who by taking her seat at Miss Love's table was obviously going to aid in the cause of the pouting battle-axe. However, no sooner than she had sat down, Miss Addiction took some kind of white powder out of her makeup bag. Within seconds and with no regard for the Bailiff, Mr. Restraint, the trollop was fervently dicing and slicing the dust with a razor blade that she had pulled from a protective case within the same makeup bag to which she returned the remaining powder. In fact, Miss Addiction winked at the emasculated Bailiff, as if she were daring the all but symbolic emotion to take some kind of action. Miss Addiction proceeded to make neat and straight line of the narcotic confection, but Miss Love couldn't restrain her contempt and let her thoughts be known.

She looked at Miss Addiction with disgust and said, "Oh for fuck's sake Miss Addiction. I thought you understood the serious nature of the commitment we have here today. That we are not only on trial for all of our lives, but for the sanity, liberty, and freedom of the entire realm and beyond. How can you possibly be indulging at a time like this?"

Miss Addiction didn't bother to respond before she took out a short little white straw, neatly clipped at an angle, from her makeup bag, and with the assistance of the device she bent over and made the larger of the two lines that she had separated disappear. As she vigorously continued to snort and leaned back in her chair, the right strap that was holding up the brassiere of her scarlet red dress fell off Miss Addiction's shoulder and left her bared naked for all the world, and jury, to see the shameless emotion's right tit and cherry red, silver dollar sized nipple.

"Really, Miss Addiction!" Miss Love pouted as she reached over to pull the fallen strap back in place upon the bare shoulder of her drugged ally.

But Miss Addiction only mistakenly took Miss Love's grab for her strap as a sign of an affectionate hug. As she attempted to return the embrace, Miss Addiction succeeded in knocking down Miss Love's arm and actually embraced Miss Love. With a wrestler's grip that held Miss Love's face to her bare breast, Miss Addiction shook Miss Love from side to side and audibly but groggily slurred, "Don't you worry honey. Momma's got you. That's right now, don't you worry."

And with the effort of a cat having its fur stroked the wrong way, Miss Love managed to wriggle free from Miss Addiction's affection. As she stood up to straighten, her disheveled sweater and skirt, Miss Love's silent gaze in the direction of the jury stand attempted to apologize to the now gawking nine emotions. As she finished smoothing her skirt, Miss Love turned to gaze from the jury towards Miss Addiction, who returned Miss Love's angry glare with satisfied compassion. Miss Love almost grew dizzy herself while she watched Miss Addiction's pupils as they grew rapidly, then quickly receded, which then caused the black dots to resemble pin balls struck by bumpers and subsequently dashed into penalty lanes.

"I've had it, Miss Addiction. I thought you were here to help, but this is the final straw!" shouted Miss Love.

"Honey, don't get your panties in a wad. You can use this straw. See, I saved you some," said Miss Addiction as she pointed the acclimated straw toward the smaller amateur line, which she had thoughtfully spared for Miss Love.

"Good God!" Miss Love screamed as she shook on the edge of a conniption fit. Then she further inquired in full rage, "What is that shit anyway?"

"Shit!" Miss Addiction hollered in tizzies and full resentment towards Miss Addiction's ungracious tirade. She annoyingly blew a wayward lock of peroxide hair that had fallen over one of her cocked eyebrows and focused her wild gaze on Miss Love, but then brought up a hand to her temple as if her ability to concentrate had been impaired.

"This 'shit,'" Miss Addiction enunciated as she attempted to gather her wits. The anxious wrinkles in her forehead disappeared but the non-cooperative eyebrow still cocked sharply on the edge of insanity alluded to the confused temperament battling for Miss Addiction's posture. Nevertheless, she plunged forward with righteous indignation and confidence to calmly repeat, "This 'shit' is the best God-damned Trail Mix I've ever put together, so I would sincerely appreciate it if you wouldn't accuse ME of not knowing just how important of a day today is."

Miss Love drew in a deep breath of air in an attempt to match the conflicted calm of the scarlet, semi-clad hussy, but was unable to capture the essence of any serenity whatsoever. She completely aborted the notion altogether and Miss Love resumed her unrestrained and angry histrionics by screaming

"What? What in the fuck is Trail Mix?"

Miss Addiction now corrected her angry mouth into a voluptuous smile towards Miss Love before she turned to face the jurors, loudly explaining in as regal a gesture as possible, with a tit still hanging out as if she were about to breast feed, "My Trail Mix today, for this most sacred occasion in which I hope to expose the celebration of 'today,'" she emphasized, then continued in oratory fashion with only a couple of audible slurs that were more akin to a lisp indulged in in a southern accent, "And let me tell y'all what. Y'all better listen now. Chickadee's, if Mr. Revenge gets his way, there may not be many more days that we're free to indulge in confections such as this."

Miss Addiction paused to focus and bring up her hand in the fashion of a four-year-old child learning to count on her fingers, then listed aloud the ingredients of her Trail Mix, "I've put equal parts of Crystal Meth, cocaine, and ketamine," and with a giggle she brought the counting hand up to her face to hide her mouth from the rest of the courtroom, as she loudly whispered in the direction of the jury the last ingredient, "and just a warm and fuzzy amount of heroin; kinda like the bass harmony of our little quartet."

Mr. Revenge only gazed back at Miss Addiction with an open mouth, astonished at both of the facts that his one-time ally could even stand up after inhaling such an intake of narcotics, much less deliver a soliloquy that was catching so much of the attention of the yet to be convened court. Miss Love stood behind the opposing table, her eyes covered with one hand as if to shade her mind from the light of this spectrum, which if taken in would surely bring about a lethal migraine. And she muttered loudly, "Oh Goddamn!"

"What!" Miss Addiction shouted as she briskly turned around from the jury to face Miss Love whose hand, which had covered her downcast eyes, now visibly began to shake.

Slowly, as if with measured effort, Miss Love removed the hand that covered her eyes and formed it into a fist. Then she dropped it to the side of her hip where it rested tightly, mirrored by the left hand doing the same. Fists clenched, her body tense and straight, Miss

Love gritted her teeth and verbally lit into Miss Addiction, "You don't actually think that shit is going to help in an emotional court of law?"

"Well, if you don't want it," Miss Addiction curtly replied, then brushed back her hair and with her free hand brought the straw to her nose and inhaled the small remainder of the mix into her left nostril.

"You bitch," screamed Miss Love continuing, "Can't you get control of yourself for just one day? Just one measly motherfucking day? Is that too much? Don't you see that you are ruining any chance we have to sway the court in our direction? For just once in our life, I'd think even you could pull yourself together today?"

Miss Love was so mad she was in tears, but Miss Addiction was not moved in any regard by the display of passionate rage. In fact she replied as calmly as a purring cat, "Now just a second, Honey, before you start calling anyone a bitch. If anyone is a known bitch, it's love." Miss Addiction cleared her nostrils and with the airways to her being a little more cleared, heightened the terse accents of her words as she slowly walked closely over to Miss Love. Audibly enough for the entire court to hear, she went on, "But let me remind you just who in the hell is sitting on this committee-hearing panel."

Miss Addiction now screamed, "Go on! Take a look, bitch!"

"Yes, I know all of them, but still, what does that have to do with your habits and disregard?"

"Ha!" spat Miss Addiction. "You think you know them. Let me tell you how well I know each and every one of them. You just have to trust me on this one thing. I've partied hard with each one of those whores on that jury, or panel, or whatever the hell they are. And you are just going to have to believe me when I tell you that when they saw me with that Trail Mix and how I freely offered it to you, Honey, that was better than a million dollar bribe. They are going to know that there are good times still ahead. And they will side right along with our case if they think there's even a chance that I'm going to share my fortunes with them."

"You really think so?" Miss Love now shyly asked.

"I know so," Miss Addiction said with the conviction of a Louisiana politician who was asked if he was going to win an election in which 20,000 dead people had cast a ballot for the crook de jour. Then she further instructed in a sugar sweet southern accent, "Now come on and take your seat like a good girl. It's almost time for this show to start."

Miss Love looked at her watch as she took her seat in still some-what reluctant compliance to Miss Addiction's case and advice. But Miss Love had to admit to herself that Miss Addiction had a point. Still, it was right at one o'clock and the trial was set to begin promptly.

"Goddamn it hell, one P.M. is one P.M. no matter which realm you slice it in. Unless of course we were set for Miami time. And I'm sure we're not set on Miami time," Miss Love mumbled aloud, referring to the well-known fact that Latinos from Miami were notorious for their "Mas or Menos" attitude toward time and punctuality. She turned to Miss Addiction and nervously continued, "Intelligence was supposed to have presided over today's hearing, and I'm worried. He should have already been here. Oh Miss Addiction, what are we going to do?"

The only response Miss Addiction gave to Miss Love's question was a shameless and subsequently loud bronchial hack that would have made any congested, snot snorting redneck blind with envy. Miss Love simply looked over at the trollop in disgust and took a deep breath, as she felt a serious anxiety attack coming her way. She began to sweat so profusely that she noticed a couple of drops as they fell from her chin onto the table at which she was sitting. In fact, her hair was beginning to feel like it had when, in many years past, she frequented beauty salons and a flippant queen would spray mist all through her flowing locks prior to the initial cut. But her nostalgia was short lived as Mr. Revenge stepped the few short feet to her table and as he leaned forward, he placed most of his weight on his stubby little hands that were only inches away from the falling perspiration supplied by Miss Love.

"Really now Love!" he rolled off with a hint of Cockney condescen-sion, "What in heaven's name did you expect to be the outcome when you accepted the assistance of this narcotic quaffing vixen to aide in your case. I can only imagine that the both of you, Miss Addiction bare breasted like some French whore imploring for liberty, and you here, sweating bullets as if you were actually about to face a firing squad, have contrived these little histrionics for either the amusement or outright sympathy from the panel nine."

Miss Addiction, one eye cold-cocked and at a loss for words as the Ketamine battled for supremacy over the Crystal-Meth, only managed a somewhat deformed attempt as she shot the rod at the masked plaintiff. Mr. Revenge pleasantly smiled in response to

Miss Addiction's gesture then focused his attention squarely towards Miss Love and his tone, though still smug, became noticeably more serious.

"What a pity. I would have thought that you most of all would have held the least expectations for our elusive Mr. Intelligence and most certainly have ascertained that he would not nor could not make an appearance, much less preside over this court with the active participation of your cohort in red. And further, her actions today have all but eliminated any hope for Mr. Intelligence to don his judiciary robes."

Miss Love, after she glanced over at Miss Addiction, could only concur with a heavy sigh, that Mr. Revenge had a good point. Though full of good intentions, Miss Addiction had to a large degree thrown any chance of a competent judge to keep the day's hearing in order and from being thrown under the proverbial bus. But all was not lost.

She held a glimmer of hope in her eyes and a sparkle of confidence in her voice when she responded to Mr. Revenge, "Well, we do still have an adequate hearing panel seated. What do you say? Let's give it a try. Normal emotional procedures will be applied and therefore you will present your case first since I am basically attempting to derail yours and the state's intentions of justice, murder, revenge or whatever you care to call this decrepit, shit for brains scheme that you've been nurturing."

"Oh do we dare?" Mr. Revenge returned in a mock attempt to persuade Miss Love to continue.

"We dare" Miss Addiction slurred as she tried to focus her attention onto one of the three Marvel Heroes she was perceiving but could not nail down as the preeminent.

"What say one? What say we all?" Mr. Revenge baited.

"It's a go" simply stated Miss Love.

"I'm in" Miss Addiction voiced as she struggled to hold up her right hand to express her game acceptance.

"Well then it's a go" Mr. Revenge conceded with an exaggerated gesture as he brought his hands poised as quotation marks parallel to his face as he mimicked Miss Love's previous verbiage of the word go.

Miss Love wondered if she was doing the right thing as she observed Mr. Revenge politely bowing and further mocking her as he stepped back from the table as if Miss Love were the Queen of

England and he dared not offend her by showing her grace his back. He was strong and she would need all the help that she could get to battle the sequined fiend. She couldn't help but take another look at Miss Addiction and the drooling mess that she made at the table.

This made her think to herself, "You know, Mr. Revenge brought out a really good point about histrionics. Let's face it, I'm sweating like a whore in church and Miss Addiction, bare-breasted and as fucked up as is, does give the appearance that she is screaming for liberation. And after all, liberation is what my case is all about. Any way you look at, good theatre is good theatre. And besides the fact that I've got to get this courtroom's attention someway or I sure this little fiend is going to wind all up in Florida State Prison. Not to mention, I'm hot as hell."

With the thought no sooner expressed, Miss Love stood up and pulled up her skirt and without any ceremony or attempt to put on a strip show, she pulled off her panties and threw them forward towards the direction of the vacant Judicial Bench. Voices gasped, some muffled, others more like a restrained scream, emerged throughout the courtroom. With the ironic righteousness of a nineteen sixties bra-burner, Miss Love straightened her skirt and looked out upon the aghast courtroom with satisfaction as she was pleased to see that she actually had the room's attention. She took another glance down at Miss Addiction, who had straightened up and looked around the courtroom as she attempted, unsuccessfully, to ascertain what had caused all the commotion.

Mr. Revenge had been right. Miss Addiction resembled the fabled if not debilitated version of the Liberty Mistress of France, Marianne. And despite the attachment that she felt towards the sweater given to her years ago from the now deceased law student, Miss Love felt compelled to follow Miss Addiction's suit. Miss Love now very much held every inhabitant of the emotional courtroom's undivided attention as she dramatically hurled the sweater she had quickly taken off towards the panties. There she stood, with nothing on but her lightly starched gray wool skirt, matching knee-high embroidered socks, black earth shoes that not even a nun would wear, and a white bra. Despite the fact that all of these emotions or traits and instincts stemmed from the psyche of Mason/Andy Caldwell, a homosexual male, Miss Love held every inch of faith in her intention of keeping their focus on her as Mr. Revenge rapidly prepared himself for his opening remarks.

And Mr. Revenge was certainly not blind to the antics of Miss Love. As he simultaneously gave one last glance to the written outline of his case and took stock of the atmosphere of the courtroom, he wondered what he would do to grab the attention of the courtroom for his opening remarks. There was absolutely no way the he was going to undress in any manner. And under no circumstances would he remove his mask.

"That's it", Mr. Revenge thought to himself, "My mask! Not only will I keep on all aspects of my attire but to state my case that 'JUSTICE' is blind, I shall make my opening remarks blindfolded."

Confident that he would be successful in countering Miss Love's theatrics, Mr. Revenge searched the courtroom for a friendly emotion who would accommodate him by lending him a necktie to use as a blindfold. But no sooner had he turned to scout the room for a formally dressed friendly face, was Mr. Revenge's seeking gaze met by wide open eyes and a combined torrent of screams and ughs. At first he wondered if he had split his seams and perhaps one of his minute testicles had slipped out of the one-piece suit. But his heart of hearts, informed by the direction of gazes and pointing fingers from the courtroom in the direction towards his right, told him that he was not the cause of the commotion. As his reptilian eyes turned to focus on the cause of the disruption, their focus brought to mind one of the most disgusting scenes that he could recall in the time of his existence. Instinctively, he brought up his right arm to shield his eyes from the image of Miss Love facing the courtroom as she boldly held her bra while her sagging tits glistened from the perspiration that accumulated into large drops around her recessed and goosebumped dark copper colored nipples. But his arm was a fraction of a second late and failed to protect his eyes from the obscenity that had been blazed upon his psyche like a permanent brand seared upon an unwilling calf. For a moment, he thought he even smelled burning hair.

And Miss Addiction, once again brought out of her semi k-hole by the courtroom din, fared much worse than Mr. Revenge. With one tit still hanging free from her dress, she sat up straight and followed the pointing fingers to the cause of the calamity and when she looked up and to her left and perceived the same sight that had recently singed the eyes of Mr. Revenge, Miss Addiction's reaction was simply to throw up. Luckily for the entire courtroom, Miss Addiction seldom if ever ate any solids so that her vomit was little more than a stream of foam. As she gained some composure from the initial hurl, Miss Addiction looked apologetically towards the seated jury panel and attempted to verbally explain the reason for her rare stomach sickness. But she was dry heaving so hard that she couldn't communicate verbally. She pointed towards Miss Love and so as not to be forced to look at the hag, Miss Addiction mocking jabbed one finger down her own throat. Some of the less compassionate members in the jury box thought this outrageously funny. The entire courtroom was now nothing less than a complete melee.

And during this entire course of events, Miss Love had managed with austere dignity to throw her bra close to the panties and sweater. Satisfied that her actions would certainly interrupt the opening statements of Mr. Revenge, Miss Love calmly walked over to her chair and as she took her seat, she leaned over and grabbed Miss Addiction's hair and brought the reluctant clod closer to her so that she could whisper over the vaguely subsiding noise, "Grab hold of yourself and let's try as we can to play the innocent but just, bare breasted victims of this creep. Can you do that?"

Miss Addiction, with a survivor's instinct of will, managed to avoid looking at Miss Love by staring straightforward. She replied through a slight gasp of air, "Sugar that should be easy. Just let go my hair."

In the meantime, Mr. Revenge had spotted the illusive Mr. Dignity who was sporting a stylish navy blue with small white dots, Brook's Brother's tie. Not only did he find that his being blindfolded might help in portraying his metaphor of justice being blind but Mr. Revenge also believed that this gesture would also be practical to aid in his defense against actually having to look at Miss Love. He had to hand it to the resilient cunt that her antics had certainly put a damper on his strategy. And as Mr. Revenge hurriedly bartered for the tie with Mr. Dignity, who in his affronted history had always sided with Mr. Revenge, Mr. Revenge noticed a subtle but sure change as it slowly became apparent in the lighting of the courtroom.

And in the emotional realm, no matter the event, lighting was king; master of all moods and could only be adjusted by the master psyche of Andy himself. And Mr. Revenge knew this cast of light, which in the physical world compared to the eerie yellowish-brown and dark moss-green that creeps upon unsuspecting North American communities prior to the arrival of many daytime funnel clouds. In fact, he stopped talking about the tie in mid-sentence with Mr. Dignity and excused himself back to his table knowing full well that he would no longer need any assistance from him or any prop in swaying the panel and entire courtroom in his direction toward the murder he had initiated. Like an unruly elementary classroom left unattended for one reason or another, when the teacher suddenly reappears, the courtroom also recognized the change in lighting and gradually subsided into an eerie calm. Even the numbed Miss Addiction with all of her comforting chemical camaraderie reached out and grasped the unsuspecting hand of Miss Love who in turn accepted the gesture by scooting her chair closer to Miss Addiction.

The courtroom was now filled with the dark-green and yellowish brown chalky dry mist. An occasional and subtle spark of light revealed a few formless shades of black that could be seen as they came in and out of focus by many of the shivering emotions and character traits that had now regretfully attended the day's hearing. And suddenly, the distant sparks became more like exploding utility transformers that produced a low reverberation that became a voice that declared through the now resolutely sickening yellowish brown and moss green light of the courtroom, "SILENCE!"

No trait or emotion present, least of all Mr. Revenge or Miss Love, had the nerve to ask the voice to identify itself. It was obviously apparent. It was Fear, God-like and unflinching in his intention to sit on the bench for this most important hearing. With lighting flashing and thunder rolling, 'IT' evolved. It was neither a he nor a she. Slowly, it took on a deep blue and black misty form, if form is what one could call it. Somehow, it seemed held together by fading shades of purple that seemed in a constant battle to hold the apparition together as it took its place on the judge's bench and announced with an omnipotent voice, "This hearing is called to order. And I will give no warnings in maintaining order. Mr. Revenge will now state his case."

"Very well, yes. Very well indeed" said Mr. Revenge as he cleared his throat in a nervous fashion and immediately stood up to proceed from his table and stand directly in front of the jury pit.

"Emotions, various Traits of our distinguished panel, Your Honor" Mr. Revenge said as he made a blatant turn to face the bench and bowed gratefully and respectfully in the fashion of Victorian gentry before turning to the oppositions table to continue. "Miss Love, Miss Addiction," he curtly acknowledged and then gave his full attention to the emotional panel. "We are here today because I want to sue for the complete and total dominance of the mind of Mason Harrison Caldwell III. I'm sure, as we are all aware, that within a matter of days, our deepest fears and concerns will be medically verified. A verification that will indeed state without reserve, doubt, and or hope that our mortal existence, which is in fact all that we emotions possess, will be coming to an abrupt end."

Mr. Revenge took a moment to pause and to let this last statement resonate then continued, "I, and only I, a one Mr. S.C.(Served Cold) Revenge will ease the pain of these last days, and give meaning to our lives and to its demise. With your support, I will deliver a final victory to Mason, AKA, Andy, and will insure the suffering of the man that must and will have justice served to him. Rick Gurnee will know not guess or estimate how we feel. On this day, I plead for you all to come into unison with me and announce, that what say we one, what say we all is that WE want REVENGE. Thank you" he ended politely and turned to bow respectfully to the bench and again backed away without showing his back to His or Her Honor.

There was only the sound of Mr. Revenge's footsteps to break the silence, brought about by the terror of upsetting His or Her Honor's decree for maintenance of order. And as well, it was obvious from the looks on the faces of the members of the panel and throughout the courtroom, that Mr. Revenge had indeed made impressions.

But Miss Love was sure that she could at least equal that little fiend's soliloquy, if that's what it could be called. After all, even Mr. Revenge had not begrudged Miss Love her talents at songs and prose. However, Miss Love's main concern was aimed at His or Her Honor. Somehow, its very presence was draining her. As she stood up to address the panel, she noticed that even her tits, which had shrunk, now sagged more. Mr. Revenge noticed her observation and gave a quick snicker under his breath. Miss Love now wondered if her tit theatrics had been such a good idea after all, but nevertheless, she began her opening remarks.

"Fellow emotions, longstanding friends, family and yes," she paused as she looked down at the seated Miss Addiction before proceeding, "and adversaries. I come to you today in desperation to plea that we all grab hold of reality."

"Objection Your Honor" Mr. Revenge bellowed.

"State your objection Mr. Revenge" rumbled the bench.

"Your Honor, Miss Love would make a mockery of your court. This is an emotional hearing. We are not here to establish reality within the physical world. That is not our aim. We are here to establish how we feel. In our emotional spectrum, there is not even room for the word reality, for we are confined to feelings. Since reality in the physical world has no concern for us, why should we even speak its name, in Your Honor's court much less, as Miss Love would have us, embrace it."

"Objection sustained," grumbled His or Her Honor. Then the bench added in a menacing tone, "Miss Love will remember the purpose of this hearing. Any reference to reality, whatever that might be, will not be tolerated. Do you understand?"

"But your honor, I fail ..."

But before she could even sustain her thought, or much less, continue her sentence, a lightning bolt shot from the bench and crashed directly at Miss Love's feet. As the ground around her exploded with ear shattering resound, Miss Love was hurled, her tits slapping her in the face, eight to ten feet up in the air. As she climaxed to the peak of her ascent, Miss Love involuntarily did a collegiate cheerleader style split giving the entire courtroom a shocking glimpse of her holy of holies. And as she crashed down with a hard landing on her ass, her legs were forced spread eagle which in turn hoisted her skirt over her soup bone knees giving the seated jurors a prolonged exposure to her withered cunt.

With her hair frayed from the recent voltage and her complexion rouged in similar fashion of a person exiting a sauna, Miss Love slowly came to from her initial daze and slowly got up off of the courtroom floor. As she walked back to her table, she weakly coughed and courageously began again.

"My um, what is the word I'm looking for?" Miss Love fumbled, her fragile mind obviously suffering from the electric admonishment His or Her Honor, Fear, had just recently administered.

"My apologies. Yes, yes that is it. My sincere apologies to His or Her Honor and the ladies and gentleman of the court. I certainly meant no disrespect. My intentions here are simply to express to all of you in these most trying of times, as best I can make of it, the truth."

"Your Honor, this is outrageous! I must object again!" Mr. Revenge exclaimed as he stood up and clamored on, "Once again, Miss Love is forgetting the very nature of our realm and who we are. We are feelings, emotion, traits, and instincts and this hearing is simply to determine the dominant sway of such and the actions that will manifest from our feelings. This had nothing to do with truth Your Honor."

"But I am the truth" screamed Miss Love as she stood up and stepped in front of her table and continued just shy of having a conniption fit, "Just listen to the God damned songs!"

Miss Love had just finished her exclamation with a final maniacal jerk when no sooner was she once again airborne. The blast emitted this time from His or Her Honor was so terrific that Miss Love had actually been knocked out of her hideous shoes. And almost comically as the tips of her fingers touched the tips of her toes which led her legs in midair splits, her face a combination of agony and surprise, Miss Love was treated to the thrill of flight that so many of her own victims had sworn to experience. Simultaneously, the courtroom was instantly filled with the camera like flash that placed Miss Love's ascent into an almost delayed but choreographed theatrical stunt. If she or anyone else in the courtroom screamed, no one heard it as there was absolutely no sound but the thunderous bang that can only be recognized as a direct lightning bolt strike. Oddly enough, it combined, with a crack in the air, made a sound similar to that released by a jet plane as it passes the sound barrier.

And once again, so as if anyone was to have missed the bird's eye view offered by Miss Love's proceeding aerials, His or Her Honor sent Miss Love ascending so high that none of the attending emotions/ traits this time could possibly miss the sight of the decrepit hag's private parts. Depending on his or her makeup, the emotions either looked away, covered their eyes, fainted, silently screamed, threw up, or simply faded into oblivion.

His or Her Honor's thunder overbearingly resonated when, at last, Miss Love began her decent and finally made an inaudible contact with the courtroom floor. Miss Love landed next to the strike's crater. Her body just missed the seated Miss Addiction. Miss Love was flat on her back with one leg twisted outward that revealed raw bone in the most awkward of angles which left all present no doubt that it would be some time, if ever, that Miss Love would walk again. And eventually the room became audible and the thunder roll slowly began to be replaced by the combined clatter of comprehensive 'aghs', 'ooO's', 'oh's' and the like so familiar within the emotional vocabulary.

Despite her failing gut, Miss Addiction was no quitter; in a para-doxical sense of course. With brave resonance, after throwing up on Miss Love from looking at her bone and flesh, Miss Addiction looked at Miss Love as she involuntarily convulsed and mumbled sounds that made no sense. Miss Addiction decided to carry on the case her-self. She straightened up her dress, daintily stepped over Miss Love, and surprisingly enough, side stepped the crater caused from His or Her Honor's bolts.

"Okay!" Miss Addiction said curtly then blew a stray strand of per-oxide-blonde hair out of her eyes as attempted to gather herself. She reached out her splayed hands on either side of herself searching for some sort of beam on which to balance herself but found only thin air. After catching her balance, she continued, "Wait a minute, wait a minute, just one second please. Okay then. Now" she said.

She calmly walked over to Mr. Revenge's table and reached deep into her hair, as if she had an itch, but produced another dime bag of trail mix from which she unabashedly made a line on the desk and with a straw she bent over and inhaled the entire amount. Mr. Revenge had a sly grin on his face and said nothing but looked up to see if there was any response from His or Her Honor, Fear, but there was none from the bench. Miss Addiction then again glanced towards Miss Love who, with her vomit soaked hair and unusable leg was now doing her best impersonation of a shell-shocked marine landing on Normandy. The poor dear crawled aimlessly using only her arms to pull her about. Miss Love attempted to speak but only produced small spittle bubbles that came from her mouth as she senselessly babbled.

"Shhh, now darling, just hush. I got this baby," Miss Addiction reas-sured Miss Love.

But Miss Love, never surrendering, continued to crawl and pull herself towards Miss Addiction. Unfortunately, Miss Love did not miss the crater and rolled down to the bottom where she mercifully hit her head and was completely knocked unconscious.

"Oh shit!" Miss Addiction exclaimed then repeated aloud, "Oh shit, shit, shit, shit. On second thought, um, Your Honor, maybe I just ought to ask for a recess."

Mr. Revenge thought quickly on this and assumed that a recess would do nothing to hurt his chances for victory, as it would give him a chance to woo Miss Addiction back to his side and thus with the assurance of His or Her Honor's precedence certain to resume court, he would be sure to proclaim, "check and mate."

"Second the appeal to His or Her Honor for recess" Mr. Revenge calmly proclaimed.

His or Her Honor was silent for a moment as the vague shape of His/Her existence appeared to be taking stock of His/Her handy-work which had indeed left the front of the courtroom looking like a World War I rendition of 'no man's land'. Then His or Her Honor announced with firm resonance, "This session is now recessed until tomorrow, one P.M. at which time I shall expect this nerve-room to be restored to proper appearances. And I must remind the jury panel that I do expect them to return, as there will be dire consequences for any participants within the jury that fail to return. I expect this matter to be resolved by the end of our next session. Adjourned!" His or Her Honor finally thundered and as he exited the room, his shadow of color gradually left with him and some lighting of normalcy gradually came back to the courtroom.

Mr. Revenge stacked his papers neatly and calmly put them in his legal case just in time to open the swing gate that partitioned the main seating area from the direct court for Miss Addiction.

"So sweet of you sir." She said to him as sarcastically as she could then shot him the rod. Mr. Revenge only returned a partial smile, as he was so very tired of the overused pun.

Everyone left the courtroom with no concern for the incapacitated, desecrated, and nearly naked old bag that was still unconscious at the bottom of one of the craters that was supposed to be repaired by an emotional repair crew as instructed by His/Her Honor for the morrow's reconvened hearing. Only time would tell if anyone would even take the courtesy to remove Miss Love or simply bury her there. Although the lighting had improved with the absence of His or Her Honor from the courtroom, this was in fact a very dark time for Miss Love.

CHAPTER 35

Fort Lauderdale, May 1992

MAKE NO MISTAKE, AFTER I LEFT THE KIOSK AND WAS WALKING HOME, I was thrilled with the news Madame Dieux Dieux had given me concerning the arrival of the poison that would bring my little endeavor to fruition. But my attitude towards Rick, and life itself, was only getting worse. This evening would be the first in the coming fourteen evenings before the HIV test results would be available. They were excruciating, not only for me, but for Rick as well. I was determined to add, as much as I could, to his genuine anxiety about my well-being. We both basically knew what the coming medical paper verdict would read. It would announce clearly and summarily: GUILTY. I was guilty for being stupid and Rick for inconsiderate homicide. At least that's what I thought because I can say that, truthfully, all I knew is what was coming out of my mind. And since the truth is what I'm after here, I have to admit that there was still a glimmer of hope that the result would come back negative.

"Positive" or "Reactive," "Negative" or "Non-Reactive," I knew some of the lingo from the several previous tests that I had endured. And if I had "Seroconverted," would I still want to kill Rick? My answer was yes, but if I was negative, would I? That was a question I could not answer.

But did I still love him? Yes, I did, as much as I can possibly fathom the word, love. Because I can honestly say these types of questions that wandered the darkened halls of my mind did not lend a hand towards romance, which I can comprehend. It is nothing remotely similar to what I would assume to be true love. And, during this time Rick had actually attempted to be romantic. He had plenty of water based lube and rubbers out when I got home one night but I just laughed at him. Boy, that really pissed him off!

It was also during this time that Rick was proclaiming some sort of solutions to our situation. We should quit drinking and drugging, or get into a gym, and just start living a healthy lifestyle. I've already mentioned in the beginning of this confession (story, exercise, journaling, or whatever the fuck I call this little quest), I was having none of his suggestions. As I also previously mentioned, Rick was reacting to my bullshit with some pretty harsh verbal postures that tended to strengthen his belief that he was superior in breeding, intellect, and social status to me. He was constantly reminding me that it was in fact, his principal qualities, which allowed me to be "kept" in his house. I don't think I can blame him, as I would probably react the same way, but I knew that he wasn't going to throw me out. But I was wearing on him.

A couple of days before Madame Dieux Dieux was to pick up the powder, Rick and I were really in each other's faces. I was about to go out to work and as I was walking out the door, he yelled, "Go on then, go sell. Sell those fucking cheesy little paintings, because God only knows, Andy, you've got no talent. You could never paint one."

That hurt, because it was the truth. Just like it did when my dad told me that he wished that I would be able to do something with myself that would help other people. I was a salesman all right—good at selling my ass. That's all I was.

So I pointed out to Rick that he was a salesman too, to which he countered, "I'm a business man, Andy. There is a difference."

"Whatever Rick, but if I could paint, my masterpiece would be an impressionist of you. That's right, and the primary scope would be just a small, teensy dick. And that's what I would title the canvass, Dick Rick."

"Oh fuck off, Andy," Rick said, then quickly put in, "If you could paint, you'd probably paint something that stupid. I swear, your ignorance is beyond excruciating. I think I'd rather have pins and needles pricking my balls than spend more time in your company with the frame of mind you've been in the last couple of weeks."

"I warned you, Rick," I managed to calmly advise him, then added quickly before I slammed the door closed, "Remember that, dude, if you truly believe that I'm ignorant?"

It had only been a few weeks earlier that some tourist shopping on my shift was talking so intensely to her friend about how close to death she had come while on a charter fishing trip—she was almost stung by a scorpionfish she had reeled in on her fishing rod and the crew of the boat had acted like the fish was Ebola. So it wasn't much of a stretch of the imagination for me to walk to Madame Dieux Dieux's kiosk and let her know that I needed another twenty minutes and would be right back.

"Not a thing, Sally," she said with a smile.

I guess she could tell I had drama on my mind and she was right. I simply walked on down A1A to the charter fishing boats and put the word out to five captains that I would pay one hundred dollars for a live scorpionfish. After work around six P.M. I had my pick of three from the first boat in. I chose the smaller one, thinking that it would be easier to keep it alive as it would use less oxygen than a larger one. I was right. The captain was nice enough to give me a little disposable Styrofoam ice chest to bring it home alive. The little bundle of "pins and needles" held on right until the end of its performance. Bless its heart.

I woke up the next morning, a Monday, in the guest bedroom. I didn't want to sleep with Rick or give him the satisfaction of telling me to sleep on the couch. (He had done that a couple of nights before when I had refused the gym membership while pouring a healthy jigger of Dewar's White Label on the rocks, explaining that I would "play with my demons.") That morning was the beginning of my extended stay in the guest bedroom. And to be certain, Selectric, Rick was furious after the scorpionfish I put in his bath. I will not bore you with the details since I began this whole account of my murderous plot with my third and feeble attempt to kill the prick at the beginning of our relationship. No, Selectric, he was not too happy with me, but at the same time, I was relatively sure that he didn't really have any clue that I was actually planning him bodily harm.

And those were just some of the thoughts that were dangling in my mind as I walked to Madame Dieux Dieux's kiosk that gorgeous early May morning. I was also thinking to myself about how much my life had changed since last year. I had still been hustling in the French Quarter, probably HIV negative, and for the most part, basically having a pretty good time with things. My mind began swimming when I took into account that it was only six months ago that I boarded the Value Jet with my trick, and had arrived in this fair city. Now, I was about to commit another murder and kill another loved one. I was going to kill a guy that I was in love with because he gave me HIV. Or did he? The test results were not in yet. But again, the voices in my head reminded me that this was not the point.

"I'm glad I finished pissing or you would have made me miss the pot," Rick had said.

That was the point. That my life had meant no more to him, my being a street hustler or not, than a drop of piss on that golden abortion of a bathroom's floor. At least that's what he'd said. And I had deduced within a few seconds of his pompous triviality, that the value of my life to him was that he was in love with me, at least as far as he could fathom the word love. Or was it as far as I could fathom the word? The word? That word?

"What is a word anyway?" I remember thinking to myself.

I guess it was at that time and place, while I was looking down at my feet in their flip-flops walking to work on the sidewalk of Sunrise Boulevard, toward my assumed momentous pick up of poisonous powder, that I got the idea to write all of this down. I would try with words to make some sense of everything. I remembered the colorful fans with their Bible story pictures stapled on the inside walls of Ella's outhouse. Somehow, my little three-year-old mind was able to apply words to those images that had made my soul soar. And now my 22-year-old mind was searching for the meaning of "The Word." I remember that I thought to myself, "In the beginning was the word."

As my feet carried me further along the sidewalk that Monday morning, I had a really good presumption of what that word would be. It would be the word, "LOVE." "But is it a verb or a noun?" I wondered.

"It simply is," I heard a voice in my head say.

My mind was racing with all of this past year's events unfolding like frames of a motion picture on the passing sections of concrete sidewalk that my eyes were cast down upon. In a flash, I knew that I had to explore this word. Yes, we would hold a recess. That's what we would do. Then we would write down everything that had happened in the last few months or so.

That would allow me to look at myself, but not ass backwards as from the perspective of a mirror image. In a written retrospect, I would confess to myself the reason and justification for my very existence. And, I would have the final word.

"You can't argue with a letter," I thought to myself and then self-proclaimed, "That's it! I'll write down the chain of events in a totally honest and shameless style, so the reality of this shit can be seen through my own eyes."

At that moment, I think that the irony of taking a recess from actually implementing my plans for murder, in order to explore the meaning of "The Word" completely escaped any frame of logic that I may have still possessed. I was in a dazzle of giddiness by the time I approached Madame Dieux Dieux who had the kiosk and the day's paintings already set up. From the way she said hello that morning, she must have noticed my disposition.

"My little Sally is happy today, yes? Today she happy and smiling," Madame Dieux Dieux inquired and stated at the same time as she did a little shuffle like a Haitian Fred Astaire in a complete circle all the way around me.

I said nothing but went over to her cooler and took out a Diet coke, popped it open, and sat down on her personal stool. She looked at me like I had turned purple and said with a hint of consternation, "The boy just come in here and plop his ass down on my stool, do he?"

I started to get up but she gently placed a hand on my shoulder to signal me to remain, and affirmed her gesture.

"No, you got da right idea. You sit. I need to sit you down and talk to you."

She looked around as if to make sure we were completely alone and went on, "It here, Mason."

I'm sure my eyes opened wide and my previous grin straightened out.

"What? I thought my Sally would smile bigger when he hear this. It what you want, yes?" she questioned with a puzzled but amused face.

"Yes, absolutely," I assured her.

"Okay then, but you listen to me, and you listen good," she said and she looked around to ensure our privacy before she continued, her Creole accent stronger than ever, "Mason, I ain't no momma mafia, but if you get caught with dis shit, you don't know where you get it from, you hear! I tell you dis for yo own good. You just need to know dis; what dey do to me not gone to be pretty if da police find out it from me. But what dey gone do to you!"

She had enunciated "you" and abruptly ended her sentence with several negative shakes of her head with her eyes closed, as if the thought were too terrible to speak. Then she went on, "Mason dis is serious. But I know you are too. Dats why I get it for you. You very special to me, Mason. I dreamed of you before you here. Yes!" she exclaimed as I was about to interrupt her with an obvious question of her dream to which she proceeded to anticipate and answer, "I tell you a secret. Dat painting I give to you on the day we met, I painted it. I sign it Madeline Le Fleur, but she is me. Kinda like you are Andy. Your street name, my art name."

Again, I started to say something, but Madame Dieux Dieux was having none of it as she put her finger to my lips and another to her own lips then continued in a hushed but dramatic tone, "Shh, just listen to me. If you get caught boy, my point is there ain't no bar code on this little bag I give you, but my friends dat gave it to me, dey gone know. Like I know you was coming from my dream, dey gone know if you get caught. You don't get caught boy! And you don't let this stuff touch you. You wear rubber gloves when you handle it. It only take a tiniest small crystal or two on his jewelry a day and in two months, his lungs gone give out and he gone die."

"Two months?" I questioned.

"Dat if you do it every day" she said then quickly added, "I axed bout da earring and dey say that is almost perfect. Da needle is perfect but might work too fast. But dis earring would work. But don't let him eat or drink dis shit. Much too obvious!"

"Who is they?" I asked in a frustrated whisper, fearing that 'they' might have too much information with regards to my plot and my name.

"They?" she repeated mocking my pronunciation then she went on to explain, "Der is no Dey. It mean like when I talk about myself and say you when I mean me," and she let her hands waive in the air and further explained, "It the invisible dey. When there is no dey, it just what da people say."

I think I got her gist and said, "I hope so."

She responded strongly, "If you talk, though, der will be a dey. Dey be on me like white on rice. Dey kill me Mason. It not gone be pretty. You get my point?"

I shook my head in sincere affirmation and quietly said, "Yes," then attempted to confirm, "I get your point" and quickly added, "Two months, right?"

"Right at about," she said.

"What if I start and stop?" I questioned Madame Dieux Dieux.

"You can stop after about a month and he might make it but after dat, dis stuff gone kill the lungs. Like pneumonia, but it not. And if he HIV, like you say he is, den it may only take a couple of doses, but it depend if he already sick. But it gonna do the trick Mason. And don't you get dis shit on you. I mean it boy. Dis shit the real deal. It deadly as a snake."

As she said this, she was looking me straight in the eyes. There was no doubt she was sincere and that she considered herself a friend to me, but I asked anyway, "Why are you taking this big risk to help me do this?"

"I'm your friend, Mason. I know you long before dis world. We meet again and again."

And again I could see she believed this. And for a moment I thought I did too. But it was a fleeting glimpse at the possibilities offered by the Cosmos, one that I sustained only for a second.

Madame Dieux Dieux turned around and walked a couple of short steps and reached into a pencil box and took out a small brown leather pouch that looked similar to a bank bag. She undid the drawstrings and inside the bag was a small black glass bottle that she took out to show me, then quickly put in back in the little leather bag. Then, as if she were a lover giving a gift, she took my hand and placed the bag in my palm, and brought my fingers to a close around the little deadly token of love.

A deadly token of love? Dramatic to say the least. But was it a perfect paradox as I now had the means to accomplish my will and at the same time explore the "word?" Certainly mine was not the only murder plotted in the name of love. Madame Dieux Dieux never spoke to me again of her gift. And I didn't share with her my desire to recess until the results of my HIV test were in. And from what she had said, I knew that I would have to be as careful with the handling of the written account of my quest as I would have to be with the poison inside that bag. But I also knew that I was glad that both options would be in my hands. And so I found myself in a contradiction of terms, as it seems I always had. Is the truth always a paradox? I was going to take a look at that question.

CHAPTER 36

Fort Lauderdale, May 1992

WHEN RICK GOT HOME THAT MONDAY NIGHT AND WAS CHANGING out of his suit, I let him know that I was moving into the guest bedroom. Rick didn't mind. He just said, "Andy, do what you gotta do. Frankly, I'd probably sleep better knowing that whoever you are these last few days isn't sharing their nights next to me in the same bed."

His saying this made me nervous. For the first time since the scorpion fish, was he suspicious that I really had it out for him? So I asked him in a chiding manner, "What, you afraid I'll do something to you in your sleep. Maybe put a snake in bed with you?"

To which he replied, "No Andy, I'm not afraid of what you'll do to me, I'm afraid of what you're doing to yourself. To be honest, I wouldn't put it past you, putting a snake in the same bed you yourself are sleeping in. Probably some fucked up notion you have where you see yourself as Cleopatra or some other grandiose bitch that goes out in the dramatic fashion from the bite of an asp on her tit. God only knows you started to tell me something about an Aunt Rheda back in Hooterville or wherever the fuck you're from, getting bit on the twat. Probably all ties in together to some fucked up fantasy you have about killing yourself."

"Rick, are you calling me a suicidal redneck queen?"

"All I'm saying is I don't know who or what you are lately. I have no idea who I'm living with?" He took a deep breath and sat down on the bed, bent over, and brought his hands to his face, then straightened up and took off his tie. Then he motioned for me come sit next to him. When I had, he looked me square in the eyes and said, "I told you, and I intend on keeping my word, that I would do what I could to help you through this. You get your test back in a couple of weeks. I say this not to alarm you, but I'm expecting that you and I are in the same boat. Both of us HIV positive, Andy."

I looked away from him, looking down, but he very gently took my chin in his direction and continued, "Andy, I've been this way for at least six years now, and I'm fine. And it may or may not be that way for you.

I don't know, but neither do you. But I do know that I'll be here for you and will do what I can to help you. Honestly, it may be best for you to stay in the guest room until you grab hold of yourself, which is something you are going to have to do on your own. I can't do it for you."

Right then is when I asked him if he had a typewriter I could use and I said, "I learned from some guys in jail that journaling was good therapy."

"You were in jail?" he said sarcastically then continued as he pointed towards his computer, "Sure, help yourself to anything. Really, use my computer if you want."

"Wouldn't even know how to turn the thing on, but I could always type well and I saw that old Selectric in the closet," I said.

I paused to contort my face and in my best, (but bad) imitation of a mentally challenged person, I tried to say with a speech impediment, "Many, many research papers, history, and English research papers."

"Oh no!" Rick stood up off the bed and backed away from me in a playful, defensive posture and continued, "At the risk of another scorpionfish, you're not drawing me in on this. I believe you. If you say you can type, you can type. No way in hell you're pulling me into this little drama again. As a matter of fact I bet you're a Goddamned Hemingway."

I laughed at this and he came and sat down next to me again and he said, "I don't think you can begin to imagine how happy I am to hear you laughing again. But by the way, what would you have done if I hadn't seen that little fuck swimming around?"

"Taken you to the hospital," I replied, matter of fact.

"Really," he said with a single lifted eyebrow. He started to say something but just stood up and walked into his closet and I heard him laughing as he continued to undress. Then he said to me, "You did warn me."

Just a little joke. One day after my third attempt to kill him, he still didn't have a clue. He didn't even suspect the first two attempts. But like I said, I was going to recess this plot until I saw the damned thing in print and until I was sure I was sick. Now that Madame Dieux Dieux had given me the powder, I had an instrument at my disposal three times the power of a gun. And like a gun, this written account would have to be kept in a secure spot, away from prying eyes. Back in New Orleans, I kept a gun, but no one knew it. (There are some dumb motherfuckers that go around blabbing to all the world that they are packing; they're more stupid than people living on street level without a gun.) Anyway, before I go off on another tirade, I had always kept my drugs and gun hidden in the kitchen. I figured that the kitchen would be the safest place here as well. Rick seldom, if ever cooked and I guessed correctly that there was an extended space behind the cutlery drawers above the pots and pans in the kitchen island that separated the living room from the kitchen. It was the perfect spot to keep a large folder.

So that night, with a hiding spot in mind and a typewriter and paper, all supplied by Rick to boot, I went to town on the old IBM Selectric Three. There I was, alone with my thoughts, and they were not pretty. I remember that I considered overdosing, but that would defeat the purpose of all that I had worked for and was now working on despite the lack of clarity and contradictions to which I had exposed myself. So I began to write, and in no time the rhythm of the old Selectric was beating me into a trance and the thoughts, as crazy and fucked up as they were, began to show up in print. I found that my timing was about two to three hours, then a break, and I was good for another hour or two at most before I went dead. No gesture intended there, but that is as close as I can describe what it was and is like getting this stuff out of me. I couldn't have been more exhausted if I had just finished a really hard work out with weights; and, I couldn't have been more relaxed by endorphins at the same time. All of this, however, was because I was being honest with myself. I couldn't work when I tried to fake it.

And the next morning when I went to work, Madame Dieux Dieux must have noticed something and told me to take a break and go back home. She said "My Sally" looked like a movie star that can't make herself cry, but wanted to.

"You just not here today, Mason. You go back and get things together. Come to think of it, take a week off. Stay home, rest."

She was sincere and I knew she was right. Madame Dieux Dieux was on a psychic balance beam of some type. I swear, I think the woman could read my mind.

And I did what she said, for the most part, but I didn't rest. I went straight back to the Selectric and found myself back in a trance till the early evening. I guess I had put the cover on the typewriter around seven P.M. and went to bed without eating or seeing Rick or anything. But I am certain that I remember being awakened by a voice that was similar to the sound dub that Scarlet O'Hara was subjected to at the close of Gone With The Wind. But instead of the big screen booming "Tara, Tara, Tara!" I heard, "Positive, Positive, Positive."

But that singular word was cannonading in a volume ten times that of a movie theatre stereo and the thundering voice caused me to bolt straight up in bed. I looked at the clock on the bed table and saw in the fluorescent red numbers that it was only 1:45 A.M. and also quickly noticed that my sheets were soaked.

"Fuck, did I piss in the bed?" I thought to myself with my panic still growing from the abrupt awakening.

I pulled the soaked sheets off and got out of bed and went and turned on the light by the bedroom door. No, I had not pissed myself. But that didn't excuse the fact that when I went to examine my bed, I could make out the image of my body from the pillow down to the sheet creases caused by my ass. The moisture from my sweat had left a virtual abstract of my body and I laughed at myself when I caught myself thinking, "The Shroud of Fort Lauderdale."

I shook my head at the megalomania that consumed my mind; I'm sure that I smiled when I tried to gauge how many other positive queens had ever compared their HIV sweat soaked sheets to a supposedly holy image of Jesus Christ. But, there was no doubt about, I had the fabled "night sweats."

It was a realization that struck me wide awake, and since I figured that I wouldn't be able to go back to sleep, much less in wet sheets, why waste good time. I sat down at the Selectric, took off the cover, turned on the switch and for a good five or ten minutes sat there in a silent stupor listening to the hum of the relic. I didn't type a word and no thought, or even a willingness for insight into my quest for the truth, of my current status in life, would even spark. My mind was acting like an impotent 90-year-old dick. So I exercised one of my more perfected talents that I had acquired since adolescence and said aloud, "Fuck it."

As I covered the silent typewriter, I couldn't help but look over at the bed and my thoughts returned to the waste of time it would be to attempt to crawl into the dampened sheets and join the shroud.

"What if there really was a Jesus and a judgment day and I stood in front of him and he asked me, 'Mason, what did you do with your life?'" I thought to myself.

"Oh J.C., I don't know. I guess I just basically said, 'Fuck it,'" was the reply that came to my mind and then it hit me like a tractor trailer carrying a flatbed loaded with bricks. "Dude, you are crazier than a Christmas turkey served with enchiladas."

I wanted to escape. But where in the world could I run to? There was no place in the world I could go to outrun these dialogues in my head.

"Who are these people talking?" I thought and then I was struck even harder with the jolt of, "who the fuck just asked that question in my head?"

For some reason, my mind reverted back to a saying that was repeated over and over by this guy who would come into county jail and host the Thursday night drunk school, "No matter where you go, there you are."

"Fuck this," I said aloud and walked out of the bedroom and sat down on the living room couch.

I turned on the boob tube and CNN was showing the same old depressing shit, but before I could start flipping through the channels, my hands, like the trained muscles of an accomplished pianist that doesn't even look at the keys, reached over to the coffee table and found the lighter and the largest roach that was lingering in the ashtray. In no time, I was exhaling a cloud of foggy anguish and one of the familiar voices in my head soon questioned again, "And what in the world were you so worried about, Sugar?"

Call it a fluke, but about the same time, CNN must have been running some kind of story on Winston Churchill and they posted a snapshot of him with a big ole brandy snifter approaching his lips, while that fat stogie smoked just inches away in an old warrior's stubby hands.

"Now there's a man that knew how to handle adversity," I thought to myself and my mind immediately reminded me that there was some good cognac in the bar along with a glass that looked hauntingly familiar to the one being held by the late great Prime Minister, Winston Churchill.

CNN went on to the next story and I went to the liquor cabinet by Rick's stereo. And in moments, I was back at the couch doing my best impersonation of Sir Winston and wondered what the likelyhood was of his ever smoking wacky weed. I knew there were smoking rumors that he was bisexual.

"God bless the man," I thought to myself.

Then I decided it was time to find something different to watch other than this news story about some up and coming fat little shit from Georgia with a grey Buster Brown haircut who was galvanizing the Republican Party.

I scrolled through the channel guide and on one of the pay per views, I caught the front end of Steel Magnolias. I decided that I would see what Madame Dieux Dieux was up to when she referred to me as "Sally Field," the actress who played Shelby's mother in the flick. Right away, the plot grabbed me. Whoever directed this thing was right on the money in capturing the pace of life and culture of Louisiana. So I watched the damn movie, and in the end, when Shelby's baby was coming out of the crazy aunt's house alone down the sidewalk, and M'Lynn, (played by Sally Fields) rushed and picked up that baby, I let out a sob that would have awakened the dead. The more I tried to hold the tears back, the more they flowed and eventually, although I tried, I couldn't constrain a wail that would have made a grieving Arab woman envious.

I never heard any complaints from neighbors but I at least woke up Rick as he came jogging into the living room in a state of alarm. But when he saw me, he just calmly sat down next to me on the couch and held me. And I let him, for a minute or two, then I got up and apologized, "Sorry to wake you. Really, its just they filmed this movie about an hour away from where I grew up." I hiccupped a sob then continued, "The accents and everything. Fuck Rick, I miss my momma."

I started sobbing again and Rick got up and held me again. I guess if anyone could have actually seen this scenario, they would have thought it hilarious. I was in fact hysterical, but not in the funny way—not to me anyway. There I was, a 22-year-old street hustler crying for his Momma and being held by his 42-year-old lover, whom I was planning to kill. And to add to the ridiculous scene, Rick asked me at that time, "You wanna go see her?"

I didn't answer right away and so he probably took this for a maybe and continued, "I can book you a flight and in a few hours, you'd be back in Louisiana."

"You're not getting rid of me that easy," I replied.

"No, I don't mean to rid of you, I mean for a visit. You live here now, Buddy," he said gently as he stroked my head and hair with the tips of his fingers.

"No, I don't wanna go home. Not yet," I said.

But what I really meant was that I don't want to die, not yet. But I also knew that I didn't want to see either one of my parents unless I knew for sure that I was dying. And if I knew that for sure, I would also be intent on killing Rick.

Like I wrote at the start of my truth venture, I often contradict myself and am not clear on the outcome of what I would find out during this little exploration. I have a better picture now. As I write this now, I will be picking up the results from Dr. Ball's office tomorrow. The results of that test will limit my options and help me to clear up the outcome of this little dance of discovery that I've been waltzing.

But the last two weeks, I've had the little IBM Selectric in a jig. Slammed into high gear I was putting all this down for my little hazel green, bloodshot eyes to review. But with the results, the music will stop and so will the waltz. But I return to the Selectric to bring this endeavor to an end.

I haven't seen Madame Dieux Dieux in two weeks, nor have I talked to her. But I have her gift. My darling Coral Snake has given me a foolproof option if the verdict for my own undoing, in fact, will read, "Guilty."

So fear not, Selectric, I suspect that you have a few more weeks to vie for my affections against those I target for the venom given to me by the colorful Madame Dieux Dieux.

"Are you kidding me?" one of my selves asks another, and I'm sure as hell not sure who anyone of them are, but I hear one of the most stupid and sappy songs ever to come through my mind in stereo, "Torn between two lovers, feeling like a fool …"

"For the love of God, Dude, you are out there," I say to Self A.

"No shit, and downright faggy too, Self A," Self B says to Self A.

"Oh Please!"

"Who said that?" asks Self A.

When there is no answer Self B firmly confirms, "Faggot"

"What? I didn't say it," insists Self A.

"Don't matter," says Self B, who continues, "Only fags say 'oh please.'"

"Huh?"

"Who said that?" say both Self A and Self B simultaneously.

But still, there is no answer.

"Night," says someone.

"Night," says someone back.

"For the Love of God," ends Self A.

CHAPTER 37

Fort Lauderdale, June 22, 1992

WHEN I AWOKE THIS MORNING, I WAS UNEXPECTEDLY CALM. A TYPE of peace came over me that reminded me of a rare mood I once had before the start of a junior high basketball game. My little girlfriend had just dumped me and hooked up with my best buddy, Waylon, whom I had a serious crush on, and he also played on the team. He was beautiful, and I don't mean in any slang sense. I mean literally beautiful in every way. I was devastated, but I guess my body and mind just reacted to the situation much in the same way as one is soothed by a really hot Jacuzzi. It takes a second to settle in, then once you are in the hot water for a moment, there comes a soothing relief. Anyway, I scored 24 of our 38 points that day. It was the best basketball game I ever played. Even Diana, who was not only the girl who dumped me but was also a cheerleader, came up and hugged me after the game and told me how proud of me she was. Then she left, hand in hand with Waylon.

I have no idea why I felt that way this morning. It's not like I had a game lined up. The last time I went to Dr. Ball's office, to take the damned test, I was on pins and needles. I even shaved really close this morning, like I wanted to look good for somebody. Again, don't ask me why, Selectric Anyway, I also put on my favorite tee shirt. The shirt was a dark, rich harbor blue, my favorite color, and I tucked the shirt into black Levi's 501 genes. I put on a black belt and black Kenneth Cole shoes. When I looked at myself one last time in the mirror, I told myself that I was probably seeing myself for the last time without knowing for sure whether or not I have a terminal disease. But I was okay, I was about to find out what I already knew. And I still looked good. What was the old saying? "Die young, leave a pretty corpse." And if I am going to die young with a disease that leaves anything but a pretty corpse, then I'll leave a path of wrath. Lookout folks, here's Hurricane Mason. Maybe that would be my ballgame?

When Rick dropped me off, the rain was pounding. He had warned me that since we were now in June, the rainy season was at hand and I

needed to bring an umbrella. I didn't listen to him, but there was a covered drive near the door to Dr. Ball's office, so, actually, I didn't need the
umbrella. As I was about to get out of the Lincoln, he also warned me
aloud, "Andy, I know I've told this before, but please remember, HIV
positive doesn't mean you're going to die tomorrow or today. I've been
that way for years and I know several guys that have had the bug for eight
years! And they're fine, dude. And who knows, they're making progress
…"

I stopped him midsentence with a kiss, then said, "Who is they, Rick?"

He looked at me with a quizzical expression then rolled closed his eyes
and slightly shook his head, then asked, "You sure you don't want me to
come in with you?"

"Not necessary," I said with a bow of my head in a bad Chinese accent,
my hands folded in prayer position at the bottom of my chin.

"Okay, I'll be back in about half an hour," he said.

"Cool, where you going?" I asked.

"Down to the beach, just walking."

"In this weather! Are you kidding me?" I asked incredulously.

"Yeah, I love walking in the rain on the beach. As long as there is no
lightning."

"Whatever dude. Make it an hour then. I wouldn't want to spoil your
fun."

"Okay," he said.

I got out and he drove off. My adrenaline was pumping and I felt like
I was in a dream, but I couldn't wake myself. And I wanted so badly to
wake up. It was such a strange reality this morning. When the elevator
doors opened, I'm sure I didn't hear them. And the committee in my
head must have been on R&R, as I wasn't having anything to do with
anything except this moment. To be certain, it was almost as if I were
high but clear headed at the same time. Go figure?

Anyway, I got to Dr. Ball's office and I walked up to the smoky glass
and rang the bell only once, as instructed. I took a seat across from the
only other person in the room, an old man who was reading some kind
of army veteran's publication. He looked up to acknowledge me, and I
returned his smile. Before I could sit down, Miss Bitch, AKA Dee Dee,
gently slid open the window. Only thing was, she was smiling today.

"Oh hi, Andy, right?" she said cordially.

This sudden change, or at least my perception of her disposition from
our last encounter caused me to think one of two things; either Miss
Bitch had gotten laid, or my test results were definitely positive. Surely

news of that magnitude in my personal despair, or nine inches of Jamaican wood, were about the only two things that could possibly brighten the perspective of the cunt who had now become a sunshine poster girl.

"Oh shit!" I thought to myself, but said aloud with what I assume was a hint of suspicion, "Right."

She responded with an "everything is normal" type of smile and said, just a little too cheerfully, "Just take a seat, it shouldn't be long. Dr. Ball's had a couple of walk-ins that needed immediate attention."

"'Kay," I said and I'm sure that I caught a tremble in my voice. Apparently I had allowed Miss Bitch and her death rays of sunshine to poison my initial state of serenity in the moment.

"Christ," I thought to myself in first person plural, "Don't start crying now. We got that out of the way last night. We knew what was coming, now get it together."

And we did. I don't know who was preaching to the choir of myself, or which self was listening, but we held up. And Miss Bitch was also right. Slightly over thirty minutes later, she opened the door and was motioning for me to come with her.

"Andy, this way" she said, smiling and chipper. I followed her back to a little exam room and she asked me to take a seat in the little chair in the corner. Before she was out the door, the good doctor had blocked her exit, and there was a slight comic shuffle as she moved around him giggling and saying, "Excuse me, heeheehee."

"Oh fuck," I thought to myself.

The door shut and Dr. Ball took a look at me and started browsing through the file. He said aloud, "Let's see what we have here. Oh yes! Western Blot, here it is. Got it back the day before yesterday.

As he was reading the paper, I almost said aloud, "Well then why in fuck didn't you just call me up two days ago."

But I didn't say a thing.

"Mr. Caldwell," he said and took a deep breath, then let it out as he spoke, "your test results came back positive."

I don't think he was breathing as we were looking each other square in the eyes, but I could see his pursed lips and stone cold sober face was motionless. I quit breathing as well and for a second. I was reeling into a void. It was a complete and total void and then in a moment, it was as if my ears popped, like on a descent in a jet, and all of the sudden, I could hear again.

"Do you mind if I see it?" I asked him quietly.

"No, not at all," he replied and politely handed me the sheets of thin identical papers, of which one, I assumed, would be a copy for me.

I browsed over the lab sheet and when I couldn't find the area, Dr. Ball reached over with his finger and pointed out the olive green shaded area and there was in big bold print, ANTIGEN POSITIVE. I didn't faint. I didn't cry. I didn't do anything hysterical. In fact, I'm not sure I'd know what my response to reading these words were if I hadn't been jolted by Dr. Ball when he said, "I'm not sure I follow you, Andy."

"Huh?" I said aloud in a state of confusion.

"You were just shaking your head with a slight grin as you said 'humph,'" he said, then quickly added as he took those papers back and tore off my copy and crisply handed to me, "That's not the response I'm accustomed to when I see young men read what you just did."

"Humph?" I recognized myself saying aloud this time.

"Yes. But I usually tell people that receive news that they have a fatal disease the same thing—whether it's cancer, leukemia, or what have you. But there is a slight twist with HIV, primarily because it is contagious. I hate to sound glib, but that's about as close to the truth as I can put it to you without getting theatrical."

And then Dr. Ball rattled it off like a fucking government "duck and cover" civil defense clip.

"Mr. Caldwell, you have tested positive for HIV, which does not mean that you have AIDS, but only means that your body had produced antibodies that confirm that you have been exposed to the virus that we believe at this time to cause AIDS. And, I am required to inform you that this is a contagious disease and, from what we know, it is spread by blood and semen and possibly saliva. I must ask you that you take this into consideration in your daily affairs and mostly in your sexual conduct, and that I will be reporting the results of your test to the state of Florida, but your name will not be disclosed. I would also strongly advise that you take care to not stress your immune system, as this is a disease that attacks T cells, and thus weakens the body's ability to fight off infections of various types. I am recommending that you immediately take some tests to see where your blood counts are so that we can have some sense about which direction to take our next steps. I'm sure you are aware, there is no known cure for this disease and it does appear to have an extremely high mortality rate, but I must also explain that the time-frame from inception of HIV to death by AIDS does appear to vary greatly. Do you have any questions?"

"Where do I take the test?" I quickly answered.

And he explained, "We can draw the blood right here and now. Can you come back in a couple of weeks?"

"Yes," I again directly answered.

He wrote some scratch on a piece of paper and said, "Call me if you have any further questions. Wait here and Darla will be here to draw blood."

He gave me a quick eye to eye glance and again pursed his lips. And for a second, I thought I heard a voice sounding like Walter Cronkite saying, "And that's the way it is folks, June 22, 1992." But there was only the sound of the door closing and I was alone in the room to ponder if I would see the end of this decade. The end of the century I liked better, as it made it seem that I had more time. But I wasn't alone with my thoughts for too long before Darla, AKA "The Vampire" cheerfully entered the room. She was respectful as I guess she had heard the news and had toned her rays of sunshine down a bit from the previous two weeks. She asked sweetly, "Which arm do you prefer, Sugar?"

I held out my right arm. Darla went straight to work with the ritual and again, the prick of the needle wasn't so bad. But I was afraid to look. As silly as this may sound, I didn't want to see my blood now that I knew it was poisonous. Darla hummed as the vials quickly filled and she pulled the needle out and bandaged the tiny wound with a cotton ball and band aide. She dispensed with the needles and marked the vials, then said in her Mississippi chipper accent as she handed me a sheet of paper, "That's it, Sugar take this on up to Dee Dee and she'll set you up for your next appointment."

"Thanks," I replied and Darla smiled back compassionately.

When Miss Bitch, Dee Dee, had set the appointment for 2 weeks later, I inquired about the payment and she explained that a prepaid amount of $1,000 had already been set up.

"Didn't you know?" she asked curiously.

"No," I said.

"Oh! Well you're all set. See you after the fireworks show," she beamed.

"Huh?" I asked.

"After the 4th. You know, the big beach fireworks, barbeque," she giggled then made quotations with her hands and said, "BEER," then arched her eyebrows in the fashion of a rascal.

"Oh right. I hadn't really thought of it," I said.

"Yep, see ya on Tuesday, the 7th. The 4th is on a Saturday. What a rip off, huh?"

"What?" I asked.

"You know. There's no extended weekend. Bummer huh?" she explained, then the phone rang, so she had to excuse herself.

"Dr. Ball," she answered then said, "Oh, hi, Mrs. Burman," and totally turned her attention to the good doctor's schedule book as she gave me a polite little twinkle of the fingers, her wave goodbye.

I walked out the door with my appointment card and on the way down in the elevator, I swear to God, the fucking music added insult to injury as the corny orchestra was playing an old Skeeter Davis song, "Why Does The Sun Go On Shining."

"Perfect," I said to myself and actually laughed aloud.

I got to the ground floor and when I exited the building, I could see through the glass doors that the rain had stopped and that the sun had come out. When I stepped outside, there was Rick in his running car waiting for me. I reached for the door's handle, as I always would, with my right hand and momentarily forgot about the band aid over the needle prick. Apparently, Rick saw it. And he started balling and didn't stop until after I had begged him to and that was ten minutes after we had parked in the condo parking garage. There we sat in his silent Lincoln, him still soaking wet from his beach in the rain walk, his eyes letting loose half the water he had soaked up.

I implored him, "Rick, really now! Come on, dude, grab hold! I appreciate all you've done Rick. And look at you, your health is okay. Why shouldn't mine be too? Right?"

Funny huh? I didn't shed a fucking tear. Not one. As a matter of fact, I was hungry.

"Come on now, dry up. We can't go up with you like this. And I'm hungry, dude. Please!" I begged.

He gathered himself together and we went up to the suite. I lit a joint and poured a healthy shot of Scotch over some ice.

"You think you should?" Rick asked with a sniffle.

"Oh please!" I said, "No need to slam the corral gate once the horses are out, babe."

And boy are the horses out! They were running wild in my head and I think my mind is on the back of one of the unbridled studs heading straight for my soul to deliver the union of heart and mind.

It's just a matter of time.

CHAPTER 38

Fort Lauderdale, June 22, 1992

The Committee

WHERE ELSE WOULD THE "HEART AND MIND" OF A 22-YEAR-OLD gay hustler unite other than a bar room located in Andy's balls; more specifically, in the heavier lower hanging left nut. It was more spacious. And the tavern was humming, full of life as the mixed jostle and conversation between the emotions, instincts and characteristics, previously engaged as spectators and jurors alike, imbibed cocktails and spirits accustomed to their various pallets. The mood seemed to have magically dismissed any recollection of the afternoon's courtroom fiasco where Miss Love, still lying about in the crater of His/Her Honor's fury, was all but forgotten.

Once again, the spectrum of Andy's emotional kingdom defied all logic of the material world as the basic verdict, just as official as any courtroom decision, would be handed down to his mind from the shenanigans that were taking place in this hyperphysical saloon. All of the courtroom participants, with the exception of His/Her Honor and Miss Love had been herded to the saloon by the call of Mr. Revenge, converted from prosecutor to British town crier on the courthouse steps ringing a bell and shouting to the four corners of the realm, "Hear Ye, Hear Ye, All drinks on me. Hear Ye, Hear Ye, to the tavern you'll be."

It was as if Mr. Revenge had used the hearing as nothing more than a mere formality so that he might draw all of the inhabitants of Andy's emotional world together. And he had succeeded.

"Lefty's" two bartenders were close to working up a sweat due to the open tab and unlimited funds secured by the masked crusader, a one Mr. S. C. Revenge. His credit card, Psychotic Express, was platinum and had passed with flying colors and was authorized by all powers that be of the emotional credit bureau that all expenses accrued, regardless of the amount, would be honored by the credit card company. Mr. Revenge was as good as his word and his credit held a perfect score of eight hundred. He had never reneged on any debt he had accepted.

And so it was an emotional Mardi Gras. The spirits filled the air, from bottles to glasses, then tummies to minds. Without His/Her Honor, the lighting in Lefty's was nothing short of perfect. The gas lit flames flickered on the old and bare brick walls and the sound of two copper dueling pianos echoed off the worn slate floors. The two pianists, Miss Talent and Mr. Ego, were taking requests from any and all in turn, which provided an electric and almost classy atmosphere. But it was still just dingy enough to hold the emotions of Andy's Psychic Realm's attention. Any inhibitions were all but gone.

That of course included verbal dialect. Mr. Morality had just expressed some of his concerns to Miss Addiction. He had tried to politely explain to her that moderation was the key aspect on which he and she should build a relationship. Her response was a flippant but loud, "Lick my hole!" which she followed with a matching acoustic slap to the face of the weak and skinny old man.

He stumbled backwards into the seat of the diva pianist and banged his head on the ivory keys to disrupt the catchy tune of "Bei Mir Bist Du Schoen" being played by Miss Talent. The boisterous middle aged hag, whom had been a legend in her own mind for many years, had just found her pipes and was singing the famous lyrics, "la Bella, belle," when Mr. Morality interrupted her rendition of the old swing song. Her reaction was swift and automatic. With only a slight annoyance, Miss Talent performed a capella while Mr. Ego covered her back from the sister piano. She didn't miss a note or make any mispronunciations as she effortlessly sunk her painted nails into the head and neck of Mr. Morality. He was bleeding profusely as she threw his body under the Steinway grand and when she returned her hands to the ivory keys, she couldn't help but notice the red stains that were blemishing the fine piano. Miss Talent had never committed, and didn't intend to start now, the unforgivable act of stopping a show tune in mid song. The ivory keys began to look like a crime scene.

All and all, the place was jumping. It was quite the scene and Mr. Revenge, upon hearing Miss Addiction's obscene language and encore slap, was already approaching the chaotic epicenter to take full advantage of the opportunity to rub elbows with Miss Addiction.

"My Dear Girl, we do have a way with words," he said to Miss Addiction as he touched her shoulder. He referred to her excessive use of the rod, "I see Miss Talent isn't the only one with good use for her hands," he said as he took stock of the Mr. Morality who was near the feet of Miss Talent and having his head beat in by the piano pedals.

"She's using her feet asshole," Miss Addiction shot back and gave Mr. Revenge the rod with her right hand.

"Oh Dear," he pondered with English calm and concern, "And not only does this Lady have a wicked slap but I see she can express sign language with her painted talons as well. So much talent, Miss Addiction."

Pretending to be bored by him, Miss Addiction looked over at Miss Talent, who was now back in full rhythm of the swing tune, and confirmed Mr. Revenge's assessment by raising her left hand and producing the middle finger ever so dramatically. Miss Addiction simultaneously flipped Mr. Revenge the bird with both hands and gruffly said, "That's right Wonder Queer, Miss Talent and I go hand in hand."

"Much too clever, Miss Addiction," he feigned in delight.

Miss Addiction had had enough and the other four fingers of her right hand had joined the extended middle finger to slap the boisterous fiend, when, as if by magic, his red super hero elbow glove extended in her direction and produced a small bullet-looking bottle that was filled with teensy white dandruff of some sort.

"To heighten our communications skills and brighten our demeanor. K, I believe," he gleamed with pursed lips and tongue in cheek.

In an instant the splayed hand that was headed for the Masked Crusader's face changed direction (in the nick of time, she thought to herself) and automatically swooped the loaded paraphernalia from the gestured crimson hand. Without hesitation and with a sense of complete familiarity, Miss Addiction brought the bullet to her right nostril and inhaled about a third of the interior concoction. She brought the bullet down and quickly placed it in her handbag, then brought her jungle red nailed index finger to press, ever so daintily, against her unused nostril so that she could give a polite snort. All to confirm the quality of his gift, you understand.

Her demeanor changed in an instant. It could not have been more obvious if a genie had appeared from a golden lamp and replaced her polyester panties with one hundred percent silk lingerie. Miss

Addiction shuffled her hips ever so subtly then exhaled through gritted teeth and growled, "Honey, my pussy feels good!"

"I beg your pardon?" Mr. Revenge politely inquired as he watched her continue to snort the remaining residue in her nostril. As her eyes crossed just enough to concern Mr. Revenge, she responded as though her mind had become attached to an asteroid hurling into oblivion, "Hmm?" she asked innocently while batting sluggish eyebrows over dilated eyes.

"Madame, you were saying something about your pussy?" he curiously asked with a hint of concern.

"Was I?" she questioned in the fashion of a Stepford Wife that had short circuited.

Fortunately, the asteroid that was taking her mind far into space was caught in the gravitational pull of Jupiter before it could escape the pull of the dazed trollop's sun. And like a slingshot held by a galactic David, the Solar superhero of the day, Jupiter, shot her mind back from the threatening abyss. Miss Addiction was back and able to salvage the moment as she had done hundreds of times before. With the effects of an overheated and simpleton Southern Belle, she rebounded, "My, oh my!" She was breathing heavily and dramatically clutching her breast.

Despite her hearty attempt to feign distress, the elated vixen could not remove a contorted and fucked up smile that resembled a clown-faced Betty Davis on acid. Had Miss Addiction been confronted with a wager of a couple hundred grand to make the attempt to go straight faced, she would have been unwittingly throwing her money into the wind. (And don't think the bet did not cross Mr. Revenge's mind. He schemed that he could probably front the cost of the afternoon's extravaganza from the trollop who was also known to exert her nature into the vice of gambling. He was also aware that the insatiable bitch never had any money so he scrapped the idea and kept to the course at hand.) But Miss Addiction did have the wits to grab an unused score of paper from Miss Talent's piano and start fanning herself as she explained, "It's just sometimes I get a little excited and when that happens ..." she paused to take in another huge gulp of air, then continued with her southern accent getting stronger by the second. "It's just that all of the day's events ... and here you come along with the answer to all my problems you sweet, dear, darling, precious, precious ..."

Miss Addiction went silent in her attempt to find the right word that would classify her current opinion of Mr. Revenge, but her scuttled mind could not grasp the thought to express her adoration for the fiend. So she simply took action and proceeded to smother the masked avenger's face with kisses.

"There, there Miss Addiction. Ha, ha, ha! Here now," Mr. Revenge giggled.

He received Miss Addiction's affections as if she were an overly playful puppy that was greeting her new master who just came home. As he gently held off further attempts of Miss Addiction's smooches, Mr. Revenge yelled out an order for champagne.

"Here now! Moet & Chandon White Star ... Quickly, quickly ... with two glasses, chop chop."

He was satisfied immediately and he let out a nervous laugh as he dismissed the waiter who had feverishly, at break-neck speed, delivered and uncorked the bottle. Mr. Pleaser, wanting so badly to be liked and appreciated, offered to pour the champagne, but was instructed by a wave of the hand of Mr. Revenge to place the bottle back in the silver ice stand. Mr. Revenge wanted to pour the glasses himself. It would give him a polite excuse to free himself from the clutches of Miss Addiction.

"Here now, love. Let me hoist you up on the piano."

Miss Addiction grabbed her chest as the invigorated masked charmer gently grabbed her with both hands, each under her arm pit, just lightly brushing her tits, and lifted her to the cat bird seat on top of Miss Talent's copper grand Steinway and Son's.

"Yeah, that's a good girl," Mr. Revenge grunted with satisfaction as he let his strong Cockney accent out of its cell to dominate his speech as it always did when he was faced with any form of manual labor.

"Having a good time love?" he asked Miss Addiction in a sincere and fond fashion.

Like a little girl that had just been placed on the carousel steed of her choice, Miss Addiction clapped her hands and squealed with delight, "Oh my God! Yes, Mr. Revenge. I can't remember having such a good time since I played with Mr. Slut/Whore."

With the memory of Mr. Slut/Whore expressed aloud, she attempted to pout momentarily, but again, the gleam in her eyes and the unstoppable smile produced something akin to what one could only presume would be the expression of a necrophiliac serial killer at the point of orgasm. Even a being of such twisted intrigue as Mr. Revenge was taken aback at the contortion Miss Addiction presented atop the copper grand. So he acted quickly to end the histrionic charade she attempted to evoke.

"Now now love, don't pout. Daddy Revenge is here to bring you back to your wondrous times of yesteryear," he said as he beamed mischievously whilst he tickled her twat with his left hand and simultaneously poured the champagne with his right.

Miss Addiction immediately took heed of his request and in fact went far beyond a change in facial presentation of a pout. With the touch of his fingers through the edge of her panties to her unshaved cunt, she squirmed, but not too far from the hand that was scratching her kitty. Her eyes popped open to the size of silver dollars as she feigned shock combined with actual delight. She made no attempt to physically stop Mr. Revenge. In fact, her legs parted ever so slightly more as her hands grabbed the edges of the piano so that Miss Addiction's seat moved closer to open air and gave the red gloved fingers a little more advantage to the task at hand.

"Oh My! Mr. Revenge you rascal!" she exclaimed then, heaving deep breaths and laughing uncontrollably. She asked, "Whatever is a lady to do in the clutches of a man like you?"

"Let's toast, I say," and he removed his fingers from under her skirt and brought a glass of champagne to her mouth.

He carefully allowed her take hold of her saucer and with his free right hand raised his glass of sparkling temptation. Their glasses, like two ships in the night coming close to a collision, steered clear just in the nick of time to stop an out and out breakage, but they did collide just hard enough to cause a little spillage and an extremely audible clink.

"To yes."

"Yes!" Miss Addiction confirmed while the only ladylike gesture she attempted was an extended pinky as she quaffed the entire glass down.

She sat the glass down atop the piano and with her index finger tapped it, signaling Mr. Revenge to accommodate her thirst. While he obliged, she wiped a bit of champagne from her mouth with the back of wrist, much in the same fashion as she would remove beer foam from her slight mustache had she been enjoying a pint. And as she reached down to take the refilled saucer, she quizzically asked,

"Exactly what are we toasting 'yes' to?" Then she took a quick sip of her champagne.

While she was in mid gulp/sip, Mr. Revenge responded, "Why to murdering Rick Gurnee of course."

"Oomph!" grunted Miss Addiction as her throat constricted and caused her to spit out the nectar, which had not freely made it through the journey to its appointment with the garbage can that describes the essence of Miss Addiction's being. In no time she was apologizing to Mr. Revenge, "Oh Good Lord! I'm so sorry," and she reached down to the champagne bucket on its stand and took the linen that was covering the ice and began to spot wipe the spittle that had found refuge on the face and mask of Mr. Revenge.

Mr. Revenge, fangs bared, growled as Miss Addiction touched his mask with the linen and she jumped back with a startled giggle and said, "Yes, of course. I'm so sorry again. Lord, I'm batting a thousand."

She had no idea what that expression meant, as she had never bet on a baseball game, but she had heard it several times used by the bitches on the afternoon soaps she found herself glued to. She knew the catch phrase was one of blunder, and took no offense as Mr. Revenge, a little too sternly, jerked the linen from her and began dousing with small little dot-dot gestures the beads and light running trails of champagne and spit that coursed his face. Within seconds, he managed to wipe the growl off his face and his expression again returned to one of Victorian cordiality.

"Really now love, no worries. What's a celebratory moment without spilt champagne?" he asked, to console the shallow cunt he needed to go along fully with his ambitions if he were to succeed.

"I know, but really, I do declare, where are my manners?" answered Miss Addiction as she gathered herself together and crossed her legs as if to guard herself against any further flirtations to her cootch.

With this retreating gesture and as the ketamine subsided, she was able to portray herself in a little more serious tone. The maniacal smile on her face was still there but had been downgraded from a clowned Bette Davis on acid to a Joan Crawford smoking an A.M. joint to dissolve a hangover while she recalled the previous night's three-way, and pondered how she was able to place two cocks up her ass at the same time. She reached over to her purse which was sitting next to her on the copper grand and, without looking down, withdrew her alligator skin cigarette case from her bag. With the style and finesse that would make any starlet of the mid twentieth century silver screen envious, she lit the coffin nail. Careful not to offend Mr. Revenge, she arched her neck and pointed her chin up and away from the host of ceremonies so as the smoke would not engulf the devious spinster.

As the smoke harmlessly joined its family near the high ceiling of the old tavern, Miss Addiction spoke her mind, "Now I'm all up for a party, ya hear, and as you know, I'm sure." She paused and took another huge drag of her cigarette and continued talking as the smoke curled slowly out of her mouth. "These kinda occasions are about at the top of my list of things to do. But fact is, Mr. Revenge, although this one here is brought on by you, it's usually Mr. Rick that brings home the goodies that keeps me a happy girl."

She took another drag off her cigarette and grabbed her purse, which still held the bottle of K. She had no intention of giving back her most prized possession of the moment as she exhaled her lung's sickening cloud directly into the masked crusader's face. She simultaneously and recklessly extinguished her cigarette on top of the piano, gathered herself together to plop off the grand, and said, "I just can't see any possibility of me joining your cause. In fact, and I'm sorry, I can't and I simply won't allow you to continue any further with this ridiculous little—" Her simpleton mind was at a loss for words and she stumbled as her feet made contact with the tavern floor. The jolt from the small jump brought her thoughts together and she finished her sentence in disgust, her face now void of the atrocious smile, and she spat, "Blame game!"

As she took a single step to walk away, Mr. Revenge gently touched her elbow and politely but firmly demanded, "One moment, Miss Addiction."

Miss Addiction did not reach for his arm but reacted by protecting the Ketamine bullet and moved her free hand over to guard her purse, which was already slung over her shoulder and neck in the fashion of a Napoleonic soldier marching with his rifle and rations. Mr. Revenge lightly smiled at her priorities, but quickly brought his expressions to portray a stone cold sober appearance that were in fact the polar opposite of Miss Addiction's previous contortions.

He said crisply, "Perhaps you missed this morning's conversation between Rick and Andy?" He began removing his superhero elbow gloves from both of his arms and hands.

"What conversation? I only heard Rick crying and you and a lot of your kissing cousin emotions enjoying some sense of satisfaction from the dear man's tears."

He politely folded the gloves and slid them into a hidden side pocket of his sequined jump suit and formed both hands into a fist. As he brought his fist firmly to his chest, he almost looked like Das Führer at the podium of a Hitler meeting as he exulted in his glory like the protagonist of a Wagner opera.

"Yes! Miss Addiction! That sense of satisfaction is me. Revenge. And I am most satisfied particularly when I am served in the fashion that Mr. Gurnee is very soon to be ingesting. Cold! Not only will Madame Dieux Dieux's powder allow me the satisfaction justice declares, but you shall as well, Miss Addiction, aide me in—"

She rudely and theatrically interrupted him as if she were the histrionic star of a silent movie and stated emphatically, "Oh no I won't!"

"Yes, you will," and he grabbed her by both shoulders so that she faced him squarely. The pianist paused and all chatter ceased as he brought the flat of his right palm and fingers loudly against the bare skin on the left of her face. It was the mother of all slaps and its sound, was quickly followed by gasping and shocked chorus that rang through the entire bar, "Hawwwwhhhh."

Miss Addiction was in shock. For a moment, she actually contemplated that she was back in a K Hole, but she soon became cognizant of the sting in her left cheek. Instead of a ketamine throb in her temples that resounded like a concert electric bass, the left side of her face began pounding and it was an unfamiliar tempo. Unlike the drug beat, this pounding was quick and urgent, like a stranger in trouble knocking at a nighttime rural door for emergency and pleading for emergency assistance. And Miss Addiction intended to answer that knock immediately.

Upon realization of the fact at hand, she quickly gathered a series of responses which she could utilize in her retaliation. She knew how to fuck with anyone or anything that toyed in her affairs. And this little piece of chicken shit had seriously crossed the line and above all, in doing so, had made a public spectacle of her dishonor. Being Miss Addiction, her first response to public humiliation would be drama. She stiffened and slowly turned her cheek to square off and meet face to face with the man who had just assaulted her. And with the tavern audience's eyes on her, she audibly and with slow deliberation proceeded to grandly question the masked avenger's audacity.

"How dare—"

But before she could finish the banality to a personal affront, Mr. Revenge, right hand still raised as he had swung through the a tennis return, reversed his motion and backhanded the vixen's right face with such force that Miss Addiction soon found herself on the floor, face to face with the comatose Mr. Morality. With the exception of the room above her in kaleidoscope, the vicious and tenacious bitch was still conscious. For a moment she actually reveled in the sensation brought about by the backward and classic hook extended by Mr. Revenge. It reminded Miss Addiction of acid and mushroom trips she had experienced in happier days. However, the inevitable ramification from the physical smack soon manifested as a pulsating twinge to her entire head that quickly shattered any congenial sensations. And the sequined and masked mug of a thug soon dominated the rotation in panoramic vision presented to the stunned and downed trollop. And, as if it were a voice from a faraway time and place, the governing facade began to speak to her.

"Miss Addiction. Miss Addiction!"

And immediately the face of Mr. Revenge was replaced by a hand that was visibly and audibly snapping its fingers. As well, the voice continued with finger snaps, "I believe you can hear me Miss Addiction. But I want to make sure that you can understand me. Please hold up any appendix of your right hand if you can comprehend my voice."

Miss Addiction meekly erred as she proceeded to hold up an index finger of her left hand. Mr. Revenge chuckled at this and called out ostensibly for champagne, treating the semi-circling crowd, which wasn't permitted to join the circumference due to the huge Steinway, as if each of them were his personal waiter. He was quickly obliged by Mr. Curiosity who had jumped up on the copper piano and squatted down, hands clasped and elbows over knees, so that he had a ringside seat in which to view the carnage. From his vantage and still squatting, Mr. Curiosity, who now resembled an intrigued chimpanzee, reached down to the champagne bucket, picked up the bottle, and clumsily poured champagne into the saucer that Mr. Revenge was blindly holding for service. With his attention and focus still squarely on the befallen Miss Addiction, Mr. Revenge cordially thanked Mr. Curiosity for his patronage and without spilling a drop, he gently dropped to one knee and with his free right hand, he gently raised the head of Miss Addiction from the bottom of a piano leg's wheel and propped her head ever so slightly against the flat side of the piano leg. Then he brought the champagne saucer carefully to Miss Addiction's confounded lips. As if she were a little girl who had fallen from her tricycle, Mr. Revenge gently caressed Miss addiction's temples with the thumb of the hand that was holding up her head and said in hushed and tender voice, "Shh, there, there. Yes, that's a good girl."

Miss Addiction attempted to say something but couldn't as the sparkling wine was already dancing over her tonsils and massaging her vocal chords.

"No, no. Don't speak Miss Addiction. Just drink," cooed Mr. Revenge. And again he softly praised her, "Yes, that's a good little bitch. You see Miss Addiction, I know you much better than you think ..."

Still in dazed confusion, Miss Addiction again tried to talk and in her attempt, she interrupted the masked brute. In true character of a thug, Mr. Revenge smoothly removed his right hand from behind Miss Addiction's head and with her head still propped against the leg of the piano, offered her a classic case of the carrot or the stick; the sting of his back hand versus the champagne that was still flowing into her mouth from the crystal glass pressed against her lips. Miss Addiction acknowledged this presentation in a haze and ceased her attempt to speak. She returned her focus to the champagne saucer and took the content as if it were mother's milk.

His stern facial question of choice was once again replaced by a tender smile, and as well, he returned his hand to pillow her head from the hard wood of the piano leg. Then he continued to coo, "My dear and tawdry child, as I was saying, I know you much better than you can possibly imagine. And being the single celled brat that you are, I know that you have turned on every single being who has crossed your path. You are without a doubt the most treacherous blight to plague our realm. But as you can see, even though you have crossed me, we can get along. The choice is yours, Miss Addiction, and I believe we could have avoided this entire scene had you only extended me the small courtesy of hearing me out."

Miss Addiction was in fact enjoying the cerebral massage that Mr. Revenge was providing and so she willingly relaxed in his grip and ever so soothingly blinked her eyes to confirm her comprehension of his dialect.

She nursed like a baby and Mr. Revenge continued, "I need you, Miss Addiction. I can't have any reservations from an influential and vivacious trait such as yourself if we are to carry out our plan of retaliation. And please, let me finish. Make no mistake, my child. I will have you, one way or another. It's only a matter of walking arm in arm or being dragged, kicking and screaming down the aisle by your thinning hair, to my altar of confirmation. Shh, shh, now. Let me finish. More champagne?"

He didn't allow her to answer as he took the crystal glass from her lips and held it up for Mr. Curiosity to once again provide a fount. His right thumb continued the temple massage, while Mr. Revenge replaced the edge of the glass to Miss Addiction's accommodating lips and continued, "I think that you will find marriage to me most enjoyable my love. And I'm further convinced that once you have heard the content of the conversation between Rick and Andy during this morning's histrionics, you will in fact grasp my hand for marriage. You see, dear, had you not been so preoccupied with getting stoned this morning, you could have paid attention to what Rick was wailing in his attempt to soften his own personal guilt from his play in the fatal situation we now face."

Miss Addiction made a motion with her mouth as if she once again wanted to comment on Mr. Revenge's words, but he quickly anticipated her response and took the glass gently from her and held it up for someone to take. That someone, who as if on cue to accommodate Mr. Revenge, was Mr. Curiosity. Still squatting in curious form as if he were a chimp, he relieved Mr. Revenge of the glass which thus gave Mr. Revenge the freedom to show the back of his hand as a warning to Miss Addiction. No longer cooing, he sternly admonished the vixen as he assumed she was returning to a state of comprehension.

"Darling, I am well aware that neither I nor anyone else, including His/Her Honor, can eradicate you, or for that matter, even banish you from this kingdom. But I can replace you, as I have done to some extent already, and I will only grow stronger as our Dear Host, Mason Harrison Caldwell III, trudges to make sense of this predicament. I can make your being more painful than any $20,000 a month rehab center ever dreamed of. So once more, let me assure you that the back of my hand you have recently felt is only a pin prick compared to genitalia electric shocks that I will torture you with, unless you can comprehend my demand that you shut up until I tell you to speak."

With the mention of rehab and genitalia electro shock, her wide open and terrified eyes conveyed the severity of her comprehension as she ever so slightly and tight lipped nodded in confirmation. Mr. Revenge did not bother to retrieve the extended glass being offered by Mr. Curiosity. Instead, Mr. Revenge roughly removed his pillowing hand from the back of Miss Addiction's head which now fell rather abruptly to thump on the slate floor. He took a deep breath and with his hands he smoothed back his hair that had become only a little disheveled from his exertions upon the insolent trollop and he elegantly straddled the momentarily domesticated tiger he now had tranquilized. To all who were watching—and all were—Mr. Revenge looked like a Friday Night Wrestling champ waiting for the theatrical referee to come and raise his hand as the winner.

But Mr. Revenge knew better. He knew in fact that the match was not yet won. That only the consent of Miss Addiction, not a referee or judge, could produce the result that he wanted. And as if he were Alexander the Great asking for the hand from the daughter of Darius and thus the keys to the great eastern empire, Mr. Revenge revealed his vision in the terms that Miss Addiction could comprehend and endorse.

"Despite the irony that I am kneeling over you, rather than to you, I suspect that you will appreciate the fact that I am kneeling, and therefore you can value the sincerity of this proposal. In truth, this is the only in way I have ever knelt. I bow to no one Miss Addiction. But I'll give you a moment to ponder this tidbit of information before I actually pop the question.

"This morning Rick, in a deplorable state of grief and guilt combined, carelessly informed Andy that should Rick die of AIDS or any complications from the disease, that all of his assets, including stocks, properties, cash and residuals, would be bequeathed to Andy, or more specifically, Mason Harrison Caldwell III."

Mr. Revenge paused and again ran both hands through his hair and brought them to clasp behind his neck so that he could enjoy the moment, as the information slowly arrived into Miss Addiction's soaked and anesthetized current of mind. Mr. Revenge took in a huge gulp of air and leisurely exhaled. He cherished the change of expression on the face of his confused and dazed little tigress he had momentarily pinned under him. He could literally read her mind, which if put into print would have said, "What in the fuck am I doing? Did I just hear this freak correctly? Did he say that if Rick dies, Andy will have his own money, perhaps a couple of million? Oh my God! I would control the mind of a motherfucker with a multi-million dollar estate. Motherfuck, can you imagine the party? And this little chicken shit that has me pinned can give me all this if I'll just marry him? Are you fucking kidding me?"

"No, Miss Addiction," he said as he stood up and extended a hand to the starry eyed and elated old tramp, "This is an honorable and sincere proposal. Marry me, Miss Addiction."

It was more of an order rather than "the question." And as she took hold of his hand and began to stand up, she never took her eyes off of the little black beads appearing in the slits of his superhero, comic book mask. They were so piercing and entranced upon her own bloodshot sockets that she almost felt hypnotized by his reptilian gaze.

And not knowing that he could actually read her thoughts, Miss Addiction pondered to herself, "Okay now, 'easy does it,' as those jackasses in some of those jail house recovery meetings Andy used to attend would say. I don't want to appear too eager. Just stay quiet for a second. Try and remember, this should be a ..."

She again found herself at a loss for description on how she would try and tag the moment she now found herself in. Miss Addiction knew she was at a pivotal point in her existence, but she had never been confronted with sincere feelings. How should she treat the man that was going to make all of her dreams come true? God knows, she didn't actually love the twit.

"Tender," Mr. Revenge said aloud as he finished assisting her off the floor.

"Why sir, if I didn't know any better, I'd swear that you could read my mind," she said with a slight gasp, her Mississippi Delta slang more apparent than ever.

"I can, Miss Addiction, and let me put your mind to rest. Love has nothing to do with this partnership. Let me remind you, she may be dead. I'm really not certain, and I really don't care. She won't interfere anymore. Of that I'm am certain."

"Tender?" Miss Addiction pondered aloud as if she were pronouncing a word in French 101 for the first time. "Like in the way I might lick a joint I just rolled?" she asked innocently but sincerely.

Mr. Revenge laughed aloud at Miss Addiction's gullibility. She reminded him of a little girl who had inquired about Santa's sleigh. He embraced her question in good spirit but had no intention of making an attempt to describe the word "tender" to his learning harlot. That would take all year and still she might never fully comprehend it. Mr. Revenge again squared Miss Addiction to himself, except this time, he gingerly grabbed her under both arms and replaced her back on the piano to her previous seat of a more cordial exchange of social graces. She giggled again like a kindergarten girl who had just received the gift of the most beautiful pony in God's creation. She could care less if Mr. Revenge could read her thoughts, which were optimistically racing through her mind as if she had just hit the state lottery.

"More champagne, love?" Mr. Revenge stated more than inquired.

"Mm hmm," she blindly responded as she stared in wonderment at all of the characters and traits enjoying the party so generously given by Mr. Revenge.

But Miss Addiction didn't really see them. It was as though she were in a room completely alone with nothing but the glory of her own good fortune. And to add spit to shine, Mr. Revenge was tickling her twat with his now bare left hand as he poured her another glass of sparkly with his right hand.

Mr. Revenge was completely amused at the moist and inviting reception that his fingers received from the tigress. Miss Addiction only entertained him more as he read her thoughts that were pouring out in hyper type, "I'm gonna get me five eight-balls, buy me a veterinarian that will sell me a case of K anytime I need it, fly direct to Amsterdam to get the best Goddamned X in the world, keep only the best of Siamese Thai Sticks to go with my morning coffee. Hell, I'm even gonna go for the China Girl more often. Why the fuck not. And to boot, I'm getting my hooch played with ..."

As the single celled harlot reveled in her future, Mr. Revenge thought it might be best to bring her back to the present.

"Um humph," he coughed, then stated what he knew would bring her out of her trance. "Darling, don't forget the little white bullet in your purse. Ahh ahh ahh," he teased.

"Oh where are my manners sir?" Miss Addiction exclaimed, not giving two cents worth of shit that he could read her mind and that she was feigning sincerity.

Miss Addiction blew Mr. Revenge a kiss and without taking her eyes off of him, she reached into her bag and quickly felt the familiar "engagement present" that she knew would soon only heighten her ecstatic senses into a stellar dimension. And again the bullet found her nostril, causing the music from the piano to double in volume. She didn't have to say anything about her pussy to Mr. Revenge this time. No child! He was on the mark.

His left hand still twitted with the opening around her clit and as his face assumed the smiling expression of a rascal at large, he plugged the top of the champagne bottle with his right hand and began shaking the trapped and carbonated wine into a bomb.

"Another toast, Miss Addiction," Mr. Revenge announced as he kept to the tasks at hands. He bellowed his formal eulogy over the pounding music to the entire room but directly to Miss Addiction, "To our marriage AND to eternal justice." He paused, and in a more hushed voice personally asked her, "What say ye, Miss Addiction?"

And in one swift motion, he opened her now steaming and moist cunt with his left hand and with his right, plunged the champagne bottle's neck to its end into the receptive cavern and let loose the trapped vintage that douched her g-spot with endless little pops.

"What say ye, Miss Addiction," he insisted again as he grinned and pumped the bottle's neck in and out of her pulsating hole.

If she had ever been at a loss for words, and she had on many occasions, this was not one of those times. The problem was that her mouth had formed into a gaping O and her vocal chords were audibly exuding the most ridiculous and heightened moan that would have been credited in most cases to the howl of a basset hound whose tender ears were being assaulted by a passing emergency siren. She knew what she wanted to say but it was as if her body had been seized by an electric volt and she had no control over any of her extremities or bodily functions. She was in sheer ecstasy and he knew it.

"Come on, Love, what say ye?" he further teased as he continued to use the champagne bottle like a greased dildo. "That's right darling! To eternal justice, our second murder, and last but not least, our MARRIAGE! What Say YE??"

"OOOOooooooUUuuuuuuuuuu   AhhhhhhhOOOoooooooOhhh-
hooooo!" Miss Addiction howled and sang, her forehead burrowed
in sharp creases. Her mouth, which resembled a Christmas caroler
statuette, annually poised to present its posture of singing the first
syllable in "O Come All Ye Faithful," was frozen in a freeze frame.

"Yes, my darling sing to me, SING! But tell me now what say ye!
NOW!"

And in her orgasm she screamed so that all the realm, inside and
out of Lefty's could in no way ignore her answer, and thus the death
warrant of Rick Gurnee.

"YESSSSSssssss, YESSssssssss, YESSsssssssss".

As Mr. Revenge removed the bottle from the Bride to Be's convuls-
ing cunt, he lifted both hands, and thus the bottle, as if it were the
World Cup, up into the air. Perhaps a more accurate picture would be
that of a victorious Superbowl locker room. Miss Addiction, through
no choice of her own, but enjoying the shockwaves that pulsed
through her body and climaxed in her womanhood, exploded like
Mount Saint Helens. It was as if the crew of SeaWorld had forgotten to
put out their signs on the unsuspecting spectators to warn that they
were in a "splash zone." Her spewing cunt gave back the champagne
now enhanced with a combined salty and medicinal character that
soaked not only Mr. Revenge, but many more emotions within the
non-proclaimed zone. Most did not mind the altercation of taste as
they opened their mouth, leaned back their heads to revel in the Ariel
font that was streaming down through the flickering gas lantern's
light like a sainted epiphany.

"I said La Bella Bella ... Boonseva!" wailed the lyrics from the vivacious voice of Miss Talent.

Those in the crowd with glasses raised their cocktails, while others politely applauded, as if they were in a private country club, the
betrothal of the host of the evening's regalia to the endeared, but
treacherous, Miss Addiction, who was at the end of her orgasm. Mr.
Revenge bowed to the room and then turned and gave the same
exaggerated gesture to Miss Addiction. With a curled bottom lift, she
exhaled a big breath and blew some of her stray hair that was covering her eyes to the side. She winked at Mr. Revenge and smiled. The
applause grew louder, and the engagement was set.

CHAPTER 39

Fort Lauderdale, June 24th, 1992

YESTERDAY, I WOKE UP WITH ONE OF THE WORST HANGOVERS I'VE EVER had in my life. And, I woke up in Rick's bed. Slowly, an element of reality crept into my mind which brought bits and pieces of the night before, the day before, and all of their revelations back to me in no rational or chronological order.

And damn it to hell, Rick had already left and gone to work. Fuck! I didn't even get the chance to poison him. But I was poisoned. Or am I poison? I think we blotted acid too? Never mind, it doesn't matter. Anyhow, I could sure tell my ass had been pounded. The bumper of K and bottle of poppers were sitting next to a quarter-filled rocks glass with no ice, but the liquid was still a dark color of vibrant potency. I thought that if I'd poured it back in the bottle, no one would be the wiser as the cocktail, from the tone of its color, never had more than two cubes of ice, if any.

Oh my God! I just remembered—too fucking funny. Rick, in true control freak mode, had taken the bottle of Johnny Walker Black out of mouth my and had slapped me on my bare ass, in teasing admonishment, before he walked over to the living room bar and poured the straight scotch into the tumbler. He then went to work on me. Holy fuck, and did he go to work on me. No kidding, I started to pop a midmorning boner just reliving the night before and the jungle gym sex that continued into the early morning. Then I whacked off, thinking of the unprotected bare back sex we had indulged in. The morning jerk off session eased my hangover a little until I shot and then the hangover was back in full form and so were the memories of the positive antigen leaflet that had thrown us into wild state of abandonment, in which we threw all caution to the wind. Like I said, no need slamming the corral gate when the horses were already out. And with Rick, had I ever slammed the gate for any reason?

But I soon became upset with myself. I had not held to my conviction that I would immediately begin using the powder that Madame Dieux

Dieux had supplied. To ease the state of disgust I felt for myself, I walked into the living room, still bare butt naked and found half a joint in the ashtray next to the half a fifth of Johnny Walker Black. What the fuck, I took a swig of the scotch, then lit the joint and sat down on the couch. And I thought to myself, "What the fuck am I so worried about. Rick ain't going nowhere. I can just catch up tomorrow."

And with that thought in mind, I turned on the boob tube and momentarily sank into an episode of The Andy Griffith Show. I thought to myself, "Fucking Aunt Bee, what a bitch she is! I'd go crazy with a voice like that in my life. Filling a freezer full of bad meat, she was a stupid bitch too. I can't take this bitch's voice."

So I flipped the tube to CNN and the news of the world began to propagate my mind with all types of worldly horrors.

"What a fucked up world," I thought to myself as I took another hit off the joint and a strange sensation of gratitude replaced my hangover and anxiety. I must have been comparing my life to the stories on the newscast. I stayed focused on the tube as I walked over to the bar with the scotch bottle, and left it there, after I took a swig. Then, I took my seat back on the couch with my good friend Doobie.

I wasn't going to jail like our bud Manuel Noriega, nor was I getting the shit beat out of me by the police like Rodney King. I laughed aloud when I saw that Vice President Quayle couldn't spell "potato." Yep, I wasn't doing so badly. But then the next bit of news broke my jollies up in half and really put a damper on things.

Anthony Perkins, the actor from Psycho, was very sick from AIDS. He was ping ponging from hospital to home, then home to another hospital.

"So Norman Bates was taking it up the ass?" I thought, and again my mind went into Q&A with itself.

"Do you think, besides being HIV positive, you and old Norm have more in common than you know?" Asked Self A.

"Oh please," said an unknown voice.

"Okay, where is the faggot?" asked Self A.

"Yeah," asked Self B, so as to confirm that he did not say "oh please."

Then Self C stated calmly, "Well it wasn't me, but I have to wonder if I'm not a psycho."

"Oh please," was heard by the whole of me again and in unison.

Selves A, B, and C proclaimed, "Who said that?"

"I did," Self XYZ said.

"Who the fuck are you?" Self A asked in consternation.

"XYZ."

"I don't think we've met," Self A said.

"We've met, but it's difficult for you to recognize me. You are always looking forward and I tend to come in on the tail end of situations. But since we are drinking this morning and looking at an actor who is near death from a common diagnosis, we kinda hooked up."

"Are you a faggot?" asked Self B.

"Sure," said Self XYZ. "We're all faggots. Been that way for years."

"I'm Bi," said Self C.

"You hold on to that honey," said XYZ.

"Anyhow!" said Self A, "You seem to have an opinion on this 'psycho' question."

"Yes, I do," said XYZ matter of factly. "We're a psychotic faggot."

"Oh please!" exclaimed Self B.

"See I told you," confirmed self XYZ, "you just said 'oh please.' Only faggots say 'oh please.'"

"I ain't no Fag," hollered Self B.

"Yes you are, and you have AIDS," Self XYZ calmly retaliated.

And in a tone that was emphatic and punctuated, Self A sternly corrected XYZ, "I have HIV and I don't have AIDS."

"Play chicken and egg all you like, but let me ask you, A—who the fuck are you to say 'I' am HIV positive?"

"Why, I'm Mason Harrison Caldwell III," Self A grandly declared.

"No, I'm Mason Harrison Caldwell III," Self B pushed in.

"I'm Mason," Self C flatly stated.

"OH SHUT UP!" A, B, and XYZ all simultaneously spat towards Self C.

And in a voice that resembled an echo bouncing through the canyons of the Alps, all four of the above selves heard a ringing, "All of you! Please! SHUT UP. I ain't none of you."

"Who rang that out?" questioned Self A to the other present three selves.

"Must be someone between C and X," XYZ rationalized aloud to himself.

And in an instant, the unfamiliar voice rang out in a scream that would have made ole Alfred Hitchcock see dollar signs. It felt as if rain were falling hard on all of the selves.

"Later dudes," said Self C.

"Yeah, later," they all said back and disappeared.

I guess the canyon that the voice had traveled through to all of the mind's selves was Rick's gold and marble tomb, called a bathroom. I caught my physical reflection in the mirror, my hands splashing water onto my face. I surmised that the vocal cords around the visible Adam's apple was what produced the scream. I thought that I had never noticed how strange my Adam's apple looked until that moment.

"It would look stranger with a straight razor slicing through it," said a new voice in my head.

But I just splashed more water on my face and refused to engage the voice. I looked at my face in the mirror, for the first time in my life, I truly didn't recognize myself.

"Who am I?" I said aloud over the running water. "What am I?" I heard the face in the mirror pronounce.

Then I came back; that's the best way I can put it. I simply "came back." I turned off the water and could vaguely hear the news from the television spouting something about Iran Contra. I dismissed the broadcast, as I didn't understand or give a damn about Iran or anything else right now except that the body I saw in the mirror was mine.

I silently thought to myself, "You won't be here long in that body. You have AIDS. Just like good ole Norman Bates and apparently I'm a psycho because I didn't give a damn about the others in the water next to Rick as I baited the water for sharks nor did I give two cents' worth of shit about the other drivers on the freeway Lover Boy was supposed to have had a blowout on."

The face in the mirror grinned at me. Then looked at me in shock. Then grinned again.

"Oh fuck, that is some good weed," I thought and then stepped away from the mirror.

I turned on the shower and stepped in and started singing old country songs, like Merle Haggard's, "I'm a Lonesome Fugitive" and Waylon Jennings's, "Rambling Man." I made up my mind right then that since I was a psycho, I could at least be true to myself, whoever or whatever that is, and be a country psycho. Shit, besides AIDS and psychosis, Norman and I had nothing else in common. Well, maybe a little, but not much else.

Anyhow, I dried off and got dressed and slightly giggled after I took another hit off of the big roach that was the previous night's doobie. No doubt, the hangover was gone. I felt like the beach. It would be good to talk to Madame Dieux Dieux.

"Now there's a woman I have some things in common with," I thought to myself.

"Oh yeah, what really?" said someone in my head.

"Oh shut up!" I said aloud.

And he did. And I slipped into my flops by the door and I'm sure I grinned as I bet their presence there had to perturb Rick as he left for work this morning.

"Good, I hope them sitting there under the framed picture Madame Dieux Dieux gave me chafed his ass and put him in a foul mood for the rest of the day," I thought to myself.

And as I got onto the elevator alone, some voice again started up in my head.

"Jesus, aren't we a petty little bitch."

"Shut Up!" I declared aloud and thought that these voices must be some residual effect of the ketamine.

The voices cleared as I got off the elevator and when I walked outside, I said aloud, "Holy Moly."

The heat and the humidity brought my senses back to the days of New Orleans and I immediately reasoned that the walk that I was about to take in this heat would help my body sweat out the chemicals that I had so willingly placed in my insatiable garbage can.

And I was correct in my assumption. To state it point blank, as I neared Madame Dieux Dieux's kiosk, I could literally smell myself. A combination of pot smoke and formaldehyde, with a sickening sweet tinge. I knew that if I could smell it, so could other people and so would Madame Dieux Dieux. But I quickly rationalized that I couldn't give two cents' worth of shit if anybody could smell me. And if they lit a match and I blew up like a Molotov cocktail? Well, I wasn't so sure if I'd enjoy that, but that was taking it a little too extreme. I giggled to myself as I saluted Madame Dieux Dieux from about fifty yards of her set up.

She was alone and sitting under the shade of the canvas-topped kiosk and waived back. She didn't bother to get up off her stool, but I could see the white of her teeth as she smiled, which of course brought me joy, knowing she was happy to see me. As I got closer, I could see that she was no longer jaundiced. And that brought me immense satisfaction. But as I got a little closer still, I could see the expression on her face change from happiness to mild disgust as she waved a hand past her face to remove the bad air that my sweating body had supplied.

"Chile!" she exclaimed, then continued, "What is it dat give da Almighty da notion dat's make you white peoples smell so bad."

Being raised a redneck hunter, I should have realized that the wind, which blew in from the north and my back, carried my medicated and bodily odor directly to the poor black woman. I'm sure a redneck hunter is what I probably smelled like. If you've never smelled one after about three days in the woods, I can't expect you to concur here Selectric but lets just say I didn't smell like spicy pine or clearwater fresh. I stank.

To say the least, my mind was erratic from the bouncy levels of serotonin and dopamine that had been thrown into schizophrenia from the combination and amounts of different drugs that I had been mixing. Although I couldn't smell Madame Dieux Dieux, I could of course see her, and a strange feeling of happiness abounded as memories of Ella flashed through my head. I was so grateful for the love that had been extended to me by her and Madame Dieux Dieux. I almost started crying and Madame Dieux Dieux caught this and said, "Oh shit. Not Sally! Please! For da love of God, today! Please! Not Sally. Mason, I just joking. Well, a little. You don't have to cry. You don't smell dat bad. Juss a little bad. You can't help it none. You know you are white?" she teased.

"And fucked up," I responded as I all but fell into small fit of laughter at what Madame Dieux Dieux had just expressed.

"Ooo Chile!" she exclaimed then slapped her knee and sneezed with a combined cough a wicked little laugh in herself. Then went on to say, "Good to see you, Mason. But I'm not so sure you been doing what's good for you?"

"Oh Madame Dieux Dieux; maybe not, maybe so. But you look great. You feeling okay?"

"Yeah man! I feel great 'cept dis heat taxing my ass like it gone take all I got. You see how many peoples out and about in dis shit."

"You not doing much business, huh?" I questioned her sincerely.

"No," she replied in a matter of fact single word sentence. She hesitated and then added.

"I tink I'm gone open up only on da weekends from de July four weekend on tru to October, Mason. You okay wit dat?" she asked.

"Yep," I replied and added, "well, at least I'm glad to know that you haven't needed me to help you out around here. It's okay with you if I continue to stay home? I have been doing something good for me there," I said referring to my journaling.

"My nose tells me not much," she stated, then added as her posture became totally sincere, "So now you know da truf?"

"I do," I replied and before I could tear up she held out a hand to stop me.

She said sternly, "Sally time over. My Mason got to man up and face dis ting, anyway you want, but you got to look dis shit square in da eye boy and accept it for what it is. And from where I stand and from what I know of dis devil, you not doing yourself no good drinking and God knows what else seeping out your pores. Da peoples back home know dis. Da people wid da sickness dat go into da ground. Dey da ones dat indulge and dey smell like chemicals. It a deathly smell and I smell it on you."

Her words hit home in my soul and grabbed my mind like a child hearing "Once upon a time" read in the opening text of any fairy tale.

And I thought silently to myself, "I smell like death?"

I knew Madame Dieux Dieux didn't mince words and always meant what she said. And I of course knew she was referring to my drinking and drugging. And just as matter of factly, I knew I had no intention of ceasing that activity. "No sir, ah ah, NOoooo. No, no, no no!" my own mind screamed silently at the not so subtle suggestions, while Madame Dieux Dieux and I meandered through the silence.

"You okay, Mason?" she quietly asked. She wasn't whispering but her voice was low and deliberate.

"For now, yes. I'm okay for now."

"'Now' is all any of us got, chile" she said as she grabbed me hard by both shoulders and looked me square in the eyes.

I admired both the physical and mental strength hidden inside the little black and thin body of this elderly woman. And although small and thin, she wasn't saying anything frail. Again, her piercing stare into my own eyes seemed to convey that she was reading my mind, and without saying a word her eyes conversed, "Paradox upon paradox. Dat da truf boy."

But nothing had been said verbally. In fact, all I could hear was a mixture of the wind blowing through the beach palms, the traffic on A1A and the muffled lap of the calypso surf. I thought to myself. "Could a little Haitian woman who spoke English in a Creole dialect honestly know the meaning of the word 'paradox'?"

Perhaps it was only my imagination, but a small crease on the corners of her mouth produced an ever so slight smile, and it seemed once again that her gaze conveyed words.

"Da ant pound for pound be da strongest ting on dis globe. Don't let yo eyes fool you. You need ta listen to yo heart."

Was I tripping? Right there in broad daylight on the remnants of last night's festivities—or this morning's pot and scotch? Festivities that were celebrating what? My HIV positive confirmation. Or maybe the life insurance policy and will/testament Rick had announced that made me the sole beneficiary of his estate.

Out loud I said to no one, "Get the fuck out of here."

Straightaway, Madame Dieux Dieux released her hold of my shoulders and began that crazy uncontrolled laugh that I remembered from the first time we had met. Except this time, it wasn't the Pillsbury dough boy, asshole tourist standing there. I was the one standing there looking like an idiot to anyone that might have been watching. But nobody was watching except Madame Dieux Dieux, doubling over and pointing at me as she tried, unsuccessfully, to stop her laughing hysterics. There she was, hissing and sneezing at the same time, and completely enjoying herself at my expense. And then she really freaked me the fuck out.

Holy shit, did the lady freak me out! She crooked her elbows and knees into as much of a ninety-five degrees as is humanly possible for an old lady and simultaneously, she splayed her hands and made her hands and fingers start a creepy crawly gesture. Even her toes were wiggling. Then she totally blew what was left of my mind and said, "I da little black ant. Uhuh! Dats me. Just yo personal little Haitian black ant."

I must have screamed. I couldn't hear it. Not yet anyway. Then a sting, as if my personal Haitian ant had stung me on the right cheek. Then another sting on the same cheek and I could suddenly hear myself screaming and once again, I could feel Madame Dieux Dieux's strong grip on my upper arms. She was shaking me and then released her left hand grip and drew back to what I could only assume was going to be a slap and I jumped back and instantly realized that she was causing the strange stings on my right cheek.

In that moment, I realized something about my friend that I had never noticed before, and I said aloud, in astonishment, "Oh my God, you're left handed?"

Her eyes were crazy wild and Madame Dieux Dieux put her hand down and a look of sane astonishment began to replace her mad gaze. But her forehead was still furrowed and she was obviously exasperated by my comment. She bent over and drew in a deep breath and before I knew what was going on, she had pounced like a fighter coming off the ropes and with a strong hook gave my left shoulder an agonizing shot with her knuckled fist.

"Dat's da truf, smelly boy, but I got good use of my right too."

"Ah?" I grunted as I held my stinging arm and jumped back to avoid any further assaults, then continued, "That's right, the truth is a paradox on top of a paradox."

"A pair of what?" she loudly quizzed in complete frustration.

"But you're not an ant? And you are certainly not laughing," I mused aloud.

Then she answered my previous personal question that I had asked myself at the beginning of this episode. Madame Dieux Dieux squawked, "I ain't yo Aunt and I for certain ain't laughing. You tripping, boy. Flat ass tripping yo little white balls off."

Now I cracked an actual smile to this and she screamed, "It not funny Mason! No way funny! Boy I thought you was about to run in front of da cars on dat street." She was hysterically pointing at the traffic on A1A then continued, "What da hell make you want to run from me, Mason? Huh? No, it not funny, boy, and you better take dat piece of shit grin off yo mouth before I give it more wid my left of what I give to yo arm."

I did as I was told and she responded in kind with a posture that barely resembled compassion. She panted, "Boy, what you running from? You ain't right, Mason! Not one ounce of right. You scaring me, Mason," she finished sincerely.

She was right, so very right. One hundred percent, right on time correct. And as her question about what I was running from sunk in, my first answer to myself was, "AIDS." That didn't make one bit of sense to me, as I rationalized that there was no running from a disease that was already in my blood. I became confounded and completely frustrated. I again started to get glassy eyed.

"I'm not playing, Mason. Playtime over," Madame Dieux Dieux said as she emphatically raised her voice, but was not yelling. She continued "You go lock Sally up. Dat bitch done had her day. No, dis not about yo tears. Dis is bout what causes dem, and don't come telling you don't know."

I again did as Madame Dieux Dieux instructed, or perhaps it was the adamant strength that she was illuminating. Whatever, I didn't cry.

Where there had been only an empty question, moments earlier, something from within me spoke up and bluntly stated, "I don't want to die."

There was the combined sound of the wind through the palms, the traffic with music coming through open windows, seagulls, and people laughing near the surf. Then a girl playfully screamed, "Stop." I guess her boyfriend was dragging her into the water. But Madame Dieux Dieux didn't say anything. At least not for about five or six seconds. Her disposition turned from tough love to unreserved compassion the second I finished answering her question. But her expression was that of genuine dismay. There were no furrows on her forehead, nor any veins protruding from her thin neck and elongated temples. She showed me the palms of her hands, which were, as far as I knew, along with the soles of her feet, the only pale skin on her body.

She calmly and quietly asked, "Then why you killing yourself Mason?"

"Am I?" I replied.

She whispered something in Creole French I had no way of understanding, then softly reprimanded me, "Mason?"

"What?" I asked somewhat perturbed.

"Boy, you got to get honest with yourself. You da only one you fooling."

"The truth is a paradox upon paradox," I said in consternation.

Madame Dieux Dieux exhaled loudly and said, "What da hell?" and while walking over to her stool, she held her hands up in surrender. Then she sat down and began fiddling with some tiny wooden carvings on her kiosk. She abruptly stopped and pouted loudly, "You wouldn't know da truf it came up and bit you right in da ass."

"It has done bit my ass, Madame Dieux Dieux."

"Turn around, smart boy," she ordered.

As always, as far as Madame Dieux Dieux was concerned, I did as told.

She continued, "Yep! You still got yo ass. And not bad for a white boy. Humph!" she grunted.

"Thank you," I replied in my best imitation of a self-conscious little boy attempting to practice taught manners.

"You not gone have dat or nu ting if you don't get inside dat head you got and make some sense."

"I'm trying, Madame Dieux Dieux. Really, I'm trying."

"Don't try. Just do, Mason."

She got up off the stool and walked over to me and reached around me and gave me a hug then asked, "Help me pack dis bitch up. It too hot today and besides, no body gone come around me anyway now dat I smell like you."

I said that I surely would and we slowly packed up the kiosk and pushed it to her shed on Del Mar. Despite the sea breeze, it was blasted hot and we didn't say anything as I pushed and she guided with a slight pull from the front. When she had finished closing the rolling doors of the shed and locked the two padlocks over the hinged brace, she walked to her car and said, "Get in. I give you a lift from dis heat."

I politely declined and as she got in the Corolla and cranked the poorly muffled engine, she spoke over the motor's buzz. Through the smell of gas fumes she said, "You gone be alright Mason. Just be good to yourself."

Then she peeled back and ground the gears and sped away.

I quickly found myself alone. "Be good to myself," I pondered silently, and a voice from somewhere within my head asked again that most egregious of all questions, "So what are you going to do now?"

"Okay then," I responded aloud and turned around to head on home.

Funny I should actually think of Rick's house as my home. Really, I don't think I've had a home in years. I guess my body is my true home. And from what I can deduce, it's a home scheduled for demolition. Oh well, my house ain't the only one on that list.

Now I feel the Selectric humming beneath my fingertips, as if hinting that she is ready for sleep. I wonder if I will live on through the print of the little typewriter. That's being ridiculous, I know, but whether I want to die or not, and I confirmed to myself today, that I don't, I have to say that I'm not afraid of the transition.

"Now is all any of us have, chile," Madame Dieux Dieux had said. I think about that tonight and it is something that hints to me that I may be headed in the right direction in discovering "truth." If the past is the past, then I suspect somewhere in the future that Death has a calling card for everyone; an inevitable invitation to a deliberate event from the time we are born. But how we drive to that party makes all the difference in the world—or does it? Anyway, Rick's hearse will start getting shined in the morning. I don't know if justice is served or not at these events, but let's just say for the sake of not knowing, it would not be justice for the man to outlive me. So, I'll begin the sentence in an oh so subtle way, provided by Madame Dieux Dieux first thing in the A.M.

I have never named this concoction of words that I've amassed here, but I'll see you tomorrow, Selectric, with a new set of the day's events. (Maybe I should name you 'Kitty' or something of the like, even though I'm not a little Jewish girl hiding from Nazis.) I think I'll just stick with "Selectric." Hopefully you offer more insight as I am beginning to see my thoughts and observe them. Something's happening.

'Night, Selectric.

CHAPTER 40

June 25th, Fort Lauderdale, Florida

RICK WAS ASLEEP THIS MORNING WHEN I WALKED INTO HIS BEDROOM. Regardless of all the recent sex and "I love you" drama, I am still sleeping in the guest room. And the digital clock radio next to his bed showed 6:08. I knew that I had almost an hour as Rick usually woke up at around seven. Anyway! Before I go off on a step by step, motherfucking Anne Rice list of details—the color of each strand of carpet and the direction his hair lay against the pillow, the sound of his breath bullshit—let me get to the act, which was so relatively simple. Oh, but I did notice that Rick stank when he slept. Maybe just gas, but I don't think so. I guess I had grown accustomed to it but just walking into the room, DAMN! The man stank.

But like I said, the act was relatively simple. So is pulling the trigger on a gun, but they are so noisy. Anyhow, I picked his earring off the purple velvet jewelry stand that sat on the dresser and walked quietly with it back into my-slash-the guest room.

I had hidden the little leather pouch in my right cowboy boot down in the toe. I took the black vial out and walked over to the dresser where Rick had an old make up application area. I guess it was for when he had female guests, or his mother. Come to think of it, I've never even asked Rick about his mother. That wouldn't make me a shallow person, would it?

For the love of God, if I can just keep my mind on the matter at hand, maybe, just maybe, I can kill this man by getting this justice applied and dried. So anyhow, the Goddamned dresser had a big ole hand held mirror in front of the wall mirror. I could watch myself sprinkling the small amount of tiny crystals on the hand held mirror. Thank God I didn't have a straw as I might have, just by habit, snorted some of the shit. First, I made sure that the A.C. vent was closed in the room and that the ceiling fan was completely still. I was taking Madame Dieux Dieux for her word that this shit was the real deal. I also had the rubber gloves from under the sink. The gloves were blue, in case anybody gives a frog's fat ass. Ha, so is the song "Love Is Blue." But what shade of blue it is doesn't matter.

So I spit on the tip of my finger and took the tip of the earring and applied the saliva. Then I placed the spitted end into the opaque, teensy crystals and walked back into the master's bedroom. I almost felt like I was in some Disney movie as I put the poisoned earring on the purple velvet. Except I don't think any wicked old stepmother from a fairy tale would be in nothing but fruit of the looms with one hand in a blue rubber glove. I quietly walked out, down to my room, took some Windex and a paper towel and with the rubber-gloved hand, cleaned off the mirror. Then I put the vile back in the bag and the bag back in the boot. End of story.

I went back to sleep and when I woke up, Rick was already gone. Madame Dieux Dieux would be closed today, so I started the day by rolling a big fat joint and plopping my ass down on the living room sofa. I saw the decanter on the bar and was about to go pour a glass of scotch when I remembered Madame Dieux Dieux telling me I smelled like death. So I told myself, "Self, no more drinking in the morning. Pot smoking, yes, but drinking no."

Then I walked into the kitchen and took some of the cold coffee that was left from Rick's morning habit and filled a mug, then got the atomic miracle of a microwave to ding with the announcement that all was as it should be—hot coffee! I plopped back down on the couch, lit the doobie and caught the final Showcase on The Price Is Right. I remember that I thought, "Do you ever think ole Bob Barker might hire some male models?"

And some voice in my head had replied, "That and a black president will be the day."

"Don't go there," I thought.

I got to tell you, Selectric, I just am having a horrible time figuring out who "I" am. Am I the voice that asks the question, or am I the smart ass that doubts that The Price Is Right will ever hire male models? I thought about that while I was sitting on the couch, but I still managed to focus on the Showcase Showdown while putting the question of "Who am I" to rest. I think I was a hundred dollars or so off and won the Caddie. I gotta get on that show. One day, Selectric, I will and I'll come back and tell you about all the treasure I looted from ole Bob and his stable of mares. Come to think of it, I better make it soon, as I'm not sure how many days I've got left. They certainly won't let me on the show with Kaposi spots and Ethiopia neck.

"Nope," I thought and then decided right then and there, "I've got to become a man of action right now."

I took another drag off the doobie and went back to the guest room and you, Selectric. I took out the work that I had been typing and read through it. It's amazing what I'm seeing, Selectric; I see just how half-ass I—whoever I am, is. Man, I really got a bad case of "fuck it's." Come to think of it, if I knew they weren't going to cremate my diseased skin bag, the perfect epitaph on my tombstone would read, "Mason Harrison Caldwell III: Fuck It."

Anyhow, as long as Rick is ashes before me—and with conviction and the help of Madame Dieux Dieux, that should be the case. I wonder if I can mix K with his ashes and snort it and fuck around with my Boy-Toys. I gotta remember that; it is gonna be perfect.

So I spent the main part of the day going back into the previous journaling and adding any thoughts by physically writing in red ink with my multi colored fat Bic pen. I gotta tell you, Selectric, I saw some of Rick's paperwork that he'd printed off his computer on the coffee table the other day—and dude, your days are numbered. It has color, font sizes, pictures … whatever I want. I may be your last buddy, Selectric. I'm sorry, that's wrong of me to try and scare you. I think I will always prefer your rata tat tat, Selectric.

I remember how fascinating the four colors of green, red, black and blue, all accessible in one pen, used to be to us kids of the Schoolhouse Rock! generation. That was only ten or so years ago that that fat Bic miracle came about. Fuck, did my fifth grade teacher have a fit with us turning in papers with green ink. She snatched up every big, fat, four-colored Bic that she could find and sent home letters to the parents about the problem being caused by the green ink. Dude, I gotta tell ya, I can only imagine a computer like Rick has in the hands of my fifth grade compadres. We would have drove ole Lady Harrell out of her behived head. She would have short circuited and looked more like the bride of Frankenstein than she already did.

I gotta say it, Selectric. You'd think with space shuttles and computers, they'd be able to come up with a cure for AIDS, don't ya?

"Who is they?" you ask, Selectric.

Well, just like Madame Dieux Dieux said, "They is the invisible they"

Anyhow, it's getting late and I've got another early morning of poisoning to get to, so let me call it a day. Selectric, I appreciate all of the insight that you are giving me. I'll be back tomorrow to fill you in with more information.

Night Selectric.

CHAPTER 41

Fort Lauderdale, June 26th, 1992

WELL, I NEARLY FUCKED UP. AND I GUESS, AFTER READING THROUGH some of my previous pages yesterday, that I'm low on fuel in the vocabulary area. I tend to say/write the word "fuck" quite often. But, oh boy, did I nearly give myself a fucking heart attack this morning.

Selectric, we nearly said our adieu's today. If you electric appliances can speak to one another through their energized currents, please do me a favor and ask the telephone to put itself on mode "Ringer Off" from midnight till 7:30. I'd do it myself but it would do no good as Rick does so much business from his phone that he would notice that the ringer was off and would certainly get pissed—or worse.

So I'll skip the step by step Anne Rice bullshit and get right to the point. There I was, about to place Rick's poisoned earring back on the purple velvet when the phone rang—at 6:30 in the morning! Are you fucking kidding me! Good God, it's been a while since I couldn't breathe. Not even the words of the good Dr. Ball knocked the breath out of me like the sound of that God damned phone. I mean, I freaked.

"Oh fuck!" my limited vocabulary mind thought to itself as I physically froze. There was no plurality of conversations between myself and Selves A-Z. Only self A stayed in this crisis. The rest are a bunch of fucking cowards and I couldn't have pulled them out of their hiding places at that moment with the bait of pure cocaine, or even K. In an instant I thought, "How in the hell will I explain this motherfucking blue glove? Much less being in Rick's Room?" I could weasel out of being in the room by a quick lie like, "I missed watching you sleep," despite how fucking creepy that would sound, but the blue glove would get me busted for sure. What would I say? That I was doing some early morning dusting?

"Run!" I heard myself say and again, there was no argument or conversation concerning this very strong suggestion; it was automatic.

I dropped the earring only hoping it fell on the padded velvet and bolted for the door. Before the second ring I was in the hall and almost inside the door of the guest room when the second ring was cut short by

Rick's voice. I heard Rick groggily breathe and say, "Hello, Uh huh, good morning, Jay"

"For real!" my mind screamed in silence. "Really, Jay, at motherfucking 6:30 in the bloody fucking morning? What kind of freak calls before eight motherfucking A.M.? We ain't selling drugs, queer."

"No, that's alright, bud," I heard Rick assure the ill-bred asshole.

I didn't bother to listen to the rest of the conversation. I silently closed the door and crept over to the open closet and placed the rubber glove down in the boot where the little leather pouch with the black glass vial were already snug in the toe. I didn't bother to clean the little mirror of any residue. And never mind that the room was stuffy as a motherfucker with the vent closed and the overhead fan still. I got into bed and pretended to be sleeping. But of course sleep was impossible. I can't remember a drug that had me as high as that phone ringing did.

Within minutes, I heard Rick in the kitchen running water and closing cabinets, already in the daily morning ceremony of making coffee. I couldn't stand it. I had to know if he saw me. So I jumped out of bed and caught myself in front of the mirror just in time to allow myself the necessary moment to slow down and assume the character of a just awakened night owl. Satisfied with my appearance, I opened the bedroom door and walked into the hallway bathroom and relieved my now aching bladder, as I silently thought, "I can't believe I didn't piss myself."

After I flushed, I walked into the kitchen and yawned a big yawn as Rick stood there in full nudity, encouraging the coffee maker to hustle.

He half whispered, "Oh dude, I hope I didn't wake you. I'm so sorry."

"No worries," I yawned and then made a motion with my hand to my ear, that it was the phone call that had got me up.

Rick closed his eyes and shook his head, then said, "I know. Dude, I can't tell you how sorry I am about that. It's just sinking in how hysterical Jay was. I mean I can't believe it!"

"What the fuck? Is he alright?" I sincerely asked. I mean despite the near bust from his phone call, and that I had nearly fed him to the sharks, I actually like Jay. But I had to fake the rest of my response as soon as Rick explained the urgency of what the call was all about.

"Yeah, Jay is fine," Rick grunted and then reached into the fridge to get out his cream, which he started pouring into the empty mug. He explained further, as he continued his morning ritual, adding sugar then placing the cream and sugar concoction in the microwave so that it would not cool the coffee that was brewing. "It's just that Steve is in a jam and Jay needs some help."

"This early?" I sleepily inquired.

"Yep," Rick responded and came over and gave me a kiss right on the mouth, morning breath and all.

I squinted and he continued as he walked back to the microwave and took the coffee mug out and placed it next to the coffee maker which was not yet half full.

"Seems our boy Steve is not quite so mountain stream-pure as we all thought," he said.

In contempt, I responded, "Don't put me in that we. I know bullshit when I see it, and that dude is bullshit."

"Bullshit in jail," said Rick.

"No shit?" I questioned and quickly had to catch my adrenaline rush that was about to betray my sleepy act.

"Yes shit," Rick said as he cheated on the undone coffee pot and in a professional and quick act, placed his cup in the spot of the coffee pot. Then in one swift scoop, he poured coffee into the mug as it sat catching the drizzle from the machine.

There was no mess, only the slight hiss of a small drop of liquid on the burner plate that had skipped the replacement transaction from the cup back to the pot. I'd hoped that the hiss drowned out my suppressed laugh as I was supposed to be too sleepy to really take all this in. So I kinda woke up a little more in response to the news and took Rick's coffee cup from him and had a sip, then gave it back and asked, "So what gives?"

"It seems Steve has been a cat while Jay sleeps through the early morning hours."

"How the fuck?" I asked a little too anxiously and further clarified, "I mean, don't they share a bed?"

"Yep," Rick said, then added "Jay has started some kind of antidepressant that seems to knock him out till six or seven. I guess Steve couldn't sleep—and no wonder!"

"What d'ya mean?"

"Steve's in jail because he bought a quarter ounce of crank from an undercover agent early this morning." And while I'm sure my jaw dropped at this, Rick let loose the bomb, "at the baths."

I bet my eyes nearly popped out of my head at that. I know that all I could conjure to say right away was, "Scandal!"

Rick chuckled and said, "You can take the belle out of the South but you just can't get her out of those hoop skirts."

"Fuck off," I retorted.

I'm certain that I must have been visibly embarrassed as Rick sat down his coffee and came over and gave me a hug with one arm and a scalp burn with the knuckles of his other fist.

Then he teased, "You be out of your Shimmies before I get home tonight, ya hear now." His attempt at Southern slang was poor and again I don't like being teased for being effeminate. It brings back too many memories of when I was four, five, and six years old. So I pulled free and went into guest bathroom and showered. All the while the asshole hollered that he was sorry and that he was only kidding.

While I was showering Rick shouted through the locked door, "Andy, come on. I was only kidding."

I didn't respond and there was silence for about two or three minutes, then Rick spoke loudly again through the locked guest bathroom door, "Hey, I'll be back in a little while. I gotta bring Jay some dough and then give him a ride up to the Sheriff's to see if he can bail Steve out or whatever."

I thought about retorting something like, "No shit" as I was astounded that Jay was going to try and get the twink out of jail. But I caught myself and remembered that I was mad at Rick and hollered back, "Whatever."

"Okay, but please, no fucking poison fish or anything. I was just kidding. Okay?" he pleaded.

I think I heard him chuckle. Regardless, at the sound of the front door slamming, I turned off the shower and grabbed a towel and raced out of the bathroom drying myself as I ran into the living room. The place looked and felt empty. So I ran back to his room and looked and saw no sign of him. I checked the bathroom to make double sure, and then I went directly to his dresser.

As luck would have it, the earring had landed and had stayed on the purple velvet. But as luck wouldn't have it, I knew that Rick had not put it on, but I surmised that he would be back to shower and get ready for the day after he helped Jay out with the speeding hillbilly quasi pseudo altar boy.

I caught myself breathing heavily. I guess it was from the running. Then I remembered the mirror in my room that I had not cleaned off and went and very carefully cleaned off any of the deadly crystals that might have avoided the pin of the earring. I sat down on couch in the living room and took a deep breath and then, of course, I lit a joint.

Selectric, I gotta say I got the journal out after Rick had gone. I spent the day reading through and adding some thoughts. One thing became very apparent. That is that I have run a lot. I think I'm even breathing heavy right now as I think about it. I'm tired; tired of running.

And Selectric, as I sit here and type on you tonight, I feel that I have finally stopped running. I find that I've stopped and breathed and am squared off and facing the bull head on. Do I have a red cape? Do I need one? So many questions you bring about, Selectric. Some answers come flying back from your little electric ball as it whirls out words of random thought, in its honest pentameter, some really good answers.

Oh, and just a quick note before I sign off from you. Even though Rick and Jay could not get the first lady of country music out of the slammer, Rick did come home and dress for work. He ignored me and left me alone in my room with you, but upon closer second inspection, after the front door had shut, the purple velvet proved to be vacant of any jewelry.

Uh huh.

Night Selectric.

CHAPTER 42

Fort Lauderdale, June 29th

GOOD MORNING, SELECTRIC. RICK JUST LEFT WITH HIS DIAMOND earring that will propel him into eternity, and he left behind the smell of his cologne which helps to keep him in my mind. My boyfriend does wear some good smelling sauce. It takes over the house in the morning. But he's gone. So here we are again.

Well, Rick has gone to help Jay find another attorney and try and get our boy Steve out of jail. I can't believe Jay is trying to get the sassy bitch out. Would I spring Rick? Hell yes. I can't poison him if he's in jail.

I'm feeling a bit more optimistic today. For one, I could swear that I heard Rick sneezing and coughing this morning, as I feigned sleep while he went through his coffee and balcony rituals, to get ready for the day. Could it mean … We'll just have to wait and see when he gets back today.

To boot, Selectric, I've enjoyed our sessions this past weekend exploring the "Committee." Someone once tried to tell me that feelings weren't facts. Bullshit. How I feel about something is about as close to the truth as I can get. If I'm not honest with my feelings, then I'm not being honest at all. And if I'm not being honest, then you and I can't possibly observe the truth, can we?

And you are to be given full credit with the new addition to the journal, Selectric. If you hadn't brought to mind, whichever mind be it, A-Z; Then I would never have even noticed the committee that apparently must inhabit all of my psychic realm. Whatever "my" is or whoever "I" am, are questions yet to be answered. "The Committee" exists and meets anywhere and everywhere and in every mind of that alphabetic psychotic realm. Of that, I'm as certain as I'll ever be.

Yes, Selectric, with your rhythmic tat-a-tat taps and whirling ball that has placed these little symbols that represent thoughts and questions, I was able to notice on the physical paper a stunning perspective. "Who" was asking the questions and "who" was answering them in my mind has not yet been made clear. But, and this is a big "but," Selectric, they are all possessed by the same characters. All aspects of the mind, which

I'm beginning to look at as one of those liquid bubble machines popping out, instead of only bubbles, but bubbles with an additional bubble machine within each bubble ad infinitum. The bubble machine equals "The Mind"?

Oh boy, I think I'm spinning, Selectric, because when I look at the bubbles when the light plays on them, they all have the same color or prism appearing on their oh-so-delicate membranes. Then they pop. But never you fear, Selectric—more are made. I suspect, and I can only suspect, that these new bubbles are Selves A-Z, possibly Selves Aa, Ab, et cetera until the popping runs us back to self A-Z all over again. And even though they have popped, selves A-Z never lose any of their previous information. They just keep coming back with that beautiful prism of color. Is their color "The Mind"?

Yes, Selectric, of course I've been smoking some really good shit this morning, but as I just mentioned, I'm also feeling incredibly optimistic about my venture. Although I haven't got the committee up to date with the rest of the journal, they are showing me an entirely new side of my being. I like them, Selectric. They are much better than talking to my image in the mirror. In fact, I believe they are much more real than my image. No, Selectric, please don't worry. I don't think I like The Committee better than you. "Why is that?" you ask, Selectric. Well, I guess it is because I have absolutely no control over the committee. Oh come on now, please don't pout.

As I said, Selectric, It takes smoking some pretty good shit and—okay, Selectric, okay!—you are absolutely right. If we are being honest, we must be honest. I did blot a tiny bit of acid early last Saturday morning. But I didn't drink any alcohol! No Sir, I was good for my word. What's that you ask, Selectric?

"How tiny was the blot of acid? Remember Mason. Honesty, honesty; that's our policy."

Well, Selectric, it was as small as any blotter I've ever done and yes, I think it may be lingering. And yes, I did a blot on Sunday too. There, happy? What's that, Selectric?

"Perhaps you should stay away from my keys until the 'tiny' blot wears off."

Please just cooperate, Selectric? And no more attitude. I might start thinking that you are flaking on me and my mission. I'd hate to throw you out the window, into the pool, and then go and buy a new typewriter—one with auto-correct!

No! I'm not threatening you, Selectric; I'm merely stating my options. They are my options; whichever "my" or "I" A-Z, happens to be controlling the fingers playing upon your sainted keys. And yes, that counts for any "I" influenced by acid or drugs of any kind. You just keep laying down the ink and we'll get through this shortly.

As a matter, of fact, I think I'll/we'll revisit 'The Committee now. Get back on track, you know. I'll get back to you later tonight on Rick's condition. Oh boy, Selectric! This is getting good!

• • •

Good evening, Selectric. I have more good news even though I feel like shit; I am not of this world. But you'll be quite happy to know that I've gotten some sleep and am not nearly as manic as I was earlier today. But dude, an acid hangover is the worst. I guess that's why the good Lord invented marijuana. Let's see if I can get my neurotic head together and bring us up to date.

Rick is sick as a big dog on Valentine's chocolate. He is full of snot, coughing and sneezing, and just plain miserable. Hell, he was so sick he asked me to do him a favor involving his business. I mean he has literally never asked me to get involved in his Real Estate in any capacity. But tonight, he came in looking like shit and put down his brief case and while he got undressed, asked me to put a Supra on a unit down on the second floor.

So I asked, "Sure dude, but what the fuck is a Supra?"

"It's the keyless lock system we use so other Realtors can get into our listings."

"What's a listing?" I asked innocently enough and he nearly blew like Mount Saint Helens.

"For fuck's sake, Andy, will you just go down to the second floor and put this blue thing on the door of Unit 209? Not hard, not complicated, it just hangs over the door handle."

"I didn't think you sold like houses and stuff, only businesses?" I wondered.

Rick took a deep breath and with forced patience briefly explained that some old couple he knows from the Condo Association is selling and wants to list, but not pay a Realtor. Rick vaguely explained that he is a Commercial Broker but since the Berkley's have been good for business, he took the listing on some kind of flat fee.

"Cool," I said pretending I understood what he said. I was vague on a "listing" but "flat fee" might well have been Greek. So I thought to myself, "Whatever," then said aloud, "Unit 209, right?"

"Yes. Thank you," he curtly replied, and took off his pants, then just left them on the floor. He walked to his bathroom and I could hear him sneezing and hacking.

So I took the blue, lost in space-looking Supra and walked out of the unit and headed for the elevator. I had never seen one like this, so when I was riding down to the second floor, I was toying with it, and long story short, I clamped the hook that was supposed to hang over the door handle. I mean, it was an innocent enough mistake to make considering my schizoid frame of mind from the acid hangover. I didn't even realize I'd made a mistake until I tried to put the thing on the door and apparently the damn apparatus had to be open to clamp over the knob. You know, I hadn't ever done anything like this before.

So I took the thing back up to Rick's and he is already in bed with the lights out and only a little evening sun seeping through the dark curtains of the sliding glass door of his bedroom. And I interrupt the blessed silence and darkness and whisper, "Rick, you asleep already? Rick?"

He groggily and somewhat irritated replied, "Not yet Andy. What is it, babe?"

"I fucked up, Rick. I clamped the thingamajig down before I put it on the door."

I must've sounded like Lenny from Of Mice And Men because either he took pity on me or was careful not to insinuate that he thought I was stupid, when actually in this case, stupid was about the only way to describe my condition.

"S, P, Y" he specifically responded, and said, "Can you do that Andy? The code is S. P. Y. Now let me sleep, dude."

"Okay, Rick. Sorry," I quietly apologized and backed out of the room.

I could tell from the tone of his voice that he was about to blow again and I didn't want that, with the strange frame of mind of an acid hangover, almost bordering on elation. But I witnessed just how sick he was and how fast the crystals were working on him.

"Holy Shit!" I thought, "Madame Dieux Dieux, I love you."

I quietly shut the front door and caught the elevator with the blue thingamajig down to the 2nd floor and found myself once again stumped. I had never seen a lock other than my gym locker which had all the numbers on a dial. This thing had various letters on three separate rolls.

I must have looked like an ape playing with a calculator. I sat down and leaned back against the wall by the door of unit 209 and brought my knees up. Dude, I gotta tell ya; an acid hangover can make the simple sequences of the ritual of a Mr. Coffee load difficult. So I worked the tumblers as I remembered that Rick had verbally spelled "SPY." So I fumbled with the sticky little rollers to spell SPY and pushed a little button and out fell a box with a key.

"Hurray" I silently congratulated myself.

But the lock box was still in no position to place on the door handle. I looked at it with more curiosity as the guts of the apparatus were exposed after the key box had fallen out when a voice in my head casually suggested, "Open the door and go in."

I was about to instantly put the suggestion into action when another part of my mind questioned, "Dude, if you go in there, that could, like, put you in a situation where you could jeopardize your plan with Rick. You know? You can't poison crystals on his earring if you are in jail."

Some other part of my mind in areas Q through T perhaps, I'm not exactly sure, tried to rationalize that it wasn't breaking and entering if one had a key. But then F, with his all-powerful word came through and said, "Fuck it."

As I stood up and was about to place the key in the keyhole, some other aspect, I would suspect Self C, politely came in and said, "Hey Dumbass, don't you think you ought to know and make sure you're just not barging in on people at dinner. Come on now, Cinderella, use that big pumpkin you have for a head. Knock, numb nuts."

"But what would I say if they answered the door?" queried Self A.

"That you didn't want to startle them as you hung the thingamajig, so you knocked."

"Good thinking," said Self B.

"Yeah, and if no one is home, we can go in and take the silver and jewels," said Self Q.

"Shut the fuck up, dumbass," said Self C, who then added, "you just gonna take the loot and stash it back at Rick's and when the police come looking for Rick, there it is and they haul Rick off to jail and he loses his job, and no income coming in, and you can't poison him while he's in jail, and …

"We get it," interrupted Self A.

"Fuck it," countered Self F, who then gruffly added, "Knock on the Goddamned door."

So I knocked. I sat for about twenty seconds and listened for any sounds of activity, then knocked again. Alas, no response so I opened the door.

The Unit was flat empty, with only the hall light on. I inspected the place and, even if I was stupid enough to rob someone, there was no furniture, no people, no silver, and no jewelry—just a great view of the swimming pool directly below the balcony. And I chuckled aloud as I thought, "Jesus, can't you imagine some old geezer getting his eyes full as he gazes on the tits and ass just below him while old lady Barkley, or Berkley or whatever, bitches at him from the kitchen to get off his lazy fat ass and take out the garbage."

And Self C, always the clever counter, sent out, "Yep he could just holler back at the old bag, 'Okay Dear, just give me a second' and then turn around to the girls on the pool and shout down in his best Bronx dialogue, 'hold on girls (giwwarls), Daddy's diving in.'"

We all chuckled at the thought, then decided that we had better get out of there before things went South. So I fumbled with the thingamajig and after a few attempts got the clamp opened and put it on the door, then shoved the key tray with the key up in the contraption. As I walked off, something told me it was not right. I turned around and looked at the door and immediately noticed that I had put the damned thing on backwards. The lettered tumblers were facing the wall.

"Awe shit!" exclaimed Self A. "Fuck it," Self F calmly stated.

I turned around and walked off. That was that, Selectric, end of the day. I'm going to go and puff a few more neuroses away, quietly as a mouse mind you, so that I don't wake up Rick. Then I'm gonna turn in, Selectric.

Night.

CHAPTER 43

Fort Lauderdale, Saturday, July 4th, 1992

A s you are well aware, Selectric, I haven't been ignoring you these past few days. You and I have been exploring "The Committee" and I have to say, Selectric, they are essential in this little quest for Truth. I've almost got them up to date. Amazing, but no matter who I find myself playing Q&A with, I find The Committee jumping around with full regalia in vivid Technicolor. I'm beginning to suspect they may in fact, be the key, if not the flat out answer, to many of the questions that have arisen since I've departed on this venture with you. You have to admit, Selectric, even though you only print in black and white, The Committee demands to be seen in color. Truly! But are they the definitive point of origin that tells my finger which of your keys to press; that in turn begins the sequence of events that ultimately becomes a letter, which in turn becomes a word that translates into thought. Is The Committee the product of thought or thought's originator?

Yes I know, Selectric, we're getting a bit "Chicken and Egg" here, so we'll get back to color. Fascinating isn't it? "It" being, color. Yep, it would suck to be color blind. Some people are. I'm told all dogs are color blind, only seeing in black and white and shades of grey. I wonder what a dog or color blind person would have made of the fireworks display that the city put on for all of our pleasure tonight.

Rick was too sick to be lured out of bed and down to the beach for the evening's July 4th extravaganza. And, I'm pretty sure that he couldn't see it from our patio. Whoa! Our patio. Did you hear that, Selectric? Uh huh, you did. Interesting don't you think, kinda like what's Rick's is Ours and Ours is Mine—my patio. What's that, Selectric? Okay, okay, let's get back to the fireworks and color. Jesus, Selectric.

What I found interesting was that the color really pounces off the black Selectric. Can you imagine if paper were black and your ink was in color? Exciting thought huh? Yes, I think it would be a bit much too. But no doubt, the fireworks certainly fare much better against a blackened night sky than in daylight. What am I getting at, you ask? I guess I'm attempting to take a stab at the notion that so many wonderful things come out of the dark. Speaking of dark, I saw Madame Dieux Dieux today.

Except for her palms and the soles of her feet, she is as black as coal. She was in flowing full force today in her scarlet Hellenistic ensemble with bright yellow accessories. She took advantage of the holiday lure the beach holds for the mass of consumer units that comprise this great city. There was Madame Dieux Dieux, peddling her wares, in vivid color and playing a role that could have only been written for her. I stepped in to assist her with the abundance of customers, which helped her out. But I didn't take any commission. As we were closing up, I finally got a chance to talk to her.

"Tank you, Mason, for de help today. Here now, you push and I try and clear us da path and steer dis bitch," she instructed, referring to the challenge we were going to face, navigating the closed kiosk through the ever-enlarging crowd that began to clog the sidewalk as evening and the fireworks display approached.

When we finally had the kiosk locked away in the security of the shed, Madame Dieux Dieux went to her Corolla's trunk to find her bank bag and returned with some bills in an obvious attempt to pay me my commission. As I said, I didn't take any money that day, but in the fading light I explained to her, "No Madame Dieux Dieux, it was my pleasure to help you out today, if only for a couple of hours. Please!" I said as I held up my hands to express my refusal to accept my commission, which I suspect would have been far too generous to begin with, and added, "But I would like a moment to ask you a few questions about …"

I paused as I knew not to speak about the poison in a crowded public place and she responded after only a second or two of semi-confusion and said, "Come sit wid me in my car."

I did as I was told and when we were both comfortably seated, she looked at me and asked, "It working already?"

"Yes," I vocally breathed out, a bit amazed that she would ask so directly, as if she already knew.

She looked at me sincerely and with an expression that translated clearly as, "Well, what'd you expect?" So I continued, "Yes, it took hold pretty quick, starting last Monday and has progressed to a really nasty, flu like …" I stumbled for a word and finally said, "sickness."

Madame Dieux Dieux shrugged and said, "So it is. What you worried about?"

"Well, I'm not 'worried' so to speak," I emphasized as I corrected her appraisal of my condition and continued, "But I need to know. Is the stuff irreversible once it's in him? You see, he hasn't been going to work and so hasn't been putting on his earring. Even if I wanted, I couldn't have doused the damned thing with the shit. He's hardly out of his room."

"Yeap," she replied in the universal Haitian conjugation to, "That's the way it goes." And with no hint of emotion she stated, "He gone die."

"So I don't have to worry about giving him anymore?" I anxiously asked.

"No, he a dead man. Go ahead and trow dat powder out, but be careful how you do it. Don't just put it in the garbage. Dat shit break and fly out; whew! Der gone be some dead people or dogs laid about."

I nodded my head in confirmation and began to consider how I would dispose of the powder when Madame Dieux Dieux grabbed my attention with an ambiguous remark. "I would say by dis time next week, you be widout."

We sat for a few seconds in silence as I pondered the word she had just said; "without." The way she said it in her Creole dialect, it rang with something akin to an emptiness that I couldn't fully comprehend in dialect. A finality, if you will, that I felt somewhere in the depths of my chest, that I had no idea existed. The silence was finally broken by the screech of a gull that pierced through the steady mumble of the growing crowd closer to A1A. What a screech, Jesus, it gave me the heebie jeebies. I still couldn't express my feelings in words so I bluntly asked the woman, "Without what?"

Madame Dieux Dieux did not answer directly in a word. She gave her head a slight cock to the left, pursed her lips and her jaws tightened to accentuate her emaciated features. Her eyes, fully open and not blinking, shot a blazing answer to my naive question.

Madame Dieux Dieux's lips slowly and ever so slightly relaxed. "Come now my Mason. Why would you ask me such a silly ting?"

I dropped my gaze from her and while looking down at the sand-encrusted floormats of her old Japanese beater, I fumbled for something to say. Funny, I felt it but I couldn't express it. There was silence. Then there was nothing. No feeling, Nothing. Nothing. NO THING. And then, as if The Big Bang theory decided to prove itself, She about gave me a heart attack when she stated much too loudly, "Hey! You hungry? I treat you to a steak, den give you a ride home, since you work for free today."

I wasn't hungry and the memories of the cardiac sensations I had from my last ride with her were vividly refreshed. I again declined her generosity and she said, "Okay den," and turned the ignition to bring the little import life.

I didn't waste a second and jumped out of the car. We exchanged no more words and I watched and heard her tear the gears of the rusty Corolla as she backed up then honked her way through the crowds on A1A; she returned any angry comments in incomprehensible French to the 4th of July revelers through the open windows of her car.

I stayed down at the beach and waited for the fireworks, Selectric. And how the Committee did come to life as I sat alone under a palm even though I was surrounded by hundreds, if not thousands, of people. Was this "Without"? I think so. But then the darkness fell. Ahhh, the color exploded in the empty and vast summer night's sky. Vaguely, I heard a little girl asking what I presumed to be her Daddy, "So how old are we today"

He replied, "You know you're four."

"No, Poppa. Us, United States. How old are we?"

When he replied, I could hear his Spanish accent as he fumbled for an answer, "We are, let me see; somewhere over two hundred years old."

I almost corrected him by saying that we were "sometime" over two hundred years old but that didn't make any since. Did it?

"Where and when are we anyway?" a voice in my head asked me.

And as the flashes of color exploded and the booms thundered, I heard the little girl squeal in delight and I could make out her silhouette as she sat atop her father's shoulder; the dazzling lights and configurations over two blankets of black provided by the ocean and the night sky. Perfect conditions, Selectric, for The Committee to spring to life. I had heard that child's ecstatic squeal before. Only that situation wasn't nearly close to being as innocent as this kid's delight.

Let's not say goodnight just yet, Selectric. Let us again explore the revelations of The Committee. Boy, can I hear them. Yes Selectric, loud and clear.

CHAPTER 44

July 4th, 1992

The Committee

SHE FELT A TRICKLE AGAINST HER CHEEK. THEN HER TONGUE, without any instruction, escaped her mouth to catch the splendid moisture and channeled the treasured relief into its domestic cavern so that it might share the joy and bring sustenance to the append-ages of a parched and battered being.

"Joy" thought Miss Love as her mind continued to manipulate her momentary experience, "Bliss".

But the delight was short lived as the wanton purity of the moment was taken away because her lips, responding in residual harmony to the melody of Joy and Bliss, ever so slightly began to produce a smile. The effect of this was to produce a sting; a rather sharp and notice-able sting. The corners of her dried lips had cracked and thus, the mother of life, water, that escaped the imperfect funnel of her tongue had allowed the liquid, acting in true form like a battlefield medic, to find its way to the clamoring wounds to provide solace and reprieve. This it did, but with ramifications drastic enough to cause the delicate sisters, Joy and Bliss, to run for the proverbial hills.

Yet, happiness remained as her tongue ignored the uncomfort-able information and continued to lap and curl the nourishing stream into the Sahara that had become the home of our dithering heroine.

"Where am I? When am I" she thought.

This thought diminished her happiness only to the extent of being; Well? Glad? The lack of any answer to her questions had created a tinge of anxiety. But anxiety too, like Joy and Bliss, can be averted through nuisance and Miss Love's cousins, Happiness and Glee, were again creating residual ramifications with her physical vocal cords. They had begun to respond to the trickle of glee her mouth was sharing with the Mississippi of all earthly mammalian creatures—the throat.

With the help of will and instinct, sounds began to lightly hum from the double edged swords that comprised the cords of that cursed component which can create so much happiness and so much pain. The sounds began as faint moans; moans of ecstasy gradually diminished to sounds that resembled an imperfect chord from a novice child learning piano. They began to sound like renditions of music that escape the night time mouth, loosened from rest by feverish dreams.

Her tongue, as if it had a mind of its own, kept to task. Although the stream felt as though it was declining in volume and thus administering a slight change of course, Miss Love's tongue was able to emit information to her central being by tilting her head ever so slightly, "this way".

The command from her tongue gained priority attention in Miss Love's central being. It trumped the anxious questions of, "Where and When am I". Despite the fact that it had been some time since the shell shocked and broken hag had moved so much as a finger, her mind conjugated the vague instruction, "This way," which had been given by her tongue. Ever so slightly but with enough determination to continue as a reservoir for the miracle that was flowing down upon her, Miss Love's head moved and her body thanked her a thousand times for the posturing adjustment that allowed heaven's nectar to nourish her heroic soul. But resounding gratitude was expressed for only a split second.

That slight movement by Miss Love's head had awoken nerves in her upper spinal area. Along with those nourishing and wet sensations received from the gift of the Nile, the nerves were now back at work as they too conveyed information. Slowly at first, then in the fashion of a Napoleonic regiment on a frontal assault, they overwhelmed her mind and her central being with more questions and attempts at answers:

"Where am I? When am I? Who am I?"

Then the "I" responded, "In a crater. In the moment. You are Love."

"Okay then," she sluggishly concurred to herself.

And as is always the case in situations that Miss Love was now experiencing, one question answered—or as in this case three, lead to hundreds more. So she quietly stuttered aloud that most common English expression of an exception or detection of Paradox, "But, But—"

But Miss Love was to receive no more answers, at least not immediately. For along with the information being directed by the recently awoken nerves there came the great wail of sirens and urgent honks from emergency ambulances, Sheriff patrols and fire trucks. They were screaming by all of the cars and trucks that had dutifully yielded to the sides of the information highway that led to Central Being. It was difficult for anyone at "C.B." to read the inscriptions on the racing emergency vehicles as they approached, but as they began screeching to a halt outside of Central Being, their purpose became clear, very clear. Their inscriptions read neither "Sisters of Mercy Hospital," "Love Patrol" nor anything else like that. No, in bright red print in spaces usually reserved for identification for relief agencies, was printed the single word, "PAIN".

The reaction from Central Being to the onslaught of approaching pain was conveyed to Miss Love in such a manner that the British have mastered in the modern information age—The Documentary. This episode rang true to the script of any footage ever made recalling the "Finest Hour" of the English people, because the footage dramatically revealed massive searchlights turned on and pointed wonderingly into the night sky in an attempt to identify the location of the aerial Nazis, as they approached the sitting duck of London. And simultaneously, the command was given to crank the air raid sirens to warn the sleeping population of the oncoming, invisible danger so that they could run for shelter into the safety provided by the caverns of the great city's subway tunnels.

Miss Love's vocal chords, which had just previously been mumbling softly and incoherently, received the orders and dutifully complied. She screamed the chorus of a thousand felines being entered by the barbed pricks of a thousand Toms. Thus, Miss Love was awoken from her merciful slumber and forced to embrace and comprehend the living nightmare in vivid Technicolor, of the conscious emotional realm.

Her eyes popped open and at once were stung by the drizzling liquid that was no longer a steady stream. She screamed in agony and blind frustration and began nipping at her broken appendages in much the same way that a stray dog, struck by a car, attacks the invisible culprit that has long sped away but has left the canine's guts visible and so the poor creature fights a futile fight against thin air. She was in fact, a fatally wounded beast.

And like any creature that dies in rage, there came that moment when all its energy had been exerted, and body and mind, in a serene state of acceptance, became still. Miss Love, still in agony, was breathing slowly; she relaxed to recognize the inevitable and she was true to her very nature. She actually began to relish her pain.

"'Allo Love," a strong Cockney dialect which had eliminated the 'H' in hello, echoed all through the empty courtroom and some twenty or so feet down into the crater where the voice was perceived by the ears of our dying and deranged heroine, Miss Love.

Calmly and without moving her head, she rolled her eyes in the direction of the Cockney hail. Their focus made out the silhouette of a fairly large, uncircumcised dick held by a small gloved hand that was shaking the obnoxious organ so that the last drips could escape to splat Miss Love right on her face and just close enough to her mouth so that her tongue, still on auto pilot from the previous delusions, lapped at the piss and brought it voluntarily inside her body.

"At a girl. Got to do what we can to keep our strength up, anyway we can at a time like this. And you're welcome Love." Said Mr. Revenge as he released the folded foreskin and folded it down to the classical depiction of Greek statutory. One would have thought that he was handling a Boa Constrictor from the way he put his dick back in his pants, adjusted himself and allowed the spandex of his tight red underwear to pop at the conclusion of the task. It was as if he were caging an unwilling serpent.

"Go to hell" Miss Love grumbled in a raspy voice that she pulled from her gut with the last ounce of strength.

"Ah Dear, lest we forget, one girl's hell is another boy's heaven." replied Mr. Revenge.

He chuckled to himself, at his cleverness, and clasped his hands behind his back and began to stroll casually around the rim of the His/Her Honor's crater. Mr. Revenge kicked a few pieces of rocky debris out of his foot path. Some of them fell on the motionless face of Miss Love and she made no movement or attempt to respond to the particles. As the heels of his Super Hero red boots slowly clicked and echoed through the empty Gothic courtroom, Mr. Revenge began to lecture the broken heap that lay silently upon the bottom of the crater floor.

"Now Love, appears that you've been momentarily refreshed so that you might, if I dare say, enjoy, a hospice of sorts before passing on."

He paused to allow her a response and he was again about to cordially explained that there was no need for her to express gratitude, as her tongue had thanked him quite sufficiently when she coarsely whispered through faint and pastel shades of blue, green, and purple, "I can't die."

Mr. Revenge unwittingly released one of his cupped hands from behind his back and swatted at the powdery orbs of information Miss Love had burped as if they were mosquitoes or gnats. The pesky apparitions disappeared and the bright glow of his red and black sequins, highlighted with a touch of yellow, gradually dominated, and lit the courtroom, akin to a disco ball releasing its spirits upon the frivolous frames of weekend skin bags worshipping a Maypole provided by the virtuous ecstasy chemist of Holland. Red and black; the colors, all but warnings of 'poison' to any beings able to comprehend Mother Nature's strange sense of mercy. These colors were without doubt the master shades of the moment, pleasing and attractive to most eyes that comprehend color, despite their natural implication of malice. Their brilliance—His brilliance—subjugated all particles of His/Her Honors courtroom as Mr. Revenge, in full glory, proceeded to embark on a soliloquy of explanation and intent.

He stopped walking and looked down, not at Miss Love, but through her, as if she did not exist, and said, "Let's take a look at this conundrum. How shall I examine it so we can better comprehend your little predicament?"

He paused and brought the finger of his hand, which had just swatted Miss Love's statements, to his pursed lips. He took a few more slow steps and clasped his hands again behind his back, and stated loudly and deliberately, "A virus! Yes, that's the proper analogy to you, Love. You don't mind me dropping the formalities do you now dear. I find that we've become so familiar that it seems almost ridiculous not to cut through the red tape of the marital status quo spoken in me native land. Yes Love, please, by all means, just refer to me as Revenge."

Suddenly he was pelted with what could only be described as machine gun tracers of deep purple fired from the core of Miss Love that screamed, "Fucker, fucker, fucker. Fucker, fucker, fucker, fucker ..."

But Mr. Revenge was so strong that the repetitive fire of anger glanced off of him with only a smidgeon of effort like the angled steel of the Soviet T 34 repudiated a shocked, an impotent, German artillery brigade.

"Oh, Ohhhh" Mister Revenge Giggled and sheepishly grinned. Then he exalted, "Even in your waning moments, Bravo Dear, Bravo. It is truly a pity that you won't be able to audition as Regan in the future remake of "The Exorcist." So much wasted talent, dear. But I can't allow pity, legitimate or masked, to dither our moment."

He paused for moment, took a deep breath, clapped his hands and as he grasped them behind his back he shouted, "Back to the task at hand. Where were now? Oh indeed, a Virus!" He calmed his posture and took on a boyishly curious temperament, then gleefully analyzed aloud, "What a strange anomaly nature has given us. It is neither dead nor alive. And like you Love, very difficult to be rid of. So how does one "kill" a virus or anything at all that is neither alive nor dead? Really, a virus acts like any living organism in its quintessential desire to procreate."

He stopped walking and bent over to look down at Miss Love and as he kicked a few more grains of debris down onto her he mused, "Peculiar, wouldn't you agree, Love? Our boy Andy doesn't wish to procreate but he is alive, for the moment, mind you, but he will be killed by an organism, that is neither alive nor dead, but does deliberately intend to procreate. Yes indeed, so paradoxical. Especially when the Virus intends to kill the very host which allows it to exist. Very much a case of the serpent eating itself from the tail end up; wouldn't you agree Love?"

Miss Love slowly pulsed like a critical care life monitor, but she was conscious enough to examine that he had asked for her agreement several times now, to his riddles. And she had absolutely no intentions of giving him the satisfaction of any positive accord. So she simply repeated herself and her peaceful but neutral response again reached him in vibrant hues of blue, "I can't die."

"Ah hah!" Mr. Revenge exulted in victory. "So you do see my analogy of circumstance?"

Miss Love gave absolutely no response to his question which vexed Mr. Revenge enough that he again took to his meditative and conjecturing walk around His/Her Honor's crater and, presumably the final resting place of Miss Love.

"No, perhaps you don't see my point Love. Nevertheless, that doesn't imply that I shan't continue killing you. Whether or not you die, I will continue to kill you dear. That is an attempt, despite how futile, I cannot refute. If I can immobilize you to the point where you are not able to enter our host mind, then, like the virus that can no longer enter into its host's cells, you are in fact, inconsequential. Consider me your Vaccine my dear girl, an unsurpassable vaccine that you will never surmount."

"Oh there you are!" Miss Addiction loudly announced as she entered the courtroom almost stumbling. "I was missing you, Puddin'," she added with an adolescent pout, "That party down the street at Lefties, let's just say, it's a little too amateur without you. It's like New Year's Eve with all those goody good two shoes puking everywhere on their one night a year bash."

Upon the interruption, Mr. Revenge looked up and immediately reversed his facial expression of virility and triumph to that of amusement and delight. His concise verbal pentameter resembling a deliberate "Checkmate" turned to flattering and refreshing informality as he lovingly proclaimed, "Ah, me woman."

"Aren't you just the sweetest!" she continued in simpleton, Southern, eye-fluttering idiocy. But she quickly feigned a pout and like a little girl who had been told, "We'll see" to a possible weekend delight at Disney World, she moaned, "Mmm ... sir you haven't made an honest woman of me yet."

"I don't think that's possible, Darling. Just being polite, but I'm certain the honest card 'tis not now nor ever will be dealt into any of your gaming hands. But happiness my Tigris, you shall have. Like a Queen of Spades with every hue of silver and black pixy dust forming a comets tail as the card leaves the dealer's skilled finger and flies obediently towards your seat, Our Lady Happiness will bless your hand. Everything your depraved heart desires, it shall have."

Miss Addiction crinkled her nose and clinched her teeth in the uncontrollable smile of a sociopath, spreading from ear to ear. She squealed in delight again and shuffled her feet in a little dance, which in all probability, must have been performed by any redneck who has struck oil. Then she brought her feet and body to a much more formal posture, held out her hand as if to "take this dance" and gaily glided down the black slate floors of the courtroom aisle toward the galley as if all present could hear the classic Disney, "Someday My Prince Will Come." Only Miss Addiction could hear the tune.

"Bravo dear child! Bravo. A picture of elegance, truly" he lied as he clapped and saluted the inebriated doxy.

Miss Addiction couldn't have looked more like Phyllis Diller after two fifths of cheap vodka, as her bare soup-bone knees struggled to hold her body up, whilst her delusional mind, that was hidden behind her dilated eyes, seemed to flow from their sockets into a stream of mascara upon her gullied face. Better yet, to anyone who could be watching which was only Mr. Revenge, Miss Addiction appeared to be in a trance portrayed by a 1950s B actress., A really bad one at that, who overplayed the role of 'Miss Lucy' as she obeys the Master, Count Dracula, and responds to his beckoning through the mist. In this case it was vibrant, almost metallic, orbs of red, black, and yellow that fluttered and floated like alien Roswell tinfoil, through a three dimensional orifice of the deep purple, common to any night time sky perceived from the lucky recipient of Mother Nature's magic spores.

And although Mr. Revenge had never digested Magic Mushrooms, He watched Miss Addiction sway and shuffle as she entered the cratered galley of His/Her Honor's court and he was struck by the strange sensation, akin to many a child of the sixties, who had 'gone a pickin in the wood' without the proper knowledge of fungi and thus suffered by their ignorant ingestion, a very disturbing experience to say the least. He was not accustomed to this sensation but he was no stranger to masking his thoughts and true intent. Nevertheless, he was thankful that he had the aid of the sequined super hero outfit that covered every inch of his body except his neck and face. Miss Addiction's entry into the courtrooms galley had stricken him, the master of control, with a case of goose bumps that were virtually as ungovernable as the Haitian populace. For the first time, his sense of confidence had been slightly shaken. As she approached him and ever so slightly ran her blood red polished nails backhanded through his hair and down the back of his neck, Mr. Revenge, ever masked, contemplated any likelihood of his ability to place Miss Addiction in the same crater with Miss Love and he quickly concluded that any attempts at her demise by him, would be as futile as a free election in Port-au-Prince. Without the aid of His/Her Honor Fear, (whom he was certain was less likely to alienate or injure Miss Addiction any more than Satan would turn on Der Fuehrer or Stalin) Mr. Revenge knew and accepted the fact that he would have to make the best of his engagement and that he would have to consummate the marriage of convenience with Miss Addiction so that his child of retribution could be born.

Slowly, as if he were a star truck Twinkie of the 80s meeting Madonna in person, Mr. Revenge took the vixen's hand and kissed it with reverence.

"Ah my Tigris, we do have a lonely finger on ye lovely hand yearning for the attention of a golden ring, Do we not?" he questioned in a strange transition to formal British curio.

Miss Addiction responded in the unique giggling that resembled the laughter and hysterical outburst of an antebellum kitchen wench which betrayed aloud, even to Miss Addiction, any resemblance of sophistication. But she neither blushed nor apologized and she didn't give an answer to her masked and sparkling Fiancée'. Instead, and with a pout common to any brat run out of candy, she produced from the chest cups of her strapless party dress for his inspection, the empty Ketamine Bullet.

"What have we here?" Mr. Revenge exclaimed aloud.

Anyone present would have thought by the tone of his outburst that the most egregious lapse of protocol had been committed by an American slob introduced to a British Royal.

"This must be remedied immediately" he further proclaimed, and like magic, as he went down on one knee and bowed head, his gloved hand opened and presented a fresh and filled crystal apparatus for her greedy hand to take and exchange for the useless empty. The 'apparatus' was in fact a ring; a golden ring set with a crystal 'Bullet'. Were it a diamond, and shaped as such, although inverted, the bullet would have been 9 karats'. Miss Addiction had not even noticed that it was a ring but she had no problem with the mechanics of the diamond shaped crystal bullet.

He took the empty exchange and clenched it tightly in his hand which he brought behind his bowed back and stated gallantly with servitude, "My Lady, in which house of worship would ye prefer to exchange our sacred bonafides of golden proclamation to adorn our significant hands as to herald to all the world, we are one, betrothed to each other in a never ending sphere?"

"Mother fuck, can't he just speak plain English?" Miss Addiction thought silently to herself.

Miss Addiction had just finished clearing her nasal membrane with a loud and satisfying snort, at the very moment that Mr. Revenge had completed his haughty prose. As he could read the trollop's thoughts, he had to fight back a grin and keep his head bowed so that she would not perceive the amusement he was generating within himself with these silly antics that he was acting out in order to permanently incapacitate, if not kill Miss Love so that his desires of retribution could come to fruition. And Miss Addiction, fully aware that he could read her mind, could no more have given two cents worth of shit, that Mr. Revenge knew that she hadn't even thought about wedding rings much less a church. And she had yet to realize herself that she had been given a ring. Frankly, she didn't give a frog's fat ass where they got hitched. She didn't belong to any religion, per say, as she could only submit to the chemical and biotic deities that dwelt upon Narcotic Olympus. She had full faith in these Gods of delusion and even if they were false Gods, they were hers. They had sustained her in modern man as graciously as they had done in the ages of the Ancients through the Rrenaissance. She saw no reason whatsoever to abandon her Pagan tribe now. Furthermore, she thought that no good could possibly come by insulting her deities by bringing herself and thus them, into a house of worship designed and modeled on Bronze Age monotheism. With a rush of warm anesthesia and gratitude towards her bowed gentleman, supplied by Goddess K, Miss Addiction again embraced the moment with kitty cat clarity. She purred, "Oh puddin, you chivalrous dear creature. But sugar, I don't much like churches and they don't like me."

"Ah me dear, I've enjoyed some of me better ploys in houses of worship but 'tis my girl that I wish to be happy at the altar. Tis your moment my love. Where and when say ye?"

"Jesus would you just stop with the bullshit" she thought knowing full well that he could read her thoughts and again not really caring. But she loved good theatre and Miss Addiction, who recognized a good set when she saw one, seized the moment as if she were a top contracted lady of the silver screen, about to go into action with an apprentice, she viewed as having no credentials to be in the same studio with her.

"Okay, here's the deal lover boy. As a quasi-pseudo Pagan demigod, I'm telling you, either shit or get off the pot. I wanna exchange vows here, in His/Her Honor Fear's court, under the twinkle of your radiant and gallant light; now!" she demanded in a growl as was the customary nature in many of Miss Addiction's desires.

She had a good thing going and was not about to fuck it up. As well, Miss Addiction, even though she could not read Mr. Revenge, in the same manner as he could her, knew that the little shit wasn't going to jilt her. But she was as eager as any metaphorical beaver to have Andy in control of Rick's estate as soon as possible. She knew Andy wasn't going anywhere without her.

And Mr. Revenge was more than happy to accommodate Miss Addiction's enthusiasm. But he was enjoying the charade he had presented as the kneeling Knight to his lady's pleasure and thus he continued the bullshit.

"Now? Right here? With no rings? A wedding without rings doesn't sound like much of a wedding. Much less, no guests. Although I guess we could give a jingle to Lefties and have the gang walk......."

He was cut off before he could verbally explain the solving of the problem of a guestless ceremony, when Miss Addiction, in true form to any circumstance that was delaying any instant gratification, stepped out of character and revealed her true essence.

"For Christ's sake! As if I ever gave a damn for Jesus even though he had a good trick with that turning water to wine. He got my attention there, but that's about as much of it as I could stomach so Honey, PLEASE, cut the crap, let me take another snort of this lovely gift, which by the way I prefer much more than a ring, and do whatever it is that we need to do to wrap this thing up."

"Darling please, look closer, it is a ring," Mr. Revenge politely revealed.

"HUMmm?" She innocently questioned.

"The Ketamine bumper or bullet or what have you there, is in fact a ring, Dear. A ring I had made special for me girl. Does my bride like?

In an anesthetized daze, Miss Addiction looked down at the gizmo she held and for the first time perceived that it was actually a ring.

"UUUuuuuu," she squealed in delight as she put on the ring whilst her feet went into a mild jig and her arm extended so that she could truly appreciate the lights reflection off the cut of crystal filled to brim with little snowflakes of Ketamine.

Mr. Revenge was fully aware that it was not dazzling lights, the fullness of the semi diamond that intrigued Miss Addiction. He feigned a serious and fatherly tone as he instructed her, "Please, never take it off."

"Honey, don't ever let it run out," she off handedly replied, still gazing in amazement at her ring.

"Deal!" he declared with zest.

And out of nowhere, the splendid purple light in unison with the sparkling wedding bullet and the dancing orbs of Red, Black, and Yellow was cut with the faint outline of an express tube that would be familiar to any mortal American who indulged in drive through banking. There was a slight, "Whoosh!" that was directly followed by the see through canister that held documents rolled up and tied by black satin rope that emanated, in sparkling luster, the unmistakable moss green and sickly yellow aura of His/Her Honor, Fear.

"Very well then!" Mr. Revenge stated as he jumped up and clapped his hands together. "It seems we've pleased His/Her Honor with our intentions. The right place at the right time, so too say. Here we are Dear Lady," he concluded.

He stood up on his tip toes and reached up and took the canister from the express tube. He removed the scrolled documents and handled the roll gingerly, as if they might disintegrate like the express tube and canister apparatus had just done.

"Our license to wed," he announced in a solemn whisper as he looked reverently into Miss Addiction's eyes.

"Okay!" Miss Addiction replied with a shrug and walked over to her former 'defense table' and with an instructive gesture of her hand, patted the table and thus informed Mr. Revenge to reveal the document there. "Where do I sign?" she asked flippantly, as if she were about to execute a gym contract. Mr. Revenge was not by any means whatsoever offended by her laissez-faire attitude and ill-bred manners.

But when he untied the luminous black cord and unrolled what he thought was a fragile article, Mr. Revenge and Miss Addiction were amazed to find the unfolding document metamorphosed from paper to stone. And the characters that comprised the words transformed from ink to engravings that were unmistakably created with the lightning bolts of His/Her Honor's fury. Both of the Betrothed were in awe. Miss Addiction's attitude was instantly charged with a respect for the moment, and followed by a state of tranquilized sentimentality she had previously saved for crying in her beer or appreciating the servicing stud as she lay spread eagle in a sling. And that was about as reverent as the old girl was capable of being.

Mr. Revenge was not unaware of the change that overcame his bedazzled bride and took upon himself a genuine desire to add more beauty to the moment that would perhaps give Miss Addiction happy memories. He presented her with a bouquet of Morning Dumps instantly cut from the intestinal shrubs and delivered by emotional flora express. Miss Addiction squealed in girlish glee and resumed her role as an Antebellum Mistress.

"Oh sir! They're beautiful! Where on Earth did you get them?" she innocently implied.

Mr. Revenge looked at her sheepishly and blushed as he didn't want to pollute the sentiment of the moment with the verbal or, for that matter, any kind of expression which would evoke the image of shit. The ruby hew of his cheeks awoke Miss Addiction's limited memory and she laughed as she recalled the questionable habitat that the flowers grew. But she quickly became quite serious as she remembered the opiate effect the purple petals with hazel magenta eyes had gifted her in the past. Immediately, she took nothing short of an obnoxious whiff of the Morning Dumps and, as if it were possible, she savored new sensations brought about by her entry into a tranquil stratosphere of conscious delight.

While she cradled the bouquet and admired the sculptured prose engraved by His/Her Honor, Miss Addiction imagined that she knew the satisfaction felt by the Virgin of Bethlehem as Mary cooed the infant savior and savored the peace and beauty of the moment before any innocents were slain or floggings and crucifixions administered.

Alas, the moment had to be broken, "Come, dear, we'll sign together," Mr. Revenge gently declared as he took her by the waist so that they both were front and center of the stone document.

"But Puddin', I don't think a pen will write on this stone."

As she said this, Mr. Revenge reached for the silver quill that was gleaming like a razor in the top right hand corner of the stone document. Miss Addiction had not noticed that His/Her Honor had not volunteered any ink. But Mr. Revenge, having dealt with His/Her Honor Fear's contracts in the past was fully aware of the mechanics involved to execute any of the contracts drawn up by the supreme attorney of horror.

"'Tis neither by ink nor signature are His/Her Honor Fear agreements confirmed dear Miss. And you shall be a Miss but a few short minutes more," he said as he reached with his free hand and took

Miss Addiction's left hand that was already adorned with the obnoxious Ketamine wedding ring.

"Awe Sugar," she wheezed with as much cheap sentimentality her congested nasal passages could afford. And with her left hand being held and her right clutching the bouquet of intoxicating Morning Dumps, Miss Addiction, simply unable to cover her face nor hold back her reaction to the intestinal opiates, sneezed a greenhouse mist of the 'little orgasm' directly into the masked face of the sparkling Bride's Groom. She didn't even bother to apologize and was unaware that she had snot running down from her nostril and the threat made by the little stream to invade her mouth as she spoke, "This ring is just fine, baby, and like I said I didn't even bother to get ... Mother Fucker!" she screamed.

He had taken the quill, which in fact was not capable of writing on paper because it would have sliced to shreds any writing substance other than stone, and made a tiny slice, similar to that made by a pediatrician's nurse to draw blood from a speechless babe, but on the left hand middle finger Miss Addiction so fondly communicated. And he had not done it gently, as he was to say the least, just a little perturbed by the nacre-snot that he had inhaled. He never had been able to handle any substance stronger than sugar very well. Drugs always brought out a mean streak in him. Nevertheless, he was Mr. Revenge and his face did not portray his feelings.

As she was screaming, Miss Addiction, clutching the Morning Dumps ever closer to make a display of what little motherly instinct she held, had managed to pull her bleeding hand from the grip of the Masked Slasher. She shamelessly wiped the blood on the front skirt of her dress then brought the finger to her mouth and found as she had suspected, it would give her a high of some sort. She sucked on the bleeding finger and despite the Absinthe effect the blood immediately administered, she was still perturbed by the sting of the tiny wound.

And for any discomfort, Miss Addiction had a solution. Only she needed a free hand to retrieve the spare quarter gram of cocaine she always hid, although not that well, in her thinning hair on the crown of her head. She shook as she wobbled to one knee and as gingerly as she could, which was in any respect reckless, placed the morning dumps on the ground next to her. Still sucking the wounded finger, she reached expertly with her now free hand and retrieved the gram of coke that was always faithfully there for just such occasions as life might surprise her with. Miss Addiction took the bleeding finger from her mouth and brought the dime bag to her teeth and as she was finagling the zip lock with her free hand, she held out her injured finger which somehow itself looked anxious, so that she could apply the white narcotic to deaden the pain, or at least what she perceived as actual pain. It was only a nuisance but that was pain for our betrothed vixen.

"It's just a little sting, my pussy cat. Let's not carry ourselves into histrionics," Mr. Revenge hypocritically said.

Miss Addiction, mascara running, snot now actually getting into her mouth, blood and alcohol spotted dress, hair a bird's nest mess couldn't avoid dramatics if she were paid to. She stiffened and arched her back in feline warning and actually hissed at her radiant groom.

"Ah me Cheshire Tigris, let's remember our primary purpose."

He had said the wrong thing. "Primary Purpose" brought back to memory all of the horror she had witnessed as she was bludgeoned close to death when Andy was forced to endure the prison recovery groups. Miss Addiction recoiled in revulsion and Mr. Revenge once again was unnerved by the Bram Stoker metamorphosis his Bride to be was wrought to turn whenever she was truly distressed. While she looked away from him and scooted on her buttocks backwards from him, Miss Addiction held up the Morning Dumps as if they might counter the Cross of the Dr. Van Helsingr words that had just been spoken aloud by Mr. Revenge held upon her.

While he watched in disgust as his betrothed moved dangerously close to the 20-foot crater where Miss Love lay pulsing like an alien larvae in a variety of weak shades of blue, Mr. Revenge couldn't help but recall conversations in which he had learned that the directors of early cinema used heroin addicts in many vampire leading roles. He rationalized how appropriate this was and made a mental note to himself to remember the phrase, "Primary Purpose" in the future event his wife became unmanageable. But he had to get the present situation at hand under control. And in his true character, Mr. Revenge ascertained, "Fight fire with fire."

His super hero sequined apparel was not only for looks. It contained apparatuses that would have made Bruce Wayne red with envy. In his line of work, Mr. Revenge had to take advantage of opportunity's knock and one never knew when one might have to whack a heroin junkie, would one? A syringe emerged from his belt the size of a Guatemalan carrot. It contained a dose, or more like a life time supply of pure heroin, that would kill a herd of elephants. But it wouldn't kill Miss Addiction he rationalized. He was also aware that the dosage in all probability would resonate through to the conscious mind of Andy and in all probability the entire realm. He pondered the ramifications of turning Andy into a junkie and concluded to himself that if we were going to go down, we'd do it in the fashion of old British rock stars.

"God save the Queen," he proclaimed as he hurled into action.

He went straight for the jugular; she was Miss Addiction after all.

"Fuck it," he said as he grabbed Miss Addiction by the hair and plunged the syringe into the neck of the onetime beauty who was now a complete wreck.

Instantly, she became as submissive as a Stepford Wife, only she still looked like shit. And in Southern simpleton form, which was no longer an act, she found herself and declared the only rational explanation for her past behavior.

"Oh my, Puddin'!" she began as she stood up, the syringe still in her neck. She straightened her dress then took the needle from her neck and began her recitation of her past delusions as if she were Dorothy and her ruby slippers had just returned her to the safety of her Kansas farm and the serenity of her own bed, "I had the worst dream. I mean it was so real. They were so callous and cruel. I was living in a halfway house sharing a small ten by ten room with two other people and ..."

As she nearly broke down in tears, Mr. Revenge straightened his own hair and could now relax as he comforted Miss Addiction, "Shhhh, shah now. You're good dear. Safe and sound on your wedding day with the blessings of His/Her Honor. Now, now." he cooed as he held her and stroked her tattered hair."

"Oh my God!" she said as she pulled slightly away from him so that she looked wild eyed into his eyes. And as if she had just recognized that she had just tried to kill herself in mid slash of the wrist, Miss Addiction ranted, "They were going to make me take a piss test, and show up for those meetings and do nothing but drink coffee. I mean it was literal hell. Oh hold me Dear man, just hold me."

Mr. Revenge did just that and while he slowly walked her back to the table where His/Her Honor's marriage license awaited execution, he comforted his distressed kitten, "Yes Darling, Yes. I will hold you from now to eternity and all will be well. No more worries dear. Now let's take care of the necessities, shall we?"

Miss Addiction sniffled a bit then giggled just a little and shook her head in confirmation like a good little girl and proceeded to look for a pen again.

"No Darling, give me your hand. This won't hurt."

She did so and he took her bejeweled hand and took her middle finger and squeezed the little slice just so the congealed blood broke and the fount began again.

"There you go, dear. Do you see the place for your mark right there?" he asked as he pointed directly to an engraved circle marked, "Miss Addiction Revenge." Then he added, "You have to do this by yourself my sweet, of your own effort and of your own volition."

Miss Addiction again nodded in innocent confirmation and gently released her hand from his and placed her blooded appendage on the appropriate place.

As Miss Addiction pressed her finger to the designated spot clearly marked for her blood, Mr. Revenge rubbed his hands together in the sinister fashion of Herman Goering which was captured on film while Neville Chamberlain signed the Munich Agreement, written on Nazi toilet paper that handed Das Fuehrer The Sudetenland, and ultimately, the whole of Czechoslovakia without firing a shot.

"Perfect," he punctually replied. "Now come here Darling; you may want to step back and turn your head for what His/Her Honor ask for the Groom's execution."

"Huh?" She stated as he was gently leading her by her elbow away from the table.

"If you think the God of Abraham pulled one on the Israelites, wait to you get a load of this."

As he was zipping down the piss trap of his complicated apparel, Miss Addiction gave a sarcastic appraisal and said, "Oh, I see. Figures. Piss from the boy but blood from the girl. Even in this day and age ..."

When the man of her dreams further produced more of himself to adore, the sight of the serpentine and obnoxious cock with the open foreskin gasping for air caused Miss Addiction to lose all train of thought and she was unable to enter into her rant about 'girl power.' He took note of this and smiled a toothy grin and replied to what was able to come out of her mouth, "Not exactly, Wife. No, His/Her Honor does not, and I repeat, does not want my piss. And let me say again my betrothed little junkie, you may want to turn your head for this."

No one could or ever will be able tell a junkie or an alcoholic what to do. This is the cornerstone of Miss Addiction's nature; always question the rationale of any direction implied or insisted her way. In this circumstance her fucked up mind was in full disregard to his suggestion. She had already seen his Dick. She had allowed him to dildo fuck her with a champagne bottle till she sprayed an orgasm of champagne and narcotic cum all over the piano tavern. In her mind, she'd been around the block enough times to be able to take anything. And in her line of work, there was not much she hadn't seen. No, Miss Addiction didn't think she would turn her head and as a matter of fact, the Morning Dumps she had earlier placed on the slate floor, now caught the corner of her eye.

When she bent over to pick them up and take another huge whiff of their fragrance, she missed the sight of Mr. Revenge placing the head and foreskin of his gargantuan penis on the spot of the license designated for himself. As she indulged in their hypnotic fragrance, she enjoyed the pleasing effects caused by the battle for supremacy between the heroin and Morning Dump. It was hands down a victory for heroin but nevertheless, the slight excursion took Miss Addiction out of the moment, just long enough for her to miss Mr. Revenge as he removed, then inserted, the scalpel like a quill pen from its little thimble, which was also equipped with a razor belt of sorts that acted like a knife sharpener to the nib of the pen as Mr. Revenge quickly pushed quill in and out. But when she did look up, what she saw was the most ghastly sights of any bad trip come to realistic fruition.

Miss Addiction dropped the Morning Dumps again on the slate floor and brought both hands into her hair and pulled like a mourning wife of a slain Muslim. But she couldn't scream. Her forehead tensed so tightly and her mouth clenched involuntarily so that every blood vessel on her head was exposed so as to scream for her. There was an instant avalanche of sweat and her own adrenaline shot mixed with the cocktail of narcotics, she had had that day, was more than she could take. She was literally going into a stand up seizure as her eyes witnessed the masked marauder circumcising himself.

"He is a merciful God! He is a merciful God!" Mr. Revenge expounded in determined agony as he sliced round the circumference of his manhood with the scalpel quill. It was so sharp that there was very little blood and within a couple of seconds, the self-mutilation was complete.

The stone contract drew the foreskin into the designated area marked for Mr. Revenge and produced an effect similar to that of the preservation of Paleozoic vegetation seen on fossilized rock. Strangely enough, He was pleased with the document and the pleasure helped to deaden the pain he felt. But he rationalized that he needed antiseptic immediately, and there was none evident. Or was there?

He turned round to see the frozen scream sketched on the bust of Miss Addiction and clenched teeth as foam rushed through the their cracks which produced the "magic soap brush" of a car wash effect.

"Perfect," he again proclaimed as he walked to his semi quaking wife.

She was as compliant as putty in his hands. He gently pushed Miss Addiction to her knees, then tenderly removed her hands and fingers from her tangled hair and placed them obediantly around his cock. With the sparkling orbs of red, yellow, and black surrounding the entranced woman in seizure, the unblinking Miss Addiction resembled a macabre epiphany that conjured Joan of Arc praying before going to the stake. And Mr. Revenge was thrilled with this presentation. He hadn't had sex in centuries. But for medical reasons, he could justify any action.

Mr. Revenge reached down and gently instructed the hands of the entranced lunatic to rub his wounded and only slightly bleeding prick against the foaming lips of the pale and ghostlike demigod. The foam produced by the saliva glands of the toxic whore could and would kill any living micro-organism or bacteria that might cause infection inside the realm. And that slight antiseptic sting to his open wounds along with the attention and gentle caress offered by the moist lips to the century's celibate and only semi erect dick, of the Groom caused Mr. Revenge to shiver and quiver ever so slightly.

"Ash ha ha, CHA, Cha, cha," he involuntarily chattered as his expressionless eyes rolled out of there perch in the holes of his mask and up into his head whilst the cock of the masked marauder unleashed a premature orgasm on the face of his hypnotic bride.

"Whew, easy darling, oh dear," he said sucking air in through his own clenched teeth as he couldn't help but respond to the grip the zombie like bride still held on his limping and dripping dick.

With the exception of her entire body in one teensy continuous spasm, Miss Addiction could make no motion of her own accord. But again the shell shocked queen of Mardi Gras was pliant to his own hand as Mr. Revenge involuntarily whistled through his teeth whilst his hand removed the grasp of Frau Drugula from his tender organ. Mr. Revenge took a deep breath when he had completed the delicate task then without a second thought wiped his dick clean in the thinning hair of Miss Addiction.

She was a desecrated sight to behold. Mr. Revenge looked at Miss Addiction, then down at Miss Love, and then did a double take of his observation. For the first time in his existence, he perceived a queasy feeling in his gut, and thought he might throw up. But then he observed the marriage license, glowing in an eerie concoction of moss green and brownish yellow on the courtroom table. The blimey glow quickly eased then erased the foreign discomfort from his gut so that with a sense of victorious satisfaction, he placed his pecker back in the trap of the sequined jump suit.

It was time to honeymoon and so Mr. Revenge took the battered bouquet of Morning Dumps from the floor and placed them in Miss Addictions outstretched hands. The flowers may have lost most of their beauty due to the harsh treatment they had received but their fragrance was still as toxic as ricin and as her nostrils again breathed in their copious invigoration, the horrid shade of pale grey began to change her natural, yet still sickly and somewhat jaundiced state. With the snap of his finger, Mr. Revenge stood like a hypnotist finishing a surgery and Miss Addiction awoke with huge intake of fresh air.

"WHOoooooo," she audibly expressed as she sucked in the air.

Her reaction to the huge gulp of fresh air was an uncontrollable cough and empty gag for she had released much of her body moister moisture as sweat and foam in her previous episode. But the old girl did not panic. She had been through many an overdose before and she was familiar with the revival process. Slowly, Miss Addiction became aware of her surroundings and she remembered the circumcision that she had witnessed by her husband.

"My Husband?" She questioned aloud as she wiped her cum soaked face then rubbed the jism into her hair as she gently massaged one of her temples. She was concentrating hard as Mr. Revenge responded to her comment, "'Tis I. Dear Wife," he said.

She looked at the strutting and muscle ripped runt and could not help but notice the glow behind him glimmering in the fashion of Disney magic. But it was a sickly glow and the radiance on the little creep's face was altogether different. She knew that look. And when she equated it with the freshly fucked look she had come to know of herself, her memory somehow found the moment of his hefty and recently circumcised semi soft prick being rubbed across her lips.

"Well, worse things have occurred in those times when I've been over served," she thought, to her true and ill bread delta white trash self.

She spit a hacker through her teeth in the same way a 19th-century riverboat captain might aim for his spittoon.

"Good God, man!" he exclaimed silently to himself. "Is it possible that I, a Mr. S. C. Revenge, a sadistic cell through and through, am allowing this precocious doxy to turn me in the direction of a sniveling masochist?"

She could not read his thoughts, but Miss Addiction could observe discomfort in a facial expression as well as any poker circuit star of Seven Card Stud, and regardless of the promising life Mr. Revenge was presenting her, she enjoyed the unfamiliar sight of the egocentric rooster in distress. While clueless as to the cause of his obvious irritation, she was just as much a narcissist as he and she expressed her incorrect consolation and self-absorbed opinion of the cause to his dismay simultaneously to the uneasy groom.

"Awe Puddin', Don't go telling me now that you're having regrets. I'm your wife," she concluded with a confident nod towards the sickly sparkling marriage license.

"There shan't be any foreign objects inserted into any orifice of my being whatsoever during the lifespan of this marriage," he proclaimed with the conviction of Louis XIV establishing protocol of Versailles.

"Wut?" her ignorant mouth expelled before thinking.

Then quickly, Miss Addiction put two and two together. As she recalled her recent memory of "worse" things, the scenarios began to add up and she expressed her contemptuous sense of humor at his ability to read her thoughts as she clenched her teeth and sucked in her cheeks and breathed out a subtle chuckle, "U Humph humph humph humph."

She put the toe of one stiletto in front of the heel of the other and confidently swung her shoulders as she glared Mr. Revenge in the eyes while she slowly approached him. Miss Addiction still held the bouquet of Morning Dumps and was softly and casually inhaling their fragrance when she found herself within range of her free hand to extend the pigeon blood red nail of her right index finger to the lips of the Masked Crusader and all but tickle him as she slowly lowered the nail down his chin, over his throat and to his left nipple.

"However you want it Puddin'. However you want it," she sensually agreed to his declaration.

Mr. Revenge let out a heavy sigh, regained his composure and confident squint. He extended his hooked arm for his bride to take and asked, "Shall we?"

"U Humph," Miss Addiction casually grunted as she took his arm and helped herself to another whiff of Morning Dumps.

Her arm and hand extended down to his elbow, they were about to make their exit through the swinging wooden gates of the court's galley when their scheming gazes into the others devious eyes was broken by a red pulse that resembled a section of an online job application that needed the applicant's attention to complete the file in order to be considered for hire. The Marriage License was literally begging for attention, as if it were Excalibur singing for the attention of young Arthur to remove it from the stone and take it with him to Camelot.

"Oh come now dear," Mr. Revenge said as he jerked Miss Addiction to a halt. "How rude can we be? In our haste, we almost left His/Her Honor's semblance of blessings and legal authority unprotected."

"Looks like we done more than that," Miss Addiction vulgarly stated as she walked with Mr. Revenge to retrieve the stone document and observed that the red warning was pulsing directly on a vacant signature line marked simply as "Witness."

"Ah!" Mr. Revenge crisply acknowledged, "Hasn't been many a wedding that our old battle axe, who lie in yonder crater, has missed. As your people are prone to say, Miss Addiction, bless her heart."

"Oh my God! Son of ... a ... bitch!" Miss Addiction punctuated loudly as her eyes widened in disbelief to the fact that she had not given Miss Love a second thought since she entered the court of His/Her Honor looking for a score from Mr. Revenge."

"No Darling, she's simply a bitch; or what's left of one," he said with a yawn so that Miss Addiction could comprehend his boredom with the incapacitated nuisance that had become Miss Love.

Mr. Revenge pointed his arm bracelet up and in the direction of a large oak beam that supported and adorned the ceiling of His/Her Honor's court. An arrow in the shape of a fleur de lis shot out of his wristband and effortlessly gorged itself into the beam almost directly over the center of the crater in which Miss Love laid. He lodged the razor quill, like a pencil he had previously used to circumcise himself, into the crest between his ear, and head then grabbed the stone contract with his free hand and held it like a school book against his sequined leg. As Mr. Revenge masterfully controlled the spring in the cable, he was propelled through the air to the craters edge and then descended as if he were a skilled mountain climber as he jumped from broken crag to jutting rock down the edge of the hole some twenty feet or so, until he found himself at the bottom, hovering over the faint pastel blue glow of the mistress of painful joy, poor Miss Love.

The salvo of a single unseen cello mourned its echo throughout the court as it intertwined the sad and repetitive Scottish ballad, "Ashokan Farewell," into the dark matter that shone deep purple and comprised the atmosphere for the betrothed and coincidently, a funeral hymn for the vanquished mother of bliss. Miss Addiction, who adored the music that had appropriately become akin to The Civil War by Ken Burns looked down at her husband as he gently propped the stone wedding contract against the broken rubble that was strewn around the motionless body of the battered and twisted corpse of Miss Love. As he now had a free hand, Mr. Revenge reached up and unclasped the arm bracelet that was attached to the cable that had allowed him his effortless entry into the rocky grey crypt. The reflection from the dangling golden arm band hung in the air over both Miss Love and Mr. Revenge, randomly shot the orbs of red, black, and yellow that floated from above into the depths of the crater where they pierced the ever faint blue pulse of the diminished Miss Love.

"Hey Sugar. You don't look so good" said Miss Addiction, quietly and with a bit of feigned embarrassment, spoke to the unmoving corpse. "Sorry, but I forgot you were down there."

When Miss Love failed to respond in any fashion, Miss Addiction became visibly nervous. In the fashion of an adolescent wishing to change the uncomfortable subject of bedwetting, Miss Addiction held out her ring, or bumper, or whatever one could name the toxic crystal token of love Mr. Revenge had placed upon her hand; she exclaimed in mixed jubilation while her eyes glistened and produced a single tear, "I got married honey. See. Isn't it gorgeous," she exclaimed with a histrionic and forced sniffle.

Miss Addiction wiped her nose with her arm that was holding the Morning Dumps and with her ring still held out, she let out slight chuckle that would be familiar to any parent who watched his/her little girl trying on Sunday shoes and was told by the salesman that she was a little princess. Miss Love, who lay like a prime contender for the services of Dr. "Death" Kevorkian, simply stared into space with her eyes wide open without moving so much as a stomach muscle to breath much less responding to any gestures or words extended by Miss Addiction. The only sign of any life offered by the Miss Love was the faint pastel pulse that emanated around her broken and twisted, piss soaked carcass. The pulse of the blue aura was diminishing quickly like the bleep on a life-detector monitoring a patient with only an estimated minute or less to live. Had they been able to witness His/Her Honor's court, Miss Love's condition would have brought the Justices of various State Supreme Courts in sympathy with the cry of Dr. Kevorkian, "Dying is not a crime."

However, Mr. Revenge was a man at work and now free from the restraints of his cable, removed the quill with its razor's nib he had conveniently lodged behind his ear. He held absolutely no respect or sympathy for his defeated adversary. With reserved disgust, he grabbed the piss and blood soaked hair of the comatose heroine and hastily slit the throat of the decrepit hag. Her throat did not present a gusher but with the last of her physical strength, the heart of Miss Love provided the wound in her neck with an ample drainage of deep blue blood for Mr. Revenge to dip the limp hand of the fallen cupid and place a blood soaked finger on the appropriate spot of His/Her Honor's stone contract. Mr. Revenge resembled a trophy hunter posing for a camera to catch the splendid moment when he had bagged a twelve-point buck. His only regret was the lost opportunity given by the hasty nature of the wedding to hire a photographer.

"There you have it, Darling," Mr. Revenge said to Miss Addiction while he dropped the head of Miss Love with a melon thump to rest on a large gray rock that quickly turned blue from the final trickle of blood. He held up the contract and displayed the sealed and sickly glowing contract to the mesmerized gaze of Miss Addiction.

Miss Addiction had crossed another line, in her history of many that had been drawn before her, by a tempting fate that dangled new experiences of instant gratification and pleasure as if they were school yard dares. She kept staring at the stone rock under the one third decapitated head of Miss Love. The once grey stone now had the glow and brilliance of a blue sapphire and it shone brilliantly as it deflected the poisonous colors of orbs that went directly through the blue chalky mist and pierced the very carcass of the dissipated Miss Love. Miss Addiction wanted that blood. She could not have been more convinced than a gold prospector consumed by his first gaze upon King Tut's death mask, that the blood on the rock would bring her riches and joys beyond her wildest dreams.

Miss Addiction was so mesmerized by the thought of ingesting her one time ally of necessity's blood that she failed to notice Mr. Revenge as he showcased the executed marriage license with one hand and placed the wrist of his free hand into the open hinge of the dangled wrist band. She even failed to comprehend the truly comical sight presented by the conundrum the masked and sparkling crusader presented as he found himself in a situation with not enough hands. The wrist band needed to be locked but Mr. Revenge was not about to put the stone validation of his ploys close to the incoherent and mutilated body of Miss Love. He had been the essence of far too many a Hollywood plot to know that even in a seemingly defeated state, the boogey man of any horror film came back to life one last time and it suckered the premature victorious slayer close enough within his reach for one last slash at the unsuspecting survivor. No, he had what he had come for and was going to get the hell out of there.

Mr. Revenge looked like a Looney Tune's bull dog as he placed the stone contract into the grasp of his teeth so that his complexion turned crimson red and the veins in his neck bulged as they begged for relief whilst his now free hand clasped the cabled wrist band securely around himself. And he quickly obliged his own neck and jaw muscle's pleads, he removed the stone contract from his dental grip and once again secured the nauseous glow of the His/Her Honor's blessing close to his ribs, next to his heart. With a free finger, he pressed the recoil button and the Buck Roger's technology of the

emotional realm zipped Mr. Revenge into the air as he leapt simultaneously towards one wall of the crater and bounced back to dance
midway through his ascent off of the opposite side of the jagged bowl
to land securely on the basin's edge just next to his entranced wife.

"Ta Daaaa," he sang in the tune of a circus band to his hypnotized
bride.

"Darling? Mrs. Revenge? Tiger Tempest?" he said as he stood up
on his tippy toes to shake the shoulders of his taller and enthralled
partner whom now ignored his presence but pleaded aloud for
satisfaction.

"Please, oh please. Please ..." She begged with puppy dog whine
for the blue gook she was certain would bring her the high of highs.

He hated to do it but he was not about to allow the chalky blue
skin bag to pull some Hollywood B-flick stunt at his moment of glory.
He saw through her ploy and for a very brief moment admired the
dexterous attempt by his arch nemesis to foil his day.

"Not in my house you don't," he yelled with conviction, as he was
for a moment himself possessed by the fury of His/Her Honor. And
then with the will of his own, Mr. Revenge turned to face his wife and
screamed in an enraged shrill, "PRIMARY PURPOSE."

Miss Addiction in turn screamed in agony as the mourn of the
single cello transitioned to a full symphony of winds and French horns
in an attempt by His/Her Honor to restore balance to their ... no "HIS/
HER" wedding. He/She had never felt gratitude but at that moment,
His/Her Honor Fear romanced the estranged emotion to the best of
His/Her ability as the sickening aura of moss green and yellowish
brown fear perverted the atmosphere of the once magic mushroom
purple air.

But the newlywed bride was in agony. The anxiety attack that
accompanied Mr. Revenge's proverbial trump phrase was again
brought about by Miss Addiction's phobia to Rehab and instantly she
was praying for relief.

"Oh God! Whoever the fuck you are, please, oh please, help me to
get this bed made. It's bad enough that you got me praying, but that
Fascist black bitch Shaniqua, disguised as a social worker, will be
here any second to inspect the bed before that vanquishing meeting
they make me attend, and as if that alone wasn't bad enough, if the
bed don't pass inspection, I won't get my Thorazine, and if that ain't

bad enough because that crap is shit but it beats nothing 'cause I can't ..."

Then turning purple herself from lack of oxygen denied by her inability to come up for air from the depths of her nightmare currents, Miss Addiction pulled on her cum crusted hair and began verbally begging aloud through her fretful whimper, "Oh Please, Please, Please ... PLLLEeeeease!"

Mr. Revenge had been through this rodeo only minutes before. Again he turned to the discarded bouquet of Morning Dumps that lay on the stone floor perilously close to the craters edge and grabbed the wilted and bruised flowers in haste, "Breathe Darling, Breath. You simply must."

Mr. Revenge reached back with his free hand and screamed "Breathe" as he ferociously slapped the now beet red and mascara streaked face of woe with all of his might.

"Uuuuuuughhhhhh," she growled as she soaked in just enough air and subsequently just enough of the fragrance of the morning dumps so that Miss Addiction absorbed the antidote to her dreadful cliché. The result again was much akin to that of an asthma attack assaulted by the quick mist released from an ever faithful rescue inhaler. And once again, Miss Addiction found the strength to lash out and return the favor to Mr. Revenge with a backhanded slap that sent the Masked Groom flying into the bottom of His/Her Honor's bench. Bent over and still grasping for air, Miss Addiction in between gulps for breath punctuated each word with the conviction of a hammer that pulverized a nail straight through to its end in a single vigorous pound.

"DON'T ... (Gasp of breath) YOU ... (Gasp) EVER ... (one huge and successful final intake of invigorating air) speak those motherfucking, God forsaken, akin to blasphemy, syphilis infected, curse of Hade's syllables in the order that comprises those; vile of pus, pox infected, electric shock reminiscent to a molten hot glass shoved in my cunt to cool then shatter to grind my guts WORDS EVER, and I mean EVER! (Breathe deeply and upon exhalation) ... again ... MOTHERFUCKER, DO I MAKE MYSELF CLEAR?"

"Perfectly," replied Mr. Revenge as his tongue took a break from rubbing the inside of his smacked jaw while he remained on his ass underneath His/Her Honor's perch and made an attempt to further explain, "Darling, Schnookums, please understand you were about to make a dreadful, if not deadly ..."

"Understand!" she screamed as she interrupted his sentence and walked menacingly towards the sparkling little fiend. With a heavy exhalation of exasperation, she asked, "What part of molten hot glass shoved in my cunt to cool, to then shatter, to grind my guts do you not comprehend?"

"Multiply that by twenty, Darling, and possibly you can wrap that psychedelic catastrophe, which captains your ship with the effect that pulverized hag's blue blood would make upon your essence. I was simply protecting you, pussy cat," replied Mr. Revenge as he wiped the blood that began to trickle from the corner of his mouth.

She was in the middle of an unsuccessful struggle and attempt to pull the wedding ring, aka bumper, from her finger. Miss Addiction had every intention of throwing the crystal contraption at her husband but his words had struck their mark. With the clarity of the blast akin to twenty Calvary trumpets, she was able to comprehend the paralyzing agony that her husband had dashingly rescued her.

"Twenty times worse than rehab?" She whispered aloud then gulped as the concept sunk in then brought about in Miss Addiction the awe and respect shown by Java natives to an erupting volcano.

She dropped to her knees. Partly because they had buckled from the thought of the unspeakable relief she felt from being rescued from the wreckage that she would have been in, had she ingested Miss Love's emerald blue blood, and partly because she wanted to come down to eye level of her knight in sequined red. When they embraced and kissed, any cop that could have watched would have arrested Miss Addiction on the spot for he would have mistaken her for a child molester of an overdeveloped twelve year old as she flicked her tongue over her miniature husband's tonsils and rubbed her hand with gentle squeezes over his manly parts. Mr. Revenge was becoming aroused, but he could no longer take the chronic halitosis common to most heroin addicts that assaulted his perception as his wife slopped around in his mouth. But he was enjoying the massage of sorts so as not to insult her, he gently removed his mouth from hers and spoke his egocentric and self-absorbed coo into her ears so that he might have his cake, and eat it too.

"Yes, me Tiger Lilly, AHhhh, I have spared you from the ill fate of Superman to kryptonite, of Soviets on Wall Street, And Lincoln at a Natchez ball. Oh my Darling, the suffering I have rescued you ..."

Miss Addiction removed her hand from his back, brought her single index finger to his lips, and said, "SHhhhh. Let's listen to the music."

"As you say, dear," he gently agreed then groaned with pleasure. "But I can ask the orchestra to come to my veranda and behind a red silk screen, we can fully indulge from any prying eyes. The musicians, His/Her Honor, and above all, any more shenanigans from that inconsolable cunt, Miss Love."

"Sounds scandalous Puddin'. Let's go," whispered and giggled Miss Addiction as she reached over to pick up the battered Morning Dumps before standing up.

They turned to exit and Mr. and Mrs. S. C. Revenge, did the best they could, given their height difference, to lock arms. The orchestra keyed up for a grand finale to "Ashoken Farewell" and Miss Addiction did the best she could to straighten her dress. Both of the newlyweds peered down into the crater and lifted their eyebrows in a curious response to the emerald blue ooze from the rock under Miss Love's head as it crept by its own volition, over the faint and chalky blue essence of Miss Love, hardening itself into a shining and jewel-like cocoon. Miss Love could be seen no more. The blue sapphire that entombed her resembled a polished gem protruding from the worthless grey stone and brought about to the mind of the victorious onlookers the sense of satisfaction felt by an exterminator after he has soaked the paper comb of a wasp nest with DDT. They were confident they would be without the nuisance of the entombed old nemesis ever again.

And in one last contemptuous gesture, Miss Addiction threw the bouquet of Morning Dumps over her shoulders into His/Her Honor's crater where upon their contact with Miss Love's emerald cocoon the flower's petals separated from their bulbs and sprinkled about the stones to create a semblance of maggots in an impossible attempt and futile endeavor to get through and nourish themselves upon the still live marrow within the emerald shell. No, Miss Love would not be able to exit the safety of her shell and if in some miraculous event she did manage to break out, the maggots of Morning Dumps would be there to consume her and overpower her essence to the point where she would remain of no consequence.

The Emotional Realm and any of its committees were now without the presence of Miss Love.

The happy couple gave each other a quick kiss and as they made their exit of His/Her Honor Fear's court, Mr. Revenge, again bombarded by the doxy's nuclear halitosis began to strategize the inevitable renewal of Miss Addiction's sexual advances and the antics that would surely accompany them and would thus require his husbandly duty.

He thought to himself as they walked together over the thresh of the courtroom door, "Man up old boy. Perhaps now is the appropriate time to try doggy style. Adapt man, that's it. I'm a back door man, yeah," and he broke into an a capella hilarious attempt to mimic Jim Morrison of The Doors.

"Yeah, I'm a back door Man. WOOoow," he screamed, but his Victorian sense of propriety failed to give him the necessary conviction to succeed in the freedom released by a rock and roll tirade. Miss Addiction looked at him like he had just lost his mind. Mr. Revenge shrugged in apology to his tall wife. He'd failed at Morrison. With his confidence a little shaken, He was only slightly concerned with his erectile dysfunction and thus his ability to enter Miss Addiction's back door. As a matter of fact, with the absence of the old bag Miss Love, He swore to himself he was already getting a hard on.

With the ceremony over and the wedding about to be consummated, His/Her Honor Fear sent in his duel crew of handymen, Hate and Malice, dressed in one piece work suits and armed with shovel and pike to fill in the crater. They did so in haste and covered the emerald sapphire so that the crater was no more and there was now a level surface to replace the shattered black slate floor of the court. Poor Miss Love. Not a sight nor sound of her once persistent eminence could be felt; but she didn't feel a thing.

And that was about as close to death as Miss Love could ever come.

CHAPTER 45

Fort Lauderdale, Tuesday, July 7, 1992

GOOD EVENING, SELECTRIC. WHAT'S THAT, SELECTRIC? YOU SAY THAT you missed me. Well I missed you too, but boy did I get some badly needed sleep, because I was up all Sunday night and way into Monday morning with you.

I just read what we pumped out about The Committee and I gotta tell you, your suggestion that I stay off of your sainted keys when I'm under the influence of hallucinogenic drugs might be a good one. I've considered the suggestion, Selectric, but I won't take that advice. I spend too much of my time fucked up to discount my thoughts when I'm in that shape. We are after the truth here, right?

Speaking of truth. You know science doesn't lie, Selectric. You say that's a Goddamned lie? Oh, you're just sassy because I'm gonna continue to paint psychedelic prose with your little black and white utilities, but just stay with me for a bit longer, okay? So speaking of truth, I saw Dr. Ball again today. Poor Rick managed to get in the shower this morning and take me to his clinic. When we got there, Rick parked the Lincoln and said, through nasal congestion, that he was gonna come up with me and see if Dr. Ball would see him about his cold. When he informed me of this I had to restrain my eyes from rolling as my mind thought silently to itself, "For the love of God, just die already."

I wonder if I haven't been living too long among New Yorkers in their tropical borough, Selectric? At least one of my A-Z minds is ending sentences with "already." Oh me sainted Mammaw Caldwell would flip in her casket if she heard me talking like the blasted common rabble from the Big Apple. I wonder what would make her spin faster; my being gay and sick with an "African blood virus," or talking like "Goddamned Yankees?" Remind me to make a note of this, Selectric, so that when (or if) I see her in the afterlife, I can confront her with the above mentioned scenarios and observe her casket upon my presentation of this dreadful information to dear old Granny. Should be a kick.

Afterlife! You ask, Selectric, if I got bad news at the clinic and perhaps am planning on doing anything foolish, like killing myself to play the little game "Is there a God," as Wednesday Addam's so wonderfully put it in one of cinema's comic attempts to make light of death. No, dear Selectric, never you fret, for the good Dr. Ball informed me today that although I did test positive for the antibodies of HIV, my immune system has suffered no difficulties at this time. But the news was not so good for Rick.

I mean, they drew his blood and won't have any results back for a few days, but dude, was that doctor concerned about Rick! He prescribed Rick some serious antibiotics and some kind of codeine syrup that should help control his coughing. However, the doctor announced right there in front us that Rick was questionably on the verge of pneumonia. Along with the medications, strict bed rest was insisted upon for Rick to recover.

And get this, Dr. Ball took me to the side before we were leaving. I guess he knew that Rick was a bit of a control freak and didn't want to make things too bad for me, but when he grabbed my arm and scooted me into a vacant examination room, he sternly told me through clenched teeth, "You are one lucky little shit, but luck runs out on the best of us. Your liver count is disturbing to say the least. Don't blow this, Andy. This is the only life you will have. Please, stay off the booze and whatever the hell else you are on. Trust me on this one little thing. You don't want to start AZT treatment."

I didn't say a word. I just looked down and when I looked up, Rick was in the doorway.

"Everything alright?" he asked.

The doctor was quick on his feet, "Absolutely, Rick. I just wanted to emphasize to Andy how serious I am about your bed rest. He's got to understand that you have to stay in bed. No getting up for anything, Rick."

"Don't worry, Dr. Ball, he's a saint. Takes real good care of me," Rick lied.

And Rick looked so pale as he stood there telling stories. He was so thin, unshaven, with a black and brown shade under his eyes that was certainly the calling card of the Grim Reaper. I knew I had not been a saint by any degree and, as I thought about this while I looked at Rick under that fluorescent hall light, I couldn't help but recall that I had not cooked a single thing for Rick, or brought him any water or anything like that. I honestly didn't know what the guy had been eating.

"Not my problem," I thought to myself as I shrugged my shoulders and tilted my head in a modest gesture for the benefit of the good doctor.

There was a Publix we stopped at on the way home. And I managed to piss Rick off when I got back in the car and didn't get everything on the shopping list that he'd put in my head before he sent me into the store for his soup and crackers. I mean, really dude, low sodium was the main thing I fucked up on. Are you fucking kidding me? He got pissed off because I didn't get the low sodium soup? Motherfucking really! I can't tell you how close I was to shouting out, "Easy, Asswipe! Trust me on this one little thing, Typhoid Mary. The last thing you gotta be worried about is motherfucking salt."

But I didn't. I just looked out the window and stared silently as he ranted, and while he was mid-sentence, I got the goddamned grocery bag and went back into the store and exchanged the goods. The heat was so terrible that I had managed to work up a sweat, so that when I got back in the air conditioned car, despite the tension, it felt great. I let out a really heavy breath of air but didn't say a word and Rick apologized.

"I'm sorry, Andy. This should have been a break for you today. You finally got some good news. Really guy, I'm happy you're okay."

"Okay?" I silently screamed to myself. "Okay, I've got fucking AIDS, dude. I've got a motherfucking time bomb that is gonna explode without any warning in me, and you're glad I'm okay?"

But I said with complete calm, "Let's get you home in bed and fed."

"One last stop at the pharmacy, first Bud," he replied as he backed out and was nearly side swiped by a Jeep with a surfer dude who was not the least bit concerned and just held up his hands to say "what?" as Rick rolled down his window to confront him.

But Rick just pulled the Lincoln back in the space and the Surfer Dude drove by without any further communication. Rick carefully backed out, then stopped at Walgreens, where we went through the drive-through and got his medicine.

I gotta say, I didn't think the guy was going to make it back to our apartment. (Selectric! Did you hear that? "Our" apartment. Hang in there buddy, we're gonna be rich any day now.) When we got in, Rick announced that he was going to take a quick shower and breathe some steam, then do as the doctor insisted and get into bed.

"Okay Bud," I said in a contemptuous mimic of him that he didn't get. And as he was heading down the hall I hollered to him, "Do you want me to heat up any soup?"

He didn't say anything back so I took it as a no, sat the bag of groceries on the dining table, and went for my never ending roach house, where I grabbed the fattest one and thought about going out on the patio with it. Then I remembered the fucking heat and just lit it up while I plopped my pretty ass on my sofa.

That's right, Selectric. My sofa. I wouldn't be surprised if Rick ever sits on it again. That man is dying.

With a celebratory thought in my head about dead Rick, I thought that a toast would be called for, so I headed for the scotch. "Fuck you Dr. Ball, and I love you Madame Dieux Dieux, but the drink of me native land be a calling and methinks it would be very rude to disregard yonder hail," I actually said aloud in what I can only guess would be a very bad Scottish accent.

You know, I guess I've got Scottish in me blood. I know there is Irish and English and, I think I heard Mammaw say that the late doctor, her deceased husband, was "Scotch-Irish." Doesn't matter, Selectric, after the shot I poured, I assure you there is Scotch in me blood now. Because I nearly took the decanter down to zero and when I went to the bar's backup cabinet, fuck, there wasn't any. And as well, my wallet was getting pretty slim. About a second or two after I had slugged the scotch, I heard the admonishing tone of Rick, clad in a towel and still wet ask, "Is it past noon already?"

I looked up over his head and lo and behold, the star shaped digital wall clock above the hallway entrance stated loud and clear that it was 12:27. I let out a deep breath and grimaced a little from the effect of the healthy swig I had just taken, then wiped a little of the leakage around the corner of my mouth with the back of my hand and answered, "Aye, 'tis me mate. By 27 minutes past, my good man."

Rick just shook his head in mild disgust and was about to walk down the hall, apparently to bed, when he glanced over and saw the paper grocery bag sitting on the bare wood of his solid black walnut table. Where he found the strength to scream, I don't know but he did.

"Oh, for fuck's sake Andy, you irresponsible piece of—" he didn't finish, but I knew what he was about to say and I also glanced over to what he was so upset about. The paper bag that the groceries were in was really damp at the bottom and sat directly on the bare wood. He walked over in a huff and picked the bag up with such a jerk that the jug of orange juice that had apparently sweated through the paper confessed as the culprit of the moisture to reveal itself and its fresh and expensive just-squeezed inner color.

You know, Selectric, It might be a good idea to ask the orange juice companies to change the name to yellow juice. Sounds like false advertisement to me and a possible lawsuit down the road for some crafty lawyer to sink his teeth into.

Anyhow, Rick took the broken bag and placed it on the counter of the bay where I hide you, Selectric. And I swear, he talked to me just like I was a puppy that had just taken a piss on some expensive rug. If he could have taken my head and rubbed it on the ever so slight water spot on the polished wood, I think that he would have. But he pointed and poked his finger at the white spot and repeated several times, "Do you see that? Do you see that?"

"Didn't go to the eye doctor today, Rick. As small as it is, yes. I can see it. Nothing wrong with my eyes," I calmly replied.

"Well, let me ask you this, Mr. 20/20, let's check out your math skills that you picked up in that glorious Eden you call Louisiana. That bastion shining on the hill like a fucking educational lighthouse. Let me see now?" Rick asked to himself in contemplative calm, then poised a word problem aloud in a tone so contemptuously gay it would have made Mr. Roger's seem heterosexual. "Andy, a stupid and sleazy drug addict gets $75 every time he sells his ass so that he can buy the drugs and scotch he loves more than anything in the world. His monthly living expenses are $700 per month and his drugs and scotch are approximately $2,500 per month. The cost of a black walnut table that he just ruined is $4,000. The landlord and owner of the table will give him the remainder of July and the month of August to pay all expenses for both months, and the equivalent price of the table. How many times in a day does the little sleazy whore have to sell his ass to keep from getting thrown out on the street?"

I didn't answer. I poured the little remaining Scotch from the decanter into my tumbler and took a small sip.

"That's your homework for tonight Andy. I'm not kidding, I want the correct answer before noon tomorrow." Rick demanded. And he began to head for his bedroom, but stopped just a couple of steps into the hall, turned around and added for good measure.

"I'll give you a hint so don't get too baffled. There are thirty-one days in both July and August, Andy."

"Okay, Rick, but you should know I've never taken my pants down for less than a bill," I told him in what I assumed was the essence of a smart ass and took another swig.

"You're not as cute as you used to be, Andy. I was being generous with $75," he replied and stormed to his bedroom and shut the door.

"Humph," I retorted as loudly as I could with a closed mouth still holding scotch.

I swallowed the scotch and grumbled to myself, "Fucking 75. Motherfucker, I am too cute." As I said this, I turned around and looked at myself in the mirror. Rick had a point. I didn't look so good. What's that, Selectric? Oh thanks, pal. Yeah, I'm sure I could get at least a bill every time I take my pants down. I appreciate your confidence in me, Selectric. But I'm not gonna have to take my pants down for anyone I don't want to, Selectric. We're gonna be rich soon, and I'm gonna sell that fucking black walnut table for firewood.

Anyhow, I wasn't too worried about Rick's ultimatum as long as he was here in the house and didn't find a way to make it to his attorney's office to change his will before he died. So I took my scotch over to the sofa and rolled a fresh doobie and turned on the boob tube.

"Oh fuck," I exclaimed when I saw the first story.

Braniff Airlines was officially out of business. That kinda pissed me off, even though I had only once been on any airline other than Delta, and that one time was on Value Jet. But Braniff had the best looking jets by far, especially that maroon color. You know, Selectric, I bet the official airline for The Committee would be Braniff.

So I was already a little pissed off when I began to think back on that word problem that Rick had presented. And he made the mistake of calling me stupid again. So I wasn't really mad, as I knew I had already gotten even, since he was all but dead. But I knew that I'd throw a good jab in before he croaked just for good measure. I started to think about what kind of jab I'd throw as the boob tube predicted that Al Gore would be Bill Clinton's running mate.

Holy Moly, Selectric, they showed a clip of Al speaking, and he talks like a fag! Hands down, Selectric, I hope Clinton beats the shit out of that prick we've got in the White House right now, and if he does, we'll have a homo V.P.

I was enjoying the thought of that and had a ball with some ideas about fucking with Rick some more when I took the final swig of my Scotch and realized that I had no more backup. I really became concerned and got flat out angry about it, but I calmed down when I reasoned that it could be remedied as soon as Rick dozed off and I got a hold of his Visa. I was broke again myself, but then I took another toke of the joint and decided that I could hold out on vodka until I made it to the liquor store. And I wouldn't be broke much longer either. So I kind of

cheered up again after I took another huge hit off of the fatty I had burning. I decided that I would get to work on my jab with Rick.

And let me tell ya, cute or not cute, math was never my strong subject.
And when I went to put pencil to paper and began to decipher the little
situation Rick had presented me, the effects of Mary Jane did not aid in
my already defunct math skills. See, I couldn't quite figure if Rick, being
a Realtor and all, wanted me to pro-rate from today or use the entire
month of July. I couldn't remember how he quite worded it, so I decided
to do both equations for him. I figured it was the least I could do before
I began to max out his credit cards.

So I did the figuring and hand-wrote Rick, in my best cursive, the
following note:

Yo Bud,
I wasn't sure whether you were talking in terms of today or backdating
this new arrangement. So I worked out both problems.

Pro-rated, I will have to sell my ass 2.47619047618 times a day at
$75 per pop.

In full months, I will have to sell my ass 2.23655913977 times a day
at $75 per pop.

But I think I'm still damn cute, Rick, so for shits and giggles, at $100
per pop I will have to sell my ass 1.67741935483 times a day at $100.

Rick, I really like think it's customary to round these figures off and
after doing so, no matter what I charge or which day you start the rental
and drug agreement, I'd say I need to sell my ass twice a day. And that's
not going to be that difficult, Bud.

So I'm off to sell my ass. Should be back home for dinner.
Feel better,
Andy

Oh how I do enjoy letters and memos. There is simply no way for
a motherfucker to cut you off and argue with you with a letter in his
hands. And with that in mind, I crept into Rick's room and found him
in codeine cough syrup land. Dude, he was out. I stopped being so damn
creepy and without any fear of him waking, I laid the letter down on his
nightstand next to his cough syrup an— wow—I noticed the motherfucking bottle was already half empty. I went to his wallet on his night
stand with impunity and took the Visa card so that I could load up on
some Johnny Walker Black.

As I slapped the wallet back down on his dresser, I turned to look at
Rick and I caught myself smiling out of the corner of my eye from the

reflection of one of the huge mirrors that hung on each side of Rick's bed. I said, "Yo Bud, no one's gonna play with my ass today, but you're about to get fucked."

And I pulled the covers back and there was Rick butt naked and out cold as he slept on his stomach with his ass staring at me like a bull's eye.

Oh come on now, Selectric, don't stall on me like that again. You're afraid of what I'm going to type? Yep, I'm a rapist, Selectric! I know, I know, Selectric. He's already a dead man and I was gonna max out his credit before he croaked, but I gotta tell ya, I may have found my calling. I mean that was one good fuck. I'm not kidding you, I popped a boner of boners and the lube was right there in the dresser and KABOOM! I fucked him. Shot a load up his ass that any porn star would have been proud to claim. What's that, Selectric? No he didn't wake up, and yes I'm a good fuck but the codeine was apparently even better. I don't like what you're insinuating, Selectric.

And it gets even better. To add injury to insult, and since I was in the mood for more shits and giggles, I went to my room and put on my right hand one of my rubber gloves and then moistened the index finger of the glove with a little bit of cum that leaked from my softening dick. I took the little leather pouch out of my boot and directly from the vial, I placed just a tad, maybe a bit too much, of the powder on my moistened index finger of the glove.

Yup Selectric, I did just what you're thinking. Just keep rat-a-tat tatting that little silver ball of yours. I very carefully and slowly, so as not to allow my index finger to touch anything, went back to passed-out Rick and his bullseye naked ass. With my free hand, I spread his cheeks so that his asshole widened and I gave our good man a booty bump of Madame Dieux Dieux's crystal death. I shoved a healthy portion of the crystals right up Sir's ass, just in case you are wondering what a booty bump is Selectric.

Oh come on, Selectric! Don't shake so. And yes I know Madame Dieux Dieux told me to get rid of that shit. I'll do that tomorrow. Okay, don't worry about how, Selectric. I've got a good idea of how to get rid of the shit so that no else gets sick. Don't worry, everything's good.

And now I have a full bar of scotch, some incredible ecstasy I bought with the cash I advanced from his VISA. How much you ask, Selectric? Only $500, but ...

You want to know how I knew his code? Oh that was easy, and no it wasn't his birthday. Can you believe it? It was SPY, just like on his lock box, except the numbers correlated to their numerical value in the alphabet. And he thinks I'm stupid, Selectric. Yep, his security code is 191725. No money problems here, Selectric. And yes, I will bang on your sainted keys in an ecstasy trip if I like. I might even have lube on my fingers as I jerk off and type. I'm kidding, Selectric, I have more respect for you than that.

Yes, I know you didn't know that I'm a rapist and you're not so sure about me anymore but relax, Selectric. You're my friend.

Night.

CHAPTER 46

Fort Lauderdale, Thursday, July 9th, 1992

WELL, I SLEPT MOST OF THE DAY YESTERDAY, AS DID RICK, WHICH left me with the opportunity to follow Madame Dieux Dieux's instructions and get rid of our lovely elixir. That reminds me, I need to go and get that script for Rick's cough syrup refilled. Whether he needs it or not, I might want to have some of that sleepy time hanging around in the event of another bad hangover, which by the way, are getting harder and harder to come out of.

But that powder of Madame Dieux Dieux's was no problem to get rid of. Simple really. I just put on my rubber gloves and took the little vial out of the leather bag and headed for the guest bathroom. And with the nonchalant tap as if it were a salt or pepper shaker, the deadly crystals went into the guest room toilet.

And don't worry, Selectric, I held the bottle very close to the blue H2O so no one else, including myself, would get a booty bump of Madame Dieux Dieux's deadly love potion. Love for me, but death for Rick. I don't know what I'd do without that lady.

Then I took the vial and carefully rinsed it out, and along with the leather bag, put it in the kitchen garbage and took it to the garbage chute. Done.

Would you relax, Selectric? No one is going to dig through the garbage before pick up on Tuesday. Jesus, you are really such a Willy Nilly. And, if for any reason they did, all they would find would be what? Nothing, okay! Rick is gonna die of AIDS-related pneumonia any day now, and that's that. But wouldn't ya know it, just about a few minutes before I contemplated getting another piece of Rick's ass, the motherfucker woke up. That was around nine on Wednesday morning. And I have to say, the rest from the codeine cough syrup did wonders for his disposition. I swear, this guy is the classic case of Dr. Jekyll and Mr. Hyde. Sweet as a charm, he called me into his bedroom and I said as I walked in, "Morning Sunshine, I have your coffee made. I bet your starving, want some—"

"Come, sit down, Andy. Please?" he asked and patted on the bed where bed where I saw my "homework" next to his hand. His lamp light on the night stand next to his bed was on, so it was apparent that he had read the assignment. I'll tell ya what else was apparent. He looked a little better. I don't know what it was, maybe the color around his eyes. He still coughed and hacked and was seriously sick but I guess the rest did a little good for him physically as well. Probably the good stiff rod I'd supplied him did the most for him.

Anyhow, I asked him if he was sure I couldn't get him some coffee and he just gently smiled and patted the side of his bed.

"Okay," I said then made the referendum, "But don't try and kiss me. You've been out for nearly a day. I bet your breath smells like shit."

He let out a deep breath like he was giving it all his effort to keep calm, and to tell you the truth, his breath was terrible as I got a good whiff from exhaled air. But he forced a smile and made a single pat with his hand and gently said, "Please."

It wasn't an order, but it wasn't a question either. So I complied.

"Yes, I will take some coffee and if you would be good enough to bring some O.J. and toast, I would definitely take it. But first, please," he said again. Then as he looked at my calculations, he apologized, "Andy, I'm so sorry. Really guy. I'm not a very good sick person, and I didn't mean a word of what I said. Can you please put it on the shelf and let it rest?" He inquired again for about the fourth or fifth time.

I didn't answer him. He went on to say, "Dude, let's start this over, okay?" he paused to wait for a response from me and when I again remained silent with downcast eyes, he continued, "Tell you what. I think we both need some time out of Fort Lauderdale. Ever been to Europe?" he asked.

I shook my head and he continued, "Do you speak French? That's what they speak in the swamps, huh?" he casually teased.

"Nope," I curtly answered.

"You might want to start a French course. Maybe that black lady you work for?"

I corrected his assessment of my beach side relationship, "Madame Dieux Dieux—and I don't work for her; I'm an associate."

"Yes, Madame Dieux Dieux. She speaks French, right?" he said as he completely ignored the ornery temperament that I had just displayed.

And my disposition didn't change when I answered him, "Creole, Rick. She speaks Creole."

"Great," he said and quickly hacked and coughed up some nasty ass green shit that he spit into a Kleenex tissue and placed on the nightstand next to his bed.

Good thing I caught my reflection in the mirror that hung over the corner of the bed. Dude, I gotta tell ya that I was grinning teeth from ear to fucking ear when I saw that green and brown shit he spit out of his mouth. Hell no, Selectric, I wasn't grossed out in the least. That was surefire evidence that the crystals were doing their work, but like I said, thank God for mirrors. I'm not so sure Rick would have bought that I was smiling so big because of my excitement that he was obviously going to take me to France.

"Sorry about that, Andy," Rick apparently apologized for the disgusting disposal of phlegm.

I made an attempt to correct his assessment for an apology as I replied, "No problem dude; One day you'll get it through your head that I'm a private contractor."

Rick, with complete disregard for my shitty character, exclaimed again, "Great! That means you don't have to ask anybody for time off when I take you to Paris and the most beautiful wine country you can ever imagine."

I guess the excitement in his voice caused him to hack up another testament to the demise of his lungs. From the encouraged effect I was certain that the booty bump had played upon his respiratory system. And again I didn't answer or react verbally to his announcement of the grand French tour but, damn it to hell, as he reached for the Kleenex, he caught the grin I couldn't hold back from the picture that came to mind of yesterday's nursing that I'd administered to Rick.

"It's good to see you smile Andy," he said as he put the second wad of green and brown slime on the night stand.

Then he reached over and tore my ass selling assignment into several shreds.

"Throw this away will you Andy? Please?"

I was still grinning when I just shook my head in confirmation of yes to his histrionic gesture for peace.

"That a boy. Keep it up. And I could use a bite and some of the coffee you offered."

"You got it, Rick," I said as I picked my shredded assignment off the floor and headed quickly for the kitchen.

And Selectric, I gotta admit to you, I didn't go straight to the kitchen. I passed it and went to the bar then threw the shredded homework in the waste basket kept under the counter and poured myself a healthy tumbler of straight and neat scotch.

"Wine country," I thought to myself as I took sip of the morning nectar.

I wish Rick would've asked me where I wanted to go in Europe. Scotland is at the top of my list. I mean really, fuck the French. But it doesn't matter anyway. I'll just change the flights and cancel the hotel reservations the day he dies. But until then, I'll "keep it up" as Rick requested. I'll smile all the time, Selectric.

"Can't afford to take this smile off my face," I said aloud to the reflection in the mirror as I watched myself swallow the prime attitude enhancement miracle.

"What's that Andy?" Rick hollered from his room.

"Nothing babe, just got a little excited about the news you gave me and let it out a little."

I heard him laugh, then immediately begin to cough and hack from his response of joy to my new attitude.

"Atta boy," I quietly said to myself in the mirror but much more softly so that it would be impossible for Rick to hear me again.

I made the toast and coffee, which I prepared in strict accordance with Rick's pallet by heating the cream in the microwave, with much optimism and happiness. When I brought it to him on a round silver bar tray, I swiped the gross snot wads and what have you off his night stand with a free hand and placed the tray down. Then I went into the golden tomb and got the waste basket and dutifully picked up the gross little balls with no recoil. When I went to place the waste basket close to Rick's bed so that he could use it for the rest of his dying moments, I picked up the empty bottle of cough syrup and told Rick, "I'll go get this refilled right away. Says you've got three more refills."

"Oh thanks Andy, really. You don't mind walking down to Walgreens on 15th and Sunrise in this heat do ya? They'll give you no bullshit. I'll call up and let them know you're coming. Get my Visa out of my wallet, will ya?"

"Oh shit!" I silently panicked to myself.

I had forgotten to put Rick's credit card back in his wallet. I took several deep breaths and went to his wallet and Lord thank you, there was another Visa. Calmly, I took it out of the wallet and turned to give it to Rick when he said, "No, just take it with you to pay for stuff."

"Cool," I said with probably too much relief.

"What, no car keys, Daddy?" I playfully pouted.

"Sorry dude, but you might want to get a valid Florida license so that you can get your passport."

"You're right, Rick," I agreed whole heartedly.

And as I left the room with the empty bottle of codeine syrup, Rick sat up and took a sip of his coffee then put it down and reached for the portable phone. I assumed correctly that he had called the pharmacist and hollered to him that I was about to start walking to the Pharmacy.

"Okay, but would you hand me my wallet from the dresser before you take off?" he yelled."

"Sure," I hollered back.

As I walked into the room he was talking on the phone, but not to a pharmacist. Apparently, he was talking French to the party on the other end and that could have meant only one thing; a fucking travel agent. Oh shit! I had both VISA cards now. Thank God, I'm fast on my feet."

When I reached for the Wallet, I took a twenty out and replaced the credit card that I still had in my hand that I had just recently removed. I showed him the twenty dollar bill and made puppy dog pleading eyes and silently mouthed as to not interrupt his conversation, "Please?"

He made a tacit nod of approval and I silently mouthed a thank you as he took the wallet and placed it in his lap and resumed the conversation with the travel agent. I turned and quickly left the room and with every step I thanked whatever gods there may be for the dumb luck they had just graced me with. Fuck that was close. So I breathed a heavy sigh of relief as I entered my room and reached for the credit card I had so stupidly left on my guestroom dresser.

And before I left the unit, I silently took the keys to the Lincoln off the peg next to the door where that systematic prick always hung them and shouted to Rick, "Back in while."

Selectric, I'm sure I must have had a smile on my face because I felt a tingle go through my body and I wasn't sure if it was the X kicking in or just the giddy reaction that I was taking Rick's car. And no, I didn't give myself away Selectric by making a quick drive to and from the pharmacy. I went and had another scotch at this little alley bar on the way that opened at ten A.M. I took my time and actually had a nice conversation about the blasted fucked up state of affairs this great country of ours is in, with some diamond strutted old straight man at that bar. Boy, he hated George Bush.

Anyhow, Selectric, I felt too good to hate anybody. The nice pharmacist even gave me two of the three remaining refills on the cough syrup. And good thing too, I'm gonna need some to sleep tonight. And it's about that time. Rick's out cold again, but don't you fret, Selectric, I have no intention of reporting another rape to you next we meet. But now, I'm off to a long codeine's nap.

Bonsoir, Selectric.

CHAPTER 47

Fort Lauderdale, Monday, July 13th 1992

Quickly, Selectric! The Gestapo, they're close and there is only a short time for us to say our farewells. But I can't leave you in the dark, for I feel you have spread far too much light upon the dismal horizons of my past and future. I'm certain that I would have no future, as limited in time as that may be given the circumstances, but I may have been in prison or killed myself without you Selectric. And it is precisely because I don't want either of those things that our separation is at hand. So let us relish this moment.

No, Selectric, I can't slow down nor can I stop shaking. What's that? You're absolutely correct. We'd established long ago that I was no Anne Frank and you're no Kitty. Yes, I'll stop with the histrionics and get to the point.

Basically, I still believe that all cops are shitty, and always will be. I've accepted that and know that a certain Detective Kaylor will be more than happy to validate my opinion, as I intend to heed his warning that he sternly issued when he left the unit with the rest of the pack of blue pricks around 2:30 this afternoon.

"You got a favorite pizza or Chinese delivery, Psycho Boy?" Hh said as he looked me in the eye.

"Yeah John, why?" I asked with complete contempt for the fat Nazi prick.

"You might as well know my name, you little cocksucker. It's Alf Baylor, and it's the name you're never going to forget," he said through gritted teeth and a greasy fat finger in my chest.

"Whoa, Alf, How the fuck could I forget the name Alf? Dude, did your parents want you to get the shit kicked out of you every day at school?"

"Listen you little faggot, I'd like to kick your ass right now, but I'm going to kick your ass right into the electric chair instead. I can't put you under house arrest but if you step one foot out of this building, I'll find a reason to bring you in. I swear, pillow biter or poo pusher, whatever arrangement you got here, you better hope Lover Boy makes it, or I'll be the last face you see before you sizzle." He jabbed me so hard in the chest that I stumbled backwards. Then he went on as the final boy in blue, other than himself, left the apartment, "So you got that? You're not going anywhere but to jail, and probably tomorrow morning. Goddamned piece of garbage like you …"

No, Selectric; no one found the crystals or your pages, so let me quickly tell you the transpired events before, once again, I find myself, in an attempt to accommodate the fortune bestowed upon me by this tropical ward of New York, another refuge sought upon the waters of the Intracoastal.

Believe me, Selectric, I've thought about how to escape this apartment and the subsequent jail or electric chair all night. Water bound is the only answer I can come up with. And that's only one of several reasons that I can't take you or our child with me, Selectric. I can't get caught with our conversations on me. Even if Rick lives, these pages would be an admission of guilt to attempted murder, if ever found. We've always known we had to be extra careful, Selectric. But I can't bring myself to burn them or shred these pages that have exposed our "Little Darlings." I have to contradict my Southern and brooding hero, Mr. Faulkner. I just can't kill all my little darlings. And like Anne Frank, I want to live forever. So it's best for everyone that you go back safely in your hiding space. But before I place you in a basket and offer you to the Nile of ages (I know Selectric, I'll try and calm down), before I put you back in the kitchen hiding place, here are our parting words. And it happened fast. You've gotta rat-a-tat tat as fast as you can too, old friend. I've gotta be out of here at least an hour or so before this morning alights.

That's because last Saturday morning, Rick got up and went to work. Yep, he got a phone call on that gas station he's had listed over in Naples since I've known him and within an hour, he was cleaned up, in a suit, and had taken his keys off the hook. I pleaded with him to get back in bed, but as he stepped out the door, he said, "Andy this deal is too much money to let slide. I've been doing really good the last couple of days and I'm not even coughing today. No fever, no snot. I'm fine. Be home by midnight."

"Midnight!" I exclaimed in complete confusion. I thought to myself, "How in the fuck can a dead man stay out in this heat and drive around the state for over twelve hours?"

Rick gave me a quick kiss and held my shoulders square with a grip that I had to admit was strong. And he looked good as he gave that million dollar grin and said, "I've got a trip to Paris to pay for, and this one deal will set us up for the rest of the year, Andy. Really, I'm fine."

And he left. When he shut the door, I was left standing in silence and shock.

"What the hell just happened?" I thought to myself as I stared at the closed door with the chain lock still swinging from the recent departure. As I walked to the bar to pour a badly needed scotch, I tried to convince myself that Rick was in his room and this was all some kind of flash back from the ecstasy that I had been eating like candy.

There was an 18-year-old closet case that was spending some summer break time with his grandparents who were always at the horse races. Man, the guy was pure sex in a bottle and after I met him at the pool, we popped a tab. He couldn't get enough of my dick. And no, Selectric, I didn't tell him that I have AIDS, and he didn't ask. Anyhow, he was new to the scene and I didn't fuck him. Enough okay? He'll be fine. I hope.

But let me get back to the task at hand since I don't have time to elaborate on Jason and, yes, Selectric, Jason is the reason I haven't touched base with you for the last couple of days and no, I don't consider you a "task" but I'm here now, so please, let's not part in regret and a fit of jealousy.

So I'm sure that I looked like a shell shocked, D-Day ghost as I walked with my scotch down the hall. And when I looked into Rick's room and saw the empty and unmade bed, it was as good as a slap in the face from an Omaha beach sergeant who urged his men forward despite the oncoming barrage of bullets that sprayed from the German machine gun nests. I took another swig of my scotch and now fully cognizant of the situation at hand, I told myself, "Yes, move forward. I don't have any other choice. But how?"

And again that most terrible of terrible questions was asked by one of my selves, probably Self C, but I don't have time to figure that out. "So what are you going to do now?"

And like Groundhog Day, I was back at the scotch. Before I knew it, I was sweating the shit out as I trudged to the beach in my flip flops; teeth un-brushed, hair uncombed, no shirt on, body unclean, no underwear. I only had on the crinkled swim suit that I had grabbed from the shower bar where I'd left it to dry from the previous day's follies with Jason. Looking back, I'm sure I looked like that pissed off hippy I'd seen in a clip from the sixties who'd walked down Haight Ashbury with nothing on but a blanket and a scowl. Maybe worse. I didn't even have my blanky.

When Madame Dieux Dieux saw me coming, she just started shaking her head. I pointed an accusing finger at my coal black friend who again was decked in flowing crimson cotton with an abundance of bright yellow and black accessories. As I stared and pointed, she stopped shaking her head and looked straight at me with paralyzing eyes. There was a very mild sea breeze but for some reason, perhaps the scotch, Madame Dieux Dieux waivered like a serpent about to strike. But no need to worry, it had become obvious to me that what I should have known all along was that Madame Dieux Dieux was a King Snake and the first words I told her as I got within five feet of the woman were, "Red on black is a happy Jack."

She didn't respond with a word or gesture but remained poised and proud. There was little or no traffic on A1A. A young shirtless man on roller blades quickly passed by in the bike lane, but other than the sound of gulls and the breeze as it rustled through the various palms, there was silence. And silence can say so much.

Through the silence, the old snake rhyme Ella chanted to me as a little boy revealed itself to me in full clarity. With the deliberation and despair of a once-happy gambler who had turned up his Full House and postured to take the pot, only to realize his opponent calmly turned one deuce at a time till the Jack in the fourth turn is fatally followed by another deuce, I announced the rhyme with a disappointment that bordered on disgust; as if it were the fourth and miserable deuce to deny me the biggest pot I had come so close to surely winning.

"Red on yeller will kill a feller. Red on black is a happy Jack."

"Maybe you put too much stock in color Mason". she said then allowed the sound of consistent breeze as it calmly fluttered through the palms and her red dress. Her silent curiosity exposed by her brow, I decided to speak plainly.

"He's not going to die, is he Madame Dieux Dieux?" I calmly asked as I returned her gaze.

"No Mason, we are all going to die," she coolly stated, then hissed with the conviction of disgust and confidence my fourth grade teacher possessed as she assured her unruly class that we would behave, "only to realize that we will live forever."

She emphasized the word "realize" in such a fizzle that I could have sworn her tongue split into a fork, like that of snake. But I was not about to allow myself the inconvenience of another flashback. I wanted answers and I wasn't going to accept the Oral Roberts idea something good is going to happen to you, yea though I walk through the valley of death, reincarnation, mumbo jumbo riddle that Madame Dieux Dieux had just presented. I wanted practical answers. Like the one she gave me in the little leather pouch with the poison vial. Except now, I wanted the truth from her. And I told her so.

"Cut the Bullshit Madame Dieux Dieux. Rick is up and at 'em on his way to pay for our mother fucking trip to Paris. How the—"

"How lovely, what a city for lovers—" she interrupted and I didn't hesitate to return the discourtesy.

I rudely and hysterically ordered, "Shut the fuck up!"

Groundhog day all over. I felt a sting before I saw the flash of her hand in motion towards my face that was followed by a force that I could have sworn would be impossible for anyone, much less that skinny old woman to exert. Literally, it knocked me off my feet and I found myself on my ass looking up at Madame Dieux Dieux as she calmly informed me, "I was about to say before I was so extremely disrespected that Paris is such a lovely city for lovers to heal."

"How the fuck would you know? Have you ever even been in love?" I screamed at her as my ass skid across the sandy cement to try and keep up with the conniption fit the rest of my body was in.

"Yessss," she hissed and then abruptly admitted, "no."

"What are you talking about?" I said and started crying.

"Oh for Christ's sake! Here we go again," she contemptuously answered. And with a disgusted wave of her hands turned for the shade of her kiosk.

Still on my ass, I watched her as she gave me no attention whatsoever. She lit a cigar and popped a cold Dr. Pepper that she had pulled from the little Igloo that she seemed never to be without. Madame Dieux Dieux sat down on her little stool under the shade of her kiosk umbrella and toyed with her radio and finally got the reception that she had been looking for. Our private bubble, which it seemed we had occupied only moments ago, was popped by the sound of a crackling island French newscast which I had no skill to comprehend. It was as much useless babble to me as the gibberish that had just been spoken in English by the little Creole woman.

I gave up my jag and had nothing to dry my tears, so I rubbed my eyes with the tops of my forearms and stood up. Who was that old woman that puffed on her cigar with the confidence of an oil tycoon? She was now a stranger to me. But she had lied to me and I wanted to know why.

"Why did you lie to me Madame Dieux Dieux?" I asked as I joined her in the shade. She looked me square in the eyes then exhaled a huge cloud of the so that it engulfed us like some sort of spell, hinged with the smell of the smoke and Madame Dieux Dieux's breath.

"You after da truf here Mason? Right? Dat what you told me when you first told me about dis insanity you done unleashed on the world. Here da truf da way I see it, Mason." She spoke my name with such and exaggerated 'S' and with her eyes so wide open that I saw her in much the same way a witch doctor might address a demon. If nothing else, she had my full attention as she gave it to me.

"You are like a wild bull let loose in da market square intent on destroying everyting in sight." And Selectric, I'm here to tell you here and now she hissed the word sight that I never saw the old lady looking more like a snake, the King Snake, that she is.

But then just as quickly, she transformed back into the old Haitian lady and she shamelessly sat down on her stool, and hunched over waiving that cigar like it were a symphony conductor's baton. Her eyebrows were furrowed and her forehead as wrinkled as the tight coal black skin would allow as she further explained, "You don't think anybody with any sense is gonna try and dart dat bull or lasso the crazed ting or worse yet, shoot it before it hurts people and quite possibly itself in the process." She paused as she looked at me as I stared back in seething rage. "And you sitting on your ass der, So self consumed. Mason, Andy, Derwood, whatever the hell you going by, you know you never have asked me bout my name, Madame Dieux Dieux, except the pronunciation, even after I tell you it means God God."

I didn't respond as I again had to concede in this moment of dire honesty that she was speaking the truth and she must have taken it as a sign that I was listening and continued, just as calm, cool, and collected as she could have possible been.

"I wasn't always been called Madame God God. Between not dying from this common shit dat we both have and what killed my little angel and the death I dealt to her father that created a reality for me that was pure terror until I became Dieux Dieux, or enlightened, as the street name given to me by my old comrades in Port-au-Prince, a literal hell on earth," and she got extremely vitriolic as she stated the description of her home city and paused. Then she went on in a matter of fact tone, "Do you even have any idea that I send every cent of profit back to my city to help feed the baby girls and boys whose milk from dey mommas being stolen by grown men. Men like the one I killed, but den now, I know, whether I'm in fact enlightened or not that, a person who glimpses the nature of truf; the first thing we know is this; we must not and will not hurt or bring suffering to anybody."

"But you lied to me Madame Dieux Dieux. You lied and that is the furthest thing from the truth as I know." I interrupted still on the my ass, and I'm certain I looked like a disheveled wreck.

But Madame Dieux Dieux went on, "And dis I know for da fact. You about to create a reality for yourself a tousand time more painful dan you could ever imagine. I know I don't want dat, Mason. I prey da truf bite you in da ass and you recognize it. And I didn't lie to you, I just gave you a bag of salt and baking powder. I looks like the real stuff I killed my man, but I was hoping you might take the opportunity to become "Dieux Dieux" in your hell. Pick up a new name, wit out even marrying me." She smiled and looked into my red and puffing enraged face. "But hey, c'est la vie." she exclaimed with a waive of her hand.

"You are fucking insane," I told her with contempt in every syllable.

This time I was not tripping and for real, Madame Dieux Dieux treated me in much the same manner that she had treated the Massachusetts asshole that first day I'd seen her. That admonishing laugh had endeared me to her, but I found being the brunt of her contemptuous wrath anything but endearing. As she came up for air in an attempt to escape her comic seizure, her eyes pleaded for me to please stop tickling her.

She breathed hard and said, "Woo Mason, Chile!" She had to stop to catch her breath before she continued; barely able to control herself from going into another bout of laughing hysterics, "If dat ain't da pot calling da kettle black, Whew! I don't know what is!"

"You're fucking crazy," I screamed at the old woman.

Nope, Madame Dieux Dieux was unable to control her amused fit and it consumed her with no mercy. I'm sorry to say that my lasting memories of my non venomous ally will be of her bent over, helplessly wiping snot from her nose and tears from her eyes as she was unable to control herself at my expense. I was not happy to amuse her and by no means was she being useful to me anymore. I was done with her. So I turned and walked away in a fit of rage that I can compare to very few that I'd ever experienced. And that includes my episode with Rick, which inspired this whole journal.

But I wasn't going to kill Madame Dieux Dieux. Within two or three steps from the King Snake's kiosk, I had the logistics worked out to perform my original fantasy of a long and final fall for Rick Gurnee. I'd show Madame Dieux Dieux and Rick at the same time "the real stuff". And I did. Probably better than I can tell you about it.

The Devil is in the details, Selectric. With a little luck, I knew Old Scratch would come through for me. And fuck me, I was so perturbed that I left the house with no money. I went back to the condo and grabbed some cash and walked right back to the trusty True Value store that I had only moments before walked past. And they had what I needed.

I'd used propane torches many times in various jobs my Old Man had given to me as his private deckhand on the old house boat that I nearly sent to the bottom of the Ouachita River. The old boat was coated with layer after layer of paint and I'd used these handheld torches many times to melt the paint before sanding wood or for repairing rusty mesh on the rails and jagged edges on the barge floor itself. I knew these things could get hot and I knew the aluminum alloy that composed the rails on Rick's sun deck should easily yield to heat of the torch. And I bought two canisters just to make sure.

And, Selectric, it was easy as pie. No problem, little sound, and quick. I even got a little theatrical as I heated the first screw and rail on the top right connection of cement and rail. I had one of Rick's new Florida Marlins baseball hats on backwards, catcher style, and the remainder of that fatty I'd just recently rolled lit right after I lit the torch. And motherfuck, the torch worked too well. I mean the aluminum around the steel screws that were drilled into the cement walls melted like plastic wrap on a hot skillet. I left the bottom right screw and bolt that went into the Western wall of the building alone. That would be the only one to support the rail. And the other two fixtures attached to the cement column that ran from top to bottom of the building that supported balcony after balcony in the Seventeen story building yielded just as easily as the first ones. The only tale was a little tilted sag in the rail and some black carbon traces on the white paint of the cement, and that was removed easily by some dish soap and a sink pad.

There was one problem. The bottom right fixture was so strong that it alone was holding the entire four-foot wide rail somewhat secure. It might be just too secure is what I thought. So I stood back and took stock of my handiwork and decided to think over the little conundrum. And that took a healthy shot of scotch over some ice to relieve the heat and the small amount of anxiety I held about the success of what I knew would be my last chance to get the motherfucker, and to show Madame Dieux Dieux.

So I took a break and relaxed in one of Rick's deck chairs and enjoyed my scotch as I studied the situation. Yes, Selectric, I was fully aware that this would not be noted by any investigation as an accident. But I had no intention on being around to watch Rick in his morning ritual perform a fatal high dive act. As much as I would like to see it and enjoy the commotion, I'd be long gone after Honey Bunch had gone to bed after his hard day's work. I'd be nowhere near Fort La da di da when the sun came up and he arose to meet the day with his new found health. And no, Selectric, no one looked up from Sunrise Boulevard and called the police. I swear! You're so paranoid. Yes, Selectric, point taken. There was good reason to be paranoid, but like I said earlier, I think God and Devil both look after a fool. And besides, these Yankee's down here don't pay attention to anything other than themselves. If any had seen me, they probably would've thought I was a maintenance man.

So as I meditated with my scotch on the chances of the bottom screw holding too securely, Old Scratch came through for me in the shape of a terracotta plant pot. It was the perfect height to support the bottom rail if I softened the metal around the steel screw to the Western wall. But I had to be careful. The rail had to stay in place.

I adjusted the flame on the torch and softened the flame just so that the remaining aluminum by the screw to the wall might be further weakened. It held and I told myself after a gentle inspection of the rail that the dice were cast. I washed off the bit of carbon that remained on the wall of the building and put the torches back in the paper sack. I had wasted money buying two. One was all I needed. But I had to get rid of these things and I was concerned about just throwing them down the chute. I knew they were combustible, so I put on my flip flops and took them to construction site next door on the Intracoastal and buried them in the huge dumpster. Then I came back to my unit and casually packed my backpack.

As I did so, I was a bit perturbed that I would not be able to enjoy the money and the condo like I had originally planned, but damn it to hell, Selectric, I was pretty much satisfied that this was gonna work. I knew I needed to be home when Rick got home. He'd expect me to be there and probably go looking for me if I weren't. And besides, I wanted to say good night to him.

And with the remorse for my lost millions, I consequently remembered that I still had Rick's visa that he'd willingly given me yesterday. I couldn't use it on the road or my new home, wherever that might be, as the records would be traceable. So I made another trek to the ATM and this time I gambled a little higher. I punched in three thousand dollars and voila, the machine dispensed the Ben Franklins. Oh, I do love Uncle Ben. How do I count the ways? That could give a little cushion till I got to wherever I was going. And if Rick got back tonight and asked me for the card, I could just apologize and say that I'd forgotten to put it back in his wallet and hand it to him. If he didn't, then I'd keep it for any other purchases I might need before I left Fort Lauderdale then trash the thing before I left town.

When I got back to the condo, I couldn't believe how well my day was turning around. The elevator opened to reveal Jason in only his swimming briefs and a towel.

"What's up, dude?" I asked as I'm sure I eyed him up and down like a piranha.

Somehow, he managed to blush through his sunburn and with downcast eyes, he just smiled a really sheepish smile.

"You heading to the pool?" I asked.

"Yes," he quietly answered.

"Cool, I could use a dip," I said as I motioned to myself and the nasty hot mess I must've appeared. "Mind if I join you?"

"That'd be great," he said.

"Hey come on up with me real quick. Let's blow a fatty. Grammy and Pappy are at the track right?" I asked to confirm that he had the afternoon free.

"Dude, you're a mind reader," he said with a grin and agreement to my idea.

Selectric, I won't bother you with the sordid and so exquisite details of the time I spent with Jason as you and I are simply short on the stuff that life is made of, to quote Gone With The Wind. But I will tell you we never made it to the pool. We took two tabs of X each and were still high, hard and naked when six P.M. pulled in. Do you think I'd risk Rick's coming in at any second with Jason and I getting down in my—excuse me—Rick's apartment? Hell no. So we took the party from Grammy and Pappy's to the Berkley's vacant unit on the second floor with nothing but lube, a beach towel, and a little boom box. Fricking lock box was still on backwards but I managed. What a bitch. Oh yes and of course Selectric, I had rubbers. No, I didn't tell him I had AIDS and he didn't ask, but I did teach my puppy the rules of safe sex, and we played safe. And yes, it was his first time to get fucked and he loved it and I dare say he is now pretty much a faggot forever. Thank you, funny Selectric. I didn't hear anyone say, "You're welcome." That's just rude.

Anyhow, come around eight-thirty or so, I really don't know, but the sun was down and Jason and I pretty much came down as well. We drank a shit load of water and kissed good night. He said that he would be leaving pretty soon and hoped to see me around Thanksgiving. I apologized to him that I was pretty sure I'd be in France, so he took one of Rick's business cards and the pen from the guest show registrar on the kitchen counter, wrote down his personal info and asked me to give him a buzz if I was ever in New York. Jason went on up to Grammy's and I locked up and went to Rick's.

But Rick still had not made it home, so I lit the fat stub of the joint Jason and I had busted and poured a grand shot of Black on the rocks. Gone With The Wind was on and I swear, Selectric, I'm such a fag. I totally relate to Scarlet O'Hara but the Goddamned soundtrack in that movie lulls me to sleep every time, and this time was no exception. That music score along with the soothing effects of the joint over the dead X and the afternoon of jungle gym sex and my trusty—excuse me—Rick's trusty couch were a combination for sleep.

Next thing I know, I heard a scream the likes Vivian Leigh had never let out when little Bonnie Blue Butler snapped her own spoiled neck near the end of the movie, the part where the little bitch tried to jump a bar far too high for her primped pony to manage. I got up to turn the T.V. off and grumbled at myself for falling asleep as I was in a fog. But a second scream that made the hair on the back of my neck stand up and the cognizant effect of sunlight woke me up to a new reality from which there was no escape.

I'm surprised that I didn't break the living room's balcony sliding glass door as I hit it so hard when I dashed in the direction of a wailing banshee. And what I saw woke me up in flash.

It did more than that, I'll tell ya, Selectric. Dude, after I slid the door back and ran on the balcony, all I saw, in the direction of the now continual scream, was a blank space of open air where the balcony rail used to be, and a twisted piece of metal still attached to the Western wall of the building, and the cement screw that that apparently held the rail by its metallic thread. And I literally pissed myself as I raced to the edge when I had to catch my balance from going over myself. Seriously, I came that close and I stumbled back from the dizzying void and landed hard on my ass after I witnessed my lover dangling butt naked with both hands clasped with veins popping out to the corner of the rail where the bars met to form a ninety degree angle.

"Jesus, Lord Jesus, HELP me! CHRIST Andy please GOD HELP!" he screamed.

I rolled over on my stomach and with my elbows, I pulled myself to the balcony's edge. I laid my chin on the vortex of my crossed arms that made my elbows hang over the balcony floor. I literally had the catbird seat to the entire scenario.

The freaking drawbridge was up and the few Sunday morning cars stuck at the Sunrise Boulevard upraised bridge emptied their passengers. They looked like circus cars from that height and clowns falling out of them as the people that got out pointed up and weren't accustomed to not watching their feet as they exited a car. And Rick, Holy Moly but I swear, my eyes could have seen an x-ray version of his face and head. It was as if the bone and vessels were going to cut through the skin any second.

"So you're a Christian after all?" I calmly inquired to my dangling and sweat drenched boyfriend.

And, Selectric, let me say that the situation Rick was in did no justice to his manhood. I swear, I think his dick and balls were nearly sucked up inside him. His cushy gold towel fluttering from the top stalks of a tall Royal Palm below pronounced the explanation of his nakedness.

"For the Love of GOD! Please help me Andy, God!" He screamed.

"Hey Rick, Did you piss and miss the pot today. Funny, Rick, I just pissed myself just looking at you hanging there," I said to him with my chin still cushioned on my forearms. I was as casual as if we laid in bed and I had my chin on his chest talking to him face to face.

And his expression changed as well, to a near calm, to a surrender to the inevitable and something much more. He looked me square in the eyes. I could hear the sirens of approaching emergency vehicles along with the screams from the onlookers below on Sunrise. Their hysterics rang to my ears with a combination of mercy and horror as Rick's silent gaze upward into my own eyes conveyed the same blend. In that moment, I believe I thought the screams were for me. And that moment, as the sea breeze cut the corner of the building and ran through our bodies, could have been a lifetime, a thousand years, or less than a millisecond. It was eternal, real, and I'm quite sure, true. A gull glided by and, I swear, made a quick ninety degree turn to hover through the breeze to gawk at Rick. The bird's eyes and expression were without love or empathy and he flew away, unconcerned in the least. I don't think that Rick even saw the bird as he was gazing into my eyes. Who knows, maybe he did? I saw a pleading tear cut through the sweat under Rick's eyes, and just above them I could see his moist hands and fingers slowly but surely losing their grip. He had accepted his fate.

"I love you Andy. Always," he breathed aloud through flaring nostrils and punctuated cheeks.

And suddenly the serenity in Rick's eyes reverted to the previous expression of sheer terror and his mouth formed wide to scream, long before any sound conveyed his feelings, as his whole being consummated the information and validations that this was it.

"Cover your head!" a strange voice bellowed in the authority of Brooklyn construction site coordinator. I recognized the voice but could not quite place its face or rationale in the scheme of this moment. And Rick let go.

I watched in what I must admit was pure satisfaction with no regret and with a strange sense of curiosity as Rick, in what appeared to me as slow motion, made an attempt with his hands to follow the instructions of the gruff voice from nowhere. And Rick didn't go straight down as I would have thought. No, he swung somewhat backwards and with a twist that didn't make any sense to my reason.

The next thing I knew, I heard a thump. It strongly resembled the sound I recognized from my high school football days of the top of our All State kicker's foot connecting with the old pigskin to punt a fifty yard beauty that saved us from our precarious field position.

I don't know if Rick was saved. Apparently, the sound I heard was his head, back, or both as he collided with the wall from two levels below. I hadn't noticed the two pair of hands, one on each of Rick's legs and gradually my mind accepted the top view of two green capped heads that were jerked into my view the split second I heard the hollow thud. Just as instantly, I saw their backs in their one piece work covers stretched down over the rail as if they struggled not to go over the edge themselves. Then the two heads disappeared under the balcony as I, still on my stomach, stretched out over the open edge to get a clearer picture of what was going on directly below me. I saw Rick's limp body being hauled over the rail of the balcony immediately under us. And I now knew the source of that forceful voice from nowhere. It was that of the maintenance man. The second capped head must have been that of his Jamaican partner.

From previous encounters on various sights of the property with both men, I knew they were giants and could, if they chose to quit their jobs, become center ring stars for Deep South Wrestling. But today, they were Rick's guardian angels. Well, at least he didn't hit the ground. Last I checked with Jay, as Sergeant Alf, wouldn't let me leave the building, Rick was in I.C.U. and Jay wasn't sure if he was comatose. It was all very sketchy.

But the second they pulled Rick to safety, my world became quite vivid. Sirens, lights, cameras and, action! Every motherfucker but Superman showed up. And there was a huge squabble with the head of the condo association as to whether I could stay in Rick's place on several grounds. One, I wasn't approved by the condo board to live on the property to begin with and, two, the President of the Association argued that the unit was unsafe for anyone to stay in. I told them I could get a hotel but Sergeant Shit Breath forcefully took the condo Nazi aside into the guest room and when they came out, no more discussion. Through all the inspectors and the bullshit, nobody ever found the packed backpack in the guest room closet, loaded with pot, X, cash, and Rick's Visa card. And there was no search whatsoever through the kitchen where they could have found you, Selectric. Actually, you, the machine, was up in the guest room closet shelf next to the backpack. Sorry Selectric, there were none, nor will there be any plans, to take you with me. Now shush, and just listen.

"Where am I going?" you ask, dear friend Selectric.

I don't know, my trusty steed, but I know I'm not going to stay here. I guess it's out to pasture for you. Again I want you to know how much I appreciate what the galloping journey and the rat-a-tat tat of your hooves have revealed to me. Funny my friend, I still for the life of me could not tag what I'm so angry, or "enraged" about. I still feel the smoldering embers down deep inside me, but not towards Rick or even Madame Dieux Dieux for thwarting my murder. Actually, she may have failed for at the moment, I'm stuck with a possibly comatose Rick. We'll see.

Anyhow, I actually hope Rick lives. Not that I'm sorry or that I'm worried about whether or not I get the electric chair. (Dude, I will slit my own throat before I go to jail again. I got a spare razor blade from Rick's bathroom and kept it in my side cargo shorts pocket before the army of pricks in blue ever got here. It's still here.) Honestly, I don't know why I wish Rick the best. And I hope he's not brain damaged or fucked up in anyway. Jesus, I think that'd be worse than death. You know something, Selectric? Right this second, this very moment, one of my selves just told me that Rick's future is not for me to decide. And another voice said that it never was.

Maybe that's why I'm so pissed off. Things just aren't, were not, nor will ever be, the way I think they should be. I'm not God, Selectric. But do I want to be? Wouldn't anybody? I don't think so. What would make me happy, Selectric?

All of these questions and partial answers, I owe to our journey. I guess the biggest revelation was given, inadvertently by Madame Dieux Dieux when she told me that the Truth is a paradox.

And I want to explore that some more. To be honest, since I need to keep that up before I leave you, curiosity of just what the hell is going to happen next is what stopped me from crossing the yellow police tape and taking a swan dive for the entertainment of the gulls to conclude what I term as my final "fuck it" temper tantrum. I'm not going to jail, Selectric.

I'm still curious. I think my curiosity, despite my foolish nature, is what keeps me alive. What is "The Truth?" If nothing else, and there has been so much you've given me, Selectric, the reflection into that question has been worth your weight in gold.

Aha, Selectric! You ask a very fine question indeed. And I'll tell you how I'm going to get out of here. At least I hope with the aid of God and the Devil, this fool will continue his quest for truth. Like I said earlier, I want to live forever, Selectric. I know, I know! Razor blades and seventeenth story high dive acts contradict that sentiment, but herein lies the Truth in a psychotic paradox.

Anyhow here's the plan. It came to me as I watched the whole damn drama unfold in real time on Rick's television. Some tourist with a Camcorder caught most of the action in a hazy and jerked film from the vantage point of the draw bridge below. Poor Rick, as he twisted there butt naked, between the poor skills of the camera man/woman, and the distance from camera to target, he looked as anatomically gendered as the G.I. Joe doll I had in my youth. And the shots of my face were just as obscure. That's a blessing, as I won't be identified as easily by anybody who watches America's Most Wanted. I kid you not, Selectric, we're already on national news. I can only guess how much attention this thing is going to get. And as I watched the news deep into the night I made up my mind that they were never going to get me in a courtroom. As I pondered the impossible situation that I found myself in, I strongly considered a leap from the balcony the news continually flashed on telly. They had removed the dangling rail that had held all the way through the aerial drama.

Now I had to figure how I was going to be removed from this scene, and not in the back one of the several police cars that I could see on television, which halted all traffic, or persons that made an attempt to come on the property. I even had to go down and meet the pizza guy in the lobby and there were two pigs there. One of the assholes took a slice of pizza from my box before I went back up to the unit and ate. Fucking prick.

Anyway, the anger I had towards the fat fuck in blue only fueled my concentration as I watched the live news reels over and over again. I made up mind I wasn't going down. And then it hit me like a charm. I'd use the Berkley's balcony. I'd jump alright, right into the Goddamned swimming pool, and hope my Gods and demons were favorable. The winch to Rick's boat is electric. I should be able to set her in the water without a sound. And dude, from the earlier views presented by live action news, no cops are on the back side of the condo on the Intracoastal. Only the front parking entrance and lobby, which is the only entrance point other than ground floor parking entrance and the emergency stairwells which also exit in the front lobby, are to best of my knowledge, being covered.

And now it's four A.M.. The best time of the day to take any kind of devious action. I'll just stay off the elevators and take the emergency stair well silently to the second floor. I'll keep the razor blade ready for a moment's notice, should anyone fuck up my plans.

And so I end our time together, Selectric. And despite your request to stop the dramatics, I'll place you back in the hiding place and cast you upon the Nile of Ages. Who knows if or when anyone will ever read our darling child, Selectric? That is not for me to decide. And again, thank you for that revelation. Whether or not anyone ever reads this, its very existence will keep us immortal. Unlike the river of time upon which you are set adrift, I'm to vex fortune's odds, if I'm lucky, upon a man-made river of sorts. I've made a full Three Hundred and Sixty from where I spent my first night in Fort Lauderdale. Back to the Intracoastal. Except this time, I will be silently adrift in the security of a boat, in harmony to whichever way the tide is flowing. I won't turn on the boat's engine until I'm well away from the Sunrise Boulevard Bridge. I just hope Rick has some gas in that boat.

Wish me Luck!

EPILOGUE

November 2010

Mariah Wolfson Choudrant

AFTER WE RETURNED TO NEW YORK IN JANUARY 2005, OVER THE urges of my husband Sean to, "let it go," I made a flaccid attempt to contact Mason Caldwell, AKA Andy. Concretely, I made an evident attempt to return property that was not mine. And, to whom the manuscript belonged, was unclear.

I made a phone call to the title company that had handled our transaction the past November and spoke with the attorney/owner of the company. He quickly explained that I should refer to my closing documents and if I did not understand them, consult a Florida Attorney of Law. As politely as I could, I explained that I understood that our title had been transferred from the estate of Richard Gurnee, but that I had a question that concerned the deceased. The lawyer quickly explained that he could give no detailed personal or collateral information about Mr. Gurnee other than he had died May 7th, 2002 and that the sale of his residence strictly adhered to the probate code of the State of Florida and Mr. Gurnee's Last Will and Testament.

He had answered one of my questions as he verified the date of Rick Gurnee's death. I made one last inquiry into the cause of Mr. Gurnee's death and, in a very aggravated and rude tone, the owner asked me to hold. I did, for about ten minutes. I wasn't sure if my call had been dropped or worse, but the click of the phone and a woman's voice replaced that of the title company's owner. She asked me to confirm that I was in fact Mariah Wolfson Choudrant. I said that I was. I assumed, from the cadence in her voice, that she read a script that informed me that she would be happy to answer any questions that concerned the closing instruments but that she was bound by Florida Law not to disclose information about any party or parties involved in the sale. I said that I understood and could she tell me who the executors of the deceased owner's estate were. She paused for a moment, then informed me that it was clear on my own documents, should I read them, that the executor of the estate was Attorney Thomas Channing, of the firm Channing, Channing and Zavslawsky.

The woman asked me if there were any other questions that she could assist me with that dealt with the documents of transaction or conveyance. I said no but, thank you. She hung up.

Perhaps I should have taken the advice of the title attorney and contacted a Florida Attorney. Or for that matter, the Florida authorities. I'm sure that was the correct legal action that I should have taken. But I'm convinced that had I contacted anyone to expose the contents of the manuscript, I would have made a moral error.

In my view, this manuscript titled "How to Kill Your Lover" belonged to its author, Mason Harrison Caldwell III. Had I managed to contact Mr. Caldwell in 2005, I'm not even certain how I would have addressed him. Andy or Mason. And further, I didn't know whether or not he was alive.

It was evident Rick Gurnee passed nearly nine years after the attempt/s were made on his life by Mason/Andy Caldwell. That is, if Mason/Andy's story were true.

I searched on Google for "Balcony, Fort Lauderdale, 1992, Gurnee," and from various action news coverage, I witnessed the event as described by Mason/Andy in his journal of sorts. And Andy/Mason's description of the tourist video that had captured the episode were accurate. I was not able to make out much more than his silhouette as he observed from the balcony floor the perilous situation at hand.

The video, saved for posterity on the internet, verified the balcony episode from "How to Kill Your Lover." It validated my concern that the document I held in my possession was, to say the least, a legal liability. But I had not brought it with me from Florida. In what I thought was an appropriate gesture, I had placed the manuscript in the same manila envelope in which it first made its appearance, that being the shelf of the second bedroom closet in the corner where, I could only assume, the I.B.M. Selectric typewriter had, at one time, occupied.

As Mason/Andy phrased it in his writings, the million dollar conundrum, "What am I going to do now," rang loud and clear in my head. From what I could fathom, I had not so far behaved in any manner outside of the law. I reasoned that although I held the manuscript in my possession, did that make it mine? Or Sean's for that matter. So far as I knew outside of the author, Sean was the only other person that knew of the story's existence.

Only minutes after I reasoned what very little I knew of the law, much less probate law of the state of Florida, I concluded that the correct action on my part would be to contact the executor of the deceased's estate. That would be an attorney by the name of Thomas Channing.

And once again, Google came to my rescue. I dialed the number on the website and within moments I again spoke with a terse voice that questioned whether I would like to speak to Thomas Channing Jr., or Thomas Channing III. I explained that I was not sure, but that the matter at hand was probate of the firm's client, the estate of Rick Gurnee.

The voice on the other end of the line stated, "One moment please"

Within a couple of minutes, the nameless secretary of Channing, Channing, and Zavslosky informed me that I sought the attention of Thomas III, and that he was not available at the moment. Instantly, I was connected to the voice mail of Thomas III and "Tom" advised me to leave a brief message, and that he would respond to all calls appropriately.

Briefly and very cautiously, I explained to the voicemail that some items of the deceased had been left behind in the kitchen of the unit that I had purchased, and that I had questions as to what to do with them. I asked that he please contact me and left my phone number and email address.

A couple of days passed until I received a confidential email from Channing, Channing, and Zavslosky that when opened briefly explained that they did not represent me. The email explained that as long as the value item/s left in the property did not substantially affect the agreed selling price by more than the contract's inspection default number, the item/s left behind transferred ownership with the conveyance of title to the buyer/buyers, unless specified otherwise in the sales contract. It was electronically signed by Thomas Channing III.

I reasoned that the manuscript did not affect the sales price of our unit. Furthermore, I concluded that my husband, Sean, according to the email from Channing, Channing, and Zavslawsky was also in possession of the physical manuscript.

I approached my husband with a brief outline of my/our dilemma. After he dropped his dinner fork, which cracked our daily china, Sean, about as terse as any of the legal secretaries I had encountered, but with much more veiled testosterone anger, explained to me that I was opening a can of worms.

"Give the Estate of Rick Gurnee the Goddamned, insane bullshit. I don't have the time nor inclination to do anything with it, enough already," he said and returned to the chicken casserole that I'd cooked.

End of discussion. And I further considered my husband's opinion and consequently, I agreed with him. I responded to "Tom's" email and stated that to the best of my knowledge, the item did not affect the sale's price of our unit, the item I held in my possession was personal in nature and should be given directly to the person/s declared to be the benefactors of Rick Gurnee's estate and that it was my aspiration that the benefactors of the estate would forward the item to its self-declared owner.

Several days passed and I received another correspondence from the desk of Thomas Channing III and "Tom" Channing explained that the succession of Richard Gurnee was not as of this time concluded and the matter was still active in the probate court of Florida. However, he further explained, should I wish to submit the item/s to his office for distribution at the appropriately legal time, as executor of Mr. Gurnee's estate, he would hold the item until such time were established.

I emailed Tom that I did not wish to submit the property to anyone other than the rightful heir of the estate of Rick Gurnee, and asked the attorney, as executor of the estate, to notify the legally established heir or heirs of the item in my possession and simply identify the item as "Selectric's Darlings."

Within four hours Tom replied, "Do what you want," and, "As Executor of the estate of Richard Gurnee, Duly noted."

The manuscript, item, journal, confession what have you, remained in the Florida condo unit on its designated shelf untouched (and unbeknownst to Sean Choudrant) for close to five years. Fast forward to 2010, when, to put it mildly, the real estate market tanked. We listed the unit with a local Realtor to save as much as we could from the impending financial loss. Actually, we were, as they say, "A day late and a dollar short," but that did not stop me from taking our Realtor's advice, which was to remove any items or articles of value from the unit during the listing period. I boxed up "How To Kill Your Lover" and placed it, along with any other documents or items that I felt might tempt a person of limited constitution, in our unit's storage locker.

We received no offers on the unit and as far as I'm aware, everything in the condo remained in place. We placed the unit under short sale status, and long story short, I still own the unit to this day. I don't know if it will ever sell. But Trick or Treat, I don't know which, I did receive an email on Halloween day of this year from an individual who identified himself as Selectric's Buddy and the legitimate and legal heir to the estate of Richard Gurnee. His email's heading was titled "Selectric's Darlings."

When I opened the email, I read in a very brief paragraph that the sender had been contacted by the Law Firm of Channing, Channing, and Zavslawsky. The sender acknowledged that after consulting an attorney in the state of his current residence, that the Florida Statute of Limitations would prevent any prosecution of attempted murder, or any one of the other felonies for which he may have otherwise qualified. The sender admitted in the paragraph that the sender's attorney's concern was the out of state status of the heir and that "Selectric's Darlings" could aid in the charge of "multiple offenses," which under various circumstances might extend the time period of the Statute of Limitations. Before the sender's attorney would allow the Grantee to be granted the estate of Richard Gurnee, the attorney advised that "Selectric's Darling" be in the sole heir's possession. The sender requested that I forward an appropriate phone number so that options to attain what I had already established were the heir's property could be discussed with more freedom. I sent the sender the number to my personal cell phone.

While in my office two days later, on November 2nd, 2010, my cell phone rang, showing a 615 area code phone number. I usually do not answer calls from unfamiliar area codes as they, without exception, turn out to be some type of seller's pitch or scam. However, I was certainly aware of the shady nature that engulfed the author of the email, "Selectric's Darlings" and I took the call.

"Hello, Mrs. Choudrant?" a male voice with a thick Southern accent politely questioned.

"Yes, this is Mariah Choudrant. To whom am I speaking please?" I asked.

"Mrs. Choudrant, I am the attorney of Mason Harrison Caldwell III. My name is Cornell Kastelka and I am calling you on behalf of Mr. Caldwell concerning your expressed desire to return property, as you have rightly declared, that belongs to my client. My client has informed me that the document you possess contains personal information which concerns the intimate relationship between the deceased grantor of estate, Mr. Richard Gurnee, and himself. Have you read the contents of Mr. Caldwell's writings Miss Choudrant?"

"I have. Yes," I replied.

Mr. Kastelka paused momentarily and further inquired, "And have you discussed any of the contents of what you read in my client's personal property with any other person or persons?"

"Mr. Kastelka, after speaking with the executor of Richard Gurnee's estate, I was informed by an attorney that the personal property of your client now technically belonged to myself and my husband. I discussed the nature of 'Selectric's Darlings' with my husband in an attempt to decide what to do with the work. To the best of my knowledge, only I am privy to the facts of the manuscript, and I have made no copies. The manuscript is still on the property where it was found and has not left the property since the date I was first confronted with its existence. I simply wish to return it to its author," I said.

"Thank you Miss Choudrant for the affirmation of your intentions. I appreciate your goodwill. May I ask you for a time, place, and date where I may meet you so that I may accept my client's property? He does not wish the manuscript to enter the federal mail."

"I'm sorry to repeat myself but my only intention is to give the manuscript directly to the sole heir of Richard Gurnee, whom I now apparently believe to be Mason Caldwell. I will not take it off property or place it in the mail or any other person's hands. I will be at my unit in Fort Lauderdale the Tuesday prior to Thanksgiving. If Mr. Caldwell would like, I will expect him, and only him, to ring the buzzer at my address at five P.M Eastern time and identify himself as Mason Caldwell. Then he can come up to my unit, where I will give him his property, and he may leave and do with his manuscript what he deems fit."

I was tired of lawyers. Mr. Kastelka may have identified my weariness.

"I apologize for any inconvenience that I've caused you, Mrs. Choudrant. You've been quite clear about your intentions from the beginning, and I appreciate your stance. However good your intentions are, I must apologize again to you as I cannot advise my client to follow your request and return to Florida to personally retrieve his property that may incriminate him. I hope—"

"Mr. Kastelka, I can appreciate your position, but do what you and your client will. I'll be observing the holiday in Fort Lauderdale regardless. Good day."

I hung up. And I must say it felt good to hang up on an attorney. The 615 number rang my cell phone again and this time, I ignored the caller as I did the two later attempts in the day by the 615 number.

On Monday, November 22nd, I caught my flight to Fort Lauderdale as planned. Sean, who would not be leaving for Florida until Wednesday night, was stuck with work. I explained, and truthfully I might add, that I intended to shop for Thanksgiving dinner on Tuesday and spruce the unit up as we had not been in it since last June. My husband did not have any knowledge whatsoever that I had invited Mason Caldwell to our unit to retrieve the manuscript. And I wasn't sure if Mason would follow the advice of his attorney or show up. I'd like to say that I didn't care, but the impression of indifference to the matter that I had expressed to Mason's attorney, was in fact a sham. I could not think of anything that would make me happier than to return the account of a deranged street hustler to the lunatic himself. And I wanted to meet him.

I was concerned about my personal safety. I knew after reading "How to Kill Your Lover" that I was not dealing with a hotbed of sanity. Frankly, I had to remember that I was dealing with an individual who, through his own admission and by video validation, might be capable of murder. And, he was no longer a young man.

Mason/Andy had never specifically stated his birthday in his accounts but he did reveal that he was a "22-year-old street hustler." If my math served me correctly, the kid that wrote his story would now be a grown man of 40. With his drug use and in my opinion, obvious alcoholism, I realized that there was a very strong probability that I had extended an invitation and opportunity for a sociopath to return to the scene of the crime.

I had taken several precautions. Again thanks to Google, I had established the identification of Mason/Andy's Attorney in Nashville, Tennessee. I printed copies of Mason's emails along with a copy of the cover page of Cornell Kastelka's web site and placed it in an envelope in our personal home safe next to documents that I was certain would have to be retrieved in the event of my demise. In addition, I purchased a stun gun and familiarized myself with the device. And I had the lobby surveillance from which I would at least be able to take a look at the individual before he came up. If he did show up, I would be able to notify him through the speaker that he was being filmed (and to please smile for the camera).

As for the matter of him actually ringing at my door, I was well aware that I had dealt myself a big "if" card. But it was a card that I believed held a chance to be designated a wild card. I reminded myself that he had originally contacted me on Halloween. Was he still trick or treating? Coincidence? I could not say.

But like the 22-year-old street hustler from 1992, I was curious, and my curiosity had gotten the better of me. And I felt morally vindicated. I had asked myself, "What if Anne Frank had been a devious and deranged slut and attempted to murder someone in her hiding place? In that fictional case, it allowed her to survive the holocaust. Would it not be morally correct for any person or person's that found the diary to ignore the contents and return the writings to their author?"

My answer and justification for my actions were that despite the written declaration by the author himself that he "was no Anne Frank," I'd have to say that with the AIDS crisis in those years, he had been exposed to a holocaust of sorts. The late 80s and early 90s were killing fields for the gay community.

I hope no one finds offense to these comparisons. Mason/Andy did speak of the author of the greatest selling story, next to the bible, of all time. Perhaps Anne Frank, and Faulkner, whom he also mentioned, were in some respect heroes for the young man of 1992. Clearly, Mason/Andy was no Faulkner either. Again, I express my desire that no one finds offense in that analogy.

It was no Anne Frank or Faulkner that buzzed my apartment door two days before Thanksgiving this year. I had completed my holiday dinner shopping and had a hen boiling with celery, bay leaf and parsley. It was essential in the stock that my Southern Mother-in-Law had taught me for her son and my husband's expectation of cornbread dressing. And I am no cook, but I can follow a recipe. The kitchen work also allowed me the benefit of an apron with a large pocket that was ideal to conceal a stun gun. I turned the stove down to simmer and went to answer the call.

As I stared into the television screen, I observed the security camera's profile of a tall but pudgy man in jeans and cowboy boots. The security system was in black and white but I could clearly make out the mug of a clean-shaven face with eyes downcast to the ground. The posture clearly made recognizable the beginnings of a double chin. His tee shirt also exposed an upper body that lacked any signs of at one time being attractive. There was an evident paunch in his abdominal area. His hair was cropped short, almost to the style of a flat top. With one hand partially concealed and rested in his front pants pocket, and the other holding the phone to his ear, he had crossed one boot over the other.

He appeared off balance as he twisted around to look back at a Mercedes that had dropped off a resident of the building. When the passenger opened the door, I recognized the young Latina neighbor that sashayed by Mason/Andy in her stiletto's. I picked up the receiver of my intercom phone and was immediately blasted by the loud salsa of the Mercedes whose driver was dutifully watching to make sure the young woman was safely in the building. Either that or he was admiring the shape of the girl. Perhaps the presence of Mason/Andy, standing there twisted in his cowboy boots and eyes downcast, concerned the driver. Mason/Andy did look like a fish out of water.

"Hello, and please look up and smile for the camera. How may I help you?" I notified the caller.

A slight smile did emerge on the face of the man as he looked up and through the black and white lens of our security system, I was able to look into the eyes and see the remnants of my author. There was no evident sign of malice in this man's face.

The neighbor woman entered the building and closed the door behind her, then signaled the Mercedes to depart. I was left with a clear and easy-going drawl to answer my greeting.

"Yes ma'am, I'm Mason Caldwell, responding to your invitation."

I buzzed the door to open and said, "You know the way."

I had to buzz him twice as he failed to catch the door on the first try, and he missed the elevator as the doors closed to allow my neighbor to come up. Mason would have to wait. I observed him from the lobby camera and he looked nervous as he fidgeted for the nearly two minutes it took for the elevator to return. I watched him enter the car and saw the doors close. I took a deep breath and, in anticipation, went to the door of our unit and waited. I heard the heavy walk of his boots as he approached. I unbolted the security locked and opened the door.

There he stood, in living color. He was a significant foot and a half taller than I was. He extended his hand and politely asked, "Mrs. Choudrant?"

"Please, Mariah," I corrected him, then asked as courteously as I could, and in a way that I hoped would hide my fear and anxiety, "Won't you come in?"

"Thank you so much," he graciously answered, in a tone that insinuated much more gratitude than would be given to the standard manners of asking a person into one's home.

I smiled back to say you're welcome, and as I moved aside, he entered the apartment. I was instantly put at ease. He took three or four full steps into the unit and stopped and looked around for about half a minute. I did not interrupt the moment. I watched him cusp his hands to the back of his head. Eventually I closed the door and the sound of the door closing must have startled the man. He giggled and turned around. His eyes watered.

"Excuse me, but that was the last sound I heard when I left this place. Do all doors sound different when they close?" he asked.

"I don't know," I replied. "I have the manuscript on the coffee table."

He turned around.

"Wow, a totally different place than Rick had used for his living room table," he said as he walked in the direction of the table and the manuscript. "I like it," he said. "This arrangement gives a better view of the sunsets. But I don't think I ever placed a coffee mug on Rick's table."

I felt a twinge of uneasiness. Mason/Andy was making himself a little too comfortable and familiar, much more hastily than my taste could afford. He looked around the room a little longer. Perhaps he was expect-ing law enforcement to pop out at any second. I don't know. Then he shook his head and laughed. "The scotch and roach table," he said.

"No, I'm sorry. The table that you see your text on, nor any furniture in this apartment, was here at the time of our purchase. That's not the same table. We bought the place unfurnished. "

"No, I meant your expression of the table here as a 'coffee table.' I found it ironic."

Mason bent over and picked the manuscript's envelope up and said, "Again, I can't thank you enough. If you ever feel the need to contact me, my attorney asked me to leave you his card."

He placed the attorney's business card where the overly stuffed legal envelope had previously sat. Almost as if it were a trade.

"Best to ya, Mrs. Choudrant," he said with a slight bow.

When he made a couple of steps to the door, I have to admit that my feelings of anxiety were heightened, but for different reasons. Now I was certain that he meant me no harm, but could I simply allow him to leave without some sort of dialogue? I felt as if I knew him. Quickly, panic replaced trepidation and I reacted like most people in panic; I panicked. I wanted to speak with him. "Oh my gosh," I shouted, "Where are my manners? Can I get you a scotch? I don't have Johnny Walker but—"

He held up a hand and said, "Please, thank you but I don't drink scotch, or any alcohol, for that matter today."

I heard the spew of the broth as it ran onto the stove's burner and I said, "I'm sorry, excuse me for one moment"

I walked quickly into the kitchen and took the top off of the stew pot that I had the chicken in. I already had the burner on simmer, but appar-ently too much heat had caused the overflow. Whatever, I cleaned up the slight mess and left the top off the kettle and returned to my guest.

He was still standing up and said, "Smells good, Mrs. Choudrant."

"Mariah, please," I corrected him for the second time.

He chuckled and apologized, "I'm sorry but old habits taught in younger days, die hard. If I say 'yes ma'am,' I hope you won't think I'm being a smart ass."

"That would depend on what you said 'yes ma'am' to, young man," I teased him.

By my calculations, I was only five years his senior. He must have recognized that we were close in age as he chuckled with downcast eyes and shuffled in an awkward awareness of the ludicrous idea of applying his childhood instructions on etiquette to me.

He changed the subject, "Smells good Mariah. Is that bay leaf and celery together I smell?" he asked?

"You have a good nose ... Andy? Mason?"

"Mason," he quickly answered and added seriously, "I haven't gone by Andy for quite some time." Then he quickly put on his smile again and said, "With a name like Choudrant, and bay leaf in a stock, my guess is you're married to a coon ass."

"I beg your pardon," I responded. I was not sure if he had insulted my husband.

Mason quickly explained, "You know, you read my story. Hell, you knew I drank Black. My apologies again, Mariah, but I meant no disrespect. Technically, I'm a coon ass. My mother was from Louisiana French. It's just a name we josh each other with, and call anybody with a Louisiana French background. It's edgy," he conceded

"Oh I see," I said as I searched my memory for any recollection of the slang, "coon ass" and what it implied in "How to Kill Your Lover."

I still wasn't certain that I approved of the term, but I moved on and said, "I'm making a stock for a cornbread dressing recipe given to me by my Mother-in-Law. Actually, they are from Alabama." I further explained.

"One of my favorites," he said with enthusiasm.

"Would you like some coffee?" I quickly asked, as I wasn't certain whether Mason was prodding for an invitation to dine, which, at that time, I was by no means willing to extend. But I was happy with his response to my offer.

"Yes please," he quickly accepted.

"Give me a moment, I'll make you some," I said as I went to the kitchen.

"Don't go to all that trouble," he said obviously thinking that I would have to make a fresh pot of Joe from scratch.

"It's no problem at all," I assured him. "I have a Keurig."

I was happy that I was serving him a cup of coffee rather than the scotch I had just offered, which looking back, was a rather stupid offer since I knew from the manuscript that he had a serious drinking problem. But I was sure that I had nothing to fear from this man. I took the apron off and along with the stun gun still hidden in the front pocket, hung it on the special brass hook specifically allocated by my husband when we remodeled the kitchen.

"A what?" he asked as I walked into the kitchen.

Since the remodeling, there was a clear view from the living room to the kitchen counters so when I reached the counter, I patted the coffee maker and replied, "A Keurig. It'll only take a second. Please sit down. Cream? Sugar?"

"No, thank you. Black, like my scotch," he inserted.

"Good one."

He certainly was not shy.

"I love the openness of the room now," he said with increased volume.

"It took a little work," I said as I closed the top of the Keurig onto the coffee pack and pressed the start button.

I turned around to face him and pointed to the open space.

"And here is where your little darlings introduced themselves to me."

From his seat on the sofa, he had turned his head so that he spoke in my direction and he slowly nodded his head in confirmation that he understood. There was about twenty seconds of silence in which time I took the coffee from under the Keurig and brought it and placed it on the coffee table next to the original legal envelope that held his manuscript. Mason reached over and placed his hand on the envelope before he took the coffee and sipped it.

"Thank you," he said again in a tone with much more inference of importance than one would generally have for a cup of coffee.

"You are more than welcome, Mason," I said as I again acknowledged his gratitude.

"So you are the only person to read it?" he asked after another quick sip of his coffee.

"Yes," I answered and then explained, "my husband knows some of the details but he has never set eyes on the text."

"That's good," he said with a heavy sigh and looked me square in the eyes. "Mariah, that was a different time, and I was of a totally different mind. I swear, I can't for the life of me, even today, identify what I was so angry about. I don't know why I didn't just burn the thing, but I was afraid of the attention a fire would have made. And I couldn't bring myself to tear up the pages. I couldn't let go of those stories. So I sealed them up in that envelope, not sure of anything or anybody at that time. I guess I had hoped someone, sometime in the future would find the sealed envelope. They'd cut the thread and take it out and read. Then perhaps they'd know the pain I had inflicted on myself and others."

He chuckled in regret and was about to say something else when I interrupted him, "Sealed. You said that you sealed the envelope. Mason the envelope wasn't sealed It was open,l ike an invitation that asked me to help myself."

"Hell, I'm sure the glue would have broken up on the envelope. By that time, I had stuffed the legal envelope to the max. But I had that red thread tied and fastened like I had seen my father do when closing home files for storage a hundred times. That I remember distinctly," he said.

"Then I'm not the only one that read your story, Mason," I said in an astonished and hushed tone.

"I'm sorry, I don't follow you." He looked concerned.

"Mason, there was nothing tied. Look for yourself. The thread was cut. I didn't cut it."

I watched him take another deep breath and set his coffee cup down next to the legal envelope. The twine was still in place from clip to clip and had obviously been cut. He sat back and ran his fingers over his face and head. When he removed his hands, tears flowed.

"Oh my God," he whispered. Mason stared through time and space, his gaze focused through the sliding glass balcony door and said incredulously, "He read it, Mariah. He fucking read it and still left me his money." Mason turned to me and said aloud, "Jesus Christ."

I looked into Mason's eyes. Bloodshot, the hazel green seemed wild, never to be tamed, but the tears that slowly streamed down his face were real. Perhaps he knew. Perhaps I didn't need to tell him. But I did, "Mason, he left you much more than money. Forgiveness is priceless, beyond description."

"Jesus Christ," He repeated in wonder, as if he had just witnessed an epiphany.

He leaned over with his elbows on his knees and momentarily covered his face with his hands. Then he sat back up and with his fist, he began to dry his eyes. Then he rubbed snot from his nose with his forearm. He looked like a little boy. I had read firsthand descriptions of his jags in his manuscript, and Mason had been dead on. I decided to lighten the mood. I stood and as I turned to walk towards the kitchen, I said, "Hold on there, Sally. Let me get you a tissue."

I heard him laugh aloud and I could tell from the sound of the laugh that I had better hurry back with tissue. And there was none in the kitchen so I grabbed a couple of sheets from the paper towel roll. I made it back just in time. He had covered his snotty face with one hand and reached out to grab the extended paper towels with the other. His voice mimicked a kid with a cold as he held back more laughter.

"Thank you," he said.

Mason blew his nose and turned his head away from me to clean his face. I started laughing. He started laughing. I believe we had driven each other hysterical, and after a good thirty seconds or so, we came down. I had to go to the kitchen and get a paper towel for myself, then thought better. I took the whole roll from the peg, tore off one sheet for myself and as I placed the remainder of the roll on the coffee table, I cleaned some tears of laughter from my own face.

"Mason, did you ever see or speak to Madame Dieux Dieux again?"

Instantly, he recovered his senses. He got very serious.

"No, I'm sorry to say. And to be honest, I took the train from Atlanta here several days ago so that I could get here early. I had hoped to hook up with her. But she wasn't there. Christ that beach front has changed."

He paused for a moment as if to reflect back to another time and another place. Then he snapped back and continued, "Last Saturday, I went to the Bonner House and I asked to speak with management. I was obliged. There was this cat about my age that came out of his office in a bit of a tizzy. Hell, I guess I had interrupted something really important. So I quickly asked him if he knew the whereabouts of Madame Dieux Dieux. He said that he'd never heard of her, and attempted to turn back to his office but I took his shoulder and said, "she used to sell island art on A1A. She was grandfathered in by old man Bonner.

"The little shit took my hand abruptly from his shoulder and I said he was sorry. The guy said that he'd been there for ten years and had heard of no such nonsense."

"I'm so sorry to hear that," I said in attempt to console him.

Mason replied, "No need, but thank you. I swear you're not gonna believe what happened next."

"Please tell me you didn't get escorted off the property," I said, imagining that he had perhaps done more than put a hand on the shoulder of the foundations manager.

"Nothing of the sort," he said with a chuckle. "Better, much better. So you know, there it was, Saturday, with no place for me to go but to the beach or back to my hotel room so I decided to take a tour of the house. I'd never done it when I lived here, so I thought what the hell. This older lady around in her late sixties, maybe early seventies led the tour and as I and three other people followed her up the stairs to the second floor, I let out a scream. And not so manly either, I imagine. I mean I was in utter shock."

He paused to laugh and apparently amused himself as he thought back to the scream from Saturday past.

"She was upstairs?" I inquired in disbelief.

Mason shook his head and held up a hand and took a deep breath to continue.

"No, that painting, the one that she had given me the first day I met her. The cloud cat that looked down on the little mice foraging for cheese on the volcanic mountain. It was right there on the wall to my right, still in the frame that Rick had placed it in. The old lady that was leading our group stopped trudging up the stairs and was somewhat irritated with me. She asked me if I was alright and I just pointed toward the painting."

"You've got to be making this up, Mason," I told him and I wasn't far from being sincere.

"I couldn't if I tried," he said. "I gotta tell ya Mariah, I was in just as much disbelief as you as I read the brass plate under the painting that was titled, 'Temptation' by Madame Madeline Le Fleur. Humph" he let out then Mason shook his head and continued, "Explains why that manager was being such an asshole, I was telling him Madame Dieux Dieux."

I was in tears as he told me this and reached for the paper towel roll. As I tore another sheet from the roll and wiped my eyes, I involuntarily and probably inappropriately declared aloud, "This is unreal."

In a very serious tone that verged on anger but only just so, Mason corrected me. "It's very real Mariah."

"I'm sorry Mason, I know. It's just ..." I stuttered, unable to find words.

"No need," he said. "That old lady looked down and quickly said, 'Oh that. Yes garish to say the least, but Mr. Bonner was an avid supporter of Caribbean art. This piece was donated after the death of Mr. Bonner by one of his favorite artists just before her own death.'"

"I gotta say, Mariah, I was floored. I know I love drama but I had to take hold of the stair rail to support myself. I think it hit me harder than the news of Rick's death."

Mason paused a bit and continued, "I asked the tour guide if she knew about when the artist had passed and she thought for a second, then said that Madame Le Fleur had passed about sometime in 1997."

"Rick must have brought her the painting," I concluded aloud.

"That's the only thing I can make of it," Mason concurred.

And his voice took on the tone of summation, as if he were adding, "Mariah, he must have found the text before 1997 and read the damned thing. He knew everything. He had so much ammo to come at me with. And yet he didn't mention anything about me in his will, other than leaving me everything he owned, which he declared was to be liquidated. And I am as well the sole benefactor of his life insurance policy."

"If I could be so bold," I prefaced, "would you think me terribly rude if I asked what he died from."

"No, of course not," Mason replied. "According to my attorney, Rick died of pancreatic cancer. And apparently, from conversations between old man Kastelka and Rick's attorney, Rick had wished that he be cremated and with no ceremony, his ashes scattered in the Atlantic."

Mason paused for a second then, "I mean I knew if he lived, Rick would probably remember what I said to him as he dangled hundreds of feet in the air by a thread of metal. My attorney says he never pressed any charges of any kind, and that all of the warrants issued for my arrest were the handiwork of Alf Baylor."

Mason made a mock spit that was so convincing that I looked on my rug and was relieved not to see any vile excrement.

"My apologies again, Mariah. I guess I need to let go of my feelings for cops," he said, then laughed, "I'm sure you would be in a shitload of trouble if they found out I was on this property. And I'm still not certain about the civil liabilities that I would face if they found me. I'm so glad you didn't surprise me with a cop coming out of the bedroom to take me to jail."

I was again moved by the sincerity of his gratitude and really at a loss for what to say. I was more moved by the actions of his deceased lover, Rick Gurnee.

"You know, Mason, letting go of our past tapes that run in our heads is about the best thing we can do. Forgiving is a powerful trait. I think we both find that evident from the actions of Rick Gurnee."

He didn't respond. As he wrote in his text, "Silence can say so much," but I wanted to know so I asked him, "Do you still love Rick Gurnee?"

"Absolutely, without any reservation whatsoever. I wish he were here."

Mason's eyes watered, but I was relieved he didn't enter into a fully-fledged jag.

"I would love nothing more than to have known when he was still alive that he didn't hate me or wish me harm. Mariah, I can't tell you how many times I came close to coming down here just to knock on his door. I don't know what I would have said, other than I love you."

"Mason, you just did," I whispered to him. "And it's evident he loves you."

"You know," he said with a sniffle, "My attorney back home—"

"Nashville?" I asked.

"Close," Mason said vaguely. He continued, "My attorney definitely advised me that this could all be a trap. He told me that through private conversations with Rick's attorney that, at the time of Rick's convalescence from the bang on his head, Rick's family had come down from New Jersey, and that's when they found out he had AIDS. My attorney tells me that his Mom and Dad left the hospital immediately, with Rick still in critical condition. My lawyer was certain from the way that Rick's will was drawn up that everything about it was more or less a way to kill two birds with one stone in his attempts for justice beyond the grave. He could slight his parents and trap me." Now Mason did go into a genuine fit and all but hollered, "God I wish I had had the courage to come down here. To have been here for him in his last days. Just to have known."

Mariah whispered to herself, "Incredible."

I got up and sat closer to him and placed my hand on his thigh as he cried like a baby. Mason responded by reaching over and placing his mouth on the nape of my neck. He was incorrigible. After a couple of minutes he calmed down and I gently pushed him away and gave him another paper towel.

"I'd like to make you a proposition," I said as he blew his nose and wiped his eyes. "That is, if you don't have to get back to 'Close' anytime soon. How'd you like to spend Thanksgiving with us and stay in your old guest room?"

He began to slip into another jag and I said, "Okay now Sally, don't make me backhand you." He laughed and I verified my genuine wish for him to stay with us. "Really, I would be very happy if you would accept."

He nodded his head in an affirmative, yes. I can only guess that he knew my elation to this as his eyes sparkled in happiness.

"You know," I said with a cautious pause, "I may have just recently established ulterior motives for this invitation."

Mason's posture of elation quickly faded, as doubt spread over his face like a black silk veil. So as not to be cruel, I quickly explained, "I don't have a typewriter. I don't think anybody does anymore. But I do have a laptop that I've brought so that I can work from home."

"Okay?" he questioned me.

"Mason, I'm an editor for a company in New York that holds several key magazines. Not that they would be interested in your story, but there's a chance somebody might bite on it, and to tell you the truth, it's just not that difficult to get published anymore. I'd love to hear about Miss Love. Whatever happened to her?"

Color quickly returned to his face, but he didn't have to say a word. I could tell he was back in his "Realm." He was off somewhere far away. And I let a few seconds pass before I tried to regain his attention.

"Earth to Mason, come in Mason," I teased.

"Oh Jesus, Mariah, I'd love to get Miss Love back," he said with hope and soft desire.

A puzzled veil enveloped his facial features, and Mason appeared like a little boy who attempted to comprehend mathematical pi. "I don't feel 'without.' I mean, I feel so much more. Honestly, I'm pretty sure Miss Love never went away. She was so right. You can't kill love. It never dies. She never dies. And I was just thinking about some of things Madame Dieux Dieux said."

"You know you got so much more from Selectric than the title of your manuscript suggests. You found so much more than the simple suggestion of 'How to Kill Your Lover,'" I said.

"Jesus, you are so right, Mariah." He supposed reverently. "'How To Kill Your Lover' was off the top of my head, and what I had on my mind in the throes of my rage. The lack of clarity or better yet, the insanity, which I referred to in the beginning of the story began to fade and the truth slowly revealed itself."

"And that is?" I asked.

Mason chuckled, "The million dollar question. The trillion dollar question!" he exclaimed. Instantly he calmed back down and thought hard through squinted eyes. "You know what the truth, as far as it relates to the title, was?" he paused momentarily to bite his thumbnail, then took his thumb from his mouth and said, "I really think I was killing Miss Love. You know, in a way, an attempt at self-annihilation."

"Perhaps" I said.

"What do you think we should call the story?" he asked.

"If you're up to it, I'd like to spend the holidays here with you, going over the text. It needs a lot work, but as for the title, that depends on you, on how you write the last chapter. What happens to Miss Love?" I asked again.

"Jesus Christ," he said, then stood up, "Mariah, can I use your john? I don't know whether it's the excitement or the coffee or what, but I gotta pee."

"Sure, of course. And by all means, check out 'the tomb.' See if it meets your approval."

He excused himself and after a couple of minutes, he walked back into the living area and stood by the glass balcony door. He was so tall. His smile held a grin that was beautiful. Surely a bladder release was not the reason for this transformation?

"Dark blue. Now that's the color a bathroom should be." he said with authority.

And I told him so. "You talk like you're an authority on decorating. I thought you didn't like authority?"

"As long as it's my own, I'm good. And I'm an authority on my own taste. And a bloody bathroom should be serene. Not a ..." He was at loss for words, then found them, "an electric-shock torture chamber."

I giggled, but his description brought to mind the reality and gravity that might await Mason and possibly myself if we were not cautious with Selectric's Darlings.

"As much as I dislike the thought of it, we had better find ourselves a good Florida criminal defense attorney, or we both could find ourselves in trouble with the wrong kind of authorities. We need good consultation or we just might find ourselves in a chamber without any tasteful accommodations. What do you say?" I asked.

As I earlier said, the boy definitely was not shy. And I say "boy," although the man was in his forties. But from the transformation that I had recently witnessed, Mason appeared younger, as if his energy flow had clamped onto youthful days rather than aimed towards his fifties.

He held no reservations, and he exclaimed in a resounding boom, "Let's do it."

LAST CHAPTER

November 2010

The Committee

SHE WAS FLOATING; SUSPENDED IN A FETAL POSITION AS IF SHE were in the womb. But Miss Love could feel no umbilical cord.

"Come to think of it," she said to herself in a language that she did not recognize, "I don't feel much of anything. However, it's the first time I've felt anything at all in I don't know when."

And she could hear. The beautiful and trouble-free strum of Georges DeLauro's "Farewell for Now" pervaded her mind with the simple genius of the French composer. Miss Love relished the new sense of awareness that now flowed through her in unfamiliar terms. She had no doubt who she was. She was Miss Love and she loved herself, as well as all others. She could not fathom any sense of negative aspirations, nor could she comprehend their purpose.

She snuggled in the warm and pliant ooze that provided one of the few physical sensations that she could understand. Even though her sense of sight was nil, the darkness did not frighten her. She was in a state of mind that comprehended serenity and Miss Love relaxed exponentially in the manner of many an American, their work week over, gently arising from the unrestrained schedule of sleep afforded by the Goddess, Saturday Morning. All was good. Good was all there was. There was no anxiety when her mind proposed a question, "What is my purpose?"

In fact, Miss Love exalted in pure joy as she nearly answered her own question simply by with the emotional response that she felt towards the inquiry. She acknowledged a slight electric vibration that ran through her being, from top to bottom, wherever and whatever that was. She was giddy, and she was curious.

Energy abounded in the old girl. She had never felt so vibrant. Miss love performed for her own enjoyment a somersault in the confines of the soothing ooze. She proceeded to clap her hands in delight and self-applause but she stumbled, not upon a problem, but more like a child's riddle.

"How can I clap my hands if I don't have any hands?"

She wasn't afraid. Her mind wouldn't allow her to make an attempt to comprehend, much less acknowledge and react to the concept of fear. But her memory did return and in a split second. Miss Love remembered the ordeal that she had endured in the halls of His/Her Honor Fear's court. Still, the pleasant electric current tingled through her to remind her that those things were no more. Miss Love simply observed the thought and no sooner than she had, it dissipated like a low morning cloud that has met the noon sun.

Her recollection of the fight she had waged and lost for the good of Mason Harrison Caldwell III did, however, bring back old questions. But now, she encompassed them with clarity, quick wit, and the delight of a language that she found so very appropriate.

"Where am I? When am I? Who am I?"

And the answer again from the self-proclaimed "I" was identical in every respect to the previous response that had enveloped her conscious mind as she lay open to the elements and the pain she had experienced in the courtroom crater; with one exception. The answer, as well as the questions she had asked, were in the language of France.

"In a crater, in the moment. You are Miss Love."

For the first time since her awakened state in the mind of Mason Harrison Caldwell III, Miss Love realized that she now thought and spoke in French.

"Aha, now I recognize the soft yet deliberate intention in melodic cadence. And the language of the Bayou!" she joyfully exclaimed.

"But can a language change the nature of the experience?" she thought to herself as she recalled the unpleasant affairs she had recently observed. She couldn't really "see" anything. She, more or less, observed the past and future for what they actually were in the present moment, which in turn, her newfound state of mind accepted with no fear.

And again, the self-proclaimed "I" answered, "Yes Miss Love, it can be a start in the change of perception."

Miss Love giggled to herself as she marveled in her instant ability to comprehend the words spoken as an endless and beautiful vocabulary with a cadence of limitless possibilities. Although it resonated in French, it was a language so much more than prose founded upon Latinate rationale. In fact, she recognized that her new vocabulary

was produced from the heart and was thus as endless as her imagination. That meant she could thrive and form any reality she chose.

"Where have I gone?" asked Miss Love.

"Nowhere," the self-proclaimed "I" responded in French.

"Please, excuse me but I feel we are about to engage in an endless summersault," she explained with childlike glee to herself.

"Go ahead." said the "I" in Parisian enthusiasm, "Twirl Miss Love!
Twirl!"

As she twirled one somersault over another in the blissful ooze,
she contemplated the sheer joy she felt in her buoyancy and her freedom to do as she chose for as long as she chose. Was it a minute or
a thousand years that she raced with joy within herself? She couldn't
know. It was in this moment of bliss that Miss Love contemplated how
wonderful it would be to share this state with another. In fact, she
contemplated the possibility of an international "Woodstock" where
she could take the stage and extend herself freely to all of those who
chose to attend.

"Then you must break out from within yourself," spoke the self-
proclaimed "I."

"How do I do that?" she asked "I" as if she had drunk twenty bottles of Bordeaux and didn't recognize herself staring into a wall mirror.

"You have to answer that question yourself," answered "I" in precarious French caution.

"Okay," she said then quickly added, "Let's think about it while we
twirl some more!"

"But of course, Miss Love, But of course!" the "I" gaily concurred
in the tone of a haughty sidewalk cafe waiter, who had just been congratulated as the instrument of, "the greatest dining experience in my
life" and been asked by the enraptured diner to speak to the Chef.

She twirled in joy with the possibilities that now abounded; she
concluded that she had always had the knowledge and ability to
break out of herself. And so she did.

The emerald blue casing that had protected the once debilitated
heroine from the nightmarish debris of His/Her Honor's court cracked
and within a moment, Miss Love found herself spilling out of the protective sapphire as she gently flopped in a completely new environment on the moss green and muddy bank of harbor blue water. And
she recognized immediately that she was able to see, that she had
eyes. She could feel as well, for she noticed the drips of violet sweet

water that plopped on her face from a lotus flower that bloomed in full glory just over her head. She released her tongue and found the moisture exquisite; she held not the slightest concern that there was any possibility that the invigorating water might be another mirage of the foul and exploitive urine that had previously profiteered from her dehydrated imprisonment.

"Another paradox?" she giggled in French astonishment. "How can it be that I observe and think of possibilities, yet completely ignore the unpleasant possible?"

"We are in a pure land, Miss Love," the self-proclaimed "I" explained, "Yes! Yes! Miss Love, only virtuous possibilities exist here."

"Am I in heaven?" she incredulously and sincerely wondered aloud, still in her new found language.

The self-proclaimed I answered in the same language, and just as incredulously said, "I don't know. Look around, Miss Love! Look! And tell me, what do you see?"

What she encompassed was more spectacular than any language could convey in any form whatsoever. She reasoned that the beauty that she now beheld could possibly be captured on canvas, but as Miss Love contemplated painting the image, and the beautiful reality that her eyes engaged, she was confronted again with the fact that she had no hands.

"What do you see Miss Love?" the self-proclaimed I whispered.

She wiggled a little closer to the water's edge. And the dark blue water provided a sheen, similar to shined metal of medieval mirrors, which allowed Miss Love to view herself as she smiled face to face at herself in a literal alligator smile.

The first thing she noticed were the huge teeth that more than accented her smile.

"What?" she said aloud as her grin widened and revealed more gleaming white teeth that were accented by the chameleon pulse of color from various blues to purples and maroons that traveled through her reptilian scales.

She could see the astonished elation in her emerald green eyes that sparkled wildly back at her from the blue water's reflection. And she asked herself in a curious tone, "What in the world? I'm an alligator? I mean, I like it. To be honest, I love it but I'm Miss Love. What do I need teeth like that for?"

"A girl's gotta eat," replied the self-proclaimed "I."

"I don't recall having to eat before," Miss Love thought to herself.

"Have you ever been an alligator?" quizzed "I"

"No, I don't think so," answered Miss Love.

"Then perhaps it's best we just accept the situation offered by the moment that's been perceived by Mason and roll with the flow. Don't you agree?" advised the self-proclaimed "I."

She didn't answer, but practiced his suggestion. Miss Love watched herself in the mirror provided by the adjacent dark blue water and became aware that although she was a hatchling, she was growing bigger by the moment, as if by magic, and was able to perceive more and more of her present environment with adolescent to teenage alligator eyes. And what she beheld of the "pure land" that was presented to her through the mind and essence of Mason Harrison Caldwell III was exquisite.

The Bayou was a symphony of colors, like her pulsing scaly hide, dominated by the blue families of the color wheel as they extend from blue to greens and blue to purples, but highlighted by a touch of the red or yellow family here and there. The giant "Bald" Cypress trees that dominated the shallow blue waters provided a silhouette against the bright but soft purple horizon. The Spanish moss that hung from the deep plum purple branches of the ancient conifers sparkled like silver metallic twine as the vivid, but pleasant golden light, from a silver-gold sun, ran through the deep green needled foliage of the great trees. This brought the warmth of the sun, and fresh and unmistakable scents of the evergreen comingled with earthy and fish spawned accents, to the indulged and growing sensory delight of Miss Love.

Here and there, a rich and dotting green of duck weed broke the smooth sheen of harbor blue water. And a patch of water lilies, lavender-white to plumb-red, themselves under a loving attack by honey bees, of the most vivid maroon and gold stripes, encroached like an army for hundreds of yards upon the open channel of the bayou as giant Oak and Magnolia trees, themselves streaming with life of every imaginable bird, squirrel, and possum, temperately battled in vain from the flat banks to thwart the sun rays from bouncing off the watery paradise. Fish abound and frogs of all sizes and every imaginable psychedelic color pattern, croaked or chattered on the moss-green and muddy banks.

As she herself grew in stature to a mature cow, as female gators are prone to be called, Miss Love contemplated the majesty and miracle she witnessed. Her chameleon scales flowed from blue to purple as our girl soaked in the warmth of the sun that felt like compassion upon the back of the intensely satisfied gator. And her stomach, if it could have, clutched for the union with the cool soft mud that indulged her lower body with a comfort and a perch from which she could take in the ultimate beauty and grace afforded to her sensory delight by the creatures of the blue bayou and soft purple sky.

And as she enjoyed the cacophony of music from the cicadas and frogs, she couldn't help but observe a great osprey providing percussion to the symphony with a splash as the mother bird extended its sharp talons into the emerald blue water and arose into the sky with the flopping and obvious objections of a sparkling silver shad.

As her curiosity took hold, Miss Love wondered to herself that if a shad could scream, what would it sound like? She spoke aloud to herself, "And if this is a land with no pain, why in the world would the shad scream; if it could scream?"

As the thought perplexed her mind, Miss Love also perceived a low and guttural laugh from what she judged, by her new and heightened reptilian electric impulse, must have come from the water about six or seven yards away.

"Hu hu huuuu ..." chuckled the huge but skinny coal black gator, "Ma Cherie Amour, it best that you accept the fact that you go hand and hand with pain. Who said there no pain?" the cheerful black gator grunted in Creole French.

Miss Love, still with no conception of fear or malice peered in the direction to see a mischievous, yet benevolent and toothy smile on the jet black head that floated just on the top of the dark blue water. Green duck weed peppered the top of the huge gator's head, which helped to accentuate the size of the gator and his total disregard for his unkempt appearance.

And the newly apparent company spoke to her in Creole French, "Ma Cherie Amour, I tell you now. Dat shad would scream, if it could, like you gone scream when I give you some good loving. Huh Hu Huuuuu," laughed the big boned yet skinny black gator.

"Come again?" Miss Love responded in perfect Parisian dialect.

"Oh yes, my beautiful violet cow. Dis Black bull here gone bring you to new heights of rapture and joy dat only an air bound shad, to nourish the tummy's of ole Miss Osprey's Children, could possibly comprehend."

"You mean to tell me the shad is going to enjoy being eaten?" Miss Love fearlessly questioned the black male gator.

"Come get in de water wid me, Miss Love, and I show you better den I can tell you."

"You're going to eat me?" Miss Love questioned, a grin still on her own face at the notion.

"Better den dat. Hu HU Huuuuuu," answered the midnight bull, as a male alligator is prone to be typically called.

Miss Love, not from fear, but by the motivation of simple wisdom did not respond to the big gator's flirtatious request to enter the water. Her curiosity tingled through her so intensely, as her green eyes met the crazed green gaze of the big skinny bull that she felt as if she had been overserved a huge shot of tickle.

"Who are you?" Miss Love asked the serendipitous toothy smile, barely visible in the dark blue water.

Which, were it not for the glowing green eyes and duck weed that gave features to the smile's coal black encasing, would have been invisible.

"Come now Miss Love. Don't you recognize me? At least my voice? Or better yet my dialect of Creole French. Only a few years back did I attempt to get you to Paris with our boy Rick."

"Madame Dieux Dieux?" Miss Love squealed in delight as if the prospect of meeting the old Haitian was a million to one.

The odds, in fact, were probably higher; probably more like a zillion to one. Miss Love, as far as her essence in the realm of Mason Harrison Caldwell III, had never met Madame Dieux Dieux face to face, but she was familiar with the old skinny woman who now corrected her in bass Creole French from the gut of a bony, black bull gator.

"No, no Mademoiselle Love. Monsieur Dieux Dieux at your service. Or to service you, Ma Cherie. Hu Hu HU Huuuu," grunted the jolly bull gator.

The scales on Miss Love's hide did their best to blush, for it was impossible for the old girl in her true state to fathom red. Her entire body turned a burgundy, plumb purple that was electric and in turn, silver sparks, like those coming off stone struck flint, radiated from the hide of Monsieur Dieux Dieux. There was definite chemistry between the two enraptured reptiles.

"Well I'll be a monkey's uncle. This is unreal," Tee-heed Miss Love.

"No no, Mademoiselle, you are a blushing young cow and dis is very real," replied the sparkling bull gator. "I see you Mademoiselle Love. What say you we make some babies? You become Madame Love-Dieux Dieux."

"So fast?" Miss Love replied from bayou's bank to the huge grinning head in the water.

"Hu Hu Huuuuu," grunted Monsieur Dieux Dieux. "Fast? Fast you say Mademoiselle! Only a moment ago, you were in dat blue egg. Now look at you." He requested in masculine vibrato as his nostrils flared to inhale a huge amount of air.

As Miss Love followed his instruction and gazed at the reflection off the water of her now adult self, Monsieur Dieux Dieux exhaled the air through his teeth with such a rush that a high pitched whistle was produced.

"Chile! You are fine!" exhaled the male gator with the last of the escaping air as he rolled a couple of times so that his entire body showed on the top of the surface to unabashedly reveal the ropy white tube that searchingly flopped freely, so that Miss Love got a good look at what qualified as his huge gator member.

After a couple of excited rolls, Monsieur Dieux Dieux returned to his position where only his toothy and whimsical smile were visible above the water line. His green eyes gazed upon the purple blush of Miss Love as the female gator involuntarily gyrated her crotch against the mud so as to scratch in vain at an itch that the old girl was unable to relieve, despite her best efforts. She was invariably aware of what she desired, but in her heat, Miss Love silently debated within herself whether she was being a slut or living up to her own notion of herself. Monsieur Dieux Dieux found the consternation on the female gator's face incredibly amusing and found himself laughing aloud as Miss Love, now in doubt of herself, witnessed from the sheen on the water her scales pulse and radiate in scarlet red. She stumbled for thoughts and words, but mind any that might wonder, there was no evidence whatsoever that His/Her Honor Fear was anywhere to be seen, heard, smelled, tasted, or felt as she witnessed herself and the color transformation as vividly as the reflection of the silver blue water would allow. And the peaceful music had stopped. A techno beat of some kind began to pound in her ears. What was happening?

"I! I! I, I, I. I don't see a preacher. I don't see a church. I! I! I don't know," she squealed in delight from the sensations she felt. "I! I!

I need you. Quick get me to a church." She added as she plunged through the dark green mud and into the harbor blue water in a fit of unknowing anticipation. She was not herself. Nor was the music offered to the realm from the mind of Mason Caldwell. The scales of the arrangement had already changed as the scales of Miss Love's hide had turned from purple to crimson and beyond. The transformation of serenity from Georges Delerue to bass thumping grind of Dead or Alive, "Bang Bang" was quite a leap in atmospheric pressure brought about by the modified music.

Whoever she was shot right past Monsieur Dieux Dieux who had to grab hold of himself after a couple of involuntary rolls of delight and guttural laughs that he could chase the cow in heat.

"Slow down, Ma Cherie Amour," he said as he swam next to the racing, red Miss Love.

"Slow down, hell you say!" retorted Miss Love as she swished her tail with all its might in an effort to get somewhere—but she didn't know where.

"Come now, Mademoiselle!" chuckled the big black gator as he swam effortlessly at her side and just as easily dodged cypress trees, stumps, and logs as he humorously implored his future mate, "I beg of you Ma Amour, please! You got to lose dis PBS puppet show view of yourself. Please just stop. Mademoiselle, you are in Bayou Love. A pure land from the mind and concoction of Mason Harrison Caldwell III. It strictly Love Bayou Code Napoleon here, chile. Now let me show you da rapture of dis place and how da shad would scream, if da shad could scream."

Monsieur Dieux Dieux did not wait for Miss Love to comply with his plea. Instead, he thrust out of the water up into the silver gold light to flop down on the racing red gator and tackle her, taking her down into the depths of the blue waters of Bayou Love. Miss Love was completely overwhelmed by the boney but physical superiority of the male gator. While she did not fight him, she did continue thrusting her herculean tail and consequently propelled the two entwined crocodilians into the plumb purple and speckled green silt that lined the bottom of the bayou like the feather pillow top of a honeymoon mattress. The once clear blue water was now murky and congested with debris from the disturbed bed of the bayou.

Miss Love found herself with her back cushioned by the silt and bottom ooze of Bayou Love, and her heart pounding against the chest of her pursuer whose great ivory claws extended from his black webbed feet deep into her still red hide. She couldn't have escaped if she wanted to. Despite the pain of his claws, she knew what she wanted and Monsieur Dieux Dieux had it, and was graciously and readily providing it. The water, racing with the cluttered silt, provided zero visibility for the two gators, but Monsieur needed no sight as his huge flimsy tube, similar in respect to a fleshy version of an Air Force mid-air refueling tanker's extended piping, as it searches for its target, through the soaring atmosphere, found the target offered so freely by Mademoiselle Love.

And like almost all penises, regardless of which species they originate in, this gator dick had a mind all its own. Monsieur Dieux Dieux let the extended ambassador of himself do his job. Ambassador Dieux Dieux was a marvel of reptilian evolution that had served the family crocodilian from prehistoric times to the present. The dick was like an alien from another solar system. It was basically a fleshy probe that resembled, to some degree, an octopus tentacle with its own little grabbers and feelers to walk and pull itself through the winding and fleshy path of a female vagina, until he found the prize that the tunnel vision mind of ambassador prick so reverently desired: the eggs.

And Miss Love didn't know that she wasn't going to pop out of her own head. As the single tentacle crept through her vagina and sucked to tickle then massage every itch or desire the old girl could possibly imagine, she let loose a scream that was so ferocious even the blue waters of Bayou Love could not muffle the exploding shriek that escaped, from the depths, to open air. Birds that were at peace on the branches of the cypress forest and oak lined banks took to flight, as if a warning siren had been administered by the R.A.F. to scramble for Kingdom's life. Fish, frog and snake all hopped, slid, or swam for cover. Bayou Love was in a frenzied state as Monsieur Dieux Dieux, according to marriage statutes of Bayou Love Code Napoleon, transformed Mademoiselle Love to Madame Love-Dieux Dieux.

Her scales had pulsed from scarlet to crimson, then Magenta to Rose as Miss Love's once maiden mind exploded into a new cosmos of awareness and satisfaction, which our old battle axe had never imagined could be sharpened and shined to such an exquisite gleam. She had never felt such pleasure. Her previous somersaults in her own embryonic ooze of the emerald blue cocoon paled exponentially to what she now experienced.

If they had been malevolent, the bubbles that encased the screams of satisfaction emitted by our writhing lady in red scales would have resembled the aftermath of depth charges released from a Navy Destroyer in an attempt of deadly and righteous vengeance toward a stealthy and subsurface metal-clad demon. But Miss Love produced the explosions from the depths of Bayou Love, a pure land, benevolent in its desire to impose only virtuous and joyful experiences upon the subjects of this realm. And so the explosions were heeded in wisdom by all creatures of the surface, just as townsfolk in the afternoon square of an old Europe village knew that the old fountains are not predictable, and thus back away when the initial bursts are displayed to the joy of passersby. The entire swamp, surface to bottom, was in flurry. It would have been a painter's delight to attempt to place the picture on canvas, when the blue fountains burst harmlessly into the air, filled with the flights and songs of birds and insects of a seemingly infinite description.

Eventually, after a moment in time that was immeasurable for the enraptured mates, Ambassador Dieux Dieux fertilized the embryos of Madame Love and concluded that his work was done and he tugged on a cord that told the body of Monsieur Dieux Dieux that he was ready to come home. The ambassador's job done, the dick released its suction and returned to base, to rearm at another moment's notice to perform his magic and do his job. As he returned home, the last of the surface fountains above exploded with a diminished shriek, like a tardy burst in a fireworks display. Monsieur Dieux Dieux released his claws from the hide of his betrothed, whose scales slowly changed from red to purples and finally back to her true color of blue. In sheer bliss, the two gators floated through the particle and silt strewn water that sparkled like a shaken Christmas globe, until they both emerged at the surface, with unshakeable and toothy smiles plastered and carved into their heads. They were happiness defined.

As far as their location in the swamp, neither of the two reptiles were cognizant. Slowly, and with steady intent, the ruckus of the creatures decreased and settled down as did the silver/gold sun in the velvet purple sky. Evening approached Bayou Love like the Islamic call to prayer, only softer, but still with the authority to witness and observe this holy moment. Nothing was more beautiful than the sunset in this pure land of happiness and virtuosity.

Monsieur and Madame Love-Dieux Dieux gradually found their bearings and cruised at a leisurely pace side by side atop the deep blue water that sparkled silver gold. For the most part, only their heads could be seen, except for the end of their gargantuan tails that would occasionally cut the water's surface. They strode as bull and cow, man and wife, mates for season, into the main channel of Bayou Love and set course for the setting sun. They swam leisurely with the ebbing tide, completely in the moment and aware in satisfaction that the moment was all there was or ever would be.

The symphony of Bayou Love tuned up for the orchestration of the same arrangement they did as every approaching evening's shade descended upon the blissful wetland.

"Beautiful! No?" commented Monsieur Dieux Dieux.

No sooner had Madame Love-Dieux Dieux answered, "Oui" than the swamp symphony erupted into a peaceful overture of Paul Mauriet's "Love Is Blue," and she giggled in a grunt that only Miss Love could possibly emit.

"Happy, Ma Cherie?" Monsieur Dieux Dieux inquired, well aware of the answer provided by the serene and violet pulse of his mate.

"Never more," She answered in earnest. Then she quizzed the skinny but huge black bull, "Will it always be this way?"

"That depends," answered the male gator.

"On what?" she innocently asked.

"On our boy Mason," he answered.

Madame Love-Dieux Dieux giggled again, and in her bashful and playful grunt said, "'Our Boy' Mason has long passed thirty. Wouldn't you say?"

"Oui," Monsieur Dieux Dieux replied and giggled himself. "But look around woman, look at dis place. Dis is Mason. Still da mind of a chile. Growing, mind you, but taking off where de booze left off. Dat boy was only thirteen or so when he stunted himself wid dat poison."

"But is it real?" she asked as she stopped swimming and looked squarely in the eyes of Monsieur Dieux Dieux.

"You tell me, Madame Love. Were the Killing Fields of Cambodia real? Was the horror of Hiroshima and Nagasaki some figment of demented imagination?"

"I've never been to or seen any of those places or events, but I've accepted them as a reality; a horrible and indescribable reality," she thoughtfully replied.

"And you never heard of Bayou Love before today. Yet here you are. Listen to that music Madame. Dis place is as real as dat music. It all made up, Ma Cherie Amor. Every last bit of it. Let's just pray dat boy stay away from da scotch and his chemical relatives. Chile!" Exclaimed the black bull gator in a warning grunt.

"Not even wine?" teased Miss Love.

"Don't even joke about it, Wife. Any of dat shit is just a portal for dat Bitch, Miss Addiction to take holt. We got to make sure we take no chances wid dat sneaky bitch or Bayou Love will disintegrate like a chalk portrait in an August hurricane. Me and you, we find our asses hurling in an abyss of fear and everyting dat His/Her Honor can conjure up. Dem two go hand in hand. We got to be diligent Woman. I beg of you! Please! Don't let dat cunt Miss Addiction fool you into thinking that she yo friend. She not nobody's friend. She a complete lie, utterly and literally your opposite. Please! Don't let her tell you tings be even more beautiful if you invite her in! I tell you—"

"I get you husband, I get you!" she said with conviction and added, "There is no place, rhyme, or reason for that deranged cunt to enter Bayou Love. She belongs in another world. Another place and time. Certainly not in this moment."

"So stay in da moment, Madame Love. Stay here wit me. It real. Much more real den any of those hells I mentioned before. Just listen to dat music."

The arrangement of Monsieur Mariette filled the dusk with absolute certainty and each species of Bayou Love contributed its own flavor to the delightful tune."

"Pure harmony," stated Madame Love.

"He close to dat. Our boy Mason, He found da Bayou again. He at home. Can you hear da shad scream, Madame?"

"I think ... I think I can," she stuttered in delight.

The only audible sound was the symphony. But, she still heard the shad and she stated emphatically, "Absolutely! I hear it, it's beautiful. Nothing short of perfection."

No sooner had she said this than a sharp pain pierced her abdomen. She did not fear the pain, only acknowledged the shot of discomfort to quickly and naturally shoot for the moss-green and muddy bank of Bayou Love which she was convinced would tender relief.

"Huh, Huh, huh Huuuuuu," grunted Monsieur Dieux Dieux.

Madame Love raced with all of her might and screamed, very close to the sound she had heard from the shad, to be dinner, and she prepared a make shift nest and hole within the mud on a high portion of the bank of Bayou Love. Then she settled her lower abdomen over the hole and let loose the pain. With the last of the eggs in the hole, she felt she knew the satisfaction experienced by the shad as there was no more pain, only life.

"Funny," she thought to herself, "pain accompanies both birth and death."

With that thought in mind, Madame Love-Dieux Dieux utilized her great back flippers, claws and tail to shove leaves and debris over her eggs, and mixed in a concoction of mud to provide a steady temperature for the coming night.

As she sat gently around her nest, Monsieur Dieux Dieux swam up next to her and assured her, "You will be alright here for the evening Ma Cherie Amor. I'm off to enjoy the night."

With that, he swam away. And she thought to herself in a serine bliss, "I don't need any assurances as to my well-being. All is good. Good is all there is. I'm so happy."

"Enjoy," she shouted sincerely and wistfully to her mate.

"Huh Huh Huuuu," grunted the boney black bull affirming aloud, that as with all things, she need not worry with regards to his happiness.

There was no place for worry in the nightly paradise of Bayou Love. She knew he would return. She closed her eyes and found comfort, satisfaction, purpose, and delight from the knowledge of her offspring that safely incubated under her. The soft music took her mind further and deeper into the moment and the blissful night. Before she knew it, she opened her eyes and it was morning. She heard the clicks and yelps of her hatchlings escape from the muddy nest to softly offer percussion to the sounds of dawn.

"Good morning," hailed Monsieur Dieux Dieux from about five or so yards from her nest as he floated in the shallows of the bayou.

"I think they are about to hatch," she said, absorbed in the miracle she was experiencing.

That was a better response than a returned "good morning" would have played upon the ears of the skinny black gator. He too could hear the anxious pod under the nest calling to one another with their various clicks and high pitched murmurs which validated to each of the other of the twelve that it was time to break out.

"Huh Huh Huuuuu," grunted Monsieur Dieux Dieux. Then he stated flatly, "Breakfast."

"Well thank you. How sweet of you, but I don't dare leave. They could come any second now," replied Madame to his statement. Little did she know, it was not a question.

"Huh huh Huuuuu," he laughed and dove under the water. In a split second he returned with a gar fish about three feet long. This particular species of gar looked so similar to Madame and Monsieur Dieux Dieux that in many places, it was known as an "Alligator Gar." It was long and silver with splotches of yellow and black and the Gar was obviously in discomfort as it writhed in the teeth of the big black bull gator. With a flick of his head, Monsieur Dieux Dieux threw the debilitated fish to his mate, who caught the gift with her own ivory choppers, threw the fish up in the air and gulped the entire gar with one bite.

"Delicious," she said with a slight belch.

"Yezzz," replied Monsieur Dieux Dieux with a toothy grin that would have salivated were it able.

"Oh! Oh! Oh!" screamed Madame with the excitement of a teen-age girl on her first roller coaster ride. "Oh my God! I see one, I see her! Oh my God," she continued to exalt in sheer wonder. Monsieur Dieux Dieux's permanent grin only widened.

Through the twigs and leaves encased in mud came the first hatchling of the twelve eggs lain. The little baby gator grunted and clicked as her light blue body fought her way through the easiest path she could find. Madame Love-Dieux Dieux was so enthralled that she called out the name of the first gator hatchling that instinctively scooted as quickly as she could into the shallow water of Bayou Love.

"Joy!" She exclaimed with vigor and pride.

The little gator's scales pulsed towards a pastel purple, as to acknowledge that her mother had gotten her name correctly. And again, Monsieur Dieux Dieux just grunted a few low laughs as he sunk just a little lower in the water. Only his eyes could be seen as he watched the nest explode as if a small army had been ordered out of the trenches to take the beach front. Madame Love squealed and grunted in delight as only she could do, and called the different colored little gators by name as they emerged and raced to the water to join their sister, Joy.

"Promise, Integrity, Faith," she named aloud to the three deep shades of blue brothers that appeared almost simultaneously. Then she hollered hysterically "Oh! Oh! Hello my little scarlet Passion, and for the love of God, would you look at you, my little yellow Modesty. Aren't you the sweetest?" Then right behind Modesty came the skinny little black Gator that looked as if he could have been picked out of the ass of Monsieur Dieux Dieux.

"Huh Huh Huuu..." grunted the black bull through the water as he recognized his progeny, and Madame Love exclaimed with a conviction, of course, "Junior Dieux"

"Huh Huh Huuuu," the male bubbled again.

From polar opposites of the nest emerged one after the other three purple males of various shades and Madame Love, as she took in a deep breath of adoration, acknowledged her darlings with reverence as they formed a straight line and marched to join their brothers and sisters.

"Ecstasy, Bliss, and Rapture. Oh, my little royals."

And struggling mightily with intense grunts and incessant clicks was the head and front claws of a pulsating pup whose scales were spotted with all the colors of the rainbow. He was having a time of it in his attempt to escape the nest. As if she were viewing the babe Jesus, Madame Love gently reached down with her mouth and cautiously moved some of the mud so that little Happiness could break free.

Madame Love was in Seventh Heaven as she watched Happiness make his way to join the pod. She counted with gusto and pride that she had eleven. And with the faith of herself, she turned to look at the untidy nest, convinced that the last of her brood would soon appear. But the nest was quiet. Nevertheless, she looked hopefully back towards her husband as if to reassure Monsieur Dieux Dieux that it would only be a second. She was sure.

"I tink dats all of dem," he flippantly grunted through watery bubbles.

The beautiful music of Paul Mauriat ceased.

And with that said, black bull and father of the entire pod lunged forward in a violent break through the water with his mouth wide and snapped. Immediately, blue blood spurted everywhere. It sprayed on Madame Love herself, over her nest, into the water and on to the bank. Not a drop of difference was in the color of blood that flew from torn and dead bodies of Scarlet Passion, Black Junior Dieux, and Yellow Modesty. Despite the difference in the various shades of scales, the blood of each of the bodies being devoured by their father ran true blue.

Madame Love-Dieux Dieux didn't say a word, scream, or physically move in any manner or attack the gator that had just committed paternal infanticide. She was in a freeze frame for a split second with eyes wide open, as if staring into the coin of the hypnotist, then she passed out. It was simply more than she could take, and as a matter of course, the realm of Bayou Love afforded the mercy of an abyss to any of its subjects before His/Her Honor Fear and any of his subordinates could enter the pure land.

And as was the nature of any phenomena in Bayou Love, time itself was difficult to measure. It was impossible for Madame Love-Dieux Dieux to know how long she had been out. As she opened her eyes, it was still the silver/gold daylight that met her gaze and eventually, she made out the remaining eight of her hatchlings and the memories of the recent and bloody blue infanticide committed by her husband sprang through her head. And again, the grotesque image was more than she could comprehend, but this time she did not pass out. She laid about groggily, like a patient recovering from surgical anesthesia, while she simultaneously thought about the possibility of a divorce under Bayou Love Code Napoleon. She listened to the words of her husband, the culprit. He didn't begin to plead innocent, for any reason, or offer an apology in the least. As husband and father, Monsieur Black Bull Gator Dieux Dieux laid down the law to his newly betrothed and bewildered love. He grunted in Creole French, "Ma Cherie Amour, we are alligators. Mind you, we live in Bayou Love—but we are alligators. And I am a male alligator. We bulls, sometimes, sometimes not, we eat our babies. Strictly natural instinct, darling. Just like the shad being eaten by birds, just like you laying eggs. You, or others here may not be able to understand it, but it is natural for a male gator to eat its young."

"But Passion, Junior, and Modesty," Madame Love-Dieux Dieux spoke, still in a daze, but she slowly emerged from her trance-like state.

Somehow, just speaking aloud about the carnage she had witnessed soothed her confusion.

"For God's sake, your own Junior. How could you?" she whispered but with no alligator tears.

"Totally random, Ma Cherie. Just how the dice landed, or better yet, where I sat my alligator mouth. Dey all taste like apples, only some are sweet, some sour, some well, velvet, for lack of a better word. Dey was in da right place at the right time."

"But they're dead. Our babies are dead," she spoke with clear cognizance.

"Nothing dead in Bayou Love, Madame Wife. No, no! Like you, nothing die here. Modesty, Junior, and love in us Ma Cherie. Dey and many oders, they come in our next brood. Really now darling, please give up dis Sunday School notion that love and marriage exist for only procreation. Love exist as surely as you do and comes in so many forms, so many faces, and so many tings. I beg of you my love, please do not query. Accept yourself. Accept your surroundings. Accept me. Accept us. Accept our journey. Please, no more expectations, Madame, please." He quietly grunted, his teeth still stained by the blue blood of his own spawn.

"I expect you not to kill and eat my babies," she growled through her teeth.

"Den you gone be firmly disappointed. Swamp Pussy, I'm a bull gator. It's what we do."

"Swamp Pussy? Swamp Pussy!" she exclaimed in confusion, through laughter and alligator tears that flowed cobalt to mix with the true blue blood of her devoured offspring that had been splattered on her face. Her scales now pulsed violet blue. Even her heckled laughter sounded blue. There was no known shade of blue for that sound. It could only be felt.

For a moment, that feeling was so extreme that Madame Love-Dieux Dieux felt as though she were about to faint. She nearly confirmed that it was light's out as she looked at her disheveled nest and noticed movement.

"Ah ha! Ground movement. And next comes the spin," she thought to herself and braced to faint. She closed her eyes expecting the combined sensations of a gyroscopic light show and a calliope in flat notes pouncing upon her ears.

But she heard a click, and then a little high pitched grunt that almost resembled a cat's meow. Or was it a whimper from a pup? She couldn't tell. Madame Love opened one eye in the direction of the sound and looked down to witness the little gleaming white choppers through a gargantuan smile, much too big for his little violet blue head that had popped through the mulch and leaves of her brood's nest.

"Rick!" She exclaimed in joy and delight so loudly that all her other brood, still in the shallows within reach of Monsieur Dieux Dieux, began to form a circle and swim around the boney but huge black bull. And the black gator grunted in laughter at their naiveté.

But Rick, as if by some divine instinct from providence, did not run for the water. after pulling with all his might and will, the little violet hatchling, who of course, would one day grow up to be a male gator, ran to the safety of his mother.

"Where do I put you, Rick, to protect you from Monsieur? I have no purse, no hands, nowhere to place you," she said as she took in and let out a heavy sigh.

Her mouth cracked open. Rick answered Madame's question for her. In an instant, the little gator had climbed though the gaps of his mother's ivory row of huge teeth and settled under her tongue. Rick clicked loudly to his brothers and sisters circling the father in the shallows. He looked like a puppy that'd hung his head out the window of a car at a stoplight in an attempt to communicate with a dog in an adjacent car as he waited for the light to change. But his siblings paid him no heed.

The orchestra of swamp sounds again tuned up. In a split second it had made a full recovery with the 1960s psychedelic, "Love is Blue."

"Come, my Swamp Pussy, Ma Cherie Amor, come," grunted the bull gator.

"Where to?" she lisped from the interference Rick made on her tongue.

"In the direction of that music, Wife. Where else?"

"Where do you think that is, Husband?" she inquired as she entered the pastel blue edge water of the Bayou Love and broke into the circle of her splashing hatchlings. She was happy to see that they, in the true magic of Bayou Love, were quickly growing. She was hoping that they'd be too large in the near future to make snacks for the uncontrollable nature of her husband. She didn't even consider the fact that some of her hatchlings were male and would become hatchling killers. Madame Love-Dieux Dieux, like Mason Caldwell, the vessel of her present continuum, was growing and maturing and in due course would learn truth. Like all creations, she would eventually submit to the truth, the ultimate authority.

"I suspect Paris," Monsieur Dieux Dieux belched through the water.

When he announced his notion of their journey, the male gator was unable to control blue vapors from the blood of his son whom he had just consumed.

"To heal?" she asked as she took care not to hurt Rick.

"Huh Huh Huuuuu," laughed Monsieur Dieux Dieux, and she joined him by his side as he turned to head towards the channel with her. "No Ma Cherie. No, NO NO! Healing time is over. It time to love, my Swamp Pussy. Just to love, live, and be happy."

"Please don't call me Swamp Pussy," she said.

"Okay," he said.

No sooner had he agreed to her requisite edict, Monsieur Dieux Dieux turned his head to the right. He effortlessly lunged forward and randomly snapped his magnificent mouth into the head of a blue hatchling, then the male bull threw the instantly dead carcass high into the air and he opened wide. As the little gator disappeared into the mouth of his father, Madame Love-Dieux Dieux stopped swimming. She was not in any way hysterical. She wasn't going to allow her husband to shock her again. But she was stern as she looked her husband in the eye and with great care, so as not to injure baby Rick, who incidentally was clicking wildly to no avail for his siblings to join him in his mother's mouth, politely demanded, "Please stop eating our babies. I believe you just consumed Promise."

"No, Swamp Pussy, I won't stop eating our babies." He belched aloud in the manner of an old diabetic retiree who'd been asked by the Missus to watch his alcohol intake.

"Really?" she asked in exasperation.

Rick kept pleading to his siblings to join him in the safety of his mother's mouth, and they continued to ignore him. Like trained circus horses, they simply closed rank and file on the empty slot where the missing blue hatchling had been snatched, and they continued to swim around their parents, bull and cow gators.

"Huh, huh huh," Monsieur Dieux Dieux laughed, and with no hint of regret, he explained in the fashion of a wine connoisseur attempting to distinguish the character of a Bordeaux from a California Cabernet,

"I'm not so sure it wasn't Integrity. Dey taste so close. So crisp and refined. Huh huhuuu."

It was at that point that Rick promised himself and his mom through a series of clicks and dolphin style grunts that when he grew up, he would never eat any of his progeny. Monsieur Dieux Dieux overheard the oath of his son and began laughing hysterically.

"Boy, what make you think you gone make babies?"

Rick was still too young to understand the insinuation his father had flippantly made.

"Really now, Monsieur. You never know," Madame Love responded in defense of her little son.

"Oh I know. And so do you, Swamp Pussy. Dat boy ain't gone make no babies."

"I won't eat anyone else's either," retorted the little gator in his mother's mouth.

And with the sass and conviction of a nouveau riche millionaire at age 16 stepping into his inheritance, Rick informed his mother and father of his intentions to teach all his brothers and sisters not to engage in the manner of his father. That he would introduce a new standard of virtue to the natural order of Bayou Love.

"Boy, what you gone do when you get too big to ride in your momma's mouth?" Monsieur Dieux Dieux asked with a mischief which implied to his son that Rick himself was indeed future nutrition for the old bull.

"I'm not going to swim in a circle around you, Pops. That's for sure," Rick popped off, still in the safety of his mother's protection.

The entire family now swam into the deep channel and turned towards the direction of the music and Paris. They appeared, by all standards of Bayou Love, a happy and functional pod doing what alligators do. Monsieur Dieux Dieux grunted a loving laugh towards the little smart ass who traveled safely under his mother's protection and announced, with a twinkle in his eye, "It all good."

Madame Love had seen that twinkle before.

"Quickly Rick, take a deep breath! Hurry, hurry!"

And with that, the huge black bull had leapt into the air and was taking his mate down to the cushion of silt where his ambassador was sure to work his magic so that the little circle of happiness that swam around the newlyweds would only grow and sustain the gators as they swam in harmony towards the city of lights.

But for now, Bayou Love was again bursting with the fountains and commotions caused by the orgasmic delight of Madame Love. Little Rick held on for dear life to the inner molars of his mother while she released atomic screams of sensual ecstasy. Rick was determined to make it. He had so much more to teach. And Madame Love-Dieux Dieux, had so much more to learn.

Monsieur was there to make sure Mason continued to enjoy himself.

The End

Acknowledgments

At the beginning, I want to thank Rick Sherman for the debate as to whether or not "love at first sight" is possible. And for gently nudging me to complete the second write of this story and remaining a friend throughout, Keith Anderson. For getting me out of the gate for the initial edit and on track, thank you Stephen Hartner. David Smith for his loving friendship and taking the whip to this pony on the back stretch and getting the initial edit over the finish line, not to mention his unwavering enthusiasm and courage in the marketing of *Killing Miss Love*. And for taking time to read through the chapters where legal wording was necessary and correcting my limited knowledge of the law, I am so grateful to Thomas Glasson. Michael Moody, thank you for your storyline edit and for killing the creative boogey man time after time when he would come out from the shadows. Your affection, patience, and encouragement have led me to better understand the meaning of friendship. And to Robert Wellington, thank you so much for your artistic clairvoyance and the perfect timing of your voice mails with their right-on-the-dime messages of faith and hope. Last, but certainly not least, I want to thank Adam Robinson for his patience, publishing and editing expertise, and kind nature that have been such a huge part in bringing this work into the public world. I am so lucky to have met you.

About the Author

Marshall Blackwell was raised in Monroe Louisiana and now lives with his dog Mason, coincidently named after the character in *Killing Miss Love*, in Fort Lauderdale, Florida where he happily plays softball and hopes he may never tend bar or take part as a real estate agent again.

photograph by Susan Purdic